A Boy Alone

BOOK I

OBSESSED

Alan John Mayer

Illustrations by Steve Lubin

A Boy Alone

A biography of twisted proportions

for young readers of all generations

"The difference between what we do and what we are capable of doing would suffice to solve the majority of the world's problems."

–Mahatma Gandhi

In search of

Joi Dyer
and
Louise Fischer

In memory of Dr. Peggy Bassett

Wolfgang Martens
Kathryn E. Mayer
Peter Knauer
Eva Rieger
Ursula Theyssen
and many more loved ones

My deepest gratitude to

Dr. Doris Palazzo Lubin
and my friend Mr. Steve Lubin
without whom this story may never have seen the light.

Board the train to Abundance, back to a gentler world, to a time of civility, courtly love, manners, virtue, vice, anger, hatred, pomp, circumstance, sin—and forgiveness. Take a trip through the United States of Consciousness: *Abundance, Bereavement, Confusion, Determination, Discord, Fear, Grace, Indifference, Insanity, Play, Possession, Resolution, Terror, Tolerance, Understanding*—and *Forgiveness.*

Follow whatever example of good you may find in these pages. Leave behind what is evil. While reading, you may find yourself elevated in thought, making you a more attractive item on the job market, and on the dating scene. Obsessed reading elevates reputation, and be most certainly an agreeable way to pass the time, but as far as believing all written upon these pages is true, that has been left for you, the reader, to decide.

This book is recommended reading for anyone who desires to read, or be read to, of the intriguing history of the United States of Consciousness and the fascinating lives lived by the citizens thereof. Rough and imperfect, this is a tale told to entertain, enlighten, and heal. Forgiveness for any mistake is welcome.

This story is written in Electra LT Std. In an attempt to accommodate the varying international rules and opinions on punctuation, the author has chosen to write, punctuate, and edit the story as he hears it, with imperfections, and has attempted to remain consistent hthroughout. Titles such as King, Queen, Ma'am, Sir and the like may be capitalized because that is how the author hears them. All characters, cities, and states are *italicized* upon first introduction. Characters introduced initially only informally (and those with nicknames or titles) are *italicized* upon second introduction. Voices of animals and objects (such as a squirrel, a squeaky door, or an elevator 'DING') have been placed in 'single quotes.' All characters are fictitious, and may or may not bear likeness to persons dead or alive. Now relax, and step into the world of Consciousness.

For more information: AlanJohnMayer.com

TABLE OF CONTENTS

CHAPTER I
End of an Era

His Majesty's chauffeur, *Ernest Crankshaft*, and place detective *Evan Scott* stood atop Blue Spruce Hill and watched, as Search & Rescue workers harnessed a team of horses to the King's roadster, resting tail up in the canal. Detective Scott got straight to the point. "Mr. Crankshaft, how did the King's roadster end up in the canal?"

"I approached the carriage house in time to see His Majesty roll down the drive. He was not ready to go out on his own. He'd had only one lesson. He wasn't familiar with the gears, the pedals, nor the instruments."

"Who cranked the roadster for him?"

"I have no idea. Perhaps he bribed one of the gardeners."

"How did the roadster end up in the canal?"

"I ran after, but I couldn't stop him. I watched from the guardhouse, as he circled the traffic ring. He came back, with his head under the dash, instead of keeping his eyes on the road. It seems he was trying to determine which pedal was the brake. He hit a pothole. I could see he was heading for the canal, so I returned to the guardhouse, and told the guard to call an ambulance, and the palace, to summon Her Majesty. I hurried back to the carriage house, cranked the Isotta, drove to the portico, opened the limousine door, and waited. Within minutes, princess *Pristine* arrived. Then the ambulance jingled onto the scene. I shared my binoculars with the princess. We watched, as two divers dove into the canal, and pulled the King onto dry land."

"You could see this from the palace portico?"

"One has an unobstructed view of the canal from the east portico, Detective. One of the divers pounded on the King's chest, while another tried to resuscitate him. They lifted him onto a gurney, slid the gurney onto the ambulance, and jingled off. Queen *Marguerite* came down the stairs at ten minutes after eleven, and I drove the royals to the hospital.

"How long were you at the hospital, Mr. Crankshaft?"

"I waited an hour and twenty minutes before Her Majesty came out. As I helped her into the Isotta, from the look on her face, I could tell the King was dead."

"Are you certain, Mr. Crankshaft?"

"I am certain, Detective. "The King is dead. Long Live the Queen."

"Long Live the Queen. This is a sad day for *Entitlement*, Mr. Crankshaft." Detective Scott extended a hand. "Thank you for your input into our investigation. Should there be any further questions, I will be in touch."

Search & Rescue grooms checked the horses' harnesses, dragged the dripping Raceabout out of the canal, and towed it out the gates to the only mechanic in the state, doing business in downtown *Contentment*. Detective Scott hopped on his motorscooter, and rode back to his precinct, where deep within the bowels of the palace, he occupied a desk.

The sound of jingling bells reverberated in Crankshaft's head—as if in a loop. In an attempt to rise above the tractor's noise, he climbed a nearby boulder, sat down, closed his eyes, and pulled his cap over his head. He took in a deep breath of freshly cut grass, and prayed for the soul of his sovereign.

The King is dead. Long Live the Queen.

♛   ♛   ♛

The doors to the palace roof fanned open. Two guards stepped out onto the tarmac, and positioned themselves with their backs against the doors. Six trumpeteers, a band of drummers, and the town crier stepped out, followed by a regiment of guards, all marching in unison. When they reached the flagpole, they turned to the captain's whistle, faced the sea, and breathed in the salty sea air. Two guards stepped forward, and lowered the banner of *Abundance* to half-staff, while another carried in the flag of *Consciousness*. They clasped the flag to the pulley, and hoisted it up the pole, where the wind caught it and sent it waving.

The town crier stepped onto the platform, and unfurled his scroll. In a voice that echoed across the valley, he issued his proclamation. "Hear ye, subjects of Abundance, residents of Entitlement, hear ye—this morning, at eleven seventeen, this seventeenth day of April, one thousand nine hundred and eleven Year of our Lord, our beloved monarch, King *Poldemire Rexus James Aloneous Goldspinner*, made his transition into the Great Unknown. Our most diligent and faithful King, having never denied his subjects one duty placed upon him, is laid to his final rest. His

Majesty was one hundred thirteen years of age. The King is dead." He rolled up his scroll. "And now, let us observe a minute of silence." He bowed his head, and closed his eyes. Sixty seconds later, he closed the proclamation on a positive note—"Long Live the Queen."

The sixteen bells of the old Saint Agarapina cathedral bell tower tolled across the valley this transfer of power. Street vendors on Cathedral Lane broke down stalls, and hastened home to mourn. The Bank of the Crown closed its doors, and proclaimed the day a holiday. The ABC Stock Exchange called it a day, as well. Workers boarded streetcars. Some went home to grieve. Others headed downtown to grieve in the publique houses. Proprietors of these taverns faced a quandary. It is a well-established fact, without spirits, a wake is not a wake. They struggled with their conscience; remain open, serve those in need of spiritual support from the tap, or close out of respect for the Crown.

Bishop *Wolfgang Martens* was called upon to give the eulogy. He chose a purple ceremonial gown for the occasion, with a cross hanging from his waist chain, a golden mitre crowning his head, and satin slippers grounding his feet. For those whose eyes lead to enchantment, before them to behold there appeared a divine body. The following morning in the palace throne room, the bishop gave a private eulogy for family and friends. That afternoon, he repeated his words for the public, from the steps of Entitlement Hall.

"Today we lay to rest a man large in body, mind, and spirit. King Poldemire professed the most important footprint one can leave behind is the service one provides one's fellow beings. Our diligent King, who never denied his subjects any duty placed upon him, demonstrated this teaching in his many philanthropic contributions for eight decades; among them, the improved working conditions in our gold mines that afford our kingdom our library, our hospital, and orphanage, the History of the States' Museum, the Park Street Zoo, and the Four-Footed Friends' League, that no animal be without a home.

"His Majesty stood loyal to every state. We thank him for strengthening our bonds with *Anticipation, Grace, Resolution,* and *Tolerance.* Today, we mourn not only the loss of a great monarch—a father, grandfather and great-grandfather to so many of us—we mourn the loss of a long and prosperous reign by a punctilious, a most consciencious monarch. Let us now place our hands over our hearts, and recite His Majesty's vow to the flag of Abundance."

Bishop Martens turned to face the flag, and placed his hand over his heart. "I pledge allegiance, to the banner of *the United States of Consciousness,* to the devotion for which it stands, many states of many colors, in one ever-unfolding awareness, indivisible, united, and aligned in liberty and justice for all, and by all." He turned, and faced the public. "Let us observe a minute of silence, as we remember our great monarch, King Poldemire." He clasped his hands, and closed his eyes.

Sixty seconds later, the royal marching band started playing the *Bereavement Hymn.* Sixteen pallbearers slid the King's casket onto the hearse, stepped in line behind the wagon, and the royal began the mile-long journey up the Abundite coast, to the Abundance State Memorial Park. Thousands followed, in carriages, carts, and on foot. Those who could afford to play with motorcars joined in.

✝ ✝ ✝

The horses turned inland, onto a gravel road, approached the Commemorative Wall of Plaques, and proceeded into the park. They circled the fountain, pranced past several crypts, and stopped in front of the Goldspinner family mausoleum.

Four guards hopped to the ground, and crunched the gravel walking to the mausoleum. They pried the massive bronze doors open—on hinges groaning for oil. Pallbearers were flanked on both sides by subjects, as they walked the coffin across the gravel. They lifted it over their heads, and with one powerful thrust, they slid it into a slot, and King Poldemire Goldspinner was put to rest for eternity—His Majesty, in a box.

The marksman stood at the canon overlooking the valley, ready to fire. Upon command from Count *Alaham Russell* of Grace, he let off the first of sixteen shots, one to represent each state of the Union.

Count Russell stepped onto a platform, as the last shot faded into nothingness. He raised his hands to the sky, and spoke words the subjects had waited to hear. *"Rex est quietus in pace, Vivat Regina"*—for the commoners among the crowd, he translated into the King's English—"our King rests in peace; Long live the Queen."

"Our King rests in peace; Long Live the Queen," teary-eyed, subjects repeated.

Count Russell let his arms fall to his sides, and assessed the crowd. "Ladies and gentlemen, boys and girls, and everyone in-between, before us stands a new world order. Now is the time each and every one of us must ask ourselves—how will I fit into that new order?"

No one could have imagined the dis-order that would follow the King's passing. The first question the subjects wanted answered was—which princess will be our new Queen?—*Erica Henriette Agarapina Regina Marguerite?*—or her younger sister by twelve minutes, *Pristine Marguerite Regina Agarapina Henriette?*

👑   👑   👑

LEGEND to the MAP of the UNITED STATES of CONSCIOUSNESS

☆ CAPITAL CITY
◉ CITY OF ONE MILLION OR MORE
● CITY OF ONE MILLION OR LESS
⑂ FALLS   ⌇ LAKE OR SEA
♣ ENCLAVE   ⋙ MOUNTAINS

◉ AHA	● FRIGHT	★ RESOLVE
● AMNESIA	● GOOD GRIEF	● RESPECT
◉ ANGST	● GRAND TREPIDATION	★ SCARE CITY
● ANTIPATHY CITY	● GRIPE	◉ SOWHAT
● APATHY	● GRIT	◉ TENURE
◉ ARMOR CITY	★ GRUNTLE	◉ TERROR CITY
● ARMORY	★ HELENA	● THUNK
◉ BOCA GRANDE	● HIGH WATER	★ TIMOROUS
◉ CACOPHONY	● HOPE	● TURMOIL
● CHAOS (KAOS)	● IMOQUAY	★ UMBRAGE
◉ CLARITY	● INSURANCEVILLE	◉ WHOCAERZ
● CLEMENCY	● ISLE OF BILE	
● COMPREHENSION	★ LENIENCY	⌇ ATALANIA
◉ DADGUMIT	★ LOCO	⌇ BAY OF CHAOS
● DEAD VALLEY	● LOST CITY	⌇ BLACK SNAKE RIVER
● DIRE STRAIGHTS	● LUGDOWN	⋙ CLIFFS OF ANTICIPATION
★ DISCONTENTMENT	● MERCY	⋙ CRAGS OF DISCORD
● DYER FALLS	◉ MINA	♣ CRYSTAL ROCK (ABUNDANCE)
● END FO THE WELL	★ MÍO/MINE	⌇ LAKE MINE
★ ENVY	● OFFENSE	⌇ OCEANIA
★ EUREKA	★ OH-WELL	⌇ SEA OF CONSCIOUSNESS
● EUROQUAY	★ PARDON	⌇ SEA OF INDIFFERENCE
● EXPECTANCY	◉ PARSIMONY	⌇ SEA OF SERENDIPITY
● FEAR FALLS	★ PERPLEXITY	⌇ UMBRAGE BAY
◉ FORBEARANCE	◉ PETRIFIED ROCK	
● FORTITUDE	◉ PLEASE	
● FOU	★ REMEMBRANCE	

CHAPTER II

Coronation Day

Three Weeks Later, Saturday, May 13, 1911

Princesss *Erica Henriette Agarapina Regina Marguerite Goldspinner*, and her twelve minute younger twin sister, princess *Pristine Marguerite Regina Agarapina Henriette Goldspinner*, first and second in line to the throne of Entitlement, had lived sheltered lives inside the palace gates, under the watchful eye of Nanny *Carabella Needlepinch*.

Due to the untimely death of the princesses parents a decade earlier, Erica and Pristine had been led down divergent paths. Whereas Pristine had been indoors, Erica had been been outside, and witnessed their parents death in front of her eyes. Ever since, she had been haunted by nightmares. The Court sent Erica to *Insanity*, several times, where she underwent a series of shock therapy treatments to help her forget the imprint. Years had passed since anyone outside the royal circle, or for that matter, anyone at the sanitarium in *Loco*, had seen either. Now that the King was dead, subjects demanded to know which twin would be coroneted their new Queen.

Solicited or not, Nanny Carabella Needlepinch was always ready with a word of proper advice. Three weeks after the King's passing, the day before the coronation, she sat down with the to-be-coroneted Queen for tea, to voice her opinion. Nanny sipped delicately from her cup, and rested it on the saucer. "Your Royal Highness—Pristine, if you can get your subjects to show up to your coronation, *and* get them to return on Sunday for the banquet, you will have them hoodwinked for life."

Pristine set her cup down. "I want the subjects to attend because they want to, Nanny, not because they have been hoodwinked."

"My dear, they won't even know what has happened to them."

Pristine pushed a button under the table. "I want another sticky bun. How about you, Nanny?—another cookie?"

7

"Thank you. I've had five, but they are small. I will have another."

Pristine sipped, and set her teacup down. "Nanny, I feel like such an imposter."

"An imposter? What the Dickens are you talking about?"

"Tomorrow's coronation should be for Erica. She is the rightful heir to the throne. I don't even want to be Queen; she does. If only she wasn't so traumatized, if her mental condition were more stable, she would make a wonderful Queen. If only Dr. *Fuehlgoed* had taken the time to understand her condition,"

"My dear," Nanny took Pristine's hand, "now you sound like your mother. Let's focus on Sunday's banquet—shall we?"

"I will leave that to *Kensington*. That's his job."

"Pristine, you cannot depend on Kensington. You need to oversee what he is doing. Mrs. *Thornecroft*, from the Communications Office should have gotten in touch with you. Did she?"

"She did," Pristine nodded.

"Good. There are a few details I want to go over with you."

There was a knock, and Kensington trundled into the room. "You rang, Ma'am?"

"I did, Kensington. Would you please bring in another plate of sticky buns, and another cookie for Nanny."

"Yes, Ma'am." The butler nodded, and walked out of the room, backwards.

That Friday night, thousands camped out in Market Square, across the street from the old Saint Agarapina cathedral. Everybody wanted to be first in line when the cathedral doors opened to the public on Saturday morning, to witness the first coronation in seventy-nine years. With a young princess to be coroneted, decades would likely pass before such an occasion would arise again. This was a once in three generations occasion, and subjects were excited.

Vendors got to work setting up stalls all along Cathedral Lane before the sun even rose. By dawn, the cobblestones were alive with hungry consumers, gobbling up sausages, fish and chips and sticky buns, and they downed it all with ale. People could not get enough coronation memorabilia—flags, photographs of the royal family, pictures of the twin princesses, salt & pepper shakers, calendars—all sold out before noon.

At nine o'clock on the dot, the two sets of cathedral double doors opened to a sunny morning, and two thousand people raced up the steps, each wanting to get into the sanctuary first for a good seat. They bottlenecked in the vestibules, pushed, and shoved like commoners. At five to ten—almost an hour later, the multitude of talkative people had still not settled into the pews.

At precisely ten o'clock, princess Pristine stepped into the spotlight on the arms of two shadowy figures, followed by four cloak carriers. All talking stopped, subjects rose to their feet; men bowed, women curtseyed. The two figures led her to her coronation chair, and disappeared into the wings. The orchestra conductor raised his baton, and his musicians started playing the Abundance state anthem, while hands over their hearts, subjects pledged deference to the Crown.

Pristine stood center stage, alone before God and the subjects.

The anthem drew to a close. The princess's favored footman, *Abel Handsforth*, stepped in, and took her right hand, while Count Russell stepped in from her left. They walked her to her coronation chair before releasing her under a canopy, and disappearing.

This left the princess standing alone on the platform. She scanned the crowd, looking for familiar faces. With her hair up, her dainty ears were exposed, each highlighted by a single pearl. Upon her shoulders rested a matching pearl strand, drawing attention to her long neck.

Three weeks mourning seems standard, she thought, as she surveyed the crowd; I am glad I decided against wearing a veil. She clasped her hands, and in an an attempt to quiet her growling intestines, squeezed them against her abdomen. This resulted in an unnatural, forced smile. "You unwelcome fluttering butterflies," she mumbled, through clamped teeth, "I command you to align yourselves in a graceful ballet—now."

Count Russell stepped forward, and placed the bejeweled scepter into the princess's hand. "Your Royal Highness," he addressed her before the crowd: "this royal scepter is a symbol of your imperial insignia. It denotes your power, your authority, and your sovereignty. May it be at your command for as long as you shall reign."

Handsforth stepped in, and handed Count Russell the orb.

"Your Royal Highness," Count Russell held the sphere up, "this orb is a symbol of the world under Christ. May it be at your disposal for as long as you shall reign." The count placed the orb into the princess's hand.

Handsforth stepped in, held up the imperial ring for all to see, and handed it to the count.

"Your Royal Highess," the count continued, "this ring symbolizes your marriage to Christ. Whether you remain single, or whether you wed, may it remain on your finger always, for as long as you shall reign." He slipped the ring on the princess's finger, and stepped back.

Bishop Martens read from the Sacred Book of Abundance. "Your Royal Highness, whereas everyone present has come to pay reverence to you that you may become our coroneted Queen—are you willing to take the sacred oath?"

"I am willing," not an eyeblink from the princess; she had been coached.

"Your Royal Highness," Bishop Martens continued, "do you solemnly pledge and promise to rule over the people of Entitlement, the citizens of Abundance, the residents of the *Crystal Rock* enclave, and all others living in all other possessions and or territories you may possess with the dignity and honor of the Abundite Crown?"

"I promise so to do," Pristine's butterflies were starting to settle.

"Your Royal Highness, will you, in mercy toward your subjects, to the extend of your power, bring about justice, law, and order, to be implemented in all your decisions and judgments, within, and outside the Court of Entitlement?"

"I promise so to do." A fly landed on the princess's hand, and crawled around.

"Will you preserve and maintain, uninfringeably, the teachings of the church of Consciousness, and its disciples, the doctrine, principles, discipline, and government thereof, as prescribed by the clergy of the church?"

"I promise so to do." The fly flew, with the princess's blessing.

Count Russell held a shield over Her Royal Highness's head, and Bishop Martens anointed her forehead, chest, and hands with saffron, myrrh, frankincense, and Holy oil, and sprinkled Holy Water over her head. He scattered gold dust in her hair, and three times blessed her, in the name of the Father, the Son, and the Holy Ghost, before reciting an ancient Latin incantation. And for the commoners among the gathering, he translated into the King's English: "with these precious aromas, I, bishop Martens, proclaim thee, Pristine Goldspinner, Queen of Entitlement, regent of Abundance, in civil voice, and in all regimental affairs."

Abel Handsforth walked in a pillow, upon which rested the crown, and held it up for all to see. Sunlight entered the sanctuary from the overhead casement windows, hitting the jewels, sending beams of light dancing across the ceiling, and causing an uproar in the pews. Count Russell held the crown over the freshly anointed Queen's head.

Thrown by its size, Pristine sized up the crown. It never looked that big on Grandpa Poldi, she thought—it must weigh five pounds.

Count Russell leaned in, "seven and a half, Your Highness."

Pristine recoiled. "Count Russell, you give me goosebumps. You read my mind." How did he know what I was thinking?—she wondered.

Count Russell leaned in, and whispered into her ear, "concentration, Madam."

"How am I to balance seven pounds on my head?"

"The way you balance everything, Ma'am—with grace."

"Grace may not be enough, Count. Should I fall, you may need to pick me up."

"Your Majesty," Handsforth leaned in, "you will never fall under our watch."

As the orchestra started softly playing *Abundant Jubilation*, Count Russell addressed the sanctuary. "The time has come to place the crown on the head of our new regent." As he held the crown over Pristine's head, the crowd cheered. He placed the crown on her head, and Handsforth escorted *Her Majesty* to the lectern, stepped back, and disappeared.

The freshly coroneted Queen stood alone before God and all. She quietly thanked the butterflies in her stomach for obeying her first command, and gazed into the sanctuary. My shoes hurt, was her thought; where is *Mina*? She was supposed to break them in. They pinch even more under the weight of this crown. *GranMarguerite* once told me whenever she finds herself standing before an audience, she visualizes them wearing long underwear, and matching stocking caps. Here we go. She leaned into the microphone, and began her Coronation speech—"my shoes are killing me."

The audience responded with uproarious laughter. "Take them off," shouted one.

The shushers raced about the sanctuary, shushing those who needed to be shushed. The freshly coroneted Queen began. "Ladies and gentlemen, beloved subjects, fellow *Entitlées*, Abundites, et al: first, I would like to thank you for all your thoughts and prayers as we put my late grandfather, *Grandpa Poldi*, your late King Poldemire, to rest. His passing has thrust me, an ignorant novice in the affairs of state, onto the world stage. I am blessed to have at my call the finest advisors available. I may not always hit the mark, but I ask for your patience as I learn the skills that are necessary to negotiate the war between *Fear* and *Terror* that seems to never end. I ask for your help, as we seek to find unity, and understanding, at a more profound level than ever before."

11

The audience joined in showing appreciation for their new Queen's honest, youthful spirit.

"The young among you may not be familiar with the geography of our Union. You should find a map inside your program. Familiarize yourself with it, and you will be able to follow along. When princess Erica and I were nine, *Grandpa Poldemire* and *Queen Mother Marguerite* took us with them to talks in *Scare City* and *Timorous*. The idea we could be detained against our will behind the *Black Snake Line* had me frightened. Erica remained calm. Both cities lay under a blanket of quiet darkness. The few lanterns on the streets sent out yellow light, in an attempt to fight the fog. It was as if both states were in mourning.

"The sun rose at nine o'clock, if it rose at all. By three, it was dark. People were apprehensive to speak. The few women I saw were dressed from head to toe in black. Beyond lemon or cream in your tea, they took no part in any negotiation. But they were happy in their situation. I felt my breathing constrict. Not until we were back in Tolerance did I breathe a sigh of relief. That experience behind the Black Snake Line taught me a lesson. Just because I do not understand Fear and Terror does not mean they do not deserve my respect. I strive to accept them for what they are— motivators. I learned in those visits an awareness of the contribution every state makes to our great Union.

"It is with this in mind that I address the Abundites among us," she paused—"the *Tolerites, Gracines, Forgivers, Confused,* and the *Determined* alike. Fear warns us of impending Terror. Terror makes us aware we have wavered too far in the wrong direction. Though it may not be possible for every subject to live *in* Abundance, it is possible for every subject to live a life *of* abundance—regardless of one's origin. We must build a world where Fear and Terror are under control, and respected for what they contribute. Those among you who are old enough to remember, think back a few years, how the *Understandées* hookwinked Fear and Terror into settling their grievances with their neighbor to the north—*Resolution.*"

Subjects cheered. They were tired of Fear's surprise attacks, and wanted to learn a new respect. They had put up with a King too old to adapt with the times. They were tired of Terror forcing its way into their schools, their churches, their hearts, and minds.

Pristine took in a deep breath, along with the crowd's adoration. The muscles on either side of her lips betrayed her thoughts. This is what GranMarguerite was talking about, she smiled, the love of one's subjects. "I would like to address the *Playmates, Possessées, Bereavées,* and the

Indifferents among us, and I do not want to leave out the *Insane*, and all those who stand in resistance to Fear and Terror. It shall be the mission of my Court to combat these unwarranted attacks, that peace may once prevail once again. However," it was so quiet one could hear a pin drop— "before my Court will consider conferring stateship upon either Fear or Terror, they must demonstrate not just in words, but in action, that they will retrain their minds, and stop their evil attacks."

The audience whistled, applauded, and rose to their feet when the orchestra started playing, and they remained standing for the seven minute rendition of *God Save the Queen*.

CHAPTER III
An Unexpected Visitor

Queen Mother Marguerite and Nanny Needlepinch sat in the front row of the sanctuary, listening to the orchestra play the seven minute rendition of *God Save the Queen*. Queen Mother removed the lid from her flask, lifted her veil, and sipped gently on her fortitude, a gentle medication—usually gin. "If I never hear that song again, Nanny, it will be too soon," she took another sip, and closed the flask, "thank God I have fortitude."

Nanny gnawed unconsciously on a cuticle. "Pristine seems taken with the tune," she said, "when it played for you, it was always *God Save the King.*"

"Not always," Queen Mother slipped her flask into her purse, "she too will come to loathe it, in time. God only knows how many times those lyrics have played in my head. Millions; every dinner, every function, every ball. Sometimes they even play in my silence."

"Look at Pristine up there," Nanny blew her nose, turned her hankie outside in, and tucked it into her belt, "how brave she is."

"You know both my granddaughers possess a commanding presence, Nanny."

The seven-minute musical tribute drew to a close, and the new Queen held her arms out palms up, and smiled.

"Look how polished she is. I cannot help but feel proud, Ma'am. You know the twins are…"

"I know, Nanny, the twins are like your own."

"She has captivated the subjects. She is going to make a wonderful stateswoman."

"You know, Pristine didn't write the speech. Count Russell wrote it. She hands him her notes, and he returns them to her as a speech."

"I know that. I am surprised he didn't write her speech in rhyme. Nonetheless, she did put her mark on it. I had forgotten Poldemire and I took the girls with us to Scare City and Timorous." Queen Marguerite—now *Queen Mother* Marguerite, held up her lorgnette. "Is that Count Russell stepping onto the platform?"

"Your eyes are better than mine," Nanny squinted.

"It is. And there's Abel Handsforth. They are lifting Pristine into her coronation chair. It looks like the Count is going to speak. Let's listen."

The pulse of the congregation buzzed, as Count Russell took the microphone. He shouted over the talking, "you know what time it is? It is time to engage our Fourth Tradition—the Wild Subjects' Dance."

Those along the aisles were already boogying. No one noticed when the vestibule doors opened, and a mirror image of the new Queen, dressed in an emerald green suit with matching coronet, stormed into the sanctuary, trailed by a tall man in a chauffeur's uniform. "Erica, I stand behind you," he assured the princess.

"That is exactly where I want you, *Buzz*," she stopped in her tracks— "I only want what is rightfully mine. I am not leaving without my crown, and my scepter."

Guards were familiar with every Goldspinner royal. They had seen them all at one time or another, if not in person, in portraits hanging from the throne room walls. Portraits of the twin princesses had been commissioned to commemorate their sixteenth birthday, years ago. Both still resembled their likeness, but the artist's stroke of the brush could not conceal truth: princess Erica sparkled, from a distance, but up close she was a royal mess. The guards recognized her immediately, in spite of having changed her hairstyle, and put on weight.

"It's Princess Erica," whispered one of the guards—"grab her."

"No," a second guard rebuffed, "we have orders not to interfere, unless there is a threat. Princess Erica is no threat."

Eighty feet over their heads, the ceiling girders creaked. The recently installed electric chandeliers over the gallery flickered, and swayed to and fro. Those seated upstairs cringed in fear. "Fire!" they yelled, and shouted, "get out!"

"Take cover," shouted another, "it's an earthquake."

Those in the back pews became overwhelmed by an overpowering scent of lavender. They sneezed, as the princess hastened by. "That's Princess Erica," shouted one, "and her hu-hu-*husband*," she sneezed.

"Bless you. It *is* the princess," shouted another.

Buzz scanned the pews looking for an empty seat, among shushers dodging the altar boys, waving enormous fans up the aisles.

"Buzz," the princess turned to her husband, "what were they thinking? — not sending me an invitation to my own coronation."

Buzz caressed the princess's shoulder, "Erica, stay calm."

The custodian entered the sanctuary, carrying a thirty-foot rod over his head. He pinned it to the overhead casement fixtures, twisted it, and the windows opened. Buzz found a seat next to the only two subjects who dared to wear white, and was about to sit down when a crazed redhead — in all probability an inmate from Loco, jumped in his face. "It's princess *Hysterica*," she shouted, "she is the real queen here. She shared her experience with us in group."

A guard prompted the woman back into her seat. Erica knew she should have kept silent in group, but Loco Rehabilitation encouraged sharing as an essential part of the 12 Step recovery program — step number four — making ammends.

"I'll wait for you here, Erica."

"Are you crazy, Buzz? Are you seriously going to sit down between to White Witches?"

"That's the only empty seat I can find, Erica."

"You find a seat on this side, Buzz," she flung him across the aisle, "I am going to go address those witches right now." She crossed the aisle, stopped before the nurses, and spoke directly into their faces. "You think because you wear little white caps with wings that you have the right to poke needles into people and force them to take medications. Well, you will never catch me again." She turned away, hastened up the aisle, and left her husband behind.

Buzz found another empty seat in a back pew, and squiggled by a pink-haired woman with glassy eyes, framed and tinted by gold-rimmed glasses. "Take a seat, Big Bones," she barked, as he passed, "you're blocking my view."

Head bowed, unrecognized, Buzz squirmed down the pew, and sat down.

As the princess dodged dancers, and passed the sandstone columns, memories of Loco came to mind. The witches followed me here, she thought, just like Security, to protect me — they say.

Nurse *Chat* tied her shoelace. "Looks like princess Erica has put on a little weight," she said.

Nurse *Chien* saw Princess Erica hasten by, "ten pounds, at least," she said, "I'd say she stopped taking her medication."

"Remember the last time the princess stopped taking her meds?"

"Lordy, lord, she drove *us* crazy."

"She is royalty. We should show more respect, Chat."

Erica approached the platform, as the thurifer stepped into the aisle with his swinging censer, filled with smouldering sandalwood. Upon seeing the princess approach, he leaped out of the way, but his censer bumped her on the posterior portion of her royal anatomy, catapulting her onto the platform, landing her hands down before the Queen. Count Russell nearly fell off the platform, he was so surprised, if not for the quick reactions of Abel Handsforth.

"Leave it to princess Erica to make a memorable entrance," the count told the footman, "she always was the athlete of the family."

Erica leaped into her sister's lap. "Give me my crown," she shouted.

Guards stepped in, but the footman was quicker. He grabbed the crown off the Queen's head, and stepped back with it.

Pristine raised a finger. "Thank you, gentlemen, I can handle this."

"Give me Mother's pearls," Erica grabbed Pristine's neck.

Pristine flinched, "I will not."

"Give them to me. Mother left them to me."

Pristine lifted her scepter. "Erica, come to your senses."

Guards held princess Erica back, while subjects twirled their partners around the platform to the music, oblivious to the events occurring six feet over their heads, on the platform.

"People are watching, Erica."

"They're not watching, they're dancing."

"What will the Press print?"

"I don't care what the Press prints, Pristine," Erica struggled, and the guard tightened his grip.

"I am going to keep you restrained, Erica, until you calm down."

Nanny turned to Queen Mother. "Your Majesty, did princess Erica not receive an invitation to the coronation?"

"She must have," replied Queen Mother. "The Press is going to have questions. You and I are lucky, Needlepinch. Most cannot tell the twins apart."

"It wasn't until the other day I noticed a mole behind Pristine's ear, while I was brushing her hair."

"Yes, I noticed that, too." Queen Mother shook her head, "after this fiasco, Erica's visits to Loco are bound to go public."

"One never knows, Ma'am. The matter could fly over the subjects' heads. Look how engaged they are in the music."

Queen Mother raised her lorgnette. "What is going on up there? Have they still not settled this?"

Erica slipped out of the guards' grip, leaped into Pristine's lap, and reached for her pearls. "I want my necklace," she shrieked. The guard pulled her back, the pearl necklace broke, and pearls scattered everywhere.

"Erica," Pristine watched the pearls roll off the platform, "now look what you have done—you tore the strand!"

Guards got on hands and knees and gathered pearls.

"Look what *I* have done? Your guard pulled me—it's his fault." Erica snatched the pearls off Pristine's earlobes, and cut her sister's leg with her ring, as she tumbled to the floor.

Pristine felt her earlobes, and looked at her fingers, "I'm bleeding."

"Ma'am," the footman reached in a handkerchief.

"Thank you, Handsforth." Pristine maintained her composure, as she dabbed blood off her ears. She clenched her teeth. "Erica, give me my earrings."

"I will not." Erica popped the earrings into her mouth, as the guards pulled her back.

Count Russell turned to the footman. "Handsforth, go get help."

"Where is my Mina? She is supposed to be here."

"Miss *Amora* has been detained, Ma'am," Count Russell took the handkerchief off the Queen's hand, "*Bereave-Track* is on strike. The trains have stopped running."

"I should never have worn new shoes." Pristine turned to the guard. "Let the princess go. She can do no further harm."

Erica turned her attention to the dancing subjects, below the platform. Buzz heard the orchestra play his wife's favorite tune—the *Discordian Waltz*. He walked to the platform, and sought her out. Upon seeing her husband, Erica leaped into his arms, and unidentified by the inebriated subjects, he waltzed her into the crowd of dancers, and around the corner.

Handsforth approached Nurse *Chien*, "Her Majesty has been injured," he said, "your services are needed on the platform."

The nurse rose from her seat. "We are on it, Sir. *Chat*, come; duty calls."

Handsforth returned to the platform. "Your Majesty," he bowed before the new Queen, "two nurses are coming to tend to your wounds. Excuse me, while I go find us some privacy. I will be return momentarily."

"Privacy?"—Bishop Martens overheard, and motioned to the stairs— "downstairs in my office is private."

19

Buzz waltzed Erica through the crowd, unnoticed. They turned the corner, and he asked her, "Erica, why did you attack the Queen?"

The princess shook her head. "I don't know why I attacked her, Buzz. Years of pent up frustration, I guess."

"Pristine is your sovereign, Erica."

"God is my sovereign—dance, Buzz."

Pristine sat in her chair, visually troubled. How am I to maintain dignity?—she wondered. Never has any member of the royal family ever participated in the Wild Subjects' Dance.

"Excuse me, Your Majesty," Bishop Martens bowed, "I suggest we go downstairs to my office where you can have some privacy."

"Very well then," Pristine rose from the coronation chair. Cloak carriers stepped in, followed by entourage, and Bishop Martens walked the Queen to the stairs.

"Count Russell, how do you think the Press is going to report this?"

"Your Majesty, if I may be candid..."

"Please, candid it the only way."

"The Wild Subjects' Dance is an opportunity for the subjects to release their pent up emotions. It is through you they take part in a bit of glory, and it looks like they are enjoying themselves. I imagine that is what the Press will report. Now let us get you down the stairs, to my office."

"My earlobe is bleeding, so is my leg."

"As soon as we get you settled in my parlor, the nurses will tend to that, Ma'am."

Nurse Chien stood at the handrail, behind the Queen and her entourage. "Your Majesty," she curtseyed, "if I may say so, it is an honor to serve the Crown."

Nurse Chat approached, discomforted by the heavy first aide kit.

Nurse Chien grabbed the handrail, and stepped down. "Come, Chat, let's get a move on."

"*Come Chat*," the nurse mocked her superior, "*get a move on.*"

"Poor Chat," Chien shook her head, "life can't be easy with two left feet."

CHAPTER IV

The Bishop's Parlor

Queen Mother Marguerite, still seated next to Nanny Needlepinch in the front row of the sanctuary, took another sip of fortitude, and closed her flask. "I know the Wild Subjects' Dance is tradition, Nanny, but I don't recall ever hearing of any family member participating."

Nanny scratched an itch. "Times have changed, Ma'am—and so has Erica."

Queen Mother slipped her flask into her purse. "What has become of her, Nanny? She seemed so well-adjusted at Poldi's memorial."

"The poor girl has still not gotten over the loss of her parents. Those shock treatments in Loco didn't help any; in fact, they did her more harm than good, and medications can only do so much."

"Perhaps Dr. Fuehlgoed is not the doctor to meet her needs. Perhaps she needs another doctor."

Count Russell and footman Handsforth escorted the Queen, followed by cloak carriers and nurses, down the steps to the bishop's office. The bishop turned to the Queen, "Your Majesty, I think it best the carriers remain outside."

Count Russell nodded in agreement, "the less the merrier, Ma'am."

"This way, Ma'am." Bishop Martens walked the Queen down a long corridor, to the door to his quarters, where Handsforth stood, flanked on either side by a guard, holding a crossed bayonet. Upon seeing the Queen approach, the guards uncrossed their arms, and Bishop Martens guided the Queen over the threshold. "My parlor is to the left, Ma'am, through this archway."

Handsforth held the crown over the Queen's head, and walked through the archway with her, into the bishop's parlor, where five chairs hugged a round glass coffee table. "Ma'am," he lowered his head, "might I rest your crown on its pillow?"

"Splendid idea, Handsforth, thank you."

The footman took the crown. "Might I rest your scepter at your feet, Ma'am?"

"Handsforth, please do," she handed the scepter to the footman—"it's so heavy. Forgive me, gentlemen, but my shoes are killing me." She used one to kick off the other, and lifted her legs, as the footman rolled in an ottoman.

"I am only in the way here," Bishop Martens stepped forward. "Ma'am, if you should need me, I will be in my office."

"Thank you, Bishop."

"Your Majesty," he bowed his head, "it is my pleasure to serve."

Nurse Chien took a seat, and got to work. "If you will allow me, Ma'am, I would like to check your vital signs."

"Vital signs?"

"Yes, Ma'am. Let us start with your pulse."

"My pulse? What is your name, Nurse?"

"Nurse Chien, Ma'am."

"Nurse is not a name. Nurse is a title."

"*Abigail Chien,* Your Majesty."

"Nurse Chien, I assure you, I am vital."

"I believe you, Ma'am, but I must take your pulse. It's procedure."

"Very well then." Pristine extended her arm "if you insist."

"I do. Raise your sleeve, if you would, please."

Chat set the ermegency kit on the table, and turned to the Queen. Without thinking, in deference, she addressed her. "Your Majesty, if I may say so, it is an honor to serve the Crown."

Pristine was beguiled, "what is your name, Miss?"

"Nurse Chat, Ma'am, *Maggie Chat.*"

Chien held her hand out, "be of service, Chat, hand me the stethoscope."

"What a lovely name—Maggie, short for Marguerite."

"Your pulse is normal, Ma'am."

"I told you, Nurse Chien, I am vital."

"Yes Ma'am. Now for your heartbeat. Open your jacket, please," Chien plugged her stethoscope into her ears, "unbutton your blouse."

"Unbutton my blouse?"

"Yes, Ma'am, the top three buttons.

"Really, Nurse, I am quite vital."

"It is all a matter of procedure, Ma'am. Inhale, please," Chien placed the stethoscope over Pristine's heart—"again, please."

"I assure you I am quite well, except for my earlobes, and this nasty gash on my leg."

"I will get to that in a moment, Ma'am. Breathe again, please," Chien moved the disc, "if I may I say so, I don't understand why Princess Erica calls us White Witches. Breathe again, please. Granted, we do wear white, but we are not witches. Another breath, Ma'am."

"My sister has led a troubled life, Nurse Chien. She must be forgiven."

"One more deep breath. That's it—nice and deep."

"The shock treatments did her more harm than good."

"Your pulse is normal, Ma'am. Your respiratory system sounds fine." She pulled the stethoscope out of her ears, and handed it to Chat. "Here, Chat, hand me the thermometer."

Chat took the stethoscope, and handed the thermometer to Chien. "I checked it," she said, "it's ready."

"Open your mouth, Ma'am—say aah..."

"Aah..."

"Under your tongue, Ma'am," Chien wedged the thermometer between the Queen's lips. "That's it. Now, let me take a look at your ears." She held out her hand, "Chat—cotton and alcohol."

"Nursh"—Pristine schlurred, "I mevah dwink alkohoe."

"Oops—no talking, Your Majesty." Chien wedged the thermometer in place. "What I meant was Witchhazel—not alcohol. Witchhazel is not intended for human consumption."

"Unless you live in Terror," Chat interjected, "I hear it gets so cold in Scare City, the subjects drink gasoline to keep from freezing."

"Thank you for sharing, Chat," Chien held out her hand, "I am waiting."

"They even drink perfume," she nodded.

"I am waiting," Chat's voice took on a melodic tone.

"Waiting for what?"

"Witchhazel, and cotton. Get with the program, Chat."

Chat handed a roll of cotton, and the bottle of Witchhazel to Chien. Chien took the bottle. "What am I to do with the entire roll of cotton, Chat? For heaven's sake—tear a piece off, and hand it to me."

"Here you are."

"Thank you."

Chat addressed the Queen, "Your Majesty, I would like to take this opportunity to wish you a long, healthy reign, and may you have many male heirs."

"Fhank you, Nursh." Why does everybody think I have to have a male heir to be happy?—Pristine wondered—aren't they aware the Goldspinner line is matriarchal?

"Now, to your earlobes. Let me see...I think this can be patched without scarring."

"Patschid?"

"Yes, Ma'am. This may sting."

Count Russell hovered over the Queen. "Don't forget the gash on Her Majesty's leg."

"I am on it, Count," Chien dabbed the Queen's earlobe.

"I just want to make sure," the count stepped back.

"There we go, Ma'am. That wasn't so bad now, was it?"

"Mo," Pristine shook her head, "mop bab aeh awe."

Chien removed the thermometer from the Queen's mouth, and held it to the light. "You have a fever, Ma'am—99.3. Chat—hand me two aspirin, and fetch a glass of water."

Pristine sighed, "it's the stress of all the preparing these past three weeks—Erica's entrance, her perfume, the loud music."

Chien handed the thermometer to Chat, and saturated a cotton wad.

"Count Russell?"

"Ma'am?" the count approached the Queen.

"Do me a favor, please."

"Yes, Ma'am, anything."

"Go upstairs, please, and check on Queen Mother and Nanny Needlepinch. I don't want them to feel abandoned."

"It would be my pleasure, Ma'am." Count Russell nodded, and exited.

Handsforth carried in a glass of water, and a silver bucket of ice. He set the ice on the table, and handed the glass of water to the Queen. "The ice should bring down your swelling," he said.

Chien handed two aspirin to the Queen. "Take these, Ma'am, and if you will lift your skirt, I will tend to that gash."

"Lift my skirt?"

"Lift your skirt, Ma'am," Chien turned to her colleague, "Chat, fill the compress."

Pristine pulled her skit up above the knee, and summoned the footman. "Handsforth..."

The footman stepped forward, "yes, Ma'am."

"Do me a favor. Ask the guards to bring princess Erica to me."

24

"Yes, Ma'am," Handsforth bowed, and exited the bishop's parlor.

"This will feel cold, Ma'am," Chat placed a compress on Pristine's forehead."

Chien sterilized the Queen's wound, and unrolled the gauze. "This is going to protect you from getting infected," she said, "have it changed daily."

"Thank you, Nurse—and me an ice cube, please." Pristine held the cube to her earlobe, and breahed in a sigh of relief, "oh—it's throbbing."

"Wipe the blood off Her Majesty's jacket, Chat."

"Count Russell already wiped it, Chien."

"Then wipe it again, Chat." Chien clamped the gauze around Pristine's leg, closed the emergency kit, and rose to her feet. "Well, Ma'am, it looks like our work here is done. One day I will tell my grandchildren of Coronation Day, 1911, when I was called upon to serve the Crown."

"Thank you for your care, Nurse Chien. I wish you well, always."

"Happy Coronation Day, Your Majesty. Grab the kit, Chat, and let's go."

Chat curtseyed, "happy Coronation Day, Ma'am."

Upon stepping into the corridor, they ran into Handsforth.

"Excuse me, ladies," the footman bowed with respect, "princess Erica is about to come this way. Would you mind taking the west wing stairs?"

"Have we a choice?" asked Chat.

"Come Chat, we don't want to upset Her Royal Highness again."

"Thank you, ladies," Handsforth smiled, "your service is much appreciated."

Princess Erica descended the staircase, on the arms of two guards, followed by a procession of fans being held back by eight more. Erica shrieked upon seeing the nurses in the corridor, "White Witches," she recoiled, and turned to the guard, "you took me away from Buzz for this? This is a trick. Let me go."

The guard bowed. "Your Royal Highness, I assure you, the nurses are leaving."

The princess was taken aback. No one has addressed me by my title in years, she thought.

The second guard bowed. "Your Royal Highness, I assure you this is no trick."

He, too, called me Your Royal Highness. She took his hand. "Alright then—take me to the Queen."

The guards escorted the princess down the steps, to the bishop's office door, where Handsforth stood, flanked by the guards. "I will take over from here," Handsforth took the princess's hand, and walked her through the doorway.

"Your Royal Highness," Bishop Martens rose from his desk, and bowed, "I am honored to receive you in my quarters."

The princess crinkled her nose. "I smell them," sniff sniff, "they're here."

Bishop Martens stepped out from behind his desk. "Who is here, Your Royal Highness?"

Erica looked at the drapes. "Are they hiding behind the drapes?"

"Your Royal Highness, I assure you there is no one here."

"The nurses are gone, Your Royal Highness," Handsforth escorted the princess to the parlor, "allow me to announce you." He opened the door. With a sweeping gesture, he proclaimed: "present, Her Majesty, Queen Pristine, Count Russell presiding. Entering: Her Royal Highness, princess *Erica Gold-runner* of *Discord*."

Erica zoomed in on the crown, resting on the sideboard, and the scepter at her sister's foot. "Are the Witches gone?"

Pristine hung on the precipice of a sneeze. Finally, no longer able to hold it in, she sneezed, "ah-aah-aaah-CHOO!—Excu-u-use me."

"Bless you, Ma'am." Handsforth reached in a hankie.

"Thank you, Handsforth, open the window, please," she turned to her sister, "Erica, must you overdo everything?"

"You like lavender."

"I used to like lavender—not anymore."

The breeze coming in through the window blew the curtain covering an alcove, leading the princess to investigate. "Are they hiding in here?"

"Who? Your imaginary witches? There are no witches here, Erica. Sit down."

"I'm not taking any chances."

"Sit down. There is no one here but us. Thank you, Handsforth, that breeze feels wonderful." Pristine turned to her sister, "Erica, three drops will do. You smell like you fell into a vat of air freshener."

"Perhaps I did splash on a bit much. I felt anxious this morning—it being Coronation Day and all."

"Now I know how Loco pinned you with the nickname *Hyst-Erica*. That was crazy, the way you leaped into my lap out there. You tore my earlobes. You gashed my leg."

"I didn't mean to hurt you, but you fought me."

"You tore my necklace."

"That was my necklace. Those are my pearls—wherever they are now. Mother left them to me."

"You could have asked for them."

"You wouldn't have given them to me."

"I guess you will never know—will you? I tell you what. I will tell Mrs. Thornecroft to have them restrung, and she will send them to you. Now sit down. Where's Buzz?"

Erica settled into a chair. "He's upstairs. If you want to see him, why did you have me summoned?"

"I am simply making an inquiry. You've gained weight."

Erica sighed, "it's my cross to bear. I eat, but am never satisfied."

"Why eat then?"

"I feel guilty if I don't."

"You know Goldspinners don't believe in guilt, Erica."

"I know, but I do anyway. Then I feel shame over having felt guilty."

"Goldspinners don't believe in shame, either. What have you to be ashamed of?"

"I overeat."

"Why do you overeat?"

"I feel guilty."

"This is about Mummy and Daddy again."

"I could have saved them, Pristine."

"No, Erica, you couldn't have. You were in shock, like everyone else."

"They cried out to me for help, and I didn't respond."

"Stop blaming yourself, Erica. The only thing you have control over is your mind—and your appetite. Sure, it was traumatic watching Mummy and Daddy die, but you have to let them go."

"I've never stopped trying to."

"Then stop trying, and do it. Put it behind you, Erica. Move on."

"That's easy for you to say, oh high and mighty Queen. You weren't even there."

"I wasn't *on* the airfield, but I was *at* the airfield with you just the same."

"You were not. You were inside the terminal."

"Erica, what has gotten into you? You seemed so with it at Grandpa Poldi's funeral."

"The world has turned crazy."

"It always was crazy. That's why you went to Insanity."

"Everything seems too much anymore. Just keeping *Norbert* and *Norbertina* in line is a job in itself. Then I have to keep Buzz out of my hair."

"It all comes down to what you want."

"I want my crown, Pristine, and my scepter."

"You mean you don't want the kingdom?"

"I don't fit in here," the princess shook her head, "I never did. I only want what's mine, the crown, the scepter, and Mummy's pearls."

"I told you, I will get your pearls after they have been restrung."

"Send them general delivery. The crocs frighten some people."

"What crocs?"

"The ones that guard the moat."

"Only my sister would have a moat to breed crocodiles in."

"We don't breed them, Pristine. They breed themselves. Buzz says crocs keep the right people in, the wrong people out. No longer is it a problem keeping Norbert and Norbertina from leaving, since we added the crocs."

"You still keep your servants locked behind bars?"

"Who says?"

"You do."

"I?"

"You told me they escaped. Buzz had to go out in the pouring rain and drag them back."

"They didn't escape. They got stuck before they even got down the crag. He brought thm back, and we came to an agreement."

"What sort of agreement?"

"Buzz bought them a radio."

"But you get no reception up there on Top of the Crags."

"Buzz installed an antenna."

"But no sender can penetrate your crags."

"A few can, when it's clear."

"Your two weeks of summer?"

"It's longer than that. You exaggerate."

"Three weeks."

"Buzz allows them free entry into the courtyard."

"But you don't allow them to leave."

"I do, but where would they go?"

"Out."

"They go out. They go to church. They eat out in town, after church."

"You need to remove the bars from their windows."

"The bars are there to protect them."

"Protect them from what, Erica?"

"Intruders. Besides, the bars have been there for centuries. You do not understand the Discordian mind, Pristine. Discordians are simple people."

"Simple or not, people need their freedom."

"My servants are free."

"Not as long as they remain behind bars, they are not."

"They have more freedom than they know what to do with. They have free room and board, free coffee, tea, biscuits, and every Friday they get a free delivery of ale. They are free to worship as they please. They are free to listen to free radio, and they have a subscription to the *Discordian Free Press.*"

"That's not the kind of freedom I'm talking about, Erica."

"How much more freedom could they handle?"

"Your Press isn't free. Only the subscription is free, not the word—and you censor."

"I do not censor."

"You do too."

"I do not. Every month, I meet with the editor. I tell him what the subjects want to hear, and we decide together what to print."

"By the time your subjects get your news, it's olds."

"It is not."

"What has become of us, Erica? We used to be so close. We used to get along. There was no jealousy."

"Who's jealous?"

"We both are. You treat your servants like children."

Erica rose from the chair. "I treat my servants like children because they act like children, and don't you tell me how to handle my staff, oh high and mighty *Princess of Perfection—Queen of Entitlement.* You spit out commands from your throne while I struggle in Discord, with Buzz."

"As of yet, Erica, I have not spit out any commands."

"You sent Handsforth to get me. That was a command."

"You are right, but I didn't spit it out."

"Am I to be held responsible for my servants' lot in life? What about my lot?"

"Erica, if I could wave my scepter, and reverse the effects of gravity, I would."

"It's my scepter."

"Let's be realistic, Erica. You crashed my coronation."

29

"It was supposed to be *my* coronation, Pristine. You didn't even send me an invitation."

"You were sent one. I had Mrs. Thornecroft place you and Buzz at the top of the list."

"We never received an invitation."

"Maybe your crocodiles ate it."

"That's not funny."

"Maybe it wasn't delivered to you up there—on top of the Crags."

"The crocs never stopped any delivery before."

"I have an idea. Why don't you stay for the banquet. I'll have the footmen set up a table under the cherry trees for just you and Buzz. You love the cherry trees, Erica."

"I do love the cherry trees."

"You can root for me while I give my speech. Better yet, you could speak a few words."

"Speak a few words? Me? Oh no," Erica shook her head, "you know I don't speak in public."

"This is an opportunity for you to lay to rest some gossip. Let people see the real Erica, the genuine, caring person I know, not the crazy woman who crashed my coronation."

"I'm not crazy."

"Who else would enter with a cartwheel, and jump into my lap?"

"It was a turnabout, Pristine. The thurifer's censor hit me in the rear. No way am I going to speak. Besides, we have to be back in *Gruntle* before dark."

"Think about it. A few words might settle the subjects' tongues. Count Russell could whip up a few words for you."

"I told you, Pristine, I don't speak in public."

"But you have no qualms about dancing around the nave with the commoners."

"That is different."

"How?"

"The Wild Subjects' Dance is tradition."

"Not for members of the royal family, it isn't."

"I don't know why I'm here."

"You are here because you want my crown, my scepter, and my pearls."

"They're my pearls, Pristine. Give me the crown and the scepter, and I promise to leave you alone."

"Why should I give you my crown? You won't even speak to the subjects. How would you rule? I wonder how Buzz handles your constant mood swings."

"What mood swings?"

"Your personality shifts."

"Buzz sees beyond shifts. He treats me like the queen I am."

"I'm happy for you. You deserve the best. Are you taking your medication?"

"The last regimen made me dizzy. I blacked out on the street in Grace while we were there. I was lucky, Buzz was at my side."

"Monsieur *Noirod* hand delivered your postcard from *Helena*."

"Who's Monsieur Noirod?"

"The cute dark man in the Communications Office—with the wooly hair. You blacked out? They ran you out of town, didn't they?"

"They called me Hysterica. They refused to call me by my title. I was hoodwinked, Pristine, and so were you. Grandpa Poldi's Court should never have sent me away. Doctor *Kindervater* and *Uncle George* are especially guilty. Even *Auntie Avorah*. She did nothing to stop them. Even Nanny could have spoken up, but she didn't."

"You cannot blame Nanny. You can't blame any of them, Erica."

"I can if I want to."

"At your own peril. It was the Court that sent you away."

"The day you tricked me into trading birth certificates with you is the day you turned me into a second-class citizen."

"I didn't trick you, Erica. I am not responsible for turning you into anything, either."

"You have no idea what pain is until you've had four people sit on top of you, hold you down, and tie you into a straight jacket. Then the White Witches start shooting drugs into you, and they force pills down your throat. They made me board with five strangers—in one room."

"I admit that must be humiliating, but Erica, you had no control over Mummy and Daddy's death. It was an act of nature. Their crying exists only at night—in your dreams."

"They exist in daydreams, too, Pristine."

"Because you keep them alive."

"They are alive."

"Millions die every day, Erica, and they heal."

"No they don't. They die."

"You know what I mean. Remember what Mistress *Sitwell* used to say: 'The healing stops when you stop healing'."

"You and your stupid Mistress Sitwell quotes."

"She was a fine teacher. She taught us well."

"She, too, is guilty. She tricked me into giving up my identity."

"You and I exchanged birth certificates willingly, Erica, and you were fully aware when you did so."

"Sp-p-pare p-parts is all I am to you G-goldspinners," the princess held back a tear, "a backup, in c-case anything should ha-happen to you. The name Erica Goldspinner will g-go down in hi-history as the monarch that never wa-a-was."

"Who never was."

"Me," the princess sniffled.

"Who never was, Erica. Not *that*, the monarch *who* never was."

"Never mind," Erica pulled out a hankie, and dried a tear.

"You think it was any easier for me, Erica?—knowing *I* was the spare? We're twins. What affects you affects me. I know how tragic this has been for you."

"You do not."

"So I don't. But I lost them, too, and I got over it."

"You are insensitive, Pristine Goldspinner. I should start a rumor, see how *you* handle things." Erica started singing, "*Crystal Rock is tumbling down, tumbling down, crumbling down...*"

"Stop singing."

"*Crystal Rock is crumbling down...*"

"Erica, I said stop singing." Pristine grabbed her scepter, and rose from the chair.

"Oh mightly Queen of Entitlement, Princess of Perfection," Erica sneered—"make me."

CHAPTER V

Treasonous Rumor

Queen Mother Marguerite and Nanny Needlepinch snapped their fingers and tapped their feet, as they watched the dancers swing partners around the sanctuary platform. Queen Mother slipped her flask into her purse, grabbed her walking stick, and shouted over the noise to be heard. "It was good of Count Russell to check in on us, and it has been fun, Nanny, but my posterior is telling me I am ready for a change of scenery."

"I am ready for my nap." Nanny planted her stick, and prepared for lift-off, "all this noise is exhausting. Let's go see the twins."

"I think it best we allow them to sort things out on their own."

"Nonsense. They already have. Our flasks are empty. Let's go."

Queen Mother rose from the pew, and shimmied down the aisle past bowing and curtseying subjects, held behind ropes by guards. She stopped at a column, and turned to Nanny. "Needlepinch—how long have we known each other?"

A lifetime," Nanny rested against the column, "I came to you before Henriette was born—God rest her soul. Seventy-six years?"

"A lifetime."

"Give me a minute, Ma'am. I need to catch my breath."

"You know me," Queen Mother raised her voice to be heard over the noise, "generally speaking, I am not concerned with what people will think. They so seldom do. What concerns me is how the Press is going to report Erica's entrance."

"They are going to have a field day with this one."

"I can already see tomorrow's headlines: PRINCESS HYSTERICA—ROYAL MESS CRASHES CORONATION. That would make for terrible public relations." Queen Mother pushed herself off the column, "let's go."

Nanny followed Queen Mother to the staircase. "I wouldn't want to be the one to face the Press," she said. "If anyone knows Erica, it is I. I know her better than she knows herself. She and Pristine both confided their secrets in me. Erica was always somewhat different. She wasn't like the rest of the Goldspinners."

"Who am I to tell her she cannot be happy married to a chauffeur?"

"You are the regent supreme of Entitlement, Ma'am, Queen Mother of Abundance, Her Royal Highness's grandmother."

"Neither Erica nor Pristine came to me with their problems. They went to you, Nanny. What a disappointment to have a chauffeur in the family."

"The sooner you accept it, Ma'am, the happier you will be."

"This is not even about Buzz. He's a good man of strong character. It's about centuries of tradition."

"Look at it this way, Ma'am, princess Erica will always have someone to drive her around."

"Small consolation." Queen Mother stopped before the staircase, and grabbed the handrail. "Are you ready to take the steps?"

"Give me a minute."

"You need another break?"

"I need to catch my breath."

"We are descending the stairs, Needlepinch, not climbing."

"I need a moment to catch my breath."

Queen Mother took the first step. "Let me know when you are ready. I will await you downstairs."

Nanny planted her stick on the first step, and grabbed the handrail. "This could take a while," she shouted.

Downstairs in the bishop's parlor, princess Erica sang her song inciting Crystal Rock in its downfall. Queen Mother stood outside the door, and listened, as Pristine reprimanded her sister. "Erica, I told you to stop singing," Queen Mother heard Pristine shout—"you are blasphemizing the Crown."

"Oh my," Queen Mother was shocked, "what a horrible thing to do."

Nanny finally made it down the stairs, and Handforth escorted the two women to the bishop's quarters. Nanny grabbed a few catalogues off the bishop's desk, in passing, and stepped back in line. Handsforth knocked, and opened the parlor door. "Your Majesty, Queen Pristine, and Her Royal Highness, Princess Erica presiding," he announced, "entering

34

the parlor, Her Majesty, Queen Mother Marguerite, and Miss Carabella Needlepinch."

"My dear," Queen Mother walked over to Pristine, kissed her on both cheeks, and set her purse down, "congratulations. You are now the most powerful woman in the world. Use your position wisely." She approached Erica, and kissed her on the forehead, "Erica, could you not have made a more respectable entrance?"

"I was pushed, GranMarguerite."

"My dear," Nanny kissed Pristine on both cheeks, "may I be second to congratulate you, our beautiful new Queen." She kissed Erica on her forehead. "Have you two talked through your differences?" she asked.

"Erica changed her mind again, Nanny."

Queen Mother sat down, "not again."

"Again Erica?" Nanny plopped into a chair, and stuck her stick inside the upholstery.

"I was only playing with you, Pristine."

"That was not play, Erica."

"Your singing sounded serious to me, Erica," Queen Mother rested her stick against the chair, "I could hear you out in the corridor. It's cold in here," she turned to the footman — "Handsforth..."

"Shut the windows, Ma'am? I am on it."

"How did you know?"

"I asked Handsforth to open the windows and let in some fresh air, GranMarguerite. Erica brought the lavender field with her."

"Pristine doesn't like the scent of my perfume."

"I didn't say I don't like your perfume, Erica. It's the dosage I have a problem with."

"You must tone it down, Erica" Nanny settled into the chair, "we followed your trail down the stairs."

Queen Mother reached into her purse, pulled out her flask, and unscrewed the lid. "Oh"—she sighed, "I forgot..."

"It's empty, Ma'am." Handsforth reached out, "hand it to me, and I will see to it it is filled."

"You are right. I forgot. Thank you, Handsforth," Queen Mother handed her flask to the footman, and he stepped out.

"I am worried about you, Erica," Nanny opened a catalogue, "have you been taking your medication?"

"I have," Erica nodded.

"Which are you taking?"

"I forgot the name. I don't look at them. I just take them. They keep changing colors."

"The pills?"

"No, the doctors."

"The doctors change colors?"

"No. The doctors change the color of the pills."

"How many doctors write you prescriptions?"

"Just Dr. Fuehlgoed."

"You are aware a change in color indicates a shift in dosage, Erica."

"I know that, GranMarguerite. I take a pink when I'm feeling anxious. If I feel too mellow, I take a yellow, and when I'm feeling mean, Buzz tells me to take two green."

"It sounds like you know your regimen, but why this morning's disruptive entrance? I watched through my lorgnette, and was shocked."

"I was pushed."

"Pushed?"

"I told you—by the thurifer's censor. I did the best with it. I turned it into a turnabout."

"Erica wants her birth certificate back, GranMarguerite."

"Not again," Nanny thumbed through the catalogue, "I thought we had settled this."

"I was just playing with Pristine, GranMarguerite. I just wanted to see her reaction. Pristine, you have what it takes to rule. I don't." Erica rose from the chair, and walked to the wall mirror. Seeing her reflection, she pulled her stomach in, and grew by a quarter inch.

"Your mood swings can be exhausting for others, Erica," Nanny flipped a page.

"What do you think they do to me, Nanny?"

"Look, GranMarguerite," Pristine indicated her ear, "Erica tore the earrings off my ears and cut me."

"Oh my, they do look swollen." Queen Mother laid her gloves out on her purse.

"And look," Pristine raised her skirt, and extended her leg, "she gashed my calf, too."

"Erica," Nanny peeked over the catalogue, "what has gotten into you since your grandfather's memorial?"

"That was a good day," Erica smiled into the mirror.

Pristine turned. "Did you hear that, Nanny? She just said the day her grandfather died was a good day."

"I did not."

"You did so. I heard you."

"What I meant was it was a good day *for me*—the memorial. It helped me grieve."

Handsforth knocked, stepped into the parlor, and handed Queen Mother her flask. "I found some Sherry, Ma'am," he whispered.

"Thank you, Handsforth." Queen Mother removed the flask's lid, and took a sip of her fortitude.

Erica returned to her chair, and sat down. "GranMarguerite, tell Pristine what the prophets predicted."

"We all know what the prophets predicted, Erica."

"They said *I* would produce a male heir."

"They never predicted *I* wouldn't. I could bear a dozen male heirs if I wanted to, Erica, but I don't—I hate children."

"Pristine, no need to be so adamant about it."

"Well, it's true."

"Girls," Queen Mother set her flask aside, "we know what the prophets predicted."

Nanny glanced over her catalogue, "tell us about this rumor you want to start, Erica."

"Erica's been singing about Crystal Rock crumbling into the sea."

"My dear," Nanny set the catalogue aside, "that's treason."

"I have a better song, and it's not treason." Erica started singing, "*Pristine* and *God-wyn* sitting in a tree, $k-i-s-s-i-n-g$."

Pristine grabbed her scepter. "Stop singing, Erica."

"*First comes love...*"

"In the name of the Crown, I command you to stop singing."

"*...then comes marriage...*"

"Erica," Pristine rose from the chair, and shouted, "stop singing!"

Queen Mother sipped, and closed her flask. "Erica, let off this nonsense."

"Rebellious is what it is." Pristine rested the scepter against the chair, and sat down. "Nursery rhymes about people kissing is child's play, but involving Crystal Rock in its downfall is insurrection."

"It's treason," Nanny grabbed another catalogue.

Pristine closed her eyes, and thought of the prince of Grace, *Godwyn Bonheur*, Defender of the Faith.

Nanny nodded. "Erica, it would not hurt you to settle down."

"I will not tolerate anyone speaking ill of Prince Godwyn," Pristine opened her eyes, "not even you, Erica. How dare you start a rumor about someone you don't even know."

"I know Godwyn as well as you do."

"You only wish you did."

Queen Mother patted her armrest. "Come sit with me, Erica."

Erica crossed the room, and joined her grandmother in her chair. "I'm sorry, GranMarguerite," she sniffled, "I don't mean to be so difficult."

Queen Mother stroked Erica's hair. "My dear, we will work through this together."

Bishop Martens popped his head in the door. "Excuse the interruption, Your Majesty, it seems the Wild Subjects' Dance is out of control."

Pristine smiled. "The reason you bring this to *my* attention, Count?"

"The plebs have been dancing in a conga line for half an hour. I think we should begin the Fifth Tradition."

Queen Mother reached for her purse, "give us a few minutes, Bishop,"

"Will you be requiring assistance?"

"Heavens no. The day I require assistance you can shove me into a box, and slide me in next to Poldemire. Come back in ten minutes. We will be ready."

"Very well, Ma'am. I will escort you to the elevator."

"We will take the stairs."

Nanny shook her head. "Not I. I will take the elevator."

"Thank you, Bishop Martens, for lending us your parlor."

He smiled. "Your Majesty, it is my pleasure to serve. Does Her Majesty feel any better?"

"Much," Pristine smiled, "thank you."

"I will be back in ten minutes," he bowed, and walked out.

Erica settled into the chair with her grandmother. "I am concerned about you, Erica." Queen Mother brushed back a lock of her granddaughter's hair, "you must be so all alone up there, on Top of the Crags."

"I'm not alone. Buzz is with me. They treat us like royalty in Gruntle."

Pristine sneered. "Only because Discord has no royal family."

"We're it, Pristine. Buzz may be a chauffeur, but he's a good man, and a good mechanic. You might see that if you would give people a chance. You will go down in history as the *Spinster Queen.*"

38

"You lie like a rug. I am going to marry Godwyn Bonheur, Erica. He's mine. You wait and see."

"It's right for you to rule Abundance. You belong here, Pristine. Give me my crown, and my scepter, continue my allowance, and I will be happy."

Nanny gazed over the catalogue. "Erica, are you sure that will make you happy?"

"It will," Erica sniffled, "I just want to feel the love."

"You are the love, my dear." Nanny set the catalogue on the table. "Listen, they're playing the *Abundance Ballad.* It's time to go."

"Chin up," Queen Mother dabbed Erica's tear with a hankie, "I feel with you, but you must learn to control your emotions—at least in public."

"Oh no," Erica looked into the hankie, "my mascara—it's all over my face." She ran to the mirror. "My hair is a mess, and look at my suit—it's all wrinkled. Why didn't anyone tell me?"

Pristine turned up her nose. "You never asked."

"You look fine, Erica," Nanny gathered the catalogues, "let's go."

"Wait a minute." Erica rubbed the mascara off her cheeks, pinched them, and they took on a healthy glow. She patted her chin, and it tightened. She threaded a stray lock of hair, and every lock fell into place. She ran her hands down her hips, and as if passed over by an iron, the wrinkles in her dress vanished. She started to arrange her scarf; it coiled like a snake, and rested upon her shoulders. "Oh yes," she turned, and smiled into the mirror, "that's much better."

Queen Mother grabbed her walking stick, and rose from the chair. "I believe you are not so much a mess, Erica, as you are misunderstood."

Pristine watched her sister admire herself in the mirror. After all she has been through, she thought, she can still pull herself together like this. She looks good, but if she doesn't want to attend tomorrow's banquet then so be it. There will be more people there than I can possibly meet.

CHAPTER VI
Queen for a Day

Queen Mother Marguerite slipped into deep contemplation while watching princess Erica adjust herself before the mirror. Pristine has so much, she thought, and Erica so little. What if I were to make Erica Queen for a Day? Ride her around Market Square in the golden carriage. But Marguerite — the ego spoke — what about the subjects? Never mind the subjects. They can't tell one twin from the other. Most are intoxicated anyway. All they will see is a waving hand. What if you were to take the scepter from Pristine, and the crown? There are dozens more of each in the attic. Set the crown on Erica's head, place the scepter in her hand, drape her in the ermine cloak, and you allow her to participate in the coronation. Word could get out — the ego spoke again — what if the public were to find out, and the Press? Who cares? "I do."

"You do what — GranMarguerite?"

"Oh," Queen Mother joined the plot, and lifted herself out of the chair. "I was just thinking. Come here, Erica. We are going to have a little fun."

"Fun?"

"On your feet, Pristine."

Pristine looked over to the sideboard, "not my crown, GranMarguerite."

Queen Mother called in the footman, "Handsforth, bring me the crown."

"Not my crown, GranMarguerite — *not my crown.*"

"I don't know what the big deal is about crown. They only give headaches and flat hair. Hand me the crown."

"Your Majesty," Handsforth held out the pillow, with the crown on it.

"Thank you Handsforth." Queen Mother took the crown. "Hand your lovely coronet to Handsforth, Erica. Handsforth, set the princess's coronet on the pillow, please."

41

"Yes, Ma'am," the footman rested the coronet, and returned.

Queen Mother gasped, as she positioned the crown on Erica's head, "my dear, on you, this crown becomes a halo."

Erica practiced her balance, "it sure is heavy. How much does this thing weigh?"

"Seven and a half pounds," Pristine snipped.

Queen Mother made a slight adjustment, "wearing a crown is a lesson in balance, my dear."

"It looks even heavier on you than it did on Grandpa Poldi."

"Pristine," Queen Mother refrained from expressing disapproval.

"Well, it's true. I was just coroneted, and you've already taken my crown from me."

"No need to get excited, Pristine," Nanny gathered catalogues, "there are plenty more in the attic."

Queen Mother winked at Nanny. "Tell me, Nanny, did Erica ever look more regal?"

"No, never."

Queen Mother smiled. "Spin for me, Erica."

"Spin?"

"Yes, spin."

"Now?"

"Yes now. Carry yourself like a Queen and people will treat you like a Queen." Queen Mother held her hand out, "give me your sash, Pristine."

"My sash?" Pristine guarded her chest, "not my sash, GranMarguerite."

"Handsforth, help the Queen remove her sash."

"Yes, Ma'am," Handsforth stepped in.

"I can undress myself, thank you very much," Pristine removed the sash, "watch my hair."

Handsforth handed the sash to Queen Mother. She rested it on Erica's shoulder. "There you are, my dear. It fit's perfectly."

"Even with your extra weight."

"Pristine," Nanny gave the Queen that look of disapproval.

"Well it's true, Nanny. She *has* gained weight."

Erica ignored her sister's remark, and twirled around before the mirror, "it looks so beautiful."

"Pristine, hand me your scepter."

"My scepter, too? No," Pristine shook her head, "no, I won't hand it over."

"Handsforth, help Her Majesty relinquish the scepter."

42

"No, GranMarguerite, the scepter is my insignia of authority. I won't hand it over."

"There are many more in the attic, Pristine. Any one of them can be yours."

"But this is *my* scepter."

"In truth, it's Poldemire's scepter, Pristine. Now hand it over. I will commission a new one be made for you."

"I will not hand it over. Impersonating the Queen—this is blasphemy."

"That may be," Nanny nodded, "give the scepter to Handsforth, Pristine. You may keep the orb."

"The orb is mine to keep anyway. Bishop Martens, in my invocation said…"

"The scepter is only a symbol."

"But it's *my* symbol."

"The only value it holds is the value you place upon it."

"Hand it over, Pristine," Nanny winked, "we'll get you a new one."

Pristine let go of the scepter—under duress.

Queen Mother positioned it in Erica's hand. "This is the same scepter Poldi held during his coronation," she noted, "he knew the origin, and the history of every jewel."

"It's beautiful."

"Hold it one third of the way up, Erica," Queen Mother nodded, "that's it—the Goldspinner grip."

Nanny mimed, "like a bat."

"Ah-ha-ha-ha," Erica laughed, "like a bat—ha-ha."

"Now stand tall, my Princess-Queen." Queen mother smiled. "That's it. Make us proud."

Erica turned to the mirror, arched her back, and grew another quarter inch, as if pulled from above by an invisible cord. "That's better," she smiled, "the scepter gives me height."

Queen Mother smiled. "You look absolutely regal, my dear. This is the Erica Goldspinner the world has been waiting to see."

"You look very regal, Erica." Nanny collected the catalogues, grabbed her stick, and prepared for take off. "We should be ready for the bishop when he returns."

Pristine contested. "What you are doing is wrong, GranMarguerite. You too, Nanny. Impersonating the Queen is treason."

Nanny leaned in, and whispered, "Pristine, give Erica this one chance."

"Hold it like a bat, Erica," Queen Mother wasn't done yet. If I didn't know any better, I would place my hand over my heart, and start singing *God Save the Queen*. Nanny," she turned—"am I right?"

Nanny nodded. "Absolutely. Erica, you look divine."

"GranMarguerite, you cannot do this. This is treason."

"Handsforth, help Her Majesty take off her cloak."

"*My cloak, too?* You gave her my crown, my sash, my scepter, and now you want *my cloak?*"

"There are plenty of cloaks in the attic, Pristine. Any one of them can be yours. Handsforth, hand me the cloak."

"But they're old cloaks, and they're worn. This one is *my* cloak."

"Actually, it was your great great great-grandmother's cloak. You may keep the orb, and the ring."

"Well, thank you—I don't care about the orb and the ring. I want my cloak."

"Hand the cloak to Handsforth, Pristine."

"I will not."

"Very well. Handsforth, go ask Bishop Martens to bring us a cloak out of the livery."

"Yes, Ma'am," Handsforth nodded, and stepped out.

"No slouching, Erica. Stand tall. You are a Goldspinner."

"Erica twirled before the mirror, her weight redirected itself to her bosom, and she smiled. "Thank you, GranMarguerite. Never have I felt so regal."

Queen Mother took Erica's hand. "My dear, you *are* regal."

"The crown, and the scepter—what I came here for."

"There is more."

"More?"

"Yes more. By the power vested in me by the kingdom and the state, as widow of the late King, the outgoing Queen, I, Marguerite Goldspinner, proclaim you, Erica Agarapina Regina Marguerite Goldspinner, Queen of Entitlement."

"Only for a day," Pristine sneered.

"That's it," Queen Mother smiled, "Queen for a Day."

The furrow in Erica's brow melted. Her eyes twinkled. She laughed, and years of trauma seemed to vanish. "I have not felt this confident since the last time I left Loco," she said, "how good life is."

There was a knock at the door. Bishop Martens carried in an ermine cloak, and presented it to the princess. "I found this in the attic, Your

Majesty. It was last worn by your great-great-gandmother, Queen Agarapina, at her coronation, in 1712. Might I slip it over your shoulders?"

"Please do Her Majesty the favor," Queen Mother smiled.

"All it needs is a minor adjustment, Ma'am."

Nanny whispered into Erica's ear, "get ready, my dear. You are about to be taken for the ride of your life."

"Yeah," Pristine tossed out a fake smile, "taken for the ride of your life."

"Chin up, bosom out. Are you ready?" Queen Mother walked the princess out the parlor, through the bishop's office, to the door, where the two guards stood, bayonets crossed. Seeing Queen Mother, they lowered their weapons, stepped back, and arm in arm, Queen Mother and princess Erica proceeded out the door. As they stepped into the corridor, the cloak carriers reappeared, and grabbed on. Nanny dropped the catalogues on the bishop's desk, and hastened to catch up.

Handsforth followed, intent on leading the entourage back to the sanctuary. "Your Majesty," he noted, "the elevator is to your right."

Queen Mother smiled. "But the stairs are to our left, Handsforth."

"Yes, Ma'am. I thought you might want—never mind."

"Climbing stairs is good exercise. It keeps one's bones strong."

"I'm not feeling that strong," Nanny shook her head, "I'll take the elevator."

"We will have arrived twice by the time you get there, Needlepinch."

"Just the same, I will reconnect with you upstairs." Nanny turned right.

Erica rested her head on her grandmother's shoulder, and whispered into her ear, "thank you, GranMarguerite. You've made me feel worthy again."

"Remember, Erica, with the crown comes responsibility."

"I will remember that," Erica kept a lookout for nurses.

The entourage ascended the stairs, as Count Russell came down. He noticed princess Erica, on the arm of Queen Mother, was wearing the crown, trailed by Queen Pristine. He spun a turn-about, and got in step. "Your Majesty," he was one of few who dared take Queen Mother's arm, "why isn't the Queen wearing the crown?"

"I will explain it to you later, Count."

"Are you sure this is a good idea?"

"You have known me long enough to know I am never sure of anything, Count. It seemed the right thing to do."

"Might I escort you up the stairs, Ma'am?"

"You mean *help* me? I may be an antique, but I assure you, I am quite ambulatory. Thank you for your chivalry, Count. I need no help."

"Of course. If I remember correctly, you have a birthday coming up."

"One hundred-and-three."

"Why the charade, Ma'am?"

"I have draped Erica in a dream that she can take home with her."

"Her Royal Highness certainly deserves a better hand than she has been dealt," the count whispered, "but is she aware this is not reality?"

"We shall find out," Queen Mother smiled, "for now, let us enjoy the ride."

"I think I understand the circumstances, Ma'am. You did right. Princess Erica needs to know the world cares for her, especially now that the spotlight is on Pristine."

Pristine waited at the top of the stairs for the entourage to arrive. As Queen Mother approached the pen-ultimate step, she released the Count's arm, took Pristine's hand, and whispered into her ear. "You have been blessed with life in Entitlement, while Erica struggles in Discord. Allow her this to carry her through the hard times."

"I've been thinking it over. It really is like you said, GranMarguerite. Erica and I may be twins, but I'm not Erica—I don't need a crown, a scepter, or a cloak to remind me who I am."

"I am glad you see it that way." Queen Mother smiled, "I appreciate you playing along, for the benefit of all."

"This is about power, GranMarguerite, nothing more."

"*You* want to tell *me* about power?" Queen Mother took Pristine aside, "I, who for eight decades traveled at your grandfather's side through every state of Consciousness?"

"That's not how I meant it, GranMarguerite. What I meant was…"

"Never mind what you meant. I believe the elevators are down this hall." They approached, and found Nanny sitting in the corridor, on a divan.

"There you are," Nanny looked at her watch, "finally. I've been waiting for you."

"Three minutes, Needlepinch—no longer."

Nanny looked looked at her watch again, and lifted herself off the divan. "Seven minutes. Let's go."

CHAPTER VII

The Golden Carriage Ride

Guards accompanied Queen Mother and her entourage out of the cathedral, down the steps to the curb, where a golden carriage waited to take the freshly coroneted Queen on her ceremonial ride around Market Square. Count Russell whispered into Queen Mother's ear, "let us hope the subjects are so mesmerized, they won't be unable to tell one princess from another."

"I realize my little charade could have consequences, Count, but if it brings light to Erica, it will have been worth it."

Princess Erica walked to the carriage on Queen Mother's arm, followed by her cloak carriers. As she passed Buzz, he blew her a kiss. "I love you," he shouted over the noise. Four coachmen stood at the carriage. One positioned a stool before the step, while another held the door open. Queen Mother put her arm around her granddaughter, "this is the same carriage Poldi and I rode in during his coronation," she smiled, "what a lovely memory."

"Both of you fit in there? It must have been tight."

Queen Mother chuckled, "Poldi couldn't keep his hands off me."

"Buzz and I would never fit in there together. I wish he was joining me. I feel so alone."

"Buzz is with you in spirit, Erica. You are never alone. Everywhere you go, God accompanies you. Remember, wave at the subjects, but lean back. Do not make eye contact with anyone but Handsforth."

"I'll do my best, GranMarguerite."

"That is all one can expect, my dear," Queen Mother smiled, "you never looked more radiant. Remember, hold it one third of the way up."

"Like a bat."

"That's it. Make it your friend."

Guards held lookie-loos at bay as the entourage approached. Erica turned to her sister. "Pristine—my sovereign, I'm not quite sure what to make of this. I feel as though I'm stealing your thunder."

"Well, you are, Erica," Pristine chuckled.

Queen Mother kissed them both on the cheek. "This can be our little secret, girls. Now get in the carriage, Erica. The world awaits you, and remember, stay snug in the cloak."

"Thank you, GranMarguerite."

"Now off you go."

"Enjoy the ride, Erica," Pristine kissed her on both cheeks. "Make them think you're me."

Queen Mother took Count Russell aside. "Tell the driver no further than around Market Square. No need for this to get out."

"I shall relay your message immediately, Ma'am," the count nodded, and walked off.

Lady *Avorah Woolsey* dragged her husband down the stairs. "Come, *George*—we might still catch her."

George Woolsey, dressed in a herringbone camelhair suit with matching cap, struggled to keep up. "Slow down, Avorah," he hollered, "can we not congratulate her when she returns?"

"I want to be first." She turned to him. "Don't you? We're her godparents."

"But can it not wait?"

"You are just like a man, George. You will never understand."

"Your Royal Highness," the coachman made a sweeping gesture, "are you ready for the ride around the Square?"

The princess smiled, as the cloak carriers stepped aside. "I am."

"Very well then," the coachman gave her a hand, "into the carriage."

With one foot inside, the other on the stool, Erica waved. Ever so graciously, the coachman gathered her cloak, and helped the princess into the carriage. Handsforth stuck his head in. "Your Royal Highness—princess queen Erica," he whispered, "may this memory always remind you of the love of friends, family, and staff, who await you here at the palace."

"Thank you, Handsforth." Erica's nose quivered, "I smell cherry tobacco." She looked out the window, and saw Lord and Lady Woolsey approach. "Handsforth, quick—it's Auntie Avorah. Let's go."

"Yes, Ma'am." Handsforth nodded to the driver, the driver cracked his whip, and the horses took off.

The subjects had been in the dark as to which twin would be their next

Queen. It was not until the coronation that the palace Communications Office released a statement revealing which.

"It's Queen Pristine," shouted one.

"It's Queen Erica," hollered another, "it's not Pristine."

"How can you tell? She's hiding inside a cloak."

"The two princesses have a different gait," shouted another.

The band conductor clicked his drumsticks. To the accompaniment of the royal musicians playing an old favorite—*Abundance How We Love Thee*—the horses pranced down Cathedral Lane. Count Russell climbed back up the steps to the colonnade, to find Queen Mother Marguerite, Queen Pristine, and Nanny Needlepinch standing in the sun. "Your Majesties," he took Nanny by the elbow, and pulled back a post, "why have you not been seated? Allow me to escort you into the shade."

Three footmen pulled out chairs, as Queen Mother assessed the situation. "This seems the perfect spot to catch this lovely breeze," she sat down.

"Finally, I can rest my feet," Nanny leaned her stick against the wall. "My bunions are killing me."

"Let us hope Erica can distinguish fantasy from reality when she returns, GranMarguerite."

"You hold that thought, Pristine." Queen Mother settled in.

Nanny sat down, and the footman pushed in her chair. "Pray on it, Pristine."

"Queen Pris-tine, Queen Pris-tine, Queen Pris-tine," to the chant of the crowd, the carriage proceeded down Cathedral lane.

Back on the colonnade, Count Russell sat down opposite the two queens. The sage count was one of few given the permission to address a royal before having been addressed. He looked up at the sky, "what a glorious day for a coronation," he said, with a sigh.

Pristine smiled, "it is a lovely day."

Count Russell zoomed in on the tiny mole behind Pristine's right ear. "Your Majesty, were it not for the weight difference between you and your sister, I myself might mistake princess Erica to be my sovereign, my freshly coroneted Queen."

"Nothing unusual about that, Count Russell; we *are* twins."

"My point is this: I have known the two of you a lifetime, and *I* often cannot tell you apart. I doubt any subject without connection to the palace could." He surveyed the hills surrounding the cathedral, and saw families celebrating on the rooftops, children playing in the streets, and a pair of lovers smooching under an old oak. "Look at them, Your Majesty," he pointed (with two fingers) "they dangle from the lamposts and fire escapes, just to get a glimpse of you."

"A glimpse of Erica is what you mean."

"No, Your Majesty. They are here to get a glimpse of *you*. They have been waiting since dawn, lined up as far back as the zoo."

Nanny shook her head in disbelief. "Look at those youngsters splashing in the fountain. Is there one sitting on the King Aloneous statue's head? Such outlandish behavior should be forbidden."

"Climbing statues is forbidden. So is swimming in fountains. It's just not enforced, Nanny."

"And one cannot expect enforcement," Count Russell nodded, "on a celebratory day like today."

"Let them have their fun," Queen Mother removed her shoes, discreetly, "as long as no one gets hurt."

"All in fun to elevate," the count nodded, "no better time than now to celebrate."

"I remember sitting at Poldemire's side, at his coronation. That was 1832, seventy-nine years ago. Some college student draped a nightshirt over the Aloneous statue, and sent the town fathers into an uproar."

Princess Erica peeked out the carriage window, as the procession turned onto Market Street.

"*Que-en Pris-tine, Que-en Pris-tine, Queen Pris-tine,*" the crowd shouted in unison.

"Oh my"—Erica jumped back, "I'll check the other side."

"*Que-en Pris-tine, Que-en Pris-tine, Que-en Pris-tine,*" the crowd blew kisses, and waved signs with Pristine's face on them.

An internal chant took over, sending Erica into a trance. '*Queen E-rica, Queen E-rica, Queen E-rica,*' like a chant, it played in her head on a loop, '*Queen E-rica, Queen E-rica, Queen Erica...*'

A man wearing rainbow suspenders elbowed his way through the crowd, and jumped onto the carriage step. "Queen Pristine," he shouted, "I love you, I love you, I love you." One of the guards hooked him by his suspenders, and flung him back into the crowd. "I love you, I love you, I love you"...his voice grew more faint, "I love you. I love you. I love you..."

The procession turned under a murder of crows looking down from the utility lines overhead, onto Telegraph Row. The bird's placement on the wires resembled musical notes on a score sheet. They seemed to be standing on guard, ready to peck the neck out of any suspicious looking feck. As Telegraph Row is lined with brokerages, and insurance firms, closed on weekends, the ride began in earnestness, but when they approached Bob's Barbershop, all ended in glee. Spirits soared when Bob's quartet harmonized with the royal marching band. Erica was elated. "Can this be real?" she pinched herself, and waved out the window, as the crowd blew kisses at her, and threw flowers.

The loud music and dancing crowd on Telegraph Row faded into the distance, as the procession turned onto Memory Lane, and Erica sobered up. "They're not here for me," she told herself, "they're here for Pristine. You had better enjoy this." The Memory Lane turnout was a crowd of parents with their noisy children, all holding up abecedarian drawings of the new Queen for her approval. Erica grabbed a few of the drawings, unable to resist, blew kisses to the children, and smiled from within her cloak—swathed warm to the neck.

As the carriage turned onto Elm Street, the sun pierced the vine-ensnarled canopy, blanketing the procession in a maya-like quality. Erica smiled, and waved all down Elm. The anxiety, the painful memories, the treatments in Loco, all of it suddenly dissipated. Erica took on a glow. In the distance, she saw a flag waving. I'd recognize that insignia anywhere—it's the flag of Insanity.

"Go Loco, go Loco, go Loco," a woman shouted.

Erica wracked her brain. Is that one of my podmates?—the one with the orange hair? It can't be. Everyone thinks it's Pristine in the carriage."

The procession approached Mayer's Jewelers, where an acrobat twirled loops around the suspension arm of the giant street clock. He flung himself onto the carriage roof, popped his head in the window, upside down, and shouted, "Your Majesty, happy coronation."

"Yikes!" Erica recoliled, and drew the curtain.

Two guards grabbed the acrobat by his ankles, but he compressed his legs like a spring toy, launched himself onto a nearby rooftop, and disappeared.

The procession then took a quick detour onto Easy Street, home to writers, musicians, and other non-conformists. Immediately, the event turned into a love-in. People in the streets hugged complete strangers—regardless of gender, color, religion, or orientation. The crowd of artists strung lutes and banjos, and blew into kazoos. They sang Abundite praises, along with the Queen's name. Erica smiled, and waved from inside the golden frame, "it's all about Pristine."

Back on the colonnade, Lady Avorah Woolsey rose from her chair. "Come George. Let's go."

"Already, Avorah?" Woolsey looked at his watch, "she's not scheduled to arrive for another ten minutes."

"I want to be there *when* she arrives, George; *not after.*"

Woolsey rose from the chair, and tipped his hat, "Your Majesties, if you will excuse Lady Avorah and me."

"Come, George. Stop doddling."

"Why can't we congratulate her at the banquet?"

"You know how uncomfortable Erica is in front of the public."

"She could have fooled me this morning."

"Well, that was unusual—even for Erica. I know for a fact, she won't show for the banquet." Lady Avorah stopped mid-step, and turned to her husband, trying to keep up, two steps behind her. "George, other than Poldemire's funeral, we have not seen Erica since before she and Buzz eloped. As her godparents, don't you think we should make an effort to say hello?"

"Of course we should make an effort, Avorah, but now?—amid thousands who all want to see her?"

"Your doddeling only takes up time, George. I am going," she turned, faced downhill, and descended the steps.

"I'm trying my best to keep up with you, Avorah. Perhaps you could slow down?"

"I see the carriage."

"I was sitting comfortable in my chair the shade. Now I'm sweating in the sun."

"Here's the carriage."

Woolsey read the signs. "Her carriage is going to pull up over there, Avorah."

"Are you sure?"

"Of course I am sure. The carriage stops at the carriage stop."

"Well, let's head over there." Lady Woolsey secured her hat, and took off.

The procession turned back onto Cathedral Lane with a jubilant princess Erica inside, totally confident, waving, and smiling at the crowd. I could get used to this attention, she thought, maybe I should have fought to be Queen.

The carriage came to a stop, and Handsforth opened the door. "Your Royal Highness," he bowed from the neck, "welcome home."

Erica saw flashy plumes flying about the crowd, and drew the curtain. "Handsforth," she whispered, "it's Lady Avorah. Get rid of her for me."

Handsforth approached the sexagenarian engineer. "Good afternoon,

Ma'am," he inched her aside, "what a beautiful hat. If you please, allow Her Majesty some space."

"I am her godmother, Lady Woolsey. This is my husband, Lord Woolsey—Her Majesty's godfather."

"I don't care if you are God Himself, Madam. Please step back."

"I want to congratulate my godchild—Her Majesty, the Queen."

"Lady Woolsey, please step back, lest I need call in backup."

Lord Woolsey tugged on his wife's arm. "Come, Avorah, we can congratulate Her Majesty later."

Inside the carriage, Erica trembled. *If I am found out, I could be tried. They could find me guilty of treason. The last person I want to see right now is Auntie Avorah. I think of an eggplant every time I see her. From her purple plumes to her purple fingernails and pumps, she's even got the shape down. How am I going to get out of this carriage safely?* She peeked out the left window, and saw Handsforth's back, standing against the window. She peeked through the curtain on the right, and saw yellow-tooth Dr. Kindervater, chomping on his cigar.

He tipped his hat, "Your Majesty, congratulations."

Erica read his lips, and closed the curtain. "Ugh—you miserable old rat. You are more responsible than anyone for sending me away."

Handsforth eased the doctor up, onto the curb, secured the guards, and opened the carriage door. "Your Royal Highness, are you ready to make your escape? The coast is clear."

"Thank you, Handsforth," she gathered her cloak, "ready as I will ever be."

"Let's go." Handsforth helped the princess with her cloak, handed the ends to the carriers, took her hand, and helped her out of the carriage, into the center of a universe of blinding camera flashbulbs.

CHAPTER VIII
Homeward Bound

Queen Pristine gazed over the rooftops, from her seat in the shade on the cathedral colonnade, seventy-eight steps above the cobblestone lane. On a distant lot, a couple romanced in the shade. On a rooftop terrace next door, a woman set a table, while six toddlers ran in and out between her legs. On another lot, framed by a large picture window, a couple argued. On another roof, two men debated how to secure a lightning rod.

Perhaps it was overexposure to the sun that got the Queen to speak before thinking. She shook her head. "Look at my subjects. They have about as much style as refugees from Confusion. Fools—all of them."

Count Russell leaned in. "Did I hear you right, Ma'am? Did you just call your subjects fools?"

"I did, Count. I suppose I shouldn't have."

"No, Ma'am; you shouldn't have. Referring to your subjects as fools is bold. It would be best if such comments you would withhold."

Queen Mother leaned in to Count Russell. "I imagine Pristine's comment was a slip of the tongue," she whispered, "I recommend we scratch the record."

"Indeed," Nanny leaned in, "Pristine—Your Majesty, you must think before you speak."

"This is your first day as regent, my dear. I imagine you are on edge." Queen Mother took Pristine's hand. "You gave up your spotlight today, a nobel thing to do. All considered, I would say it has been a magnificent coronation."

"Except it wasn't mine. It was Erica's, GranMarguerite."

Nanny patted the Queen's hand. "You shared your thunder, Pristine. That was noble of you."

"I think Erica creates these scenes intentionally, to draw attention."

Queen Mother cleared her throat. "I don't believe it's intentional."

"It is. I *know* it is. She's my twin. I understand her like no one else can."

"Pristine, Erica's circuits are merely overloaded. It's her P.T.S.O."

"This goes beyond circuits and P.T.S.O., Nanny. She gets a thrill out of provoking me."

"Why would Erica want to provoke you? You're her sister—her twin."

"Exactly. She wants to throw her discord onto my kingdom. I won't let her do it."

"If I may say so, Ma'am," Count Russell intervened, "princess Erica wants to be loved and accepted, like anyone else. We must live as Forgivers, sincere in thought, word, and deed, extending care to those who are in need."

"Forgiveness seems a never-ending journey, Count."

"Indeed, Ma'am," the count nodded.

"I am tired," Nanny grabbed her cane, "I'm hot, and I want my nap."

"I, too, am ready to leave." Queen Mother reached for her purse, and a footman hastened in to pull out her chair.

Count Russell held out a hand. "Your Majesty, might I walk you to your carriage?"

"Thank you, Count Russell," Queen Mother nodded, "this time I will accept your offer, as we are descending the stairs."

A footman stepped in, and assisted Nanny out of the chair. She thanked him, and grabbed Count Russell's arm. "I will take you up on that offer, as well, Count."

The count saw no choice but to oblige Nanny Needlepinch, and addressed Queen Pristine, as they began the long descent down the cathedral steps. "Your Majesty," he commended the Queen, "you committed a noble act today. I feel assured that will pay off, in every way."

"Thank you, Count. At first, I was pretty mad at Queen Mother."

"You alone may have restored Erica's confidence with your act, and the way you executed it, Your Majesty, it was pure Goldspinner tact."

"Thank you, Count."

Nanny nodded. "I agree. She did a wonderful thing."

"The doing was GranMarguerite's, Nanny."

Queen Mother wondered. I hope I did the right thing.

"Of course you did, Your Majesty," the count heard without words. "Watch this step, Miss Needlepinch—good is as good does."

Queen Mother took the steps with precise caution. "Sometimes I feel responsible for Erica's condition."

Nanny shook her head. "Don't be ridiculous."

"Hear me out. I let Erica down. She and Pristine were left under my care."

"No, Your Majesty," Nanny grabbed Count Russell's arm, "I was on payroll. It was my job to look after the twins."

"Your Majesty, watch the step. Nothing you could have done would have brought different results to anyone."

"I didn't feel it was my place to question the doctors' diagnoses."

"Ma'am, it was not a woman's place to speak up, much less to question three male doctors."

"I remained silent. That is what troubles me. As consort, I really had no power beyond the boardroom, and the bedroom."

"I'm tired," Nanny stepped onto the cobblestones, "where is our carriage?"

"Smile, Miss Needlepinch. The carriage will be here in a while."

Nanny nudged the footman. "Handsforth, go see what's keeping our carriage."

"It should be here, Miss Needlepinch. Nothing I can do but wait."

"I don't want to hear should. Go and check, Handsforth."

A carriage pulled to the curb at that very moment. "Is this it?" Nanny checked her watch.

"This is it, Miss Needlepinch."

"Twelve minutes we have waited. A black carriage—for Coronation Day?"

"The sedan has a broken axel, the landau is getting springs replaced, and the other two are out on loan," said the coachman. "You are going to have to share."

"Share? With whom?"

"With the maids."

"The maids?" Nanny grumbled, "as if this day hasn't been long enough, we have to share a carriage with the maids."

"Ladies' maids, Miss Needlepinch."

"Well, at least it's not the scullery maids." Nanny nudged Queen Mother. "Get in, Majesty."

Handsforth opened the carriage door. "Your Majesty, Miss Mina is among the maids."

"Mina—finally," Pristine smiled.

The coachman lowered the step.

Count Russell poked his head inside, "welcome home, Miss Mina—Miss *Uppsola*," he nodded, "Miss *Cocoa*."

Uppsola Pumba, and *Cocoa Rocco,*" Nanny moaned—"the last two people I want to sit in a carriage with."

"Six in the carriage may be tight," Count Russell addressed the maids, "move in closer, ladies, and it should be all right."

"Count Russell, let us hope the subjects awaken tomorrow without any recollection of today." Queen Mother entered the carriage first.

"Trust me, Your Majesty, once they have filled up on pints and quarts, no one will believe their distorted reports."

"I hope you are right," Queen Mother settled in.

"Your Majesty, Queen Pristine," Count Russell nodded, into the carriage."

The maids bowed, as the two monarchs stepped into the carriage. "Welcome home, Mina," Pristine smiled, "I never realized how much I could miss you."

"I am so sorry I let you down, Ma'am."

"No more sorry than I. My feet are killing me."

"I forgot to walk in your shoes. Forgive me, please."

"Already done."

Nanny clamped onto Count Russell's arm, hoisted herself into the carriage, and complimented the maids, as she feel onto the bench. "What lovely hats you have on."

Queen Mother removed her gloves. "Thank God, no one was hurt today."

"I was hurt," Pristine checked her ears, "my earlobes are still throbbing."

"I am sorry I failed you, Ma'am."

"I managed—in spite of my pinching pumps."

Mina sighed. "I tried to get back yesterday, Ma'am, but *Bereave-Track* is on strike. I returned home by omnibus. I heard the coronation on the radio."

Pristine pouted. "It was humiliating."

Nanny smiled. "I thought it was a lovely coronation."

"For Erica it was."

"When are we going to leave? Uppsola, ring the coachman."

"Why me?"

"Because you are seated under the bell."

"Oh," the maid rang the bell.

Mina noted a feather blowing in—"three o'clock, Your Majesty— Lady Avorah."

"Quick—draw the blind."

Lady Avorah nearly tripped on the curb, as she approached. "Hold your horses," she shouted, as the carriage lunged forward, hurling her into Count Russell's arms.

"Pfft," the Count blew back a feather, "let me steady you, Lady Woolsey."

"That certainly was a charge," Pristine chuckled, as the carriage departed, "I hope Auntie Avorah didn't get hurt."

"That should teach her to keep her nose out of other peoples' business."

"Uppsola, guard your words."

"I lose an hour every time that woman visits."

"I know what you mean," Pristine chuckled, "forgive me, ladies. I have to remove my shoes. My feet are killing me."

"Something about Lady Woolsey sets me on edge, always has been." Queen Mother set her gloves on her purse. "This morning she referred to Princess Erica as poor," she paused—"I hope it wasn't wrong of me to crown the princess in an illusion. Normally, I would not discuss such matters in front of you ladies, but I figure, over the years, you have heard enough dirty laundry."

"I understand why you did what you did, GranMarguerite. I want you to know I'm okay with it."

"Thank you, Pristine. It comforts me to hear you say that."

"Forgive me, *Y.M.*, but princess Erica's entrance this morning was a scene straight out of Discord."

Miss Cocoa was confused. "*Y.M.?* Why you no call Queen Mother You Majesty?"

"Y.M. saves time. It takes four syllables to say Your Ma-jes-ty, only two to say Y.M."

Cocoa's ears perked. "I hear tambourines," she looked out the window. "Dare are dancers on de side of de road. You Majesty, dey celebrating you."

Pristine waved, as the carriage blanketed the dancers in dust.

Queen Mother took her granddaughter's hand. "Pristine, you were a knockout today," she corrected herself—"you *are* a knockout."

"Thank you, GranMarguerite. I believe *knocked* out better describes how I feel."

"I am tired. I'm ready for my nap."

A hovering hum over the carriage caught Uppsola's attention. She stuck her head out, and scanned the sky. "Your Majesty, look—it's a blimp."

Cocoa craned her head. "Eet say *Long Live de Queen.*"

"I have seen a blimp before, Miss Cocoa."

"No like dis one."

Pristine looked out the window." You're right. It is big."

"There must be hundreds of lights on it," Mina gasped, "I've never seen anything so big."

Cocoa was mesmerized. "Eets berry, berry beeg,"

Queen Mother shook her head. "What will they think of next?— talking boxes?"

CHAPTER IX

Terrorist Attack

Truckers pulled to the curb to witness the tail end of the carriage ride around Market Square. They watched, as princess Erica stepped into the blinding sea of flashbulbs. No one wanted to miss the opportunity to catch a glimpse of their new Queen. Covered from neck to toe in her ermine cloak, princess Erica waved to the crowd, and smiled for the cameras, while Handsforth helped guards hold rubberneckers at bay. Across the street from the cathedral, an idling Locomobile with out-of-state plates spewed lavender tufts of exhaust. "Your Royal Highness," Handsforth whisked the princess through the crowd, "Sir Buzz awaits you across the street, at your limousine."

The princess smiled. "Thank you, Handsforth."

Sir *Buzz Runner*, dressed in grey chauffeur's livery, stood proud as a peacock at the open limousine door.

Suddenly, princess Erica was overcome by fear. "I hope there are no Terrorists about, Handsforth. They could rally against me for impersonating the Queen."

"Your Royal Highness, you are safe with me."

A sudden explosion in Market Square turned the crowd into a mob. The Terrorists were on the warpath again, determined to attack Fearlings, and anyone else who did not approve of their way of life, among them, princess Erica. The hoodlums grabbed potatoes, and coal briquettes out of the trucks, idling at the side of the road, and hurled them at the princess. "Imposter," they shouted—"traitor."

Handsforth hastened the princess across the street as fast as he could. "Your Royal Highness, we will be out of this in a jiffy," he assured her.

"That's not our Queen," a woman hurled a briquette, "you ain't never gonna fool no *Terrorist*."

"Stop throwing stones" a *Fearling* shouted—"it's the Queen."

61

"That is not our Queen." An Indifferent tossed an apple. "It's princess Erica. Apprehend her."

"She's not my Queen," shouted another. Mid-throw, he dropped his briquette—"or is she?"

Truckers were concerned for their cargo. They put their trucks into gear, and drove away, passing police paddy wagons, as they left town. "Your Highness," Handsforth shouted over the racket, "you must forgive them. They are not worth your thought."

"I never would have believed this," cried the princess, "what did I ever do to them?"

"Ma'am—remember only the love bestowed upon you during your ride around Market Square."

Arms extended, Buzz ran across the cobblestones. "Erica, get in," he shouted.

"Thank you, Handsforth," the princess kissed the footman on the cheek, "take care of yourself."

Handsforth bowed from the neck. "Your Royal Highness, it is my pleasure to serve the Crown." He smiled, and returned to the carriage stop.

Erica waved the scepter. "Look, Buzz, I got the crown, too."

"I see that, Erica. Give it to me, and hand me your cloak." He spread her cloak on the bench, set the scepter on it, adjusted her crown, ushered her into the limousine, shut the door, stepped into the driver's seat, and locked the doors.

Erica knocked on the separation window, and it descended. "Look, Buzz, I got the sash, too."

"I am so proud of you. You got what we came here for. Your dignity has been restored." Buzz released the handbrake, "let's go."

"Go. I've had enough of Entitlement to last me a lifetime."

Buzz looked in the rear view mirror. "It looks like the police are arresting the attackers."

"Heartless bastards. They deserve to be locked up."

Dancing feathers caught Buzz's attention. "It's Lady Avorah."

"Step on it, Buzz. I don't want to see her."

Lady Woolsey was fast, but Buzz was faster.

"Your Royal Highness," Lady Avorah's voice faded, "will you be joining us for the buffet?"

Buzz shifted the limousine into second gear, and watched Erica claw at the cloak, like a fox making her bed. "Being Queen is exhausting, Buzz," she projected through the open separation window, "even for a day."

"Aren't you glad it's not for you?"

"I'm tired. I want the world to go away."

"Your wish is my command," Buzz shifted into third, and took off.

Back atop the cathedral steps, Count Russell stood, hands over his forehead, eyes closed, sending out healing vibrations over Market Square. A leftist gang, the '*We Who Once Fell for Anything Now Stand for Something,*' group, collected potatoes and briquettes, and clobbered the remaining Terrorists with their own ammunition. The Terrorists ran off, while Fearlings hid, content to have not been arrested.

Count Russell remained standing, until the last paddy wagon jingled off. Lord Woolsey, drawn back up the steps by Count Russell's humming, huffed, as he approached. "Your incantation seems to have dispersed the crowd, Count," he paused, and caught his breath, "well done."

Count Russell let his arms fall to his side, and opened his eyes. "All it took was a little time away, Woolsey. Sometimes, all we need do is pray."

"I would like to know how the hooligans got into town. Every street, avenue, lane, and boulevard leading in and out of Contentment was set up with a road block."

"What an assault," Count Russell shook his head, "I shall check with Detective Scott to see who is at fault."

"Let me know what you learn, Count."

"I will do that, Woolsey."

"I'd better get back to Avorah. I told her I'd be back in five minutes. It took that long just to climb the stairs. Say, will you be attending the banquet?"

"I will be there," Count Russell nodded.

"Well then, see you tomorrow," Woolsey tipped his hat.

Count Russell stood atop the steps, surveying the aftermath of the attack, watching Lord Woolsey descend the steps. Street cleaners collected potatoes, briquettes and vegetables, to be sent to the needy in *Indifference*. Estimates of the Coronation Day crowd size ranged from five to seven thousand, depending upon one's source. Merchants who worked the memorabilia stalls that day brought in more than they had in months. The publique house proprietors who remained open, for those in need of spiritual support from the tap, brought in enough that day to hand half their earnings over to wives. Those who remained closed, out of respect for the Crown, if not in attendance at the coronation, spent the day family and friends at the beach, building sand castles, snorkeling, and collecting seashells.

CHAPTER X

Home at Last

The carriage stopped before the gates, where a crowd of gift-bearers had gathered. The coachmen jumped to the ground, and collected flowers and an assortment of gifts, which they passed to the royals through the open window. They secured larger gifts to the boot—and eventually, the roof. Queen Mother chuckled, as the coachman passed yet *another* bouquet to her through the open window. "Look at this, Pristine. They love you."

Nanny was amazed. "How many does that make?"

"Cocoa has five. GranMarguerite has four. Uppsola, how many do you have?" The footman appeared at the window with another bouquet.

"Another bunch of flowers?" Pristine could not believe it.

"I have four bouquets."

"I have five," Pristine counted—"that makes eighteen. Can you believe it? Eighteen bouquets."

"Your Majesty," the coachman appeared at the window, "I have another stuffed animal for you."

"Another?" Pristine laughed, "what is it this time?"

"A giraffe, Ma'am."

"Good heavens—an artiodactyl—where shall I put it?"

"The boot is full, Ma'am, and we can fit no more on the roof."

"Leave it with the guard."

"You can't do that, Pristine," Queen Mother whispered, "it would be an insult to the one who gave it to you."

"Very well then, send it in."

Head first, the coachman shoved the giraffe through the window.

"This feels awkward," Pristine fidgeted with the flowers, "sitting here, being watched, while we wait. I wish the coachman would take off already."

"Me too," Nanny yawned, "I'm past due for my nap."

"I know what you mean." Queen Mother turned to the Queen. "You are their sovereign, Pristine, their Queen. However uncomfortable, you must emanate only well-being, at all times."

"Even in the privacy of my carriage?"

"Even in the privacy of your carriage. Now smile, and wave."

"If I must."

"You can do better than that—look happy."

The second coachman secured the last gift to the roof while the first addressed the subjects. "Ladies, and gentlemen, on behalf of the royal family, I thank you for your many cards following the passing of King Poldemire. As well, Her Majesty would like to express her gratitude for your gifts," he paused—"Long live the Queen."

"Long live the Queen," men bowed, women curtseyed. The coachmen hopped onto the footboards, and the palace gates fanned open before them. The horses pranced past manicured lawns, dotted with blooming flowers. Butterflies fluttered about from blossom to blossom. Two squirrels played tag, circumnavigating a tree trunk. An opposum waddled by with twelve cubs clinging to her back. Miss Uppsola came to a realization, as the gates closed behind them. Most never even get to see the gardens of Entitlement, she thought, and here I wake up to them every morning.

Nanny covered her yawn. "I am tired, and so hungry I could eat a horse."

Nanny's comment did not go over well with the horses. They responded with a unanimous neigh. The experience at the gates left Mina troubled. She could tell some of those giftbearers were immigrants from Fear. It reminded her how she and her family, with their two goats, swam across the *Black Snake River*, how they had slithered across the *Black Hills Trail* on their stomachs, just to escape Fear, and start a new life in Tolerance.

Queen Mother's vision was sufficient to appreciate the shirtless *Gardener* triplets, working in the garden. The eldest, *Bob*, sat on the tractor, mowing the lawn. The middle brother, *Rob*, raked in grass clippings, while the youngest, *Tob*, stuffed the clippings into a large compost bin.

"Why are the gardeners mowing on a Saturday?" asked Pristine.

Queen Mother breathed in the scent of freshly clipped grass. "Apparently, they don't think of gardening as work," she replied.

Mina smiled. "Breathe in that honeysuckle. Isn't that heavenly?"

Nanny sniffed. "With all these flowers in the carriage, I can't discern a honeysuckle from a rose."

Uppsola chuckled. "Neither can I."

"Poldi and I planted those honeysuckles together."

"*You* didn't actually plant them, Y.M.—did you?"

"Yes, Uppsola, we planted them together." Queen Mother wondered—what will my life be like now that Poldi is gone? Am I to spend the rest of my life with Uppsola questioning me?"

"Look," Mina pointed, "the bougainvillea are in bloom."

"What ees so especial ebout de boganveea bloom?" asked Cocoa.

"They weren't blooming when I left on Wednesday."

"Mina, take these for me, please," Pristine passed her bouquets, "I need to put on my shoes."

"Ho-hum," Nanny yawned, "this has been the longest day. I cannot wait to get into my bed."

Footman *Fenewick Twickenham* hastened down the steps, as the horses pulled up. While Twickenham opened the carriage door, second footman *Gowen Fetchett* lowered the step. "Your Majesties," the footmen bowed, each extending a hand, "welcome home."

Queen Mother addressed them. "Take the flowers first, please, Twickenham," she handed him several bouquets, "then help our younger travelers exit. Miss Needlepinch and I shall follow."

While the coachmen untied the gifts, third footman *Randall Quigley* hastened in, laid the bouquets neatly on a cart, and delivered them to the kitchen, to be arranged in vases, and distributed around the palace.

"Finally some fresh air," Pristine smiled, as she stepped out, "the first thing I'm going to do is take off my brassiere then I am going straight into the tub for a hot soak."

"Thank you for sharing, Pristine."

"You are welcome, GranMarguerite. I will see you at supper."

"I'm going straight to bed," Nanny grumbled.

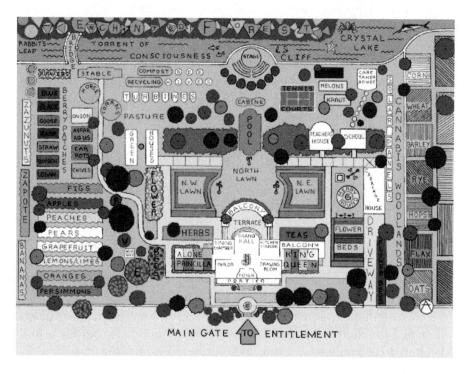

Map of the palace and grounds of Entitlement

CHAPTER XI

Sunday, May 14, 1911

The Coronation Banquet

Queen Mother Marguerite's prediction of Sunday's headlines was close to spot on. Word was out. The Sunday morning *Times* bold headline read: PRINCESS ERICA CRASHES CORONATION. Due to the unexpected death of King Poldemire—though at one hundred-thirteen, palace chefs *Maurice Le Souffle*, and *Fradenzo Kookje* were prepared, they had only three weeks to arrange the biggest social event of the year—*the* first coronation banquet in seventy-eight years. With a budget befitting Abundance, and an army of workers at their disposal, the cuisenaires orchestrated a feast fit for a king, or in this case, a Queen. One hundred round tables dotted the north lawn, each draped by a white linen tablecloth, covered in an umbrella, and accentuated with an orchid centerpiece. Ten times as many chairs waited to be warmed.

At three o'clock, the guards opened the gates, and granted entrance to anyone who could present their embossed invitation. Uppsola Pumba sat next to Mina Amora at the domestics table—the ladies' maids' table. She heard a noise in the bushes, craned her neck, and would have sworn she saw the Defender of the Faith—Prince Godwyn Bonheur. "Psst," she whispered, "Mina."

"What is it, Mina?"

"I just saw the Prince of Grace pop his head out from behind that bush." Mina looked around. "I see no prince, and why would the prince hide?"

"I don't know, but I saw him."

"You're seeing things, Uppsola." Mina reached for her spectacles.

"I *am* seeing things. I know I just saw Prince Godwyn."

Mina set her spectacles on her nose, and looked. "I see no prince."

"Look again—there," Mina pointed, "he stuck his head out again."

"Why would Prince Godwyn be hiding in the bushes?"

"Maybe he wants to keep a low profile."

"I would think after the long drive from Grace, he'd want to sit down."

"Spectacles won't help you, Mina, unless you're willing to see."

Pacing on the platform inside the coronation tent, Pristine tried to settle the butterflies in her stomach, while stroking her ermine jacket cuffs. She stopped before the wall mirror, and extended a leg. "GranMarguerite was right. This dress *is* short. But I have shapely calves. Thanks to Nanny's magic stockings, not even I can tell I am wearing a bandage." She stopped at a brass ring in the tent flap, and looked through it. "Good heavens," she watched the guests settle into their seats, "they're lined up as far as the stairs to the terrace. I wish I had slept better last night. I'd better take a moment to relax." She sat down in her throne, took several deep breaths, and reflected upon the previous day's coronation. Count Russell was right—I shouldn't have referred to my subjects as fools. I am the fool, for having spoken without first having thought. I must learn to engage my brain, before I engage my tongue."

Handsforth poked his head inside the tent. "Everything okay, Ma'am?"

"I'm nervous, Handsforth. I haven't spoken in public since I was ten."

"You will do fine."

"My neck is stiff. I didn't sleep well. I tossed and turned all night."

"Nothing I can do about your sleep, Ma'am, but I *can* relieve your stiffness."

"Please, do."

"Turn around, please. Clasp your hands behind your head."

Pristine let her cloak cascade into the footman's arms, "like this?"

"Exactly," he caught the cloak, "now, I am going to cradle your neck."

"Oh, that feels good."

"I have yet to begin."

"What are you going to do?"

"I'm going to lift you by your jawbone, and bounce you. Are you ready?"

"Yes. Oh, whoo-oo-oo-hoo!"

"Hold steady."

"O-o-oh—Ha-ands-fo-orth tha-at fee-eels wo-o-on-de-er-fu-ul."

"I am going to set you down now. Are you ready?"

"I guess I am."

"No. Don't stop."

Handsforth lowered the Queen to the ground, as if resting her on feathers.

"Handsforth," she smiled, "you are blessed with a healer's touch."

"Shake your arms out, Ma'am. It will get your energy flowing."

"Like this?"

"Exactly. It should calm your nerves."

"I sho-ou-ould do-o-o thi-i-is mo-o-ore o-o-of-ten."

"The world awaits you, Ma'am. Are you ready to give your speech?"

"Those butterflies have taken over my stomach again, Handsforth."

"Make them dance, while I check on something. I'll be back in five minutes."

"Butterflies," Pristine cradled her abdomen, "fly in formation."

The orchestra piped in *God Save the Queen*, and subjects rose to their feet.

As promised, Handsforth returned. "Ma'am, this is your cue. Are you ready?"

"As ready as ever. Thank you, Handsforth."

"Good luck." The footman walked the Queen to the lectern, and stepped aside.

Two workers pulled up the tent flaps, revealing the young Queen standing behind the lectern, wearing a Gracine-cut suit with ermine hem and cuffs. She wore on her head a simple diamond coronet, with a matching chain resting upon dainty shoulders. The butterflies were starting to obey, and she remembered Queen Mother Marguerite's words: 'Visualize your audience wearing red long underwear, and matching caps.' She smiled, and watched, as latecomers settled into their seats. As the music drew to a close, the garden fell under the command of silence.

Pristine leaned into the microphone. "Thank you," her first words transmitted screeching feedback, cueing the electician to jump onto the platform, and make an adjustment. He jumped off the platform. She stepped back to the lectern, and smiled. "Let me try that again. Thank you."

The crowd went wild with whistles, and applause.

"That sounds much better," she connected visually with every person in the garden. "Beloved subjects, fellow citizens, comrades in Consciousness, first, I would like to thank you for your kind cards and words, as we laid King Poldemire Goldspinner, my late grandfather, to rest. For me, these past few weeks have been a time of great reflection. I have decided it shall be the mission of the neo-Goldspinner Court to solicit the backing of Parliament that we may build more schools, libraries, and hospitals, particularly in the eastern cantons of our state. You may wonder, where does the Queen intend to find the funds to do so? According to the royal accountant, the Abundance War Fund increased last year alone by four percent. I have decided Parliament will take a vote on extracting the proceeds out of the AWF."

The subjects applauded. An entire generation had seen how war destroys character.

Pristine continued. "During the early years of my grandfather's reign, too much was invested into the illusion war was the solution to solving society's problems. War does not solve problems. It creates them, for the problem lies within us, ladies, and gentlemen, not outside."

"We need better childcare," cried a mother.

"We need more parks," shouted the ranger.

"Health care for all," shouted the Nurse's Union crowd.

"*We want to smile*," sang the young, "we need dentists."

"We wann moah Engrish teeshers," cried the E.S.L. group.

"The neo-Goldspinner Court will see these services are improved upon, but it takes time. Every parent," she choked on the word—"every parent must have access to childcare, healthcare, dentists, and parks." How did I miss *parent* in practice—she wondered. "It is unfortunate I must now address the Fear-Terror war, years after we thought we had brought the conflict to an end. If there are any Fearlings or Terrorists around, or any who hear this, I speak to both when I tell you your attacks will no longer be tolerated. Not here, nor *Forgiveness, Play, Determination*, or Resolution, not in any state of our Union. Your vicious dogs patrolling your border, your vultures circling the skies, they do not frighten us."

Count Russell stood at the bar, in the shade of the old magnolia. He had been writing speeches for royal family members for decades. He clung to every word the Queen spoke. Lord Woolsey approached, pipe clenched between his teeth, and lit up. "Wonderful day for a banquet, isn't it?" he slipped his lighter into his pocket.

"Judging by the applause, I would say the Queen is in tune with cause."

"Another good speech, Count," Woolsey puffed, "perhaps Her Majesty will end the conflict once and for all."

"The day shall come when Abundance is blessed again." Count Russell pulled out a handkerchief, it morphed, and flew off into the treetops.

Woolsey stopped puffing. "Did you see that?" He pointed.

"See what?"

"Your handkerchief," Woolsey turned to the Count—"it flew away."

"How many drinks have you had, Woolsey?"

"Just the one. Did you, or did you not just pull a handkerchief out of your vest pocket, Count?"

"I did."

"And did it not turn into a dove that flew off into the treetop?"

"A dove? Into the treetop?"

"Never mind," Woolsey sipped his drink, "I'd better get my eyes checked."

"Your eyes are fine, Woolsey."

"Fear and Terror been have been at war how long?"

"Forever, it seems. The spark of Fear has never been killed."

"And here our new Queen takes a stand on Day One."

"Not much we could expect out of Poldemire, at his age, Woolsey. Let's listen to Pristine speak."

"Yesterday, she said, if need be to end the conflict, she herself would go behind the Black Snake Line."

"One never knows what to expect of a Goldspinner."

"She wouldn't dare cross over the line alone." Woolsey pulled up his britches.

"I imagine she would send an envoy."

"Little Pristine, and here she is Queen," Woolsey puffed on his pipe, "I hear you read her like a book, Count. How you do that?"

"Patience and perception, Woolsey. Let's listen."

Pristine sent well-beingness into the crowd. "First, I must address Princess Erica's entrance yesterday. Some of you may have noticed it was she who stepped out of the carriage yesterday, not I. Princess Erica's claim is true. She *is* the rightful heir to Entitlement, but as she admits, her state of mind, resulting from the traumatic experience endured upon witnessing the loss of our parents, makes it impossible for her to rule. Even the best doctors, here and in Loco, have not been able to help her."

The crowd was silent. Subjects had waited years for an explanation from a palace Communications Office that refused any information.

"Yesterday, I passed the crown to my sister, but not with the intent she rule. I gave her my crown, but not my kingdom. I gave her my scepter, but not my sovereigncy. There are more. I shall rule Abundance in good faith, and princess Erica shall rule Discord, as she has already been doing so successfully. My beloved subjects, those too young to remember, you deserve an explanation."

73

Woolsey puffed on his pipe. "This should be interesting."

"Ten years ago, a warm day in Forgiveness, princess Erica watched, as an earthquake swallowed up our parents. As you might imagine, this sight sent her to Insanity. I was lucky. I was in the terminal with Nanny, while Erica stood on the open airfield with the adults. In an attempt to alleviate her nightmares, visions of our parents crying out for help as the earth closed in on them, she agreed to undergo shock treatment in Loco. Now she experiences memory lapses. For no reason, she feels guilt and shame. She believes she could have saved them, had she acted. These are the thoughts of one who is troubled. No one can save anyone from an act of nature. Dr. Kindervater, the palace pediatrician who has known us since before we were born, has identified princess Erica's nightmares as P.T.S.O., or *Post Traumatic Stress Occurrence*. This diagnosis has deemed Princess Erica unfit to rule. Many years ago, at the Court's coaxing, backed by doctors, princess Erica and I agreed to exchange birth certificates. To this day, she remains haunted by memories she cannot erase.

"Mental health is a struggle that affects millions of our citizens on a daily basis, and we need to address it more openly. These are our *parents*"—she choked on the word again—"they are our children, our husbands, wives, brothers, sisters, grandparents, neighbors, and war-torn veterans, so many who have fought bravely for the freedom we take for granted. I ask princess Erica not be judged by yesterday's run-in with the thurifer's censor. Let us ask ourselves what we can do to help those afflicted by mental illness, that we may heal our families, our community, kingdom, and state. Your support is imperative."

By applause, the crowd reflected unanimous support. Lord Woolsey, still puffing, joined in. "Good living is a challenge mastered in increments," he said, cap under his arm, "bravo to our new Queen."

"No man is an island." A snapping branch in the bushes caught Count Russell's ear. "Did you hear that, Woolsey?"

"Hear what?"

"You didn't see Prince Godwyn poke his head out of the bushes? It couldn't be—what would Prince Godwyn be doing in the bushes?"

"If the prince were here, Count, Avorah would know about it."

"I heard the prince is shy in the presence of princess"—he corrected himself—"*Queen* Pristine."

"Where is princess Erica now?" a royal aficionado shouted to the Queen.

"Why is the princess not here?" shouted another.

Woolsey turned to Count Russell. "Why *is* the princess not here, Count?"

"Your guess is as good as mine. Let's listen, Woolsey."

Pristine continued. "I asked my sister to share a few words with you but in her fragile condition, doctors have instructed her to keep public appearances to a minimum."

"Fragile condition?" shouted one, "she leaps and dances."

"She showed up yesterday," shouted another.

"Princess Erica was pushed."

"When will she address us?"

Pristine smiled. "My sister may be a dancing fool, ladies, and gentlemen, but I assure you, she will continue to receive the best medical treatment available if I have to go to Loco and administer it myself."

Count Russell chuckled. "The crowd is bewildered. They don't understand Pristine's humor."

"Yet—how could they?"

"Here it comes." Count Russell smiled. "They got the joke."

"As I said in yesterday's speech, I intend to rule with truth and honor. God bless the kingdom of Entitlement, the state of Abundance, our Crystal Rock enclave, every state of Consciousness, and every one of you." She extended her hands, palms up, and smiled. "Thank you."

"God save the Queen," guests cheered, and shouted, "Long Live the Queen."

The orchestra started playing *God Bless the Queen*. Subjects rose to their feet, and placed hands over their hearts. Pristine took this opportunity to relax. Now that this song is playing for me, it *does* seem rather long, she thought.

In time, the notes lingered. Workers released the tent flaps, and the first coronation banquet address in seventy-eight years closed to shouts, whistles, and applause.

Handsforth stepped into the tent. "You were brilliant, Ma'am. They loved you—you *are* brilliant. They love you."

"Thank you, Handsforth. My mouth is dry. Could you get me…"

"A glass of water?" he handed her a glass, "your wish is my command."

Pristine sipped. "You are a man of anticipation, Handsforth. I admire that."

"To your health, Your Majesty."

Pristine took another sip, and set the glass down. "I got through the speech."

"You got through the *coronation,* Your Majesty. They love you."

"I want them to love Erica, too."

"That will come. Give it time. Staff is going to raise the buffet screens in twenty minutes."

"Thank you, Handsforth." Pristine took another sip, and handed him the empty glass. "I need to regroup."

"Take your time, Ma'am," he took the glass, "I will return in ten minutes."

Pristine sat down in her chair. I know I give more credit to my handsome subjects than I do to the lesser, she told herself, that Abel Handsforth is my tall, dark commoner—my good luck charm."

Back at the bar, Woolsey relit his pipe. "She has them charmed," he puffed—"totally charmed."

"No reason why they shouldn't be. Her Majesty is a firecracker."

"Parliament is going to want to know how long her fuse is."

"You shall have to wait to find out, Woolsey."

Busboys cleared the tables, while a dozen footmen rolled in carts filled with scrumptious sweets, followed by waiters carrying trays of champagne flutes, and for the more serious drinkers—martini shakers.

Count Russell buttoned his jacket. "Excuse me, Woolsey. I will be right back."

When the orchestra started playing *The Sun Rises on Abundance,* Woolsey walked to the microphone, anxious to be the first to toast the new Queen. Lady Avorah brushed a feather aside, grabbed a flute off one of the passing trays, and handed it to her husband. "George, take this. You can't make a toast without a drink in your hand."

Woolsey tapped the flute with a spoon, steadied himself against the lectern, and began. "I feel honored to toast our new Queen. Your Majesties, ladies and gentlemen, fellow guests, gazing into the sea of faces, it saddens me to see gloom, at a time when my friend Poldemire would have wanted us to celebrate life. Were Poldemire with us today, he would tell us to reach for the light. He reached for that light every day, until the day his Raceabout ended up in the canal. Poldemire's light lives on in his granddaughters, Her Majesty, Queen Pristine, and Her Royal Highness, Princess Erica Gold-Runner of Discord." He raised his flute. "Godspeed to my goddaughters," he downed its contents, and looked around for a replacement.

Lady Woolsey took the empty flute off his hands, set it on a passing tray, grabbed another, and kissed her husband. "That was wonderful,

George," she leaned into the microphone, and turned to the crowd. "Ladies and gentlemen—wasn't that a wonderful toast?"

From the table of liquid friends there arose a clatter. Flutes clinked, "*ai ai ai ai ai—we will drink to that.*" They downed the contents, and summoned a footman for refills.

Lady Avorah leaned into the microphone, and encouraged the crowd. "Was Lord Woolsey's toast not touching?" The crowd settled, and Lady Woolsey began. "I, too, would like to toast our new Queen, and Princess Erica. Lord Woolsey and I have had the honor of knowing the Goldspinner twins since before they were born. We are blessed to be their godparents. When these two extraordinary princesses fell into our lives, we had no idea how to raise children. We did our best to meet their needs. We failed, but authentication expresses itself as result. Nanny Needlepinch was always there, ready with a word of advice—solicited, or not."

Members of the inner circle chuckled.

"George and I never had children. We were foolish to think Nanny could handle everything, but she did. She did it with courage, and strength of spirit, and she did a fine job." Lady Woolsey raised her flute. "To you, Carabella Needlepinch, until the *next* set of Goldspinner twins arrive."

The crowd burst into applause. Nanny smiled, and waved her martini glass. Those at the table of liquid friends saw one of the waiters carry in a fresh tray. They grabbed more flutes, downed the contents, and sang, "*ai ai ai ai ai—we will drink to that.*" Another bar, and they burst into laughter.

Count Russell stepped up to the lectern, dressed in an olive green suit, grounded by matching olive green stockings, and shoes. He grabbed the microphone. "Ladies and gentlemen, to those who subscribe to the doctrines of Terror and Fear, might I remind you, this is not your place here. Long ago, Fear and Terror decided to follow a darker path. Rather than conform, they hold onto their wrath. To the brave souls among us who withstand, and resist—we must keep our eyes to the light, truth will persist. This light shines in our beautiful new Queen. Your Majesty," he raised his flute, "this toast is for you, our beautiful sovereign—Queen Pristine. To our new monarch who dares take on Terror and Fear, it looks like 1911 is going to be a very good year. Bottoms up."

"Here, here," the guests emptied their flutes, and sang, "*a long reign to our Queen.*"

From the table of liquid friends came the chant, "*ai ai ai ai ai—we will drink to that.*"

Carabella Needlepinch was determined to be next at the microphone.

She rose from the chair, brushed her cape aside, and knocked her martini glass over, saved from falling only due to Quigley's swift reflexes.

As hard as Pristine tried not to show emotion, disapproval found her face. "Nanny," the Queen shook her head, "have you not had enough?"

Nanny stood at the microphone, grabbed a spoon, and clanked her glass. "Thish toasht ish to my shignifigent udder," she stuttered—"prin-chesh Prish-teen Gold-schpinner."

Lady Avorah whispered into the nonagenarian's ear. "Nanny, it's *Queen* Pristine."

"Whatzat?"

"*Queen* Pristine, Nanny—not princess."

"Oh, eh, well then—*Queen* Prish-tine, I love you and Erica like my own daughtersh. May your reign be a long, and happy one. Cheersh!" She raised her glass—"to ebryone."

Lady Woolsey took the empty glass out of Nanny's hand, and set it on a footman's passing tray. "Don't you think you have had enough, Nanny? Come, let me accompany you back to your seat."

"I kin make it on my own."

"I know you can. But I want to talk with you."

"What about?" Nanny grabbed Lady Woolsey's arm, and Lady Woolsey helped her off the platform. Nanny sniffled. "I losht my shecond girl today, Lady Woolshey, my life will never be the shame."

"No need for shame, Nanny."

"I'm schlurring my wordsh."

"That's okay, Nanny. I know this is hard for you. You will feel better when this is over, and you can lie down."

"It'ch been an exshaushting weekend."

Lady Woolsey led the old woman through the crowd of good-humored guests, laughing amongst themselves, as busboys cleared the tables. "Here we are, Nanny, back at your seat."

"Finally," Nanny let go of Lady Woolsey's arm.

"Ouch—for a nonagenarian, Nanny, you certainly have a grip."

Nanny planted her stick. "Jusht becaushe I'm ninety doesh not mean I'm not fit, Lady—*Avorah*."

"I feel it. Let me fluff your donut before you sit down, and remember—you've not lost a princess, you've gained a Queen."

"She'sh no longer gonna need me."

"Shit down—I mean *sit down*, Nanny. Pristine has become an independent grown woman. Wasn't that your purpose in raising her?"

"You're right, she'sh grown," Nanny nodded, "she'sh all grown up."

"It was *you* who prepared her for this moment."

"The princhesshes have been my life."

"Sit down. Let me get you a hankie."

"I have one," Nanny pulled one out, and dabbed her tears.

"I know how troubling Poldemire's death was for you."

"No you don't. I knew him for more than half a shentury."

"I can only imagine your pain. Just three weeks ago, you lost your King, and now you have had to let go of your life companion. Such loss would trouble anyone."

"My heart achesh," Nanny sniffled, "what'sh gonna become of me?"

Lady Woolsey put her arm around Nanny's shoulders. "Pristine will look after you. This is an opportunity for you to take care of yourself for a change."

Nanny finished her martini, and started coughing.

"Nanny, are you all right?" Lady Woolsey stepped back.

Ever on the alert, Twickenham hastened in from behind, jabbed his hands under Nanny's armpits, and hoisted her into the air. He clamped onto her abdomen, gave a powerful thrust, and out popped a cocktail olive, hitting Lady Woolsey in the face. Horrified, the crowd watched, as Nanny wheezed. When they had been informed regular breathing had been restored, they applauded, and went back to celebrating.

Uppsola was next on the platform. She brushed back her scarf, held up her flute, and tapped it with a fork. "It's my turn." She raised her voice, and the crowd settled. "This September, I will complete seven decades of service to the royal family, and I must say, these have been *the* most rewarding years of my life."

The orchestra piped in a quick bar of *Seven Decades of Happiness.*

"Thank you," the nonagenarian maid smiled. "How about a big hand for our orchestra conductor and his musicians—for what is life without music?" The old maid joined in the applause, "I have had the honor of getting to know the Goldspinner twins since 1887, the year the stork dropped them off here at the palace. These extraordinary sisters have taught me life is but a series of changes. The best we can do is adapt." From the distance, she locked eyes with the Queen. "Your Majesty, may your reign be a long, healthy one."

"Thank you, Uppsola," Pristine nodded.

"Ladies and gentlemen," Uppsola raised her flute, "to our new Queen—and may we all be invited to attend a royal wedding soon."

Alan John Mayer

The orchestra piped in with a bar of *Here Comes the Bride.*

"A royal wedding?" guests were perplexed. Was it Pristine who caught the last bridal bouquet? Was princess Erica to have a post-nuptial church wedding? There had been no royal wedding for the princess. King Poldemire had refused his granddaughter permission to marry his former chauffeur. Erica and Buzz had eloped. What's in the works?—everyone wondered.

CHAPTER XII

H.R.H. Prince Godwyn Bonheur of Grace

Pristine watched from her table by the bushes, as guests amused themselves, when something tickled her neck. Being an entomophile, she loved insects, and did not want to hurt the creature, so she brushed it aside. "Shoo, my little friend," she whispered, looking back, "move on."

"Move on?"

Pristine flinched. "Godwyn—where did you come from?"

"Hello beautiful. I'm sorry I frightened you."

"I thought you were a bug."

"I didn't want to miss this opportunity to greet my Queen."

"Where have you been hiding? I haven't seen you since Poldi's funeral."

"I've been in your bushes."

"Why?"

"Everyone seems to want a piece of me, wherever I go."

"I can see why," her eyes twinkled, "but why in the bushes?"

"I am avoiding the Press. They've been after me to comment on yesterday's attack on your sister."

"Terrible, isn't it? I intend to put an end to these attacks. You missed the coronation."

"I did. I'm sorry." Godwyn pulled up a chair. "*Grace-Trans* is repairing the infrastructure on the G-5. The bridges are bottlenecked. I left *Leniency* early, but found myself stuck in traffic. Once I realized I'd miss the coronation entirely, I turned around, and drove home."

"You heard about Erica's entrance?"

"I did, on the radio. I heard about the attack, too. Here I am, talking about me again." He took Pristine's hand, "how was your coronation?"

81

"Fine—until Erica showed up. She took my crown."

"She took your crown?"

"GranMarguerite gave it to her, along with my cloak, and scepter."

"Why?"

"She wanted to make her Queen for a Day."

"Are you still not used to your sister's off the wall behavior?"

"I worry about her. She's so fragile."

Godwyn smiled. "Erica will be okay. I would like to kiss you."

"Right now?"

"Right now."

"Be my guest." Pristine held out a hand.

"That's not what I had in mind."

"Not in public, Godwyn. You may kiss my hand."

"I guess I have no choice but to oblige," Godwyn kissed her hand. "You smell lovely."

"Why are you so late?"

"I got stuck in traffic again. The report said west bound traffic would resume, it being a Sunday, but it was bumper to bumper. I arrived at the west gate, and it was closed. I drove to the south gate, entered, walked through the orchard, and here I am—late."

"Won't you stay for the dinner?"

"I can't. I have to be back to Leniency. *Possessa* and *Gezealous* are giving a recital. They'll kill me if I don't show."

"I hope not."

"It's just a phrase," he smiled. "You take everything so literally. I guess that's what I love about you—your innocence."

Pristine blushed. "You flatter me, Godwyn."

"You deserve to be flattered."

"How are Possessa and Gezealous?"

"You know how tweens are. They're bickering brats."

"I wasn't a brat. Neither was Erica."

"I wasn't referring to you. My girls have been fighting all weekend."

"That's what teenage girls do, they fight. Do they play anything?"

"Records."

"Besides records. I meant like a musical instrument?"

"They do." Godwyn nodded. "Gezealous plays the violin, and Possessa plays the cello, but they lack motivation. They complain their instruments are old."

"I always thought the older an instrument, the better it plays."

"That's what I thought, but it's better not to get into an argument with them. They know everything better."

"Sounds like tween-agers."

"Every device I use for business, they use for pleasure—the telephone, telex, wireless."

"What young girl would not be enticed by the many electronic devices on the maket today?"

"My daughters certainly are."

"Are you sure you won't stay for dinner?"

"Not today, Pristine. I regret missing your coronation, and the dinner."

"It was more like Erica's coronation, Godwyn. She took the carriage ride around Market Square."

"That was magnanimous of you."

"Queen Mother gave me no choice. The good part is it got me out of smiling and waving for an hour."

"People outside the gates have gone mad buying up memorabilia— matchbooks, flags, calendars, photographs—you name it."

"They're not mine."

"The photographs?"

"The proceeds. All of the proceeds go into state coffers."

"But the photograph is yours."

She smiled. "The photo is me. When will I see you again?"

"I don't know, but next time, I want to be with you alone," he smiled—"without a chaperone."

"So we won't have to lose Nanny in the Spook House?"

Godwyn chuckled. "That's right. By the way, I heard your speech on the radio. Your message had a sincere call to action."

"Thanks. I choked on the word *parents.*"

"You made a smooth recovery. Your subjects will love you for having a fault." He rose from the chair, "I have to leave."

"Already?"

"I have to be in Leniency before seven."

"You just got here."

"I know. I wish I could stay, and nibble on your neck."

"Oh, Godwyn, you are silly."

"I'll telephone you next week. We should go away."

"We're not married."

"What difference does that make?"

"None, I guess, as long as we maintain separate accommodations. We'll have to keep an eye open for the Press. We could visit Erica."

"I would love to see princess Erica again. And I want you to meet my family. I'll call you before the week is out."

"I will be expecting your call, Godwyn."

"Goodbye, beautiful."

"Green lights, Godwyn. Happy trails."

Godwyn left the Queen in a dream state, as if hypnotized. Only the sound of Nanny clearing her throat pulled her back into the plot. Outside the gates, the Press ambushed the prince, as he walked to his motorcar. "Your Royal Highness," the reporters vied for his attention, "as Defender of the Faith, what have you to say about yesterday's attack on princess Erica?"

"Gentlemen, I have asked you politely, numerous times, to set up an audience with my secretary. Instead, you ambush me. I have only this to say: attacks are fundamental in nature. Not only do attacks come from Terrorists and Fearlings, Mother Nature attacks, in the form of earthquakes, floods, tornados, volcanos, storms. One must also consider attacks from outer space, meteors, asteroids, flying space junk. When Mother Nature attacks, it comes from the highest source. When man attacks, it stems from the primitive flight or fight response that goes back to our primordial ancestors. Attack is a part of life, and it never ends."

The reporters clamored for the prince's attention. One over the other, they shouted, "what have you to say about last week's attack on Timorous?"

"We must see to it the culprets of any attack are apprehended, and returned to their state of origin. I gave you your statement, gentlemen. Allow me to pass."

"One more question, Sir," one reporter persisted in a more personal direction, "how do you respond to the rumor you fancy the new Queen?"

"I neither confirm nor deny. I dare any one of you who does not fancy Queen Pristine Goldspinner to step forward." Godwyn appraised the lot. "I thought not. Not one of you stepped forward. Now go back to your bedrooms, gentlemen—where you belong."

The reporters were left speechless by the prince's statement. They rolled up their cords, stuck microphones into their cases, tossed everything into their motorscooter baskets, and rode off.

News travels fast. Back on the palace lawn, Mina Amora turned to Cocoa Rocco. "That really *was* Prince Godwyn you saw in the bushes. I heard the Press ambushed him, and asked about his attraction to the Queen."

"What Hees Roial Highness sayed?"

"I don't know what he said. I thought you might have heard."

"I no heared no-thing."

The table of liquid friends clanged spoons to flutes, and sang another round of "*ai ai ai ai ai— we will drink to that.*"

The orchestra conductor lifted his baton, and the musicians played a few bars of *God Save the Queen*, prompting the crowd to rise to their feet. An electritican hastened in to raise the microphone, then leaped off the platform. Lord *Draggelsdorp* approached, and raised his flute. "I would like to make a stately toast to a beautiful young woman," he looked at the Queen. "Your Majesty, may the wind be always at your back, may the Lord hold always you in the hollow of his hands."

Pristine took a flute off Lady Woolsey's hand as she approached the microphone, and raised it into the air. "Will you please join me in saluting our conductor and his talented musicians—what would life be without music?"

"Here here," guests clinked their flutes, and drank up, while the table of liquid friends laughed, a bit slower now.

Pristine stood at the lectern, holding her flute. She nodded to Mr. Kensington, and waited, while he lined up his staff of handsome young footmen. "Is everyone here? Not everyone, I see. I would like to thank everyone who worked so hard on such short notice to put this terrific banquet together. I salute our cuisinaires superbs—Mr. Maurice Le Souffle, pasty chef Mr. Fradenzo Kookje, our butler, Mr. *Kenneth Kensington,* our footmen: Mr. Abel Handsforth; Mr. Fenewick Twickenham; Mr. Randall Quigley; Mr. Gowen Fetchett; Mr. *Mishigawa Munchipoo;* Mr. *Andrew Harrison,* and," she looked around—"where are the rest?"

Handsforth spoke up. "They are in the kitchen, Your Majesty—at work."

"Let us applaud our hard-working staff, too many to mention, who upon such short notice orchestrated a buffet fit for a king, or, as in this case, fit for a Queen."

"Long live the Queen," guests raised their flutes.

Pristine continued. "I would like to thank my sister, princess Erica, and her husband, Sir Buzz Runner. May happiness shine upon Gruntle always, and lastly, but not least, please join me in a big round of applause to you, our guests, for showing up. Thank you for your support."

Count Russell escorted the Queen to her seat. "Your Majesty," he spoke over the applause, "be it work or fun, you remember to thank everyone."

Pristine spent the next hour shaking hands, and kissing babies. By the time the sun kissed the treetops, most of the guests had left. A few stragglers descended upon the tables, when no one was looking, and pocketed matchbooks, centerpieces, spoons—anything that had not been carried away.

As dusk descended, guards ushered loiterers out the gates. Workers canvassed the lawn, gathering trash and donations for Lost & Found. Sixteen trays of food were collected. They were wrapped, and taken to the station to be loaded on the night train to Timorous—a donation to the New Hope Shelter.

Queen Mother was delighted to be able to spend a private moment with her granddaughter, the new Queen, even is it was while climbing the steps to the terrace. "What a relief to be done shaking hands, and kissing babies," Pristine shook her head, "why is it everyone thinks their baby is the cutest?"

"I don't know what it is. The ego sees itself in a carbon copy."

"I think all babies are ugly."

"Of all the royal duties, shaking hands and kissing babies were always my least favorite, even while wearing gloves. You never know where a person's hands have been."

"Never mind hands. It's the babies I'm concerned with, GranMarguerite. They slobber. They're so gross."

"Pristine, stop." Queen Mother examined the Queen's dress.

"What?"

"What's that on your shoulder?"

"Shoulder pads?"

"Not your pads. What is that? Is that snot?"

"Ew," Pristine touched the mucus by accident, "gross—baby snot. GranMarguerite, get rid of it for me."

"Hold on. Let me pull out my hankie."

"Eew," Pristine squirmed—"that is gross."

"Stop moving." Queen Mother wiped up the mucus. "There we are, all gone. Remember, Pristine—only well-beingness."

"You mean I can't react to baby snot?"

"Not if you want the subjects to love you," Queen Mother shook her head, "only well-beingness."

"Yuck. I hope you're going to get rid of your hankie."

"Why would I keep it?" Queen Mother chuckled. "I will toss it at the first opportunity. Now, let's go in. You are going to be shaking more hands tonight, after dinner."

"More shaking hands?"

"After tonight, you will be free until the next event."

"When is that going to be?"

"Summer Solstice Tea, at the lily pond.

The Monday morning Abundance Times newspaper headlines read:

MANY GUESTS LEFT CORONATION BANQUET FILLED FULL
BUT ONLY A HANDFUL LEFT FULFILLED.

CHAPTER XIII
Neo-Goldspinner Court Holds Session

After King Poldemire's passing, Queen Mother Marguerite and her life-long companion maid, Uppsola Pumba, moved into adjacent freshly refurbished suites in the palace attic, where, overlooking the gardens, *Crystal Lake*, *Mount Majesty* and the *Troubled Forest* in the distance, they looked forward to peaceful retirement.

Uppsola stood at the sink in the kitchenette, holding the kettle under running water. "How about a nice foot soak, Y.M.?" she asked Queen Mother, seated in her favorite chair.

"Uppsola, you read my mind," Queen Mother's legs rested upon an ottoman, toes spread. "I think I may be getting a bunion."

Uppsola turned off the faucet, flicked a flintstick to a burner, and set the kettle on the stove. "A hot soak should ease your pain, Y.M."

"I wish you would stop calling me Y.M., Uppsola. You know how it annoys me."

"Y.M. is just more efficient than having to say *Your Majesty*."

"Call me Ma'am, or GranMarguerite, at least in public."

"Uppsola counted, "Gran-Mar-gu-er-it-e—that's six syllables."

"Three, the final e is silent—Gran-Mar-guerite, or Ma'am" Queen Mother held up a finger—"Ma'am is one syllable less than Y.M. Why not call me Ma'am?"

"By the way, Ma'am"—Uppsola mocked, "would you please tell the fire boys to keep the furnace burning. Every time there is no hot water, I have to heat it up, and run back and forth between the kitchen and the bathroom to fill your tub."

Queen Mother set her *Radio Talk* on the table. "Tell Kensington, Uppsola. He will take care of it."

"Here I come. Remove your slippers."

"I already did. Are you going to massage my feet?"

"I am." Uppsola set a tub of hot water at Queen Mother's feet. "Step in."

"You've not massaged my feet since..."

"Since before Poldi died, Ma'am."

"There; you said it again."

"Said what?"

"You called me Ma'am. Was that so difficult?"

"Just a slip of the tongue, Gramma—don't get used to it."

Palace butler, Mr. Kenneth Kensington, spent months distributing the late King's personal possessions. Tradition states finer items, such as watches, cufflinks, snuffboxes, and shoehorns be bequeathed to the butler, the valet, and favored footmen of the deceased. Mr. Kensington donated the extra large clothing to *The Holy Ghost Charity Shoppe* in Indifference, where unconcerned subjects have no qualms about wearing oversize fancy clothes to everyday drab occasions. It is said: *'As long as the Indifferent is shielded from rain and sun, he cannot be bothered with what to put on'.* Check out the world's shortest book on mode at your local municipal library—*The History of the Indifferent Fashion*—three full pages, in color—each dedicated to a gender.

It took Pristine no time at all to settle into her newly renovated quarters in the east wing—Queen Mother Marguerite's residence, before her move upstairs. The new Queen took immediate command of the Court. With a staff of experts at her call, she was determined to cement her identity in the pages of history. She had an agenda, and she planned to carry it out without compromise.

The first session of the neo-Goldspinner Court met on Monday, September 18, 1911—*National Consciousness Day.* At six o'clock in the morning, four guards wrenched open the twenty-foot tall oak and bronze doors to the palace throne room, and eager Parliamentarians walked in, and headed to their desks, in preparation for the day's session.

In the last session, Parliament had elected Lord *Manton Cnute* to preside over this historic day. He arrived early, and walked down the rows of desks, filling inkwells, distributing programmes, picking up the occasional piece of litter, when he noticed the Queen was to arrive in five minutes. He finished his rounds, and proceeded to his position at the lectern.

At nine o'clock, the petite strawberry blonde stepped into the throne room, to the accompaniment of *God Save the Queen.* Parliamentarians rose from their desks, bowed, and curtseyed. Heads turned, as she walked up the aisle, dressed in a rust-colored faux-suede suit with matching heels, bangles dangling from one arm. Closer inspection revealed she wore a pair of diamond-studded haircombs, one on each temple.

The Queen's private secretary, *Tusnelda Thornecroft,* seldom seen dressed in anything but brown, followed Pristine and her favored footman, Abel Handsforth, to the stage. Handsforth led her up the steps to her chair, center stage, facing Parliament, and disappeared. Pristine remained standing for the remainder of the song, then sat down, and assessed her Court. This is an assembly of Parliamentarians I might respect, she thought—predominately male, elderly, and silent. They all need a Nanny to tell them how bad they have been. Let's see how long it takes for me to whip them into shape.

Mrs. Thornecroft set her bifocals on her nose, and opened the State Ledger, while waiting for Lord Cnute to open the session. The good Lord finished polishing his spectacles on his ascot, set them on his nose, and nodded to the secretary. Mrs. Thornecroft nodded to the Queen, and the session began.

'BAM.' Cnute slammed his gavel on the lectern. "Order in the Court. The firsht shession of the neo-Goldshpinner Court ish now in shesshion. I, Manton Cnute preshiding over thish hishtoric event, the firsht meeting of the neo-Goldshpinner Court, with our lovely young Queen." He lowered his head, "Your Majeshty, the floor belongsh to you."

"Thank you, Lord Cnute. Before we get started, I am told you have an update on the fate of the attackers on princess Erica, and many other innocent victims, following my coronation this last thirteenth of May."

Mrs. Thornecroft leaned in to her microphone. "Your Majesty, the Fear-Terror Attack case was closed in proxy, in the last session of the Poldemire Court."

"Why was I not given notice to be present?"

"The Court voted by mail, Ma'am, and the majority ruled you were not to be disturbed."

"I still do not understand why I was not informed."

"Your Majeshty, under the shircumshtanshesh, the Court took a vote not to trouble you with what the conshidered to be unneshseshary informashion."

Mrs. Thornecroft took the mic. "I have the sentence results here, should you wish to hear them, Ma'am."

"Yes. Read me what you have."

Mrs. Thornecroft brushed her scarf aside. "As to the Saturday, May 13th, 1911 attacks perpetuated upon Her Royal Highness, Princess *Erica Gold-Runner* of Discord, and seventeen commoners of various states, and colors; 98.63 percent of those arrested pled guilty as charged. The attackers are now enrolled in rehabilitation prison."

"And the Fearlings?"

"That figure includes Fearlings, Ma'am."

"The terms?"

"Three years rehabilitative labor in *Fou.*"

"Well that should be nice for them." The Court chuckled. "And the remaining 1.37 percent?"

"They took the Insanity plea. Those six individuals are now serving time in Fou, under the same terms, and conditions."

"That should teach them a lesson."

"Yes, Ma'am."

"Thank you, Mrs. Thornecroft." Pristine aligned her posture. "It is a shame to see young people getting into trouble for no reason at all."

"At your service, Ma'am."

"While I have the floor, I would like to thank our Parliamentarians for executing justice in this case. Thank you, gentlemen, and—Lady Woolsey. Lord Cnute, I turn the floor back to you."

"Thank you, Your Majeshty. Nexsht on today'sh shillibus—Caishe Number 009-23-58, the Cryshtal Rock Lighthoushe Dock and Pier. I believe Count Russhell shined up to shpeak fhirsht."

"Thank you, Lord Cnute." Count Russell approached the lectern. "Ladies, and gentlemen, and everyone inbetween, welcome to this historic gathering of the neo-Goldspinner Court. What a year it has been, eh? Those who have ever heard me rehearse, know that at times, I break into verse."

The Court chuckled.

"If the Court will indulge me, I would like to open today's session with a riddle." He looked about the room. "I see no opposition, so I shall proceed. What do *Possessée* solicitors wear to court?"

The Parliamentarians shook their heads. "No idea." They shrugged their shoulders. "We give up." One finally admitted no one had a clue. "What *do Possessée* solicitors wear to court?"

"Law suits." Count Russell waited for one to explain to the next, until chuckles emerged from the sea of dark suits. "Serious now, Your Majesty, Parliamentarians, subjects of every state, we address Case 009-23-58—the

Crystal Rock lighthouse and dock. This small Abundite enclave on the *Understanding Strait*, held by Abundance since 1408, annexed to the kingdom in 1703, is now in danger of being washed out to sea." He paused to let the severity of the situation sink in. "Ladies and gentlemen, the time to move the lighthouse was yesterday. If we wait much longer, it is not going to stay — mark my word — it will be washed away."

Cnute leaned in to his microphone. "Count Russhell requeshtsh the Court give input. Who would like to be firsht?"

"I will, Mr. Chairman," Lord *Morningstar* rose from his desk.

The gavel struck, 'BAM.' "The Court recognishes Lord Morningshtar."

A mysterious looking man with long braids approached the lectern. "Count Russell, would not a taller barrier wall keep the waves out?"

"Good question, Lord Morningstar. The project engineers have made the calculations, adaptations, and accommodations — all leading to a final resignation." Count Russell shook his head. "Waves cannot be held back by a taller wall. We must move the lighthouse, we must move it before fall."

'BAM.' Down went Cnute's gavel. "The Court recognishesh Lord Woolshey."

George Woolsey rose from his chair, and steadied himself on his desk. "Thank you, Lord Cnute. According to the chief engineer on this project, my wife, Avorah Woolsey — and what an engineer she is — within ten years, a fortified barrier wall would risk a fall, in addition to draining state coffers. Nothing we can do will stop Oceania's waves from rising. We must find a new home for the lighthouse, further inland. Thank you."

Count Russell took back the floor. "Every year, Oceania's great waves rise in height. The fight to save our lighthouse has become quite a plight. The stairs leading up the hill have been washed away, the old wooden dock is in decay. The time for discussing and waiting has long passed. We must move the lighthouse, and we must move it fast."

"Thank you, Count Russhell. Lord Woolshey, I shee your hand ish up."

Woolsey steadied himself at his desk. "Ladies and gentlemen, our lighthouse has served us with loyalty and glory for four hundred years. Now we stand to lose it. Should we not serve it with the same loyalty and glory it has served us? We must act now, before the foundation crumbles."

Pristine got lost in thought. That's what Erica was singing in the bishop's parlor — Crystal Rock is crumbling down. Could she have put a spell on our lighthouse? That cannot be. This is Mother Nature releasing her fury for the way humanity is destroying the planet.

'BAM.' "Count Russhell, I return the floor to you."

"Thank you, Lord Cnute. Crystal Rock may seem no more than a small enclave of our state, but this small enclave has served our citizens since 1708. The tariffs collected at Crystal Rock keep our parks green, our streets lit, our libraries in stock. Without these tariffs, our streets would go dark, our parkland would turn brown, and society would go into shock."

"We must move the lighthouse to higher ground," came a cry from the 4:20 Club, upstairs in the gallery.

"There is no higher ground," shouted one.

"There is," shouted another, "it's three miles inland."

"Raise the foundation," cried one.

"Raze-it," cried another.

"A new dock first."

Count Russell looked into the gallery, raised a hand, and silence befell the audience. "The Court seems to be in agreement now. We must move the lighthouse, the question is how? I leave the surveillance of this task to Lady Woolsey, and the Court, that we may find a solution quickly, and close this report. Lord Cnute, I turn the floor back to you." To applause, Count Russell returned to his seat, without further ado.

Cnute consulted his syllabus. "Here to dishkush with ush the progressh of the move, schpeaking for her team, Lady Avorah Wool-shey."

'BAM.'

The Court applauded, as Lady Woolsey approached the stage, hand securing her hat. "Thank you, Lord Cnute. Your Majesty, Parliamentarians, ladies and gentlemen of the Court, I feel honored to serve as the Crystal Rock Lighthouse project manager. Our study has concluded that the existing pier, built in the late fifteenth century, will not withstand the weight of the machinery we need to move the lighthouse. Before we can consider moving the lighthouse, we must first build a new pier."

"But that would mean having to destroy the old pier," said one.

"Exactly."

"Why not have two piers?" cried another.

"Exactly."

"Lady Woolsey," the Queen leaned forward, "could we not build a pedestal for the lighthouse?"

"A pedestal is one idea, Ma'am, but it would still require moving the lighthouse. Where it stands, it will always be slashed by waves, as would be any pedestal or foundation we might build. We have no option but to disassemble the lighthouse, and move it to higher ground."

"Disassemble? You mean, take it apart?"

"Yes, Your Majesty, floor by floor."

"Which higher ground has been considered?"

"Three miles inland, Ma'am, six hundred feet above sea level."

"And how do we go about transporting the lighthouse?"

"The move will require several stages. The lighthouse will need to be transported in pieces, horizontally. Our contractors have already drawn out blueprints for the construction of the new dock. If anyone has any further questions, please see me. Thank you," Lady Woolsey smiled, returned to her desk at her husband's side, and sat down.

Pristine issued her first official decree: "I order the lighthouse be moved as soon as the new dock is completed, before this coming spring."

Lord Morningstar rose from his desk, "but Your Majesty…"

'BAM.' "The Court recognishes Lord Morningshtar."

Lord Morningstar hastened to the lectern, and took the micropone. "Your Majesty, my team and I have been in charge of the logistics to this move. Next spring is an impossible target date."

"Impossible, Lord Morningstar?"

"Impossible, Your Majesty."

Count Russell rose to his feet. "Your Majesty, it will take us at least six months to finish the dock, and that is working six days a week around the clock."

"Six months won't do it"—Sir *David James McClure* did not mind speaking out of turn. He walked straight to the lectern, dressed in an elegant white suit.

"Shir McClure, you musht wait to be recognished."

To whistles, and shouts, Sir McClure took the microphone, and waited for the audience to settle. "Your Majesty, ladies and gentlemen of the Court, my forty years experience moving lighthouses tells me Lord Morningstar's calculations are absolutely correct. To expect the work to be done by spring 1912 is overly optimistic."

Hand in the air, Lord Draggelsdorp rose from his desk.

'BAM.' "The Court regognishesh Lord Draggelshdorp."

A lanky man in a gray flannel suit stepped to the microphone. "Your Majesty, a more realistic goal is winter, 1913."

"Winter? Lord Draggelsdorp, Count Russell, gentlemen, are you hard of hearing? Shall I summon Queen Mother's audiologist? I said the dock shall be finished by spring 1912, and that is what I meant. I thank those of you who have offered your opinions and calculations. The case is closed until next session."

While the Court bantered over how to meet the new Queen's demand, Pristine dreamed of Prince Godwyn's kiss on her hand, as he left her last spring at the banquet.

'BAM.' "Your Majeshty." The gavel struck again. 'BAM.' "Your Majeshty," and again.

The third strike caught Pristine's attention. "Godwyn," she opened her eyes, "oh—Lord Cnute—it's you." She corrected her posture, and straightened her dress. "Forgive me, I seem to have dozed off."

"Ma'am, how dosh Her Majeshty vote?"

"What was the question?"

Cnute peered over his spectacles. "Wash that a yesh, or a nay, Your Majeshty?"

"Yes, nay—what?"

"The vote to reshtore the dock by coming shpring, Ma'am."

"Oh, yes—that was a yes vote from me."

'BAM.' "Caishe closhed. Mrs. Thornecroft, ish there anything elsh on today'sh shyllabush we have not covered?"

She buttoned her cardigan, as she checked the ledger. "We seem to have covered everything, Lord Cnute."

"Thank you," Cnute lifted his gavel.

"Wait!"—a lanky man in cargo gear stepped onto the stage, and took the microphone. "Your Majesty, Parliamentarians, if you will lend me your ears."

"The Court recognishes, eh," Cnute leaned over—"whatsh your name, Shon?"

"*Martin Becker,* Sir."

'BAM.' "The Court recognishes Shir Martin Becker."

Sir Becker addressed the Queen. "Your Majesty, I represent a non-profit organization called *Save the Trees.* Perhaps you have heard of us."

"I have, Sir Becker," she nodded. "What can I do for you?"

"We do what our name implies, Ma'am, we save trees."

"Sir Becker, say your piece. Court has adjourned."

"Your Majesty, just one minute, two, please, if the Court would oblige me."

"Very well," the Queen leaned into her microphone. "I ask that you stay and hear what Mr. Becker has to say."

"Thank you, Ma'am. Thank you, members of the Court. *Tele-Co-Communications* has plans to fell the trees on Main Street, in Contentment, and replace them with telegraph poles. We see this as a

96

declaration of death, a war against animals. Trading live trees for dead trees to satisfy investors, without taking into account the merchants, shoppers, and the many species of animals who enjoy the shade these trees provide, and call home, this is against our principles. Trees provide shade; telegraph poles do not. Trees emit oxygen; telephone poles do not. Polls are dead trees with unsightly overhead wires, Your Majesty."

"I could not agree more, Mr. Becker. Please, continue."

"We at Save the Trees stand in opposition to this proposal. We believe a row of telegraph poles supporting wires down our main street would be an assault to the eye—in particular the tourist eye. Personally, I myself see their plans as exterminating animal life, turning Main Street into a graveyard. *Tele-Co-Com* reasons, dead or alive, a tree is a tree. If they have their way, the felling of the trees will have a disturbing effect upon the mental and physical health of our citizens, not to mention it would destroy the habitat of thousands of insects, birds, and animals. We cannot allow this extermination to happen."

"I imagine this would have quite an affect upon not only birds and bugs, but tourist income, as well."

"Oh, Your Majesty, yes, in a big way."

"And where would they strike next?"

"Yes, where will their next target be? Ma'am," he leaned forward, "I understand you are an entomophile."

"Why yes, I do have an affinity for bugs. I see you have done your homework. I assure you, Sir Becker, I will not allow the destruction of life on Main Street for the sake of *Tele-Co-Com*'s profit."

"That's the spirit, Ma'am. We ask that you help us—Save the Trees."

"I am glad you brought this to my attention, Sir Becker. I wrote a letter to *Tele-Co-Com* recently, suggesting they *bury* their telegraph lines. Mrs. Thornecroft, was that letter posted?"

"It was," the secretary checked the ledger, "I posted it on July 31st."

"Lord Cnute, would you take a vote."

"Shertainly, Your Majeshty." 'BAM.' "All thoshe in favor of shaving the treesh, raishe your hand, and shay 'aye'."

Every hand went up. Out of every mouth came an 'aye.'

"Thoshe opposed?" Cnute surveyed the floor "I hear no objectshions." 'BAM.' "The Main Shtreet Maple treesh shall be shaved."

Mrs. Thornecroft slipped her bifocals into an étui, and finished buttoning her cardigan. "I shall send a duplicate letter to *Tele-Co-Com* tomorrow, Ma'am, informing them of the Court's decision."

97

"Thank you, Mrs. Thornecroft. Please make sure the trees are *saved*—not shaved."

"Yes Ma'am," she smiled, "consider it done."

Pristine leaned in to her microphone. "In conclusion, I would like to thank Parliamentarians, and the members of the Court for your attendance. Lord Cnute, would you close today's session, please."

"Absholutely." Lord Cnute looked at the clock, "three-forty, looksh like we can all be home in time for tea." He grabbed the gavel. "Goldshpinner Court ish adjourned until Monday, October 23rd." 'BAM.'

CHAPTER XIV

A Visit to Puerto Loco

Y our Majesty..." the butler trundled into the Queen's parlor.
"What is it, Kensington?"
"Sir Runner called while you were out. Princess Erica has gone into relapse."
"Another relapse?"
"Yes, Ma'am. Her Royal Highness is at the Celebrity Center in Loco."
"I knew something was wrong. All day I have felt off kilter. Tell the captain to prepare the Consciousness, Kensington. We sail tomorrow morning at seven."
"Right away, Ma'am."
"Tell Mina to pack light. Inform Miss Needlepinch and Mrs. Thornecroft they will be accompanying me, please."
"Yes, Ma'am," the butler bowed, and walked out, backwards.
The following morning, after a two-hour ninety-mile journey in the Isotta Fraschini, Crankshaft pulled into the new Crystal Rock harbor parking lot, at 0:6:48. Ten minutes later, the ship cast off, and the HMS Consciousness sailed to *Puerto Loco*, on the southern tip of the Discord-Insanity peninsula.
The next afternoon, Buzz Runner met his sister-in-law, the Queen, at the Celebrity Center Café, surrounded by Security officers hiding behind columns, planters, and badges. He bowed, out of habit, "Your Majesty, Pristine, hello."
"Hello, Buzz. I am glad you are here to greet me."
"How was your crossing?"
"Rocky, at best. No one got seasick. How is Erica?"
"She is in stable condition. This has been a difficult week."
"It has been for all of us. Where is she staying?"
"She's at the Celebrity Center Hotel. She's in training right now."

"Let's go see her," Pristine nodded, and a porter rolled in a baggage cart, "she wants support, let us give it to her."

"This way, Ma'am—Pristine—I don't know how to address you."

"In public, I prefer you call me Your Majesty upon first interaction, and Ma'am thereafter. In private you may call me Pristine. It must be a challenge to have not one, but two of us in your life, Buzz."

"It is complicated, but well worth it."

"What a nice thing to say. This is not a good time for me to be away from Entitlement. There is so much going on."

"Erica apprecitates you coming—as do I."

"When will they release her?"

"The doctor said as early as Friday."

"I cannot stay past Wednesday."

"I think all Erica needs is to know you showed up, Ma'am."

"She seems drawn to this place. You must keep her away from here, Buzz. I can't hop on the ship every time she has a relapse."

"She finds comfort here. I guess it's because she hears other peoples' stories, so she connects with common folk."

"The streets certainly are clean."

"Thanks to the OCD patients. Their assignment is litter patrol."

"It seems well-lit. The grounds appear to be well-maintained."

"No crime, thanks to all the pan-sexual artists who call this home. When I am here, I have not a care in the world—except I have too much time to think."

"All Erica talks about over the phone is how much value she finds in pod. What is pod?"

"It's group sharing, in a circle."

"I imagine there is something to be said about airing your dirty laundry in front of a group of strangers. Only my sister would do that."

"For Erica it's about family. Sharing in pod makes her feel she is surrounded by people who understand her."

Pristine stopped, "and we don't?"

"Of course we do. Turn here, to the right. I was thinking of hiring her a live-in caregiver."

"What's wrong with Norbert and Norbertina?"

"They're servants. Erica needs a registered nurse, and that's tricky. You know how Erica feels about nurses."

"Like a pitfull loves the letter carrier. This center is massive. I see they finished the glass roof."

"They did that in 1908."

"It's marvelous architecture."

"Buzz looked at the girders, "it's sixty feet up."

"This campus seems huge."

"Twenty acres. Staff here treats every disorder there is. Sixteen languages are spoken here, including *Insane-a-Sign*."

"Insane-a Sign?"

"Sign language, it's how the deaf communicate."

"I see. How do you know all this information?"

"I attended their free orientation class. Every board and sign is translated into sixteen languages."

"Seems an ideal location for a scribe, or a translator."

"Insanity is the only state to hold no language boundaries. Here we are, Ma'am, through the double doors."

Two doormen stood guard at open glass doors. Buzz followed Pristine into the reception lounge, followed by Security. Buzz looked at his watch. "She's still in pod. It's 11:28. They should be coming out any minute."

The door flung open. "Pristine," Erica ran to her sister and embraced her, trailed by an elderly nurse wearing mint green. "Pristine, am I glad to see you."

"Hello, Erica. Did you have to drag me here? Let me take a look at you." Pristine stepped back. "You've lost weight."

"Nine pounds."

"And you're wearing my dress."

Erica spun before her sister, wearing a mint green Grace-cut suit, and giggled, "we're wearing the same outfit."

"Where did you find it?"

"On you. I liked it so much I had Norbertina sew me a copy. You told me you never wear the same outfit twice."

"I don't. I am so fond of this cut, I had Mrs. Taylor sew me two."

Erica took Buzz's hand, and dragged him to the sofa. "Let's talk. How are things at home, Pris?"

"Nothing out of the normal. Court held it's first session last week—well, it's *my* first session. Your attackers were sentenced. They're serving time in labor camp—three years."

"Good. Serves them right. The bastards deserve ten. Imagine, tossing coal and potatoes at *me*—a royal princess, from the house of Entitlement."

"Erica, how is your recovery coming along?"

Buzz smiled. "Erica is always excited after pod."

"Pod gets my blood flowing. It gives me insight into the troubles other people have. You know—the common folk—I'm sorry, Buzz. You know I don't mean you."

"Oh, Erica, all I could think of these past few days was you. Kensington called, several times, but all he got was a busy signal."

"We got hit by another hailstorm. The lines were down again."

"One hail ball hit one of our crocs on the head, and killed him."

"Yeah, it was the size of an orange."

"Erica, you exaggerate."

"No, Ma'am," Buzz shook his head, "she's not exaggerating."

"Isn't that a misfortune. I came as soon as Kensington gave me Buzz's message."

"My handsome husband." Erica cupped Buzz's cheeks, and kissed him. "Buzz has come to see me every day."

"What else could I do?" he shrugged his shoulders, and smiled.

"Dr. *Zirko* says I can go home Friday."

"He said *maybe*, Erica."

"He said Friday, Buzz. Pristine, how long are you going to stay?"

"I have to leave by Wednesday. Erica, I can't believe how good you look."

"You were expecting me to look bad?"

"Of course not. Well—you *are* here. How did you lose the weight?"

"Medication. It takes away my appetite. When I don't eat, the guilt goes away."

"Well, it produces results."

"Sweetheart, go chat with your podmates for a bit," Buzz kissed Erica's cheek, "Pristine and I need to have a word with the director."

"A word with the director? About what?"

"Your release."

"What about my release?"

"A small matter of the bill."

"Go talk with your podmates, Erica. Buzz and I will be right here. Shoo," Pristine waved her arms, "go."

"Ten minutes," Erica walked through the swinging door. Meanwhile, a door on the opposite wall opened. "Your Majesty, Sir Runner," the receptionist curtseyed, and stepped aside. "Dr. Zirko will see you now." She ushered them into a paneled office. "Make yourselves at home. Doctor will be right in." She walked out, and closed the door.

The in-laws sat down in two chairs facing an enormous desk,

punctuated by a black naugahyde chair. Buzz whispered, "Pristine, look at all the knickknacks."

Pristine set her purse on the desk. "Look at all the trophies, and certificates. The man has more degrees than a thermometer."

"Read the nameplate, Ma'am — Pristine."

"Doctor *Zeke Zirko*, Director of Admissions, Celebrity Center Institute for the Very, Very, Troubled — that is a very, very long title."

Pristine removed her gloves, and set them on her purse. "I have a feeling the doctor is insecure."

Buzz chuckled, "very, very insecure."

A man of disadvantaged height in a black suit entered, and closed the door behind him. "Your Majesty," hand extended, he bowed, "Sir Runner, I am Doctor Zirko. I am very, very pleased to meet you."

Buzz shook the man's hand, "pleased to meet you, doctor."

Pristine nodded, "a pleasure, Doctor, I am sure."

The man sat down in his chair. "Now, to Princess Histe — eh, Princess *Erica*, Her Royal Highness has successfully completed the last series of treatment. She should be ready to go home Thursday."

"Thursday? *Dr. Pastilla* told me Friday. Is she ready?"

"I assure you, Sir Buzz, the princess is ready to go home."

"I would rather she stay an extra day, Doctor, than have her experience another relapse."

"I assure you, princess Erica is fine. She may feel a bit edgy, at first. That should wear off in a day or two."

"Was it necessary for me to come all this way?"

"Prist — *Your Majesty*," Buzz corrected himself, "if you had seen Erica last week, she was a different person."

"Yes," the doctor pulled on a knob, and his chair rose three inches, "Princess Erica has made quite a recovery. Doctor Pastilla has her on a new regimen."

"Another medication regimen?"

"She's been on it for nearly a week now, and she is doing fine."

"Any side effects?"

"A little nausea perhaps, some dizziness, vomiting."

"Vomiting?"

"Only severe cases," Dr. Zirko spun around, and opened his credenza. "I will give you each a pamphlet. It should help clarify the Post Traumatic Stress Occurance condition. It is important you not re-act to any outburst she may have. You must be pro-active — not reactive."

Pristine looked up, "will she still experience mood swings?"

"It's likely, Ma'am. Any questions you may have should be answered in the pamphlet." He handed each one.

"Will weight loss have any negative consequences?"

"You will find answers to all your questions in the pamphlet," the doctor leaned over the desk, "Mr. Runner, see to it the princess gets plenty of rest—and no surprises."

"That leaves out the Spook House."

"There you have it, Buzz. Life may calm down yet."

"Love will carry us through. It always has."

"I must warn you, Mr. Runner, anything can be a trigger."

"How can I recognize a trigger?"

"Usually it's alcohol, or a drug. Or sexual misconduct. You will find a chapter on triggers and how to avoid them in the pamphlet. Although Fear and Terror have called a truce, I would refrain from travel there."

"Any truce behind the Black Snake can only be temporary."

"I could not agree with you more, Ma'am."

"Anything else we should be aware of, Doctor?"

"Things should be fine. Just try to remain on the peninsula. You might consider a live-in nurse. I could arrange one for you if you like."

Buzz shrugged his shoulders, "what do you think, Pri-?"

"It couldn't hurt," Pristine nodded, "any nurse, as long as she does't wear white."

"Let me see," Doctor Zirko grabbed a clipboard, "you have a preference?"

"Not racial, no one in white."

"The princess has an aversion to white uniforms. Her suspicions started here at the Center."

"I am aware of that. The princess has made her preference known: no White Witches."

"Unless it's a wedding, and hopefully there would be no witches," Buzz leaned over the doctor's nameplate, "she hates nurses in white."

"I understand. See to it she adheres to her medication, and you should have no problems."

Pristine grabbed her purse, slipped into her gloves, and rose from the chair. "I hope this will be her last visit to Loco. I can't keep coming back."

"I understand," the doctor nodded, "we are here for you should you need us."

Pristine extended a hand, "I hope never to see you again, Doctor, at least not here."

"My feelings exactly, Ma'am. I would rather administer shock treatment to a hundred Fearlings and a thousand Terrorists than to treat one Abundite," he bowed from the neck, "thank you for coming."

Pristine looked at all the panels, each identical. "I seem to be confused as to which panel is the door," she said, "they all look the same. Can you help us out?"

"Sure, which panel did you come in?"

"I don't know. That's my point."

"Your Majesty," the doctor stepped forward, "allow me to show you to the exit."

Buzz took the I-5 to the D-2, and by noon Friday, he and his princess were back home, in their castle in Gruntle. A day later, Queen Pristine and her entourage docked in the new Crystal Rock harbor. After the two-hour drive home in the Isotta, Pristine was exhausted. Speaking with Mina on the drive home, she moaned, "I am exhausted. All I want to do is take off my bra, get into bed, and sleep."

"Shall I unpack now, or later, Ma'am?"

"Just my robe."

"Which robe?"

"The flowered one Auntie *Envie* gave me for my birthday." Pristine lay in bed, and studied the angels on the ceiling, reflecting on her trip to Insanity. I spent two and a half days there. Imagine if I had to deal with Loco every day, the way Erica does, or Discord. I am blessed."

Mina carried in a robe. "This one, Ma'am?"

"That's the one," Pristine let her head drop back onto the pillow.

"I'll hang it over the screen."

"Mina—do you think I am weak for wanting a man in my life?"

"Not at all, Ma'am. A beautiful young woman like yourself needs a man in her life. What good is a kingdom without a king to share it with?"

"Court, and all the affairs of state keep me so busy, and Erica's needs, I never know when a trigger will set her off. I've not even found time to call Godwyn, and I *still* haven't removed my brassiere. I'll do that right now."

"Perhaps you should call him in the morning, Ma'am."

"Aaah—that feel good. What a relief." Pristine rolled onto her stomach. "Godwyn is my solution. Growing up, Erica and I shared our dream of marrying a prince. A consort would not do for Erica. He had to be a prince. Now look at her—married to Grandpa Poldi's former chauffeur. What does he do now? He invests."

"Princess Erica found her prince, Ma'am. He just happens to be a commoner, but he is a good man. Any man who raises animals must have a good heart."

"Can a kingdom be complete without a king?"

"You are complete without needing a king, Ma'am, but it would be nice."

"I feel incomplete. There is only one man who can complete me—Godwyn of Grace."

"You have had your eye on the Defender for years."

Pristine sighed, "a century, Mina."

"Shall I draw you a bath? A tub full of bubbles might help you forget your troubles."

CHAPTER XV

Demi-tour Without a Chaperone

Your Majesty, the Prince of Grace is on the phone."

"Thank you, Kensington. I'll take it in the phone room."

"Pristine," Godwyn whispered, "let's go on tour together."

"Only if you agree to separate accommodations."

"Only if you leave your nanny behind."

"In the Spook House?"

"No." Godwyn chuckled, "at the palace."

"That can be arranged. When shall we depart?"

"How about the first of the month?"

"I will have Mrs. Thornecroft set a week aside."

"A week? Are you kidding, Pristine? I'm thinking a month."

"A month?"

"I told Nanny *Bickerstaff* I would be leaving the girls with her for a month. Tell me, what could you have on your calendar that is more important than your happiness?"

"Court."

"Cancel it."

"I can't do that."

"Yes, you can."

"I can't."

"Then we will leave after Court adjourns."

"That could be arranged. Where shall we go?"

"You said you want to visit your sister."

"I do, in Discord. She lives in Gruntle, with Buzz, at the top of the Crags."

"Sounds interesting. I want to introduce you to my family, in Grace. My parents are going to love you."

"As long as we're traveling north, I'd like to visit my Aunt Envie in Resolution, but only if we maintain separate accomodations."

"Pristine Goldspinner, you are so old fashioned. Underneath, you want it as much as do I."

"Want it?"

"You know what I am referring to."

"What is it? What do you think the Press would make of it if they were to find out we were sleeping together?"

"You make it sound dirty."

"People talk."

"Fine, we'll stay in separate accommodations. You can lock your door. I will remain a man of honor, and you a woman chaste, and we can both remain anxious."

After agreeing upon a date, the twenty-five year-old Queen and her thirty-eight year old love interest, Godwyn Bonheur of Grace, set sail. After a rocky ride across the *Sea of Serendipity*, trailed by entourage and Security, they arrived at the home of Pristine's aunt, the Countess of Remembrance—*Envie Goldspinner*. They spent a day hiking with Envie's six bloodhounds, and cat, more in tune with canine identity than any mundane feline dream. They dined out twice, in restaurants closed to the public. One afternoon, the women shopped in stores closed to the public, while Godwyn relaxed with a book, and a glass of lemonade, on Aunt Envie's deck on the lake. The next day, like children, the three slid down boulders like children in a contest to see who could make the biggest splash.

The last evening, after a delicious meal and several bottles of wine, Godwyn floated in the lake, with Pristine in his arms, under the dancing Northern Lights.

Five days into the tour, they boarded HMS Consciousness and sailed north to Discord, to celebrate the Queen's birthday with her twin sister, princess Erica. A powerful tailwind brought the ship into Gruntle Harbor early. A chauffeur waited to drive them up the crags to a three centuries-old castle on *Top of the World*—the residence of Mr. and Mrs. *Buzz Ulysses Runner*.

Pristine saw Erica on the drawbridge, as they approached, feeding crocodiles with her maid, Norbertina. "There she is," she leaned through the partition window, "Driver—honk your horn."

The driver pulled the hand brake, and tapped his horn.

"Louder. She couldn't hear you."

"He can't honk louder, Pristine."

"Longer. Honk longer."

The noise startled Princess Erica. She dropped her pail. "Pristine is here," she shouted, "Norbertina, go tell Buzz they're here."

"Yes, Ma'am," the maid set her pail down, and picked up her mistress's pail and meat cuts. She dropped the cuts in the pail, set the pail down, and walked away.

Erica removed her gloves, jumped up and down, and draped them over the post. "They're here," she exclaimed, "Buzz, come down."

The chauffeur opened the door, and Pristine stepped out of the cab. Arms extended, she ran to her sister. "Erica, you've kept off the weight."

"I have," Erica embraced her sister, "you've arrived early."

"We had a tailwind. Happy birthday, Sis."

"Happy birthday, Pris."

"You remember Godwyn."

"Of course I remember Godwyn," she kissed his cheek, "how long has it been?"

"Ages."

"Come in, come in," Erica pushed the pail out of the way, as she walked them across the drawbridge. "We weren't expecting you until dark."

Godwyn studied the sky. "It looks dark to me."

"I mean really dark."

Pristine looked at her watch. "It's not even three o'clock. It feels like six."

"It feels like evening to me, too."

"It's our winter. The sun will come out again in March."

A second vehicle pulled up the hill. "That's my staff, and my Security."

"Security? You don't need Security up here."

"Aah, the Court insists."

"Come, follow me across the drawbridge. Stay center."

Godwyn took Pristine's hand, and reeled her in. "Keep your hands and feet close to your body," he whispered, "we still need you."

"The crocs are always hungry. Just don't dangle anything."

"Only you would breed crocodiles, Erica."

"I told you, Pris," Erica turned around, we don't breed them. We just keep them. Buzz says, pound for pound, crocs are the best security you can buy." She led them into the courtyard, "this is what we refer to as our front yard."

"Bougainvilleas—at this altitude?" Godwyn was amazed. How can they thrive?"

Erica smiled. "You arrived at just the right time. Buzz was going to put them in the greenhouse tonight."

"But it's so cold. Don't they need sunshine?"

"Buzz installed electricity in the greenhouse, and in the guest rooms. He's got all sorts of bulbs in there, plants, and lights. The constant imitation sunlight almost fools the plants into staying in bloom. Turn right, here, and it will take us into the heart of our home."

"You really do live on top of the crags."

"That's what they call it— *Top of the Crags*. You know what they say—location, location, location."

"Your castle has true character."

"Thank you, Godwyn. Built in 1602. The work is never-ending."

"Are those mulberry trees?"

"They are. Planted in 1887."

"The year we were born."

"That's right," Erica put her arm around her sister, and kissed her cheek, "happy birthday, Pris."

"Happy birthday, Erica," pat, pat, pat, "you can let go now."

"Of course," Erica twirled away. "Let me show you the foyer. Maybe we'll find Buzz—*Bu-uz-z-z.*"

"I love these sconces, with the recessed lighting."

Erica turned, "this is our foyer, as you can see, it's tiled."

"I expected a castle to be drafty, but it's comfortable in here."

"Buzz insulated most of the first and second floors. He sealed off every crack, and replaced the windows, but we still keep the doors shut. No need to heat the entire thing. The windows we tore out were installed in 1692? Can you believe it? He installed heaters over the entryway, too. I cannot tell you how happy I am to see you—both of you. Do you know how long it has been since we celebrated our birthday together?"

"Let me think—nineteen-O-three."

"That's right. It was nineteen hundred and three—our Sweet Sixteen."

"That was some party. I am so proud of you for keeping the weight off."

"Don't I look fabulous?" Erica took a spin, "I take my medications, I don't eat, I stay skinny, and everyone is happy."

"You had me worried last I saw you. I'm sorry I did didn't stay longer."

"I understand. You have a kingdom to run, and a staff. I just have Buzz."

"Did Dr. Zirco send you a caregiver?"

"He did. Her name was Emily. Buzz let her go."

"Why?"

"She was filled with drama. Poor girl. *I* ended up looking after *her*."

"You don't need people to look after, Erica."

"I know. I have enough just keeping these three busy."

"I imagine so."

"Living here on Top of the Crags is therapy in itself. It's wonderful to not have neighbors; no cars, no barking dogs. Sometimes the wolves howl at night, but it blends in with the wildlife. No one has ever made it up here on foot. At least not that we know of." She turned around. "Where is Norbertina? I thought I sent her to get Buzz. That girl has no motivation whatsoever."

Buzz stood overlooking the foyer, from the wrought iron balustrade, upstairs on the mezzanine. "Hello, hello—Majesty Pristine, Prince Godwyn," he checked the clock, "you have arrived early."

Pristine looked up. "Hello, Buzz."

"Sir Runner," Godwyn nodded, "hello."

Pristine stared. "Are you going to come down and greet us, Buzz, or are you going to just stand there, looking handsome?"

"Of course I'm coming down," Buzz descended the stairs.

"We blew in early on a tail wind."

"And that is good," Buzz stepped onto the parquet, and kissed Pristine's hand, "Your Majesty, Pristine, you look ravishing, as always."

"Thank you, Buzz. You remember Godwyn."

"Of course, the Prince of Grace," Buzz shook Godwyn's hand, "Your Royal Highness, how good to see you."

"Just Godwyn will do."

"Sir Godwyn."

"Just Godwyn, Buzz, no sir. I hear you have been working wonders here, installing electricity, and such."

"I love building, in spite of all the unexpected challenges."

"Buzz gets impatient. Don't you, dear?"

"When things don't go as planned, yes, sometimes I get impatient."

Mrs. Thornecroft slipped into the foyer, handed the Queen a box, and evaporated. Pristine took the box, and handed it to her sister. "Happy Birthday, Erica."

"For me? I have nothing for you, Pristine."

"I want for nothing."

"What is it?"

"Open it, and find out."

Erica peeked through a corner, "it's a cake—a birthday cake."

"Your favorite—angel food, with strawberry crème."

Erica laughed, "there goes my diet."

Buzz whispered into Pristine's ear, "angel food is no longer her favorite."

"Angel food has always been Erica's favorite."

Buzz whispered, "it's devil's food now."

"Devil's food?"

"Thank you, Pristine, but at nine hundred calories a slice, I've dropped cake from my diet."

"Godwyn's the one who thought of it. I'm the one who chose angel food. I'm sorry."

"Sweet of you to think of it, Pristine, you too, Godwyn. Staff will enjoy it." She leaned into the hall, held her hand to her cheek, and shouted, "Norbertina!—where is that girl?"

"I should have asked about the cake."

"Norbertina could be settling in Pristine's staff. She'll come at her own pace, Erica."

"That could be tomorrow, Buzz."

Buzz peeked into the box. "That looks good. I'll have a slice or two. Maybe three."

"How long are you going to stay, Pris?"

"Until you cut the cake."

Godwyn chuckled. "Pristine is teasing you, Erica."

Norbertina stepped into the foyer. "You called, Ma'am?"

"Where have you been?"—Erica handed the box to the maid. "Norbertina, this is my sister, Her Majesty, Queen Pristine."

The maid bowed, balancing the cake, "hello, Your Majesty."

"And this is her"—Erica turned to Godwyn. "What are you to Pristine?"

"I would describe myself as Her Majesty's love interest."

"This is Prince Godwyn of Grace, Her Majesty's love interest."

The maid curtseyed. "How do you do, Sir?"

"Hello," Godwyn nodded, "no need to curtsey."

"Set the cake on the coffee table in the living room, Norbertina, and make coffee."

"Yes, Ma'am," the maid curtseyed, and carried the cake out.

"Did you put the kettle on?"

The maid turned. "Not yet, Ma'am."

"What are you waiting for? Put the kettle on."

"Yes, Ma'am," the maid scurried down the corridor.

Erica stuck her head in the corridor, and shouted, "and tell Norbert to come here. I want to see him."

"Godwyn and I agreed we would stay three days."

"But you said you would stay five."

"I lied. I have to get back for Court, and Godwyn doesn't want to leave his daughters alone with their nanny for too long."

"Who knows what trouble they might get into, right?"

"Well," Erica pouted, "we'll make the best of it."

"You know what Mistress Sitwell used to say about fish and company."

"They stink. You and your Mistress Sitwell quotes." She looked down the hall. "Where is Norbert? Sometimes I think it would be faster to do everything myself. Follow me to the living room. I'll have Norbertina set you and Godwyn up."

"We are not sleeping together, Erica."

Erica turned. "And so?"

"We require separate accomodations."

"You are so old-fashioned. You are concerned word will get out."

"No, but…"

"You are concerned what the Press will print."

"Godwyn and I agreed we would stick with tradition. It's better that way."

"All right then. You sleep in the Salmon room, and I'll put Godwyn up in the Green room. Your staff will sleep in the attic, and we'll house Security over the carriage house." She stuck her head down the corridor, and shouted, "Norbert!"

A dark-skinned man with long limbs and wooly hair stepped into the corridor. "You called, Ma'am?"

"About five minutes ago. Where have you been?"

"I was gathering vegetables for tonight's salad, Ma'am."

Godwyn turned to Erica, "in the dark?"

"Buzz installed lights, Godwyn. Weren't you listening?"

"You can gather vegetables later. Set the basket down, Norbert. I want to introduce you to my sister, Her Majesty, Queen Pristine."

Norbert set the basket on the table. "Your Majesty," he removed his cap, and bowed, "it is an honor."

"And this is Her Majesty's"—she turned to Godwyn, "what are you again?"

"Her Majesty's beau."

"This is Prince Godwyn, Her Majesty's beau."

Norbert bowed, "it is an honor, Sir."

"Hello, Norbert," Godwyn smiled, "no need to bow."

"My beau." Pristine took Godwyn's arm, "I like how that sounds."

"Norbert, I want you to prepare the rooms in back of the carriage house. Tell Norbertina to prepare four rooms in the attic. Then go change the sheets in the Green room, and in the Salmon room."

"Yes, Ma'am."

"I want them ready by six o'clock."

"Yes, Ma'am," the butler nodded, and walked out.

"Come with me," Erica grabbed Godwyn's arm, and led him down the corridor, "turn left at the columns."

Mrs. Thornecroft stepped in, handed the Queen a parcel, and disappeared.

"I almost forgot." Pristine handed the parcel to her sister, "happy birthday, Erica."

"Another gift—for me?"

"It is your birthday."

"It's *our* birthday, Pristine," she shook the box, "what is it?"

"Open it, and find out."

Erica tore the paper off, tossed the ribbon, and snapped the box open. Her jaw dropped, "Pristine—Mother's pearls—you had them restrung." She ran to the mirror, lifted her hair, held the strand to her neck, and tried to lock it. "It's like new. I can't see what I'm doing. Buzz, come clasp me."

Buzz fidgeted with the clasp. "I've almost got it, Erica. If you would just stay still."

"Your hands are too big. Let Pristine do it."

"I can do it, if you will just stay still."

"I should get my earrings."

"Stop moving, Erica."

"I'm only moving my mouth. Let Pristine do it, Buzz."

"Erica, stop talking, and let Buzz clasp the necklace. You can get your earrings when he's done."

"I'm sorry I fought you over them."

114

"It's water under the bridge."

"There." Buzz kissed her neck, "you're clasped, my birthday girl."

"They're as lovely as ever," Erica turned, and studied them in the mirror. "Weren't there two larger pearls in the middle before you broke it?"

"I broke it?" Pristine's eyes opened wide, "you—never mind. You also noticed they're missing. The jeweler pinched the two biggest pearls. I noticed it as soon as I opened the box. He has yet to deal with me. When I find out who he is, he will never jewel—or whatever it is called that he does—restringer—he will never restring in Abundance again."

"Before you accuse him, Pris, you might consider, the pearls could have gotten lost when the strand broke."

"The two largest ones? Coincidentally?"

"Godwyn is right, Pristine. No jeweler would pinch the crown."

"Or would he? Maybe one of the guards pinched the pearls."

"Erica is right," Buzz agreed, "the guards could have pinched them when they gathered them."

"Or the custodian, at the cathedral," Godwyn added, "he could have found them, and stuck them in his pocket."

"Godwyn is right. The custodian could have pocketed them when he was cleaning the sanctuary."

"There is a simpler explanation."

Erica turned to Buzz, "and I imagine you are going to explain it to us."

"They got lost."

"Buzz is right. They got lost. That is what I am going to believe." Erica turned to the mirror. "They are exquisite, aren't they?"

"They look lovely on you, Erica."

Buzz extended a hand. "No use crying over scattered pearls. Let's sit down."

"I have something for you, too, Pristine. Come with me," Erica grabbed her sister's hand. "You guys go sit down."

"The pearls are from Godwyn, too, Erica."

"Thank you, Godwyn," Erica blew him a kiss. "Buzz, show Godwyn your man cave. Come, Pris."

"This way, Godwyn."

Godwyn followed Buzz down the hallway. "This is quite a place."

"Let me show you our new circuit breaker."

"Circuit breaker, eh? I've never seen one. What does it do?"

"It breaks circuits."

"I guess that was a foolish question on my part."

Erica led Pristine to the kitchen, where the kettle whistled on the burner. "Does that woman not hear?" Erica turned the stove off, and set the kettle on a back burner. "Where is she?" she stuck her head into the hall, "Norbertina!"

The maid came running, "Ma'am."

"Did you put the kettle on the stove?"

"I did."

"Did you not hear it whistling?"

"Was it whistling?"

"When the kettle whistles, you take it off the burner."

"But the kettle *is* off the burner, Ma'am."

"*I* took it off the burner, Norbertina."

"Yes, Ma'am. I'm sorry."

"Where is our coffee?"

"I haven't gotten to it. You asked me to prepare the rooms."

"After you serve coffee, Norbertina."

"Yes, Ma'am."

"Now get to it. Make coffee first, then set the table."

"Yes, Ma'am."

"Pristine, come here. I found this divine new tea from Bereavement I want to give you."

On the morning of the fourth day on *Top of the Crags*, Buzz cranked the Locomobile, and drove Erica, Pristine, and Godwyn down to Gruntle Harbor, to bid adieu. Pristine and Godwyn then boarded HMS Consciousness, and sailed on to Grace. The following morning at dawn, the ship docked at *Refinement* Harbor.

On Sunday, the family coordinated a bar-b-que, held on the lawn of the Bonheur family compound, outside Helena. It was there Godwyn introduced Pristine to his family.

"My mother, Duchess of Helena— *Florence Bonheur.*"

"Hello, Duchess," Pristine lowered her head.

"Please, call me Florence, Your Majesty." The duchess curtseyed, "we met when you were a little girl."

"Yes, I remember," Pristine nodded, "it was the Pasqua egg hunt."

"Yes. Your Majesty, you were a beautiful child."

"Is she not a beautiful adult, Mama?"

"Yes, my son; quite beautiful."

"Pristine," Godwyn took her by the elbow, "I want you to meet my father, the *Duke of Refinement.*"

"Your Majesty," the Duke bowed his head, "call me *Maurice*, please"

"How do you do, Maurice?" Pristine nodded.

"How do *you* do, Ma'am?"

"I am pleased to be in Grace, once again. I haven't been here since I was a little girl."

"Pristine, let me present my five brothers: *Kitzio, Edgar, Gerald, Herbert,* and *Francis.*"

"How do you do, Your Majesty?" the brothers bowed in unison.

"How do you do? Godwyn, you have such handsome brothers—all six of you. Godwyn has told me much about you."

Only one brother dared step forward—Francis. "Your Majesty, I am enchantée to meet you," he bowed again, because he could, "I love your dress—is it silk?"

"Why yes," Pristine smiled—"it is silk."

"It looks like a Mío original."

"It is from Mío. You're right."

"House of Miss LaRue?"

"It *is* from the House of Miss LaRue. What fashion sense you have, Francis."

"Please, Call me Francene. I don't really have any fashion sense. I just like things that are gay, gay designs, gay colors—they light up an otherwise boring existence for the people."

Godwyn whispered into Pristine's ear. "Francis is a clothes whore."

"Well then, Francis and I share something in common."

"Your Majesty, I would love to see the rest of your wardrobe."

That Friday night, twenty-seven members of the Bonheur family showed up to play charades, and did not leave until the wee hours of the morning. On Saturday, Godwyn and Pristine went canoeing with his brothers, down the Helena River. On Sunday, all nine rode horses across the Gracine countryside, feasting on kumquats along the way. Monday Maurice and Godwyn proclaimed Father-Son Day. While Florence and Pristine embroidered on the terrace, in the shade, Maurice took his oldest son fishing.

The two sat in the boat, each with a line in the water. "I am concerned about your youngest brother, Francis, Godwyn."

Godwyn made an adjustment. "What about Francis?"

"He's different than you and your other brothers."

"He always was. I knew that since he was seven, when he insisted on dressing as Snow White for Halloween."

"Your mother and I fought bitterly over that. She let me go to the party as Snow White. She is far too relaxed. It's not normal. He reads womens' magazines—Women's Wear Daily—and dresses in womens' clothing. Last month he showed up in church dressed as Little Bo Peep."

"Holy Toldeo—Little Bo Peep? Lady Donna would love it."

"I was horrified. Your mother wasn't too pleased either. Mostly because he went through her wardrobe."

"Where did he find shoes that big?"

"He didn't. He glued daisies on his sneakers."

"Daisies?"

"He thinks he's a princess, Godwyn. He insists we call him *Francene.*"

"He told me. Patronize him, Dad."

"I am not going to call my son Francene."

"To be honest, society holds a double standard, Dad. If women wear pants when it's cold, why shouldn't Francis wear a dress when it's warm out?"

"If he were petite, I might be able to deal with it, but he's six-foot-two, weighs two hundred pounds, and is a baritone at that. It frightens me when he wears a dress and make-up, then opens his mouth and speaks."

"I can understand that."

"I want you to have a talk with him."

"Why me?"

"You're the oldest. He respects you."

"What do you want me to tell him, Dad?"

"I thought you would know."

"I think he's double-spirited."

"Not to my knowledge. He just feels more comfortable wearing womens' clothes."

"Woah, I think I've got a bite."

"Hold your line steady, son."

"What do you want me to tell him?"

"Talk some sense into him, Godwyn. Tell him to dress and act like a man. Hold your line steady."

"He's pulling hard. This is a big one."

"Easy, don't tug. It is a big one."

"He's pulling like a tugboat."

"Lean back, Godwyn," Maurice grabbed the pole, "lean back, lean back."

"He's too strong," Godwyn leaned back, "he's pulling me in. Grab onto me, Dad—oh no!"

"Let go—let go of the line."

'SPLASH!'

Godwyn spent three days in bed, recovering from a cold, while Pristine and Francis familiarized themselves with each other, looking over her wardrobe, playing games. On Friday, Francis gussied up, and took Pristine shopping to Fashion Island, closed to the public, where they spent the afternoon trying on clothes—an hour trying on bridal gowns at Bob's Bridal Shoppe. "A girl can dream," said Francene.

On the afternoon of their last day in Helena, twelve family members showed up to play croquet on the lawn, among them Francis, wearing a tri-tier pink gown with five hundred beads, bobbles, and bows on it. Now fully recovered, Godwyn and Pristine continued their tour. Godwyn smiled. "I have another surprise for you, Pristine. I hope you will like it."

"What sort of surprise?"

"If I were to tell you, it wouldn't be a surprise."

"Give me a clue."

"It's in Grace."

"That's no surprise. We're in Grace. I know. You're going to take me to visit Pawlish."

"Nope." Godwyn shook his head.

"You're taking me to Leniency to meet Possessa and Gezealous."

"Nope. Not this time round."

"I give up."

"Nope."

"Tell me."

"You will find out when we get there."

CHAPTER XVI

Queen Pristine Gets Down on One Knee

Here we are—surprise!" Pristine stepped out of the cab, and Godwyn removed her blindfold.

"Oh, Godwyn, I felt the precipitation." She read the sign, and focused on the waterfall. "Dyer Falls Country Club? Why are we at the Dyer Falls Country Club?"

"I rented the course so we could be alone."

"How romantic, but I don't know how to play golf."

"Neither do I. At least not well. We'll learn together."

"Now I know why you bought me this funky striped outfit."

"You look adorable. Come with me to the clubhouse. You need shoes."

"I'm wearing shoes."

"You need golf shoes. You can't golf in espadrilles."

"Is it worth it, just to kick a ball?"

"You don't kick the ball, Pristine. You hit it with an iron."

"Why would anyone want to play a game trying to hit a ball with an iron?"

"Not a household iron, Pristine. It's a hard wooden club. It's called an iron."

"If it's of wood, why is it called an iron?"

"I don't know. It's just that way."

"This sounds like could become a good promenade interrupted. You're not going to make me play, are you?"

"I am."

"You really are full of surprises."

121

Twenty minutes later, new golf shoes on their feet, clubs and balls in hand, the couple was on the green, followed by Security, and a caddy. Before they even got to the eighth hole, Godwyn was frustrated. With a score even lower than Pristine's, he tossed his club into the bushes, and hoped he didn't hit one of the guards. Next, Pristine shot her ball into the sand pit. She slid into the pit to retrieve it, untied her shoelace, and removed the shoe. "I've got sand in my shoe," she giggled.

Godwyn followed her into the pit, and held his arm up to shade her eyes from the sun.

Pristine looked up at him. "I know what you are thinking."

"What am I thinking?"

"You think I am going to propose."

"Why would I think that?"

"Because." She put her shoe back on, tied the lace, rose to her tiptoes, and kissed Godwyn on the mouth.

"Your Majesty"—the golden speckles in Godwyn's eyes flickered like a fire, "I have waited a long time for that."

"I have waited even longer for *you* to kiss *me*—Defender."

"It is my understanding it is up to the Queen must make the first move."

"And it is *my* understanding it is up to the man."

"Ah-ha-ha-ha-ha," they laughed so hard they fell to their knees, and rolled in the sand.

Godwyn looked up at the sky. "When have we ever been alone?" He stopped laughing, and caught his breath. "Your nanny was always tagging along. Even while we were visiting your Aunt Envie, she never left us alone."

"Aunt Envie is a lonely old widow with no children. I respect that."

"I *like* your Aunt Envie. She's adorable, but she hovers."

"She thinks the world of you. She told me you are the best thing that's happened to me since I was crowned Princess of Perfection."

"Wow," Godwyn stood tall, "that's some compliment."

"My Defender, my G.L. What was it you called yourself?—my beau?"

"The Queen's love interest."

Pristine's eyes met Godwyn's, and she got down on one knee. "Godwyn Bonheur of Grace, Defender of the Faith, how would you feel about adding king consort to your list of titles?"

Godwyn ignored the Security officers rustling in the bushes, and the teenage caddy, standing by with the eager eyes. Godwyn smiled, and took Pristine's hand. "My precious Pristine, my sovereign, my Queen, there is nothing I would like more than to be your consort, your lawfully wedded husband in body, mind, and spirit, for the rest of my days."

Pristine fluttered her eyelashes, and kissed Godwyn on the lips for what seemed like a very long time. Nanny's bell would have lost it's clapper. "I have waited years for this moment, Godwyn, to be able to share my soul with another."

"As have I, waited longer than you." Godwyn puckered. "Now let's try it from the left."

They made a minor adjustment, and gave the position a try.

"That worked too," Pristine licked her lips. "Now let's try it from the right."

Godwyn puckered, closed his eyes, and waited under the hot sun.

"It won't work if you're smiling, Godwyn. You have to keep a straight face."

"I can't. All right, give me a moment to get serious." Another minor adjustment, and they tried again. "That worked," Godwyn smiled, "that worked quite well."

"It did, actually. Aaah," content, Pristine lay back on the sand.

"It worked left, right, *and* center." Godwyn pulled a small box out of his pocket. "I came prepared for this moment."

"What's this?"

Godwyn handed the box to Pristine. "Open it."

Pristine opened the box. "It's a ring. It's lovely, but why?"

"Are you going to just look at it? — or shall I put it on your finger?"

"I don't need a ring."

"Yes you do. You're a woman. Women like things that sparkle."

"I'm flabbergasted. I didn't get *you* a ring."

"I don't need a ring. The world knows I'm in love with you."

"You're right, women do like things that sparkle. I wouldn't be a Goldspinner if I didn't. I shall wed you as my king consort, and we shall spend the rest of our days together. Just do me one favor, Godwyn."

"What favor is that?"

"Try not to be so shy."

"Shy?" Godwyn pulled her out of the sand, "I'm not shy."

"It took you thirteen years to kiss me."

"You were seven when we met, Pristine."

"I mean later. When I was an adult."

"That's because every time I tried, your nanny rang her dang bell."

"She rang it to keep us pure."

"And it worked. I have never felt more pure in my life. It's time we sully, Pristine. Besides, I didn't kiss you. You kissed me, and when I did

123

have a chance to kiss you, I didn't, because I thought it was up to you to make the first move."

"Well, now you know."

"Yes, now I know," he laughed, "kiss me again, my Queen."

"Not now, Godwyn. The caddy is watching."

"That caddy has been watching since the first hole, Pristine. Let's give him something to watch."

"Stay on this side of the pit, and he can't see us."

"Let me embrace you," Godwyn tried to put his arm around her.

Pristine primped, "I need to compose myself. All this smooching has messed up my hair."

"You look flush."

"I'm fine. And for God's sake, Godwyn, promise me you will never get fat, go bald, or lose your teeth."

"Lose my teeth? You want to check, like I'm a horse?"

"Don't be silly."

Godwyn got down on one knee. "Your Majesty, Pristine, I shall make it my mission to maintain all my body parts, and if not, I assure you, you will never find out."

"How do you intend to hide fat from me?"

"I will never have any to hide, and I promise you I will keep my teeth. All my life I have been true to them, so they will never be false to me."

"You are clever. Ever since Grandpa Poldi and GranMarguerite took me to Fear, when I was a little girl, I have been able to identify false hair, teeth, and breasts from a mile away."

"A mile? What good eyesight you have, Ma'am."

"Well, maybe not a mile, but a hundred feet."

"Kiss me again, Your Majesty."

"The caddy is watching, Godwyn."

"You are so proper. One would think you were from Pawlish."

"I need to think this through."

"What is there to think through?"

"Mrs. Thornecroft crossed the first week of June off my calendar. I wonder if she knew you were going to propose."

"I've had no contact with your secretary."

"Can you work it into your schedule to wed the first week of June?"

"I can't the first week. Possessa and Gezealous are giving a recital. I promised them I would be there."

Pristine did a mental scan of her appointment book. "We could wed the following week, the thirteenth. No, the thirteenth would be a bad omen. How about the following week—the twentieth of June?"

Godwyn nodded. "That works for me."

"Good. I'll have Mrs. Thornecroft cross the second week off my calendar as well, for our honeymoon."

"A week for a honeymoon? I'm thinking three."

"Three weeks for a honeymoon? What would we do?"

"You tell Mrs. Thronecroft you are going to be gone the entire month of June."

"I like it when you act like a mogul," Pristine smiled, "where shall we honeymoon?"

"Anywhere you like." He grabbed her from behind, "kiss me, quick—the caddy's back is turned."

Pristine looked, to make sure the caddy's back was turned, closed her eyes, and puckered up. Godwyn kissed her from the left, from the right, from center, until they tumbled into the sandpit, like giggling children. "Oh my"—Pristine caught her breath, "I feel like a giddy schoolgirl."

"I love your giggle, Pristine." Godwyn helped her up, and brushed the sand off her shoulder. "We have a wedding date."

"We have a wedding date. I have been thinking, Godwyn, I would like to invite Possessa and Gezealous for tea so we can become acquainted with one another. After all, I am going to be their stepmother. Oh," she stopped—"that has a terrible ring to it."

"You supercede the stepmother label, Pristine." Godwyn lifted her onto the grass. "I think it's a wonderful idea. A visit to the palace will give them an opportunity to see what life will be like once we move there."

"It will give them a head start."

"They're going to want new wardrobes." Godwyn took her hand. "Let's take a seat on that bench, and discuss this."

"How do you think they will react to calling me their stepmother?"

"They have been trying to remarry me for years. They always knew you were the one," Godwyn wiped the bench, "sit down."

Pristine sat down. "I want to be a good mother to them, Godwyn, more a friend than a stepmother."

"That doesn't sound like a good idea. You would do better to befriend Fear and Terror than to befriend my girls. They are troubled, Pristine."

"That's why I can relate to them. I too am troubled. Think of Erica, how troubled she is. I can be a thousand miles away, whatever she feels, I feel it, too."

"But Possessa and Gezealous are not that easy, and they're not twins."

"What are their ages?"

"Twelve and thirteen."

"Godwyn, I am the sister of the queen of Discord. We grew up together. I have experience handling troubled teenage girls."

"I'm trying to protect you, Pristine. I don't recommend you start a friendship with them. They are bound to let you down."

"Are they not musicians?"

"In a way," Godwyn nodded, "they are musically inclined."

"Well there you have it. Music is the universal language. You told me Possessa plays the cello, and Gezealous plays the violin—right?"

"I might add, they play piano, beautifully."

"You told me they said they cannot play better because their instruments are old."

"Antique is the word they used. It makes no sense to me. I always thought the older the instrument, the better it plays, but at that age they know everything better."

"That is what I thought."

Godwyn chuckled. "I see you've met my daughters."

"I'm going to commission the craftsman to build them new instruments. You can give the specifics to Kensington over the phone."

"That won't be necessary, Pristine."

"It is. I want to do this, as my wedding gift. I believe I can establish a positive relationship with my new stepdaughters through music."

After a romantic dinner at the Dyer Falls Country Club's Golden Goose restaurant, the couple headed to bed—in separate accommodations. The next morning, they departed, bringing the demi-tour to a close. Godwyn saw Pristine, her entourage, and Security off on the *Crooked Spine Express* for a five hour ride through interesting terrain. Prince Godwyn returned home in separate transport, and the HMS Consciousness returned empty to Crystal Rock harbor.

Back at the palace, in spite of dissent from left, right, and center, Pristine continued to rely on Carabella Needlepinch for advice. It was the Parliamentarians in particular, who tried to cut the tie—Pristine being well over the age of requiring a nanny, but it takes more than a pair of scissors to cut the ties of a lifetime.

Pristine invited Nanny into her chambers for Saturday afternoon tea to plan the upcoming audience with Godwyn's daughters, *Possessa* and *Gezealous Bonheur.*

"Sugar, Nanny?—two cubes, right?"

"Three. I have gotten sweeter with age."

"You eat too much sugar, Nanny. It's not good for you."

"I'm an old woman, Pristine. I know what I'm doing."

"I imagine you think you do." Pristine dropped three cubes into Nanny's teacup. "Just like Godwyn's teenage daughters."

"I do," Nanny stirred, and set the spoon down.

"They told him they couldn't play their instruments better because they are old."

"You just said they are teenagers."

"I'm talking about the instruments, Nanny. The instruments are old."

"Nothing wrong with old instruments." Nanny squeezed a lemon wedge into her tea, "as long as they are of quality."

"That's what I say, but these girls are tweens."

"What's a tween?"

"Youngsters, between the ages of eleven and thirteen."

"You said the girls are teenagers."

"I was off a year. Forgive me."

"Two years, Pristine."

"Two then."

"At that age, they know it all."

Pristine sipped. "That's what Godwyn said. If they were to have new instruments, they would have no excuse for not playing better. I am going to have Monsieur *Carpentier* build some."

"With young blood in the palace, the corridors should be filled with music again."

"That's what I thought."

"I am happy for you, Pristine. You found a soulmate in Godwyn."

"I don't quite know what to expect of this, of him, of myself."

"Can Carpentier produce instruments upon such short notice?"

"He has them in waiting. All he needs to do is personalize them."

"Listen to me, Pristine," Nanny sipped her tea, "music is a good venue through which to connect, but I advise you to be careful. I know you. You want to be a mother to these girls to make up for the mother you lost. You want to be a sister to them to make up for the sister you lost in Erica, but these Bonheur girls are not your blood."

"Neither are you, but we're close."

"That's different, Pristine. You need to produce heirs of your own blood."

"From what I saw in Dr. *Fingerling*'s medical journals, I think I'll put that idea on hold."

"You cannot allow the gynecologist's reference books to determine your fate—or the fate of the kingdom."

"I am not prepared for the motherhood experience. I don't have it in me."

"That is why you have a nanny."

"I see no use for children. They rob you of time, energy, and money. They give you wrinkles, and stretch marks. The only purpose children serve is to look after one when one gets old."

"Would I could birth them for you, Pristine."

"I wish you would."

"We'll cross that bridge when we get to it."

"We already crossed it. You gave me that talk on my twenty-first birthday, remember?"

"I do. To get back to the girls, has their visit been cleared?"

"Mrs. Thornecroft took care of it."

"Will the nanny be accompanying them?"

"I hope so."

"What is her name?"

"*Nellie Bickerstaff*, I believe."

"Oh yes. I've heard of Nellie Bickerstaff."

"What have you heard?"

"She's a chatty woman, and loose."

"Loose?"

"She's been married, twice. Divorced both times."

"Well, be that as it may, Crankshaft is going to pick them up from the station at noon, and drive them back to catch the six o'clock back to Grace."

"Six hours alone with two tween-agers?"

"An hour of that is travel time, Nanny. I invited Auntie Avorah and Uncle George to join us, as backup. Avorah has a degree in Music from *Play*, and a Masters in Engineering—of course you know all this."

"I am aware of Lady Woolsey's credentials. Is she over her vegan phase? Or is the kitchen going to have to provide her with a special diet again?"

"Don't remind me. That cake she presented us with was dreadful. I took one bite, and spit it into my napkin while no one was looking. I carried it around with me all afternoon because I couldn't find a way to dispose of it."

Nanny splattered, and nearly dropped her cup. She tittered, "I did the same. I spit mine out in the planter in the hall."

"She can be annoying with her big hats and feathers," Pristine chuckled, "but deep down, she's a good soul. You know she's a VISTA patron."

"What's Vista?"

"The *Visually Impaired Service Training Animal* program. She sits on the board. She sits on three boards."

"I give her credit. She did a terrific job as chief engineer on the Crystal Rock project."

"Your memory is good, Nanny. That's been years."

"I do my best to keep up, crossword puzzles and such."

"I hope the sisters' visit will be a memorable one."

"I hope they can take care of themselves. The last thing I need is unpaid children to look after."

"I imagine they are independent. They lost their mother at an early age, just like me, and Erica. Erica and I."

"How long has it been since Godwyn was widowed?"

"Seven years. The girls were just babes. Forgive me, Nanny, I need to cut this meeting short." Pristine pushed a button under the table. "I need to have a talk with Mr. Kensington. We won't be needing two butlers."

"Two butlers?"

"Kensington is overdue for retirement, as you know. Godwyn wants to keep *his* butler, *Orderic Tibbons,* so that works out well."

Orderic Tibbons? I've known Orderic forever. He's a good man, honest, loyal to the core. But how do you think Handsforth will feel being passed over?"

"You know I love Handsforth, but Godwyn will be giving up so much, I can't deny him his butler. I am going to promote Handsforth to under butler, and give him a raise. That way Twickenham can move up to first footman."

"How much?"

"How much what?"

"How much raise?"

"Six percent?"

Nanny shook her head. "Ten."

"Very well then, ten." Pristine rose from her chair, and held her hand out. "Thank you for helping me work out the logistics, Nanny."

"Any time, my dear." Nanny grabbed Pristine's hand, kissed it, planted her stick, and lifted herself out of the chair. She walked to the door, and turned. "If you need me, you will find me in my parlor. Now that the rainy season is behind us, my rheumatism isn't so bad anymore. There's a sweater I've been knitting since before the coronation. I think I'll see if I can finish it."

CHAPTER XVII

Visitors from Leniency

Heavy rain fell on the Grace-Tolerance basin all week. By Thursday, the low-lying thoroughfares of Leniency resembled canals more than they did streets. Children freed from attendance at school delighted in splashing one another. They surfed the tide on innertubes and rafts, but the Bonheur sisters, Possessa and Gezealous, arrived dry, and on time, at Leniency Station. Her Majesty's chauffeur, Ernest Crankshaft, picked the entourage up at the station. After a leisurely drive through the countryside, he pulled into the palace drive, stopped at the guardhouse, and waited for the gates to fan open.

Nanny Bickerstaff was amazed by the variety of flora and fauna on the grounds. Possessa and Gezealous were amazed by the shirtless Gardener triplets, Rob, Bob, and Tob, trimming the hedgemaze. Crankshaft pulled up to the portico, secured the handbrake, and shut off the engine. At the banister waited Mr. Kensington. The centenarian butler saw no need to descend steps he would later have to climb. Footman Quigley opened the passenger door, bowed, and stepped back. "Welcome to the palace, ladies."

Possessa studied her surroundings, as she stepped out of the limousine. "This looks welcoming enough," she mumbled.

"My name is Quigley, Miss. Please let me know if there is anything I can do for you."

Possessa smiled. "Thank you, Quigley."

Gezealous noticed the handsome footman stepping onto the portico. "This is nice," she smiled, "it's so cool here."

Nanny Bickerstaff saw the stairs. More steps to climb, she thought.

Quigley escorted the sisters inside. "Ladies, I deliver you to the care of our butler, Mr. Kensington."

Kensington nodded. "Welcome to the palace, Miss Bickerstaff, young ladies. Miss Needlepinch is anxious to meet you. Quigley, show Miss Bickerstaff to Miss Needlepinch's parlor."

"This way, Miss Bickerstaff," the footman nodded.

Nanny Bickerstaff stepped forward. "Mr. Kensington, I should not let the girls out of my sight."

"They will be tended to, Miss Bickerstaff."

"I would like to meet the Queen to discuss the fate of our young ladies. Perhaps you could arrange an audience for me?"

"I will see what I can do, Miss Bickerstaff."

"Thank you, Mr. Kensington."

"This way to the elevator, Miss Bickerstaff."

"The girls are my responsibility, Mr. Quigley. They must remain with me at all times."

"Not to worry, Miss Bickerstaff. The sisters will be looked after by Her Majesty herself."

"I imagine that will have to suffice."

Mr. Kensington waited for Quigley to lead Nanny down the corridor before addressing the Bonheur sisters. "If you would follow me, please, ladies, Lord and Lady Woolsey await you in the drawing room." He led them down a long corridor.

"Who are Lord and Lady Woolsey, Mr. Kensington?"

"He didn't hear you, Gezealous. You have to speak up."

Gezealous raised her voice. "Mr. Kensington—who are Lord and Lady Woolsey?"

"You have to shout, Gezealous."

"I'm not gonna shout. Why do you always get announced first?"

"Because I'm the oldest."

"*Older*, Possessa. There are only two of us. It's not fair. You get everything first."

"Quiet. The butler will hear us arguing."

"He wouldn't hear an earthquake rumble under his feet."

Kensington led the sisters to the ladies' wardrobe, one. step. at. a. time, and opened the door. He took their hats, coats and umbrellas, rested and hung each appropriately, umbrellas in the urn, raincoats on hangers. "Now," he trundled to the door, "if you will follow me, I will show you to the drawing room."

"Psst, Possessa."

"What?"

"Another long corridor."

"I know. The place is filled with them. Did you see the footman?"

"Bad teeth—the Scare City look?"

"Not Quigley—the other one."

"What other one?"

"The cute one."

"What cute one?"

"Never mind, Gezealous." Possessa studied the portraits on the wall, "look at all the paintings."

"I see. How long does it take to get down the hall? This butler makes Mr. Tibbons look young."

Kensington opened the door to the drawing room, and stepped aside. "Present in the drawing room, Lord and Lady George Woolsey." He announced their arrival, "entering, Miss Possessa Bonheur, and Miss Gezealous Bonheur."

Kensington walked out, backwards, and shut the door behind him. George Woolsey rose from the chair, extended his hand, and greeted the sisters. "Possessa and Gezealous, how do you do?"

The sisters curtseyed. "How do you do, Sir?"

"Hello there." Lady Woolsey approached, hand extended. "I am Avorah Woolsey, and this is my husband, George. You must be Possessa."

"Yes, Ma'am," Possessa shook Lady Woolsey's hand, "pleased to meet you."

"And you must be Gezealous." Lady Woolsey shook Gezealous's hand. "How delightful. Please, take a seat. How was your train ride?"

"Lovely, thank you."

"Delightful creatures," Woolsey kissed the sisters' hands, and returned to his chair.

"What do you want us to call you, Ma'am?"

"I imagine Lady Woolsey should do," she smiled. By their elbows, she directed the sisters to chairs.

"You may call me Uncle George," Woolsey puffed, "my friends do."

Lady Woolsey released the girls into chairs. "You should be comfortable seated here."

Gezealous took in the atmosphere. "Where's the Queen?"

Possessa nudged her sister. "Gezealous, that's not a polite question."

"Her Majesty should be down momentarily," Lady Woolsey returned to the sofa, and sat down. "So, it looks like we are going to be family."

"Yes," Woolsey relit his pipe, "a close family."

"Must you smoke, George?"

133

George consulted the sisters—"do you mind?"

They looked at one another, and shook their heads, "nope."

"Sometimes Papa smokes."

"Put your pipe away, George. We have company."

It didn't take long for Possessa to analyze the situation. Whoever these people are, I had better face them, she thought; that way they can see how pretty I am.

Lady Woolsey pushed her purse aside. "George and I have heard so much about you. Is this your first outing on your own?"

"We're not on our own." Possessa settled into the chair.

Gezealous nodded. "Nanny Bickerstaff is with us."

"Is this your first time at the palace?" asked George.

Possessa nodded. "First time at *this* palace."

"I hear Leniency is flooded."

"It's been raining all week," Gezealous took note of the paintings.

"Papa said Tolerance hasn't flooded like this in fifty-two years."

Woolsey puffed on his pipe. "Other than the flooding, how do you girls like Leniency?"

"It's real boring," Possessa straightened her dress, "there's nothing you can't do there."

Gezealous nodded. "Papa thinks it's cool, but he's old."

"Really?" Lady Woolsey smiled, "how old *is* the Defender, Gezealous?"

"He's like thirty-six."

"He's thirty-eight, Gezealous."

Lady Woolsey stroked the velvet armrest. "It may take a while for the two of you to get used to Entitlement. Noblity has its price, you know."

"I don't know about price," Gezealous studied the plumes on Lady Woolsey's hat, "I'm not very good at math."

"I'm the smart one, and the pretty one."

"Possessa only thinks she is. Lady Woolsey, I adore your hat. What kind of feather is that?"

"Grouse, I believe." She checked to make sure, "yes, it's grouse."

Gezealous giggled. "Your hat's still on your head, Lady Woolsey."

George puffed. "You girls may want to listen to what Lady Avorah has to say. She's a woman around town."

Lady Woolsey tossed her husband a look of disapproval. "Never marry a man who makes you sound ancient, girls. You will live to regret it."

Woolsey chuckled, "what I meant was, my wife is well-rounded and knows everyone and anyone worth knowing."

"Put your pipe away, George. Pristine is going to come in any minute. We don't want the place smelling like tobacco."

"It already does."

Gezealous was stunned. "You call the Queen by her first name?"

"Put your pipe away."

"Stop nagging me, Avorah."

Lady Woolsey turned to Gezealous. "My dear, Uncle George and I are Her Majesty's godparents. Have been since she was born. At times, in private, we sometimes refer to Her Majesty by her given name."

"Lady Avorah and I have been fixtures here since before the Queen was born." Woolsey emptied his pipe into the ashtray, "we're like furniture."

"I wonder what's keeping Pristine."

"It will be interesting to see how you girls adjust."

"Why?"

"What Uncle George means is he hopes Entitlement does not spoil you."

"Why should it spoil us?"

"What Lady Woolsey means is, there is nothing more unattractive than a beautiful girl who is spoiled."

"What Uncle George means is beauty is only skin deep. Ugly is to the bone."

"To the bone?" Gezealous's eyes lit up, "what is that supposed to mean?"

"It means, if one does not possess beauty within, no beauty without could ever be."

"What-ever," Possessa sneered.

"No beauty within, no beauty without. Know beauty within, know beauty without."

Lady Woolsey smiled. "Uncle George likes to play with words."

"You girls must forgive Lady Woolsey," George slipped his pipe into his pocket, "she can be wordy."

"So, what can you girls teach us about Tolerance?"

"I don't know. It rains a lot."

"I was just thinking about the time Avorah and I walked into this little café in Leniency."

"Possessa and Gezealous are not interested your stories, George."

"I *enjoy* recalling happy memories, Avorah."

"They don't want to hear it."

135

"There *is* a point to my story."

"Well they don't want to hear it."

"When is Her Majesty going to come down?" Possessa looked at the clock on the mantle, "I'm tired of waiting."

"Me too. I'm hungry."

CHAPTER XVIII

Float across the Parquet

The drawing room door opened, Mr. Kensington trundled in, and all rose to their feet. "Entering the drawing room," the butler announced, "Her Majesty, Queen Pristine Goldspinner." Lord Woolsey bowed. Lady Woolsey and the sisters curtseyed.

Stitched into a silver lamé skin tight gown, Pristine floated across the parquet floor. "Auntie Avorah, Uncle George, hello"—she exchanged kisses, and slithered to the back wall. "My dears, how delightful. You must be Possessa, and you are Gezealous."

Blinded by the Queen's lamé gown, Gezealous covered her eyes.

Pristine walked to the sofa. "It is a pleasure to meet you both. Please, take your seats. I want to hear all about Leniency, but first, how is your father?"

Gezealous glanced at her sister. "Go ahead. You're *always* first."

"He's fine, I guess. He's busy a lot."

"He's gone *a lot* of the time."

"My dears, a lot is a plot of land, or a collection of jewelry—expensive jewelry. What you mean to say is *often,* or *quite a bit.*"

"Yeah," Gezealous nodded—"that's what I mean."

Uncle George played with his pipe. "Pristine, you strolled across the parquet like a ghost. It looked like your feet didn't even touch the ground."

"They didn't. I hovered, Uncle George. Forgive me for having kept you waiting. As I was on my way down, one of the footmen called me to the attic to investigate some repairs. The roof is over a hundred years old, and it leaks."

"One hundred years," Woolsey nodded, "*now that* is durability."

"I have good news."

"What news is that, Pristine?"

"Goldspinner stock is up."

"That *is* good news." Lady Woolsey smiled.

"I imagine Uncle George has been entertaining the girls with tales of your travels?"

"Of course. You know George."

Possessa spoke first. "We were talking about the weather."

"Lady Avorah was telling us how we are going to have to adapt."

"Excuse me. Pristine—is Kensington going to bring in tea?"

"You know Kensington always serves when staff is away."

"He is so slow, Pristine." Lady Woolsey removed her hat, and set it on the sofa.

"I have to let him do something."

"When will he serve?"

"He will get to it when he can."

"Don't you think it is time you retire him?"

"Speak softly. He'll hear you."

"He couldn't hear a train coming at him, Pristine. Why not let one of the footmen serve?"

"They have all gone to town. I forgot, until the last minute. I haven't the heart to tell him he is no longer needed."

"But he *is* no longer needed. You need someone strong, a butler you can depend upon, someone who can balance a tray."

"The footmen do all the heavy lifting."

"Where are they when you need them?"

"I told you. They're in town, at the exhibition."

"Your Majesty, excuse me," Gezealous leaned forward, "I thought Mr. Tibbons, was coming to live with us."

"Mr. Tibbons has been offered the position. I am waiting to hear if he has accepted."

"Pristine, how do you think Handsforth is going to feel about being overlooked?"

"He will be disappointed, of course, but I have decided to promote him to under butler, and give him a raise."

While waiting for tea to be served, the afternoon's conversation ranged from art to zoology. The discussion encompassed astronomy, courtly love, music, entomology (Pristine being a bug lover herself) and the plight of starved children trapped behind the Black Snake Line in Fear and Terror. Pristine rose from the sofa, glided to the door, and pulled on a cord hanging from the ceiling.

"This is the third time you have rung, Pristine."

"He's probably busy, Auntie," Pristine returned to the sofa, "be patient."

Lady Avorah laughed. "He can't hear the bell."

"Mr. Kensington has served this family since before Poldemire's coronation, Auntie. I can't just let him go."

The door opened, the bespoken trundled in, and bowed from the neck. "Beg pardon, Your Majesty, I cannot find the key to the teabox. Handsforth must have moved it, and with everyone gone, well, there is no one to help me find it."

"Very well, Kensington. We will have coffee, "Pristine looked at the sisters. "Perhaps you would like a soda?"

"Soda's fine," Possessa nodded, "please."

Gezealous nodded. "I would love a ginger ale, thank you."

"Coffee for the adults, Kensington, sodas for the young ladies, and plenty of biscuits."

"Yes, Ma'am," the butler stepped back.

"Kensington…"

"Ma'am?"

"Handsforth said he would be back before two o'clock. When he arrives, ask him to bring in the instruments, please."

"Very well, Ma'am," he stopped, and turned, "oh, eh, forgive me the key."

"Run along now."

Lady Woolsey leaned in to Possessa, "as if he could."

Kensington trundled out, and closed the door.

Gezealous looked at Possessa—"what instruments?"

Possessa shook her head, "I know as much as you do."

Handsforth returned at one-forty-seven. Within minutes, tea, coffee, soda, biscuits, and sticky buns were served. Halfway through seconds, the footman bowed before Possessa, and presented her with a hand-crafted violin—"with Her Majesty's compliments."

Possessa was confused. "But Sir, I don't play the violin."

"Handsforth," Pristine nodded, "the violin is for Miss Gezealous."

"Beg pardon, Miss."

"Yeah, I play the cello. Gezealous is the one who plays the violin."

Handsforth handed the violin to Gezealous, "for you, Miss."

"A violin? For me?" Gezealous's eyes lit up. She peeked in the *f*holes for a label, "how can I ever thank you?"

"You can play beautiful music for us."

George Woolsey set his spectacles on his nose, and pulled a periodical out of his vest pocket. "I may as well read while they play," he said.

Gezealous examined the instrument's inlay, more importantly, the bow. She beamed. "Your Majesty, how can I thank you?"

Possessa sat by, in contemplation. All this attention over Gezealous and her new violin. She gets everything because she's the baby.

"George, can't you say something to Gezealous about her new violin?"

"Yeah, it's nice." Woolsey doubled his periodical.

The door opened, and Handsforth rolled in a teakwood cello—a *Primavera*. Possessa leaped out of the chair, as he approached. "This one's for me. Your Majesty," she grabbed the instrument by its neck, "thankyouthankyouthankyou."

"Now you can both perfect your playing."

"This is swell," Possessa ran her fingers down the instrument's neck, "now I can play *a lot* better."

"A lot is a plot of ground, Possessa—a plot of ground, or a collection of jewelry."

George glanced over his periodical. "This should provide incentive."

"Like you always say, Auntie Avorah, a quality instrument brings about quality music, and quality music brings about quality living."

"And I stand by that," Lady Woolsey smiled.

"Your Majesty, I promise to practice every day, every day but Sunday."

Gezealous nodded, "Me too; every day but Sunday."

"Remember, girls, the music does not stop playing until you stop playing the music."

Pristine smiled. "Auntie Avorah, ever the music teacher."

"This is swell," Gezealous played with the strings.

Handsforth poured seconds, while the sisters ran bows across their new instruments. Kensington trundled in a plate of raspberry biscuits, set the plate on the table, and trundled back out, backwards, one. step. at. a. time.

Lady Woolsey whispered, "Pristine, are you not spoiling them before they even arrive?"

"I need them to be my allies, Auntie Avorah."

"George," Lady Woolsey whacked his periodical, "put away your journal."

"It's not a journal."

"Whatever it is, put it away."

"It's a periodical."

"Put it away. Possessa and Gezealous are going to play for us."

"Can I not read, and listen at the same time?"

"Uncross your legs. You are cutting off your circulation, and set your periodical aside." She turned to Pristine, "later he is going to complain he has cramps."

"Very well. If it makes you happy, I will put my periodical away."

"Thank you, it does." Lady Woolsey sat down on the sofa, next to Pristine. "Your idea to connect through music was spot on," she whispered, "I am having a delightful time."

"I am doing this to please myself, Auntie. I have a tin ear, so I appreciate talent in others. Erica's no better."

"Soon you will have a *family* of musicians, Pristine."

"It will be nice to hear music in the halls again."

Lady Avorah played with her feather. "They could perform at your wedding. What better venue is there?"

Possessa approached, bow in hand, "Your Majesty, I am ready. What would you have us play?"

"Something soothing, perhaps."

"Soothing, " Lady Woolsey nodded, "for us old folks."

Possessa pulled the bow across the cello strings, played a bar, and stopped.

Lord Woolsey applauded. "That sounded very nice."

"It did," Pristine nodded. "Why did you stop?"

"I chickened out. I thought I could play, but I will only disappoint you."

"Possessa is right, Your Majesty. We need to acquaint ourselves with the instruments before we can play in public."

"You are making excuses. What you played sounded beautiful."

"We need time to build a relationship with the instrument."

"Besides, neither of us is very good."

"Stop putting yourselves down. You played beautifully. Didn't they, Auntie Avorah?"

"Absolutely, they did."

"I played out of tune."

"Nonsense. George, did you hear out of tune?"

Woolsey looked up. "No. Not at all."

"Half the world is out of tune, Possessa, yet everyone plays."

"Don't force them, Pristine."

"Nonsense. I want them to play."

"Your Majesty, I cannot perform under pressure."

"Pressure creates diamonds, Gezealous; heat, time, and pressure. Shall I turn up the heat?"

"Play a few bars for us, huh?" Lady Woolsey winked, "for me?"

Reluctantly, Possessa positioned the cello, and drew the bow across the strings. Gezealous joined in, and within seconds, their trembling notes took on a musical quality. George Woolsey set his pipe, and his periodical aside, and closed his eyes.

"You see?" Pristine applauded, "that was lovely."

"You play better than you think," Lady Woolsey smiled. "George, wasn't that lovely?"

"Terrific. You girls have talent."

CHAPTER XIX
The Golden Clef

Kensington carried in a silk pillow upon which rested a golden music clef. He presented the clef to the Queen, and trundled out, backwards. Pristine rose from the sofa, and approached the Bonheur sisters, with the clef in her hands. "Before you leave, I would like to present you girls with a token of what is important. Music crosses every barrier, and in doing so, it brings people together." She held the clef out.

Possessa grabbed it. "Your Majesty, I will treasure this always."

Lord Woolsey slipped his periodical into his vest, and removed his spectacles. Musical instruments are not enough, he thought, they need a golden paperweight, too?

Why should Possessa get everything? Just because she was born first. "It's mine, Possessa," Gezealous ripped the clef out of her sister's hand, "she was going to give it to me."

"But she gave it to me." Possessa tore the clef out of her sister's hand.

"Papa said we have to share."

"Girls, where are your manners?" Lady Woolsey rose from the sofa.

"Possessa, hand me the clef." Pristine held her hand out.

"But you gave it to me, Your Majesty." Reluctantly, Possessa handed over the clef.

Pristine handed the clef to Gezealous. "Gezealous will be in possession of the clef for six months then it will go to Possessa for six months. Then back to Gezealous, and so on."

"Excellent solution," Woolsey uncrossed his legs, "that way both of you can enjoy it."

Possessa changed her tune. "I guess we can share it."

"Thank you, Your Majesty," Gezealous admired the clef, "it's really beautiful."

Lady Woolsey was bewildered by the sisters' behavior. "You two remind me of Erica and Pristine when they were your age. You must stop arguing. It is not becoming of young ladies."

"I promise to give Possessa the clef in six months. Thank you, Your Majesty, and thank you for the lovely violin."

"And for my cello, too. I'm sorry I was nasty."

"I accept your apology. I expect you both will honor the instruments." Pristine looked at the clock. "Good heavens, look at the time. It's almost four. I promised your father I would see you on the six o'clock train. We have ninety minutes. What to do?" She looked about. "If you are interested, Mr. Kensington could give you a quick tour of the palace."

"Interested?" Gezealous rose from the chair, "that would be swell."

"Cool, what should we do with our instruments?"

"One of the footmen will place them in the Isotta for you." Pristine rose from the sofa, glided across the parquet, and pulled on the golden cord.

Handsforth appeared seconds later. "You rang, Ma'am?"

"Yes. The girls are interested in a tour of the palace, Handsforth. I thought you might ask Mr. Kensington—the abridged version?"

"Yes, Ma'am. I will summon Mr. Kensington right away."

Minutes later, Mr. Kensington appeared at the door. "If you ladies would follow me, please. Oh, eh," he turned back, "Ma'am, Miss Bickerstaff would like a moment with you."

Lady Woolsey shook her head. "It seems everyone wants a piece of you, Pristine."

"Have Handsforth send Miss Bickerstaff in, Kensington."

"Very well, Ma'am," he turned to the sisters. "Follow me, please."

"Come, Gezealous."

"I've got goosebumps."

"Keep them to yourself. Come on. He told us to follow him."

With the elevator in disrepair, the tour came to an abrupt end when Kensington collapsed on the seventh step of the grand staircase. The sisters yelled for help, and tried to hold the old man up, but he was too heavy for them. Twickenham hastened up the steps, as Miss Cocoa came down. She checked Kensington's pulse, established he was alive, and the two carried the butler to his bedchamber. To the sisters' delight, Abel Handsforth stepped in to finish the tour. Upon completion of the tour, he made the visit even more memorable by arranging for the sisters to ride with Bob Gardener on the tractor, while he mowed the palace lawn.

Back in the drawing room, Pristine stood at the window, watching the sisters on the tractor, shouting with glee, as the gardener raced them around the lawn. "Well, I will say this, Auntie," Pristine returned to the sofa, "they are a handful."

"You will have them under your control in no time, Pristine."

"I hope you are right." Pristine sat down. "I wasn't expecting them to be so aggressive."

Just a bit of sibling rivalry. Avorah and I observed the same with you and Erica."

"Erica and I weren't so disagreeable."

"You are twins. That made for an entirely different set of circumstances." Lady Woolsey pinned her hat to her head, and rose from the sofa. "Come George. Grab your pouch, and let's go. Pristine has better things to do than entertain us old folks."

"I am tired," Pristine held back a yawn. "Excu-use me. Those girls exhausted me."

"Their energy should soften with time." George Woolsey kissed Pristine's forehead, "be well, my dear, until we meet again."

"Thank you for coming to support me, Uncle George."

"My pleasure to serve."

"Excellent handling of the situation, Pristine." Lady Avorah kissed her goddaughter on the cheeks. "You sealed your fate with Godwyn today."

"Thank you, Auntie." Pristine pulled on the cord, and Quigley appeared.

"The afternoon was a success," Lady Woolsey smiled, "goodbye, my dear. See you in Court."

Quigley led Lord and Lady Woolsey to the wardrobe, while Twickenham entered the drawing room, with Nanny Bickerstaff in tow. "Ma'am, Miss Bickerstaff is here to see you."

"Thank you, Twickenham. Send her in." Arm extended, Pristine slinked across the floor. "Miss Bickerstaff, come in, please. I have heard so much about you."

"Nanny curtseyed. "Your Majesty, this is an honor. Thank you for seeing me."

"Do sit down, Miss Bickerstaff. We can watch the girls mow the lawn."

Nanny looked out the window. "Mow the lawn?"

"The gardener is taking them on a tractor ride."

"Well, I imagine no ill can come of that."

145

"I understand you have accepted a position in Fou."

"Yes, caring for seven girls."

"Seven girls? Take a seat, please. That is a handful."

"Oh yes. I hope I've not taken on more than I can handle. Possessa and Gezealous no longer need a nanny."

"I guess not. I wish you good luck in your new adventure."

"Thank you, Ma'am."

"Would you care for a cup of tea?"

"That would be lovely."

"Let me ring the footman."

Bob Gardener raced the sisters around the lawn until Munchipoo summoned them back to the portico. "Your train to Tolerance leaves in forty minutes." He pointed to the bench, "if you will take a seat here, I will get Nanny Bickerstaff."

"Thank you, Mr. Munchipoo."

"My pleasure," the footman nodded, and walked away.

"Please thank Mr. Handsforth for arranging the tractor ride."

"I will do that. I shall return momentarily with Miss Bickerstaff."

The sisters watched, as Quigley placed their instruments into the boot of the Isotta. Possessa turned to Gezealous. "We survived the day without having to give a full recital," she said.

"As far as I'm concerned, today was a recital—in protocol."

"We shouldn't have fought over the clef."

"You started it."

"You're right. I'm sorry."

"Papa told us not to argue, at least not in public."

"But she did give the clef to me."

"There you go again, Possessa; we're supposed to share."

"Once we move, we'll probably be sharing rooms again anyway."

Quigley approached. "Excuse me, your instruments are in the boot."

"Thank you, Quigley."

"I wish you *un bon voyage*."

"Thank you. You too."

The footman nodded, and disappeared.

Possessa checked to make sure the air was clear. "Do you think we can like her?"

"Like who?"

"The Queen, who else?"

"She's not so bad, for an old person."

146

"She dresses swell. Her dress is like skin tight."

"I could see every curve."

Possessa giggled, "I saw more."

"The gardener sure is cute."

"You pushed me when he drove around that big tree."

"I did not."

"You did so."

"I lost my balance. I fell on you."

"You pushed me on purpose."

"You stepped on my toes."

"I did not."

Nanny Bickerstaff approached. "Move over," she barked, "you, too, Gezealous."

"Did you meet the Queen?"

"I did."

"Did she talk to you?"

"She did."

"What did you talk about?"

"You."

"Oh great," Gezealous sneered. "You talked about us behind our backs?"

"Move over, Possessa."

Crankshaft approached. "Shall we, ladies? Your train departs in forty minutes."

"Yes, Sir," the sisters jumped to their feet, and stepped into the limousine, followed by Nanny Bickerstaff.

"Bon voyage," Quigley closed the door.

Crankshaft shifted into gear, stepped on the gas, and opened the speaking tube. "Good afternoon, voyagers. Our destination is Entitlement Station. Travel time approximately seventeen minutes. Please take note of the security ropes to your left, right, and center, under the separation window. Should we make an unexpected turn, you will find them handy. Now sit back, and enjoy the ride." He closed the tube, shifted into second, and took off.

CHAPTER XX
Death Revisited

Pristine sat before the open window, at her secretary, writing in her journal. Godwyn's eyes are as clear as the water of *Crystal Lake*, she wrote—his hair smells like Baby's breath. I liken his lips to a fuzzy succulent peach, waiting to be devoured. No man but Prince Godwyn is more eligible to help me rule my kingdom. We proposed on the golf course, and have set a date to wed June 20th. My love for Godwyn is like..."

A knock diverted her attention. She closed her journal, and capped her pen. "Come in."

"Eh-em,"Nanny Needlepinch poked her nose inside. "Pristine, do you have a moment?"

"Come in, Nanny. What can I do for you?"

"Eh-em, my throat is dry."

"Shall I ring for a glass of water?"

"I'm all right—just a little phlegm."

"It's all the dairy you eat."

Nanny sat down. "I've heard your lecture before."

"And I stick by it. You don't drink enough water," Pristine pushed the call button.

"I get my water from tea and coffee," Nanny wheezed.

"Tea and coffee don't count. Neither does fortitude."

"My fortitude is one-hundred percent pure distilled vegetable drippings."

"It's one-hundred percent pure alcohol is what it is. Your kidneys have to filter all that alcohol. They need water for that."

"Pure distilled vegetable drippings is what I drink. Don't try to teach an old dog new tricks. Eh-hem."

A knock brought Handsforth into the room. "You rang, Ma'am?

"Yes. Bring me a glass of water, please."

"Yes, "Ma'am."

"You needn't bother Handsforth."

"Bring me a glass of water, Handsforth."

"Yes, Ma'am."

Pristine sat down. "You are not a dog, Nanny. What's up?"

Nanny got comfortable. "Pristine, you must never concern yourself with what people think."

"Generally speaking, I don't."

"I saw how troubled your mother was. Henriette was so unlike GranMarguerite, always worrying what people were thinking. I used to tell her: 'Henriette, you will give up worrying what people think when you realize how little they do'."

"You've told me this before, Nanny."

"That did not stop your mother from worrying. Eh-hem."

"I have a feeling there is going to be a lesson in this."

The door opened. "Your water, Ma'am."

"Thank you, Handsforth."

Pristine handed the glass to Nanny, "drink this."

"If you inisist. Eh-hem," Nanny took two sips, and set the glass on the table.

"You feel better now?"

"Yes, thank you. I remind you, many nights your mother paced the corridors into the wee hours of the morning, asking herself, 'what if?' Even as a girl, she had to evaluate everything. Who said what? Why did they say it? Should I have responded differently? What if I had said this, or done that? Did she say what she meant? Did she mean what she said? It used to drive me mad."

"I can imagine."

"She would take me along for the ride. It was crazy being in her company. Not crazy like your sister Erica, mind you, but strenuous nonetheless."

"Go on."

"Your mother could not rest her mind. Everything troubled her."

"I remember when I couldn't sleep, looking for her in the middle of the night. I'd find her pacing the rug in the corridor."

"She had forgotten the Golden Rule."

"The golden rule?"

"The Goldspinner Golden Rule."

"Why have I not heard of this rule?"

"I have told you this before."

"Not that I remember. What's the rule?"

"She who has the gold makes the rules."

"Okay. Now I remember."

"Doctor Fuehlgoed was called in every night to prepare a concoction."

"So Mummy could sleep."

Nanny nodded. "So your mother could sleep."

"You know, Nanny, I sometimes get the feeling Mummy is with me."

"Your mother is always with you, Pristine."

"I mean like here, now, like she's alive."

"She is alive. She lives in our hearts, in the air we breathe. My point is this: You must answer to no one but God. Put your trust in Her. She will protect you every time."

"I have been taught to suppress my emotions as far back as I can remember, Nanny."

"Let the face not betray what the mind is thinking."

"Speaking of mind, Nanny, did I tell you Count Russell sees right through me."

"What do you mean? He sees right through you?"

"He reads my mind."

"Count Russell has a talent for the unexplainable. You must guard your thoughts in his presence. Even if you should decide to take the train across the Black Snake Line, you must never allow Fear or Terror to take hold."

"Mummy used to say that. I bet she heard it from you."

"You would be wise to heed your mother's words."

"GranMarguerite says emotion is a luxury a Queen cannot afford."

"Your grandmother should know."

"Sometimes I experience feelings of inferiority."

"What are you talking about?"

"I think it stems from the belief I was abandoned by my parents."

"Your parents did not abandon you. Their death was the result of an act of God. They had no say in the matter, nor did you."

"You know what I mean. Losing both parents in one day, growing up without a mother *or* a father—it was hard."

"Of course it was hard. It was a shock to your system, even more so for Erica."

"You and GranMarguerite were always there for us. Auntie Avorah and Uncle George, too, though they were gone much of the time."

"I know."

"Ever since Mummy and Daddy died, I have felt a void in my heart."

Nanny took Pristine's hand. "My dear, you are the Queen of Abundance. You have no reason to feel inferior."

"Maybe it's because I'm short."

"You are not short."

"I'm not tall."

"Short, tall, it's all dualistic thinking. Do your feet touch the ground?"

"I guess so."

"What do you mean, you guess so?"

"They do."

"There you go. You are five foot five, average height for a female Abundite. First Erica goes off to Insanity, now you're telling me you feel abandoned, and inferior. Please don't put us through what your sister put us through. You'll put me in an early grave."

"I don't want that. I do my best to keep my feelings under wrap, but I still feel guilty. I've never spoken of this to anyone but you."

"Erica feels guilty. Now you, too? Guilty for what?"

"I feel like a fraud, like I'm faking it."

"Perhaps you should talk with a professional."

"I could never share my feelings with a stranger."

"What about Count Russell?"

"Never. He would know what I was thinking before I open my mouth."

"You speak with me, and I'm no psychiatrist."

"I know you're not, but I know you, and you know me."

"Aren't we all faking it, a bit? What reason would you have to feel guilty?"

"I feel somewhat responsible for Erica's fate."

"That's silly. Clear your mind. You had no more control over the earthquake than the wind has control over the sea."

"I feel like I cheated fate. I could have been more supportive. Erica should be Queen, not I. How can I enjoy my reign when the true regent suffers in Gruntle?"

"Come to your senses, Pristine. There are worse places to rule over than Discord. Erica has a fine life with Buzz. You should be happy for her."

"I am, but she and I used to be so close. We shared all our secrets. Now we speak twice, maybe three times a year."

"Everyone, and everything, is susceptible to change. I tried to instill that in you when you were toddlers."

"I know I'm not responsible for the earthquake, but you should know, as you know about twins, when one experiences pain, so does the other. What Erica experiences is reflected in my mind. We may be separate in body, but we have always been one in mind."

"Of course you are. You spent the first nine months in the same womb."

"I'll never forget the day Mummy and Daddy died."

"Best you not think of it."

"How can I not? If Erica is troubled, I am troubled. That day must run through her mind endlessly. Unless I work through Erica's troubles, I will never be free. But I need her to work through the emotions with me, and I can't ask her to relive her nightmare to satisfy my need."

"Is that why the two of you don't speak more often?"

"That, plus we're both busy. We no longer live carefree lives."

"You shouldn't let that get in your way."

"Tell me one more time, Nanny, and I promise to put it to rest. How can the earth just swallow people up?"

"If I tell you, will you promise to let it go?"

Pristine nodded. "I promise. I have to work this, or I will never be able to put it behind me."

"You were there, so you will remember most of what I tell you."

"My memory is fuzzy. There was so much going on."

"It was springtime, a sunny day in Forgiveness. Your grandmother Poldemire, your grandfather Marguerite, and I were standing on the airstrip."

"It's the other way around."

"What did I say?"

"You said grandmother Poldemire, and grandfather Marguerite. You mean grandfather Poldemire, and grandmother Marguerite."

"Well, anyway, your mother Henriette, your father Alistair, Miss Amora, Miss Pumba, you, Erica, and I arrived in *Clemency* early to watch the Grand Airship Abundance take to the air. It was a beautiful day. Not a cloud in the sky."

"I remember the birds were singing."

"A select crowd was standing on the airfield, when you told me you needed to respond to a call of nature."

Pristine chuckled. "I almost peed my pants."

"I remember. I left Erica in the care of Miss Pumba, and hastened into the terminal to the little girls' room with you. You had barely sat down on your kid seat cover, when the earth started to rumble."

"I remember the stall shook, and the pipes started gurgeling. It sounded like a train coming down a mountain. I'm sorry. I didn't mean to interrupt."

"The shaking lasted several minutes. The field split open. One by one, the earth swallowed up every tree in its path. When the trembling stopped, the trees were gone, and one section of the field lay twenty feet higher than the other."

"I remember the trees were uprooted. Erica said there were four people on the airfield."

"There were six. The earth swallowed all of them."

"Erica said she saw the earth close across their chests. She said they waved, but no one ran to help them."

"They were a hundred feet away, on trembling ground. What could anyone have done? No human can outrace Mother Nature, not even your GranMarguerite."

"Erica still hears them at night. She says they scream."

"She has shared that with me, many times."

"Why was I spared, and not Erica?"

"The endless question, why? Remember your mother, Pristine — why?"

"That was the last Erica saw of them. May they rest in peace."

"Yes, they rest in peace."

"At least I remember them whole. Erica remembers them as halves."

"God takes the regent and the commoner alike, Pristine. She offers no itinerary, posts no class distinction. One could say a visit to the throne spared you your sister's fate. That is why you rule Entitlement today, while Erica rules Discord. Look what holding on has done for her."

"No good."

"She refuses to let go. You, too, must let it go, or these thoughts will interfere with your relationship with Godwyn. This is Erica's trauma. Not yours."

"I think I did just let it go."

"It warms my heart to hear that."

"Thank you, Nanny, I needed to hear this from you."

"You think, therefore it is. Now, about that talk on womanhood."

"Womanhood? We had that talk when I turned twenty."

"I am speaking of marriage, Pristine."

Pristine looked out the window, saw the shirtless Gardener brothers trimming the hedge maze, and smiled—until the groundskeeper, *Villyum Snibbles,* intervened.

"Sunday will be your big day. We must discuss your wedding night."

"My wedding night? You aren't planning on being there, are you?"

"Of course not." Nanny smiled, "but on this, the second most memorable day of your life, the world will allow you one emotion. Be sure it is not anxiety."

"What then? Joy?"

"Fulfillment, well-beingness. You must express fulfillment, and it shall return to you."

"I'm worried about Erica's appearance. You know how jealous she gets."

"Why should Erica be jealous? She has a husband who loves her, a castle on top of the world, servants, a beautiful Locomobile, a chauffeur— need I go on?"

"We both had a crush on Godwyn growing up."

"Oh for heaven sake, that was years ago. Why would Erica have any interest in Godwyn now?"

Pristine sat down at her vanity table, and sprayed perfume on her neck. "Erica settled. She could have waited, but after that second series of shock treatments, all she wanted was to get away from here. In the end, she couldn't stand it anymore."

"I know. Your parents' empty rooms, the silent corridors, even the gardens were too much for her." Nanny took Pristine's hand. "My dear, you are going to be a lovely bride."

"I told Mrs. Thornecroft to send Erica's invitation return reciept."

"Was it returned?"

"Yes."

"Signed?"

"It was."

"Good." Nanny rose from the chair. "Then I believe Erica will be on her best behavior."

"This medication she's on seems to be working."

"Good. June 20th is going to be a magnificent day."

"It's been weeks since Erica and I spoke."

"Perhaps you should call her. Hand me your brush. I want to brush your hair. What do you two talk about over the telephone?"

Pristine handed Nanny the brush. "I avoid questions about health, anything that involves Loco."

"What *do* you talk about?"

"Girly things; bows, buttons, Buzz," she looked in the mirror, and giggled—"Godwyn."

"It's so cold in Discord. I don't know how she stands it."

"She loves the cold."

"I prefer to visit the snow rather than have *it* visit *me*."

"Last time we spoke, she said she and Buzz were taking skiing lessons."

"Skiing lessons?"

"Ouch, careful Nanny, you're pulling my hair."

"I'm sorry. You want me to stop brushing?"

"No, just be gentle."

"It's my rheumatism." Nanny kept brushing. "My muscles give, and I lose control. Erica has never been on skis."

"That's why she's taking lessons."

"Not to change the subject, Pristine, but I would like to speak with you about Godwyn."

"What about him?"

"You are aware your relationship is going to be legendary."

"The thought had crossed my mind."

"As Defender of the Faith, he will be a great benefit to you, and your kingdom. I feel it in my bones."

"You feel everything in your bones."

"I feel it, because I know you are in love with him, and it is obvious the feeling is reciprocated."

"You mean he's in love with me—not himself."

"Of course. You *have* been in love with him since the day he bumped into you at the Fair."

Pristine smiled. "It was the Pasqua egg hunt. I have never revealed my feelings about Godwyn to anyone but you, and Erica. It feels good to move through my insecurities. I'm growing."

"It feels good, once you get to the other side."

"I keep praying Godwyn will fill my void—at least somewhat."

"You yourself must fill that void, Pristine. Godwyn can only guide you."

"Sometimes I worry I may not be able to fulfill my royal obligation."

"Which royal obligation?"

"My dy-nastic du-ty—ouch! Nanny, be gentle."

"I had better stop. I'm sorry." Nanny set the brush on the table. "It's my rheumatism. Perhaps we can discuss your duties tomorrow, at the lily pond."

"First I suppress my emotions, then I pray people will not read me. Count Russell reads my mind. I pray I think only good thoughts in his presence. The first time I noticed it was at the coronation, when he responded to my concern for the crown, without my having spoken. I'm glad Erica took that thing with her. I cannot imagine having to balance seven pounds on my head," she chuckled, "besides, GranMarguerite is right. Crowns give you headaches, and flat hair."

"I doubt Erica even wears it. It's more an emblem of validation for her."

"I think you're right."

"Count Russell possesses the rare quality of anticipation. I heard how he cleared the mob after the attack on Erica. Last time I held an audience with him he said to me: 'wisdom strikes when the ego is on retreat'."

"Wise words."

"He gave me a list of books to read."

"What sort of books?"

"I started reading the first one: *How to Live the Spiritual Life*. Then there's *The 48 Laws of Power*."

"My dear, you are the Queen of Abundance. Should you be reading self-help books?"

"They're just books."

"You shouldn't be reading such nonsense, Pristine."

CHAPTER XXI

Never Trust a Man

Pristine sat in her boudoir with Nanny Needlepinch, discussing the upcoming wedding. "I read one of Count Russell's books," she said.

"Which book is that?"

"*The 48 Laws of Power.* That got me thinking."

"About what?"

"You know how the only emotion I have permission to display in public is well-beingness."

"Yes."

"I believe the world might be a better place if more people *did* express their emotions."

"That is debatable. What else did Count Russell recommend?"

"*The Book of Emotions.* That got me thinking how the prophets predicted I would give birth to a male heir."

"They predicted a *healthy* male heir."

"That goes without saying. Godwyn is the oldest of six boys. That should guarantee me a male heir." Pristine looked into the mirror at Nanny—"what's wrong with females?"

"Nothing."

"Lately, I've been feeling need more than any other emotion. It feels terrible this need, but a kingdom, by very nature of the word, calls for a king. What is a kingdom without a king?"

"A queen-dom."

"A queen-dom is not a kingdom."

"Is it Godwyn you desire, Pristine? Or is it his masculine gene? Has history led you to believe you need a penis to be taken seriously by the Court?"

"Nanny," Pristine spun around on her stool. "That which you take into your mouth, I do not take in my hands. Apologize now."

159

"Your Majesty, forgive me your virgin ears." Nanny smiled. "If *I* don't speak honestly with you, who will?"

"Godwyn will. Auntie Avorah speaks honestly with me, usually."

"To speak of the male appendage is nothing to be ashamed of. It is merely a tool, designed to serve a function—no different than a hammer, or a woo-woo. The female equipment may be concealed under stucco, but it is not unlike that of a man."

"A woo-woo? No one says woo-woo anymore, Nanny."

"What do they call it?"

"You're trying to make me blush."

"Tell me."

"All right." Pristine whispered into Nanny's ear, "they call it a concha."

"Good heavens," Nanny slapped her lap, "ho-ho-ho. Now you have *me* blushing—ooh."

Pristine chuckled. "You're turning red."

It took a while for Nanny to stop laughing. "Oh, ho-ho—that tickled my funny bone. Back to our topic." It took a while for Nanny to stop laughing, "for a quick recap—oh, that was funny. I must maintain my composure. Anyway—you will remember much of this from our talk on where babies come from. During the early stages of a pregnancy, the fetus grows balls, and a projectile muscle. If the fetus is to become a female, the balls are infused with estrogen, at which time they turn into ovaries. The projectile remains under plaster, in the sac, with the ovaries. The sac splits, and becomes a woo-woo. If the fetus is to become male, the balls get an injection of testosterone, become testicles, then drop. The projectile receives the same injection, penetrates through the plaster, and emerges from the ballsac as a penis."

"There you go again. That's not the word Erica uses."

"What does Erica call it?"

Pristine leaned in, "a pi-pi."

"Oh, ho-ho," Nanny chuckled, "this new generation terminology. We've been through this lesson before, Pristine. The female equipment may be concealed under stucco, but it is not unlike that of a man. In this sense, every man and woman is bisexual by nature: men for having begun life in female form, and women by nature of giving birth. As the male matures, he diverts his energy into playing rough games, and sports. This gives the ego permission to touch another male without feeling threatened."

"That must be hard on the soul, to feel one has to hide."

"Hard on the soul, and the body. Why should it be acceptable for women to kiss each other upon greeting one another, yet of a man the group would say it is unnatural. By virtue of the mother instinct, women are no less bisexual than men."

"That leaves me out."

Nanny sat down. "Listen to me, Pristine, during the long reign ahead, upon which you have only begun to cement your name in the pages of history, at times you may find you do not have the balls to get a project off the ground, but you have the boobs to carry it off."

"If only I had. Your lessons are always so memorable."

"It's true. You have the boobs to carry a project off. You moved the lighthouse."

"That was Auntie Avorah's project. Sir David James McClure and his workers moved the lighthouse."

"You initiated the project. You oversaw the progress, and you gave final approval."

"From the throne room. Not on location."

"Your insistence got that lighthouse moved before it crumbled, Pristine. It was your insistence that got the new dock built ahead of schedule. Think of the care you give the stray wiafs, when you visit the orphanage."

"I feel bad. I haven't been there in over a year."

"Think of the trees you saved, and all the homes."

"What homes?"

"The maple trees on Main Street you saved from being felled. The homes of the birds, the squirrels, and the insects. You oversaw all of these projects, and you made it seem effortless."

"I would hardly say it was effortless."

"You know what I mean. You made it look easy by expressing one emotion—well-beingness. At this point, you should have proven to yourself—when you set your mind to a project, you have the boobs to carry it off."

Pristine giggled. "And the woo-woo. Nanny, in case haven't noticed, I'm not particularly well-endowed."

"You will be once you give birth."

"That's the last thing I want. I have no motherly instincts."

"Wait until you are expecting. Your bosom will blossom again. You will feel like you are sixteen all over again."

"A fuller bosom hardly sounds worth the pain and of a pregnancy."

"You don't need Godwyn, Pristine. You want him. There is a

161

difference." Nanny walked to the door, and turned. "Good night, my dear. I shall see you in the morning."

"Good night, Nanny. Thanks for the talk."

The door opened, and Nanny walked out.

The morning of the day before the wedding, after a restless night's sleep, Carabella Needlepinch awoke early. With the wedding on her mind, she had not slept well, and was bathed and dressed by six. By ten to eight, she could no longer wait to begin the day, and proceeded to the Queen's bedchamber. She knocked on the door, and poked her head into the room. "Pristine, are you up?"

Pristine sat in bed, leaning against the headboard. "Nanny, good morning. Come in."

"Good morning," Nanny shut the door, and approached the Queen's bed, "our lovely bride."

"I've been up since dawn, reading." She turned back the comforter, and slipped into her slippers. "Let me put on my robe," she said.

"I have been up since four. I didn't sleep well either." Nanny pushed a button, and the drapes opened. "Had I known you were up, I wouldn't have waited until eight to come see you."

"I've been thinking," Pristine returned, wearing a robe, "I wonder what life will be like once Godwyn and the girls move in. I've been thinking about Possessa, Gezealous, and Count Russell."

"What about the count?"

"I told you, he reads my mind. Even when I'm not thinking about anything, he reads my thoughts. It's scary."

"Pristine, what you are experiencing is pre-wedding jitters." Nanny looked around, "where is Mina?"

"I asked her to go to the library in town to look for some books for me."

"These books cannot be found in our libraries?"

"Apparently not or Mina would have found them."

Nanny looked out the window, and saw two squirrels scamper up a tree. "It's a beautiful day," she turned to Pristine, "let's talk in the lily garden."

"I don't know why I put on my robe if we're going out. Let me slip into some walking clothes." Pristine walked off, "I'll be right back."

"I'm not interested in walking, Pristine, not with my wobbly knee."

"We'll take it slow."

"I'll be lucky to make it to the lily pond. It's a beautiful day for discussing the responsibilities of a wife."

"What would you know about the responsibilities of a wife, Nanny? You've never even been married."

"I've been around the block enough times to understand the responsibilities of ten wives, Pristine."

Pristine walked into the room dressed in slacks, and a cardigan. "Are you ready?"

"Ready as ever."

"Let's go." Pristine reached for the doorhandle, and the door opened. "Munchipoo," she greeted the footman, "good morning."

"Good morning, Your Majesty," the footman bowed from the neck, "good morning, Miss Needlepinch."

"Morning," Nanny grumbled, "not so fast, Pristine."

"We'll take the elevator. Here, take my hand."

Nanny clamped onto Pristine's arm. "You know, Pristine, having never been a wife did not exclude me from gleaning some good advice."

"I guess not," Pristine counted the lily repetitions in the carpet, as they walked. down. the. corridor. "What are you going to teach me today?"

"Some good advice."

"Go ahead. I'm listening."

"Wait until we get outside."

"Tell me now."

"When we get out of the elevator."

'DING.' The cage door opened, and Quigley bowed from the neck. "Good morning, your Majesty."

"Good morning, Quigley."

"Miss Needlepinch."

"Eh-em"—Nanny cleared her throat, "morning, Quigley."

"Main floor?"

"Please."

'CLANK—WHOOSH...' Quigley put the elevator into gear, and they descended, one. foot. at. a. time.

'CLUNK. DING.'

"Good day, ladies," Quigley opened the cage door, and stepped aside.

"Good day, Quigley. Nanny, you go first. I'll follow."

"Not so fast, Pristine," Nanny clamped on, "give me your arm."

"Pristine walked down the corridor with Nanny on her arm, "we are out of the elevator, Nanny. Assign me your advice."

"Never trust a man. Let that suffice until we get outside."

"I trust Godwyn. I have to. We're getting married tomorrow."

"Trust me, Pristine, never trust a man. Take Henderson for example, holding the door." Nanny whispered, "the good-looking ones—like him."

"Henderson?"

"Yes, Henderson. Quiet, he'll hear."

"Good morning, Henderson."

"Good morning, Your Majesty." The footman nodded, "good morning, Miss Needlepinch."

Nanny clamped onto Pristine's arm, and they crossed the terrace.

"So I should never trust a man."

"Place trust in no one but yourself, Pristine."

"But *you* just told me to trust *you*. If I trust *you*, it reasons I should trust others, too. Just because a person is good-looking and male doesn't mean he can't be trusted."

Nanny grabbed the handrail, and they descended the steps into the garden. "Listen to me, Pristine, love Godwyn with all your heart, but place your trust in God. She pays high dividends, every time."

"Henderson is a loyal servant. What reason have I not to trust him?"

"He is a man, and a good-looking one."

"He can't help his looks. He's like Kensington, you, or Auntie Avorah and Uncle George—you're family. If I can't trust a servant, whom *can* I trust?"

"My dear," Nanny got foothold on the gravel path, and loosened her grip, "you must be discerning in your choices."

Pristine watched workers set up tables on the lawn. "I am discerning."

"So much noise, as the workers prepare for our big day. Let's escape."

"We are unanimous in that thought. It looks like they're cleaning the lily pond. Let's go sit in the jacaranda garden."

"Fine with me. It's closer."

"Here we are. That wasn't such a long walk, was it?"

"We made it." Nanny drew back a bush using her stick, and they approached a bench. She pulled out a handkerchief, wiped the dew off, and rested her stick. "You may sit down now," she said.

"Thank you." Pristine tapped her parasol to the bench. It sprung open, and she sat down. "I like the sun, but not in my eyes."

"Pristine, I give you my best council." Nanny tucked her handkerchief into her cloak, and sat down. "Never trust a man."

"You're repeating yourself."

"Never trust anyone, man or woman—not even me."

"Whom can I trust? I know—God."

"Only God. People are fallible," Nanny lowered her hood, "the most fallible are the ones who need love the most. You must love them even more."

Pristine twirled her parasol. "Why did you never marry, Nanny?"

"I almost did marry, once upon a time," Nanny pulled pins out of her hair, and let her faded tresses fall.

Pristine delighted in the sun shining through her parasol, "you never told me this."

"You never asked."

"So why did you never get married?"

Nanny loosened her braids. "I was born in *Armory*. I grew up there—you know that. Every first of the month, one of father's vendors would pull up in a fancy white carriage, drawn by four white horses. He was a wealthy gentlemen form Possessaion, Sir James Schloesser. He took a fancy to me." She combed through her hair with her fingers. "He asked Father for my hand in marriage."

"How old were you?"

"Thirteen. Father refused him," Nanny shook out her hair, "he was not going to let go of me."

"He loved you that much, huh?"

"Loved me? Ha," Nanny let out a chortle—"he was not going to lose his maid."

"You grew up without a maid?"

"You *do* have a sense of humor, Pristine. I *was* the maid."

"You had no sisters?"

"Are you kidding?" Nanny parted her hair, "I *was* the sister, to eight brothers, all younger."

"Did Sir Schloesser kiss you?"

"He was three times my age."

"I didn't ask his age. I asked if he kissed you."

"That is a personal question."

"Well," Pristine turned to Nanny, "I can tell he did."

"Yes, he kissed me, once."

"Only once?"

Nanny twisted her hair into tresses, "okay, twice."

"I bet you were pretty."

"The name Carabella means beautiful face. I was a catch. Look at me now."

"You're still beautiful."

"All the beauty is on the inside. The more ones' outer beauty fades, the more it appears within."

"What was it like growing up in Armory?"

"Nothing to tell. After Mother died, I raised my brothers, all eight."

"Eight brothers? That must have been dreadful."

"They taught me to box, and defend myself." Nanny rolled her braid into a bun, and pinned it to her head.

"That's probably why you became a nanny. You were programmed to take care of other peoples' children, so you became a nanny."

"That makes sense. It's a man's world out there, Pristine. You must claim it, and you must be resilient."

"Resilient? I don't even know what the word means."

"You must be hard-wearing. At one time or another, you may experience a scandal involving those from whom you least expect it. Parliament, defeats in Court, public opinion, acts of nature, a family member, it's all a breeding ground. Once you've been stretched and compressed, you must recoil." Nanny finished braiding, rolled her tress into a bun, pulled the last pin out from between her lips, and pinned the bun to her head. "You must be prepared for a scandal at any time."

"You're referring to Erica."

"Not only Erica. Scandals arise from any source."

"Well, I'm not going to think of that now. What about the second time?"

Nanny raised her hood. "What second time?"

"The second time you almost got married."

"Oh, eh-em. I was in my late twenties, and I was stuck in Terror. I read in the paper about a university lecturer. I decided to attend. The speaker was a young man from Anticipation. Sir *Ronald Baudish* was his name."

"What was the lecture about?"

"Women's Reproductive Rights."

"Back then?"

"He was a trailblazer. It was an attempt to get people to take the overcrowding of the planet seriously. He advocated women keep their bloomers on, men keep their zippers in the upright, locked position. He wanted women to understand they could be more than just wives, mothers, caretakers, and nannys. Where do you think I learned this baby stuff?"

Pristine stopped twirling, "Sir Ronald Baudish?"

"That's right." Nanny nodded.

"So why didn't you get married?"

"We courted for three years."

"Did you trust him?"

"I did. I am telling you, so you will learn from my mistakes."

"What was Sir Baudish like?"

"He was a tall, handsome fellow with long, slender arms, and broad shoulders, the sporty type—a cross-country skier. He embraced me, and I felt safe. One day he asked Father for my hand in marriage."

"Your father refused him."

"No," Nanny shook her head. "Father conscented. He blessed the union."

"How old were you?"

"I was twenty-six, and in full bloom. I spent hours signing my name in my diary to Ron's surname. I wrote it with a flourish—*Mrs. Ronald Baudish.*"

"So why didn't you get married?"

"A telegram arrived. Ron had been trampled by horses."

"How awful."

"He fell off the coach, and broke nearly every bone in his body. It was agonizing. It took months for him to die."

"How horrible."

"I stayed by his side, day and night, until he drew his last breath."

"I am sorry to hear that."

"I grieved for three years. Then one day, I read Queen Marguerite was expecting. That was my ticket out. I had no money, so I tore the curtains off the rod, pulled out Mother's old Singer, and sewed myself a new dress. I polished the only shoes I had—with a hole in the sole. I stole Father's grocery money, bought a ticket to Entitlement, and never looked back."

"You *never* went back?"

"No," Nanny shook her head.

"Not even on vacation?"

"What vacation? I've spent every day of your life with you. Why should I have gone back? Mother was dead. My brothers were married. They didn't need me anymore. I sent the grocery money back to Father with my first paycheck. A few years later, he had a heart attack, and died."

"Did you get an inheritance?"

"My brothers squabbled over the inheritance. The oldest took half for himself, claiming it was his through primogeniture, because he was born first."

"I know that song."

"One of my brothers is an evil solicitor. He wrote his name next to every stick of furniture worth owning. I never saw a copper penny."

"I imagine you were left out anyway, as a woman."

"You got that right. Your grandmother hired me as an assistant to Nanny McMeane, to look after your mother before she was born. My arrival at the palace was the most important day of my life. I had escaped Terror, and I never looked back. Everyone here was so friendly, so helpful."

Pristine let her parasol rest on her shoulder, "what a story."

"My blossom eventually faded, but your grandfather kept me on. When the little Goldspinners grew up, I accepted a position in Resolution. I spent seventeen years with a family there. When their children left the nest, your mother called, told me she was expecting, and asked if I would come back. That was you, and Erica. You two became the most important stars in the universe to me, so important I never had children of my own. I guess you could say, I never had it in me, either."

"What a story." Eyes closed, Pristine looked to the sun. "You should submit it to *Nanny's Life.*

"They already published my experience—after my first tour. They entitled it *Nanny Royale.*"

"What an interesting life. I would never have suspected."

"I would never have told you, had you not asked. You see what happens when we ask?"

CHAPTER XXII
Nanny's Pre-Wedding Jitters

Pristine and Nanny, sitting on the bench under a tree, are t-a-l-k-i-n-g—regrets. Nanny shook her head. "I don't know what happened, Pristine. It seems I went to bed one night at 39, and awoke the next morning 93. Listen your yourself, Carabella—spewing regrets. The truth is, we all die alone."

"Not when you have loved ones at your side."

"Loved ones cannot take the journey with you, Pristine."

"I will see to it you are never alone," Pristine twirled her parasol.

"I am grateful for all you have done for me—you, and the family. As for becoming a parent, and it will happen whether you prefer it or not, Pristine, there are a few points I would like to make."

"How many points?"

"I want you to enter this marriage prepared. There is no manual on how to be a good wife, or a good parent, at least not yet. Perhaps someone will write it one day. It could be you."

"Me?" Pristine laughed, "write a book on parenting? Aha-ha-ha. Nanny, how many times do I have to tell you—I don't have what it takes."

"One never knows until one makes the attempt."

"I can write a letter, or a journal entry—but a book? Never."

"It is as you say." Nanny pulled her flask out, unscrewed the lid, and took a healthy sip of fortitude.

"You told me you gave up drinking."

"This is medication, Pristi—hic—excuse me." Nanny replaced the lid.

"You know alcohol puts a strain on your liver."

"What use is my liver when no one can see it?" Nanny slipped the flask into her pocket. "I am not concerned with internal organs, Pristine. I wouldn't even know I had a liver, if not for Dr. Fuehlgoed. Look at my arms," she pointed to a dark spot, "they're covered in liver spots."

"They're sunspots."

"Look at my leg," she pointed out a discoloration, my purple veins stick out like rivers on a map. If all it takes to consign ease upon my tired old bones is spirts, then I say let me be."

"A sip or two is fine, Nanny, but you exceed your limit. I'll bet those sunspots are from drinking alcohol."

"What are you talking about? — *hic.*"

"Nanny!"

"Excuse me."

"We are talking about your alcohol intake. I'm not only concerned about your liver, I'm concerned about keeping you on your feet, and gin, and Brandy don't help."

"It's not gin, or Brandy, Pristine. It's bourbon. Now, what were we talking about before?"

"Your alcohol intake. Writing a book."

"Yes, writing a book. It takes a commitment. It can take years, even a lifetime. The speeches you have given, over the years, were spot on, *hic*— excuse me. You could compile them, turn them into a book."

"Count Russell writes my speeches, Nanny. You know that. I cannot claim authorship for somebody else's writing."

"It's the idea *behind* the writing people are interested in, Pristine — not the validity."

"I do no more than hand the count notes, and he returns them to me as a speech."

"But *you* are the one who delivers the speech. You give his words meaning, and tone. You credit him for the words."

"I would rather collect bugs."

"Writing could be your legacy, Pristine. All you lack is experience."

"And talent."

"That depends upon one's perspective. Meanwhile, you are going to need an heir—and you are going to need a spare. If you are lucky, like your mother was, you will deliver twins."

"Good God no. Giving birth to one bowling ball seems more than plenty. What reason would anyone want that?"

"To secure the future of the kingdom? Pristine, it is your duty to provide Entitlement with an heir."

"I don't want to talk about this." Pristine watched, as an opossum crossed the lawn, with twelve cubs hitching a ride. "Look at that," Pristine pointed, "why would *anyone* choose that experience consciously?"

"No one says you must produce a dozen at a time, Pristine. That is why you have a Nanny."

"Children seem such an inconvenient must."

"Two will do."

"Motherhood frightens me. I want no part of it."

"Of course it frightens you. You're about to get married. Take life one step at a time."

"It's more than that. I'm afraid I won't be a good wife, and an even worse mother. I'm afraid of the pain in childbirth. I'm afraid Fear and Terror will attack again. It terrifies me I may have to ring true to my coronation speech promise to go there in person."

"Pristine, childbirth is as natural a thing as there is. With a few shots of Brandy, and me by your side you have *hic*—nothing to fear. Excuse me."

"You're excused."

"Thank you."

"You know I have no motherly instinct. And I don't like kissing babies."

"Do you remember how afraid you were before your coronation?"

"I was terrified."

"And look how well it went."

"You've obviously forgotten Erica's entrance. And the Terrorist attack."

"I would have wet my pants if I had been sitting on that platform."

Pristine giggled. "I almost did wet my pants, Nanny, and if you ever tell anyone I said that, I will deny it."

"You carried it off with true Goldspinner tact."

"I crossed my ankles, shut off the plumbing."

"You see? Fear is a motivator. When properly addressed, it motivates us to change for the better. One must use it to one's benefit. Pristine—you wear the crown more regally than any monarch ever, more regally than Queen Mother Marguerite, and if you ever tell her I said that, I will deny it."

"Thank you, Nanny. That's sweet of you to say."

"I mean it, Pristine. You rule the Court. The Parliamentarians respect you even moreso, because you are a woman. Your subjects love you. The gold mines are booming. You secured the Crystal Rock lighthouse and dock for centuries to come. The maple trees on Main Street are alive; tourism thrives. What more could a Queen want?"

"A heir and a spare, without having to go through the motions."

171

"You are living in a dream world, my child. Men and women together serve a purpose."

"What if I am not fertile? What if I am barren?"

"What if? Now you sound like your mother. Remember what I told you."

"What did you tell me?"

Nanny turned to Pristine. "Do you not listen? Do not trust him."

"Oh yeah—that. I haven't forgotten that. But what if it turns out Godwyn is infertile?'

"What it? Why the doomsday speculation? He is the oldest of six boys." Nanny shook her head. "I doubt it."

"What about his brother Francis—*Francene?*"

"The one who has has abandoned male dress?—a quirk of nature, most likely, a double spirited pansy. Godwyn will be fruitful, but remember, you are a magnificent Queen without a king at your side. With your king consort, you will be even more magnificent."

"Thank you, Nanny. I needed to hear that from you."

"You are going to be a terrific wife, and mother. I see a male heir in our future. I feel it in my bones. You shall christen him *Aloneous Rexus Poldemire Alistair Goldspinner Bonheur*, after your succession of male ancestors, and the Defenders family name, and you shall add to his prénom as many more names as you desire."

Pristine smiled. "Nanny, you're making this up."

"Of course I am making it up; it's divine prophecy."

Pristine twirled her parasol. "You are trying to make me smile."

"And it is working. Your heir shall possess his father's faith, and height, and his mother's charm, and good looks. In his time, he will bring light to the world, as you are now doing in yours."

"One day, Nanny. One day at a time. Every day, I think about Erica, up there in Gruntle, cold, dark, windy, in Discord." Pristine stopped twirling, "Fear and Terror are never off my mind."

Nanny closed her eyes, and breathed in the jacaranda aroma. "I'm not sleeping. I am merely resting my eyes."

"I didn't say anything."

The sunlight hit Nanny's face and hands through the tree canopy, in blotches. "I am trying to think of anything but Fear and Terror." She quirked a smile. "One day, when I am dead and gone, you will hear my voice and you will remember our conversation."

A flock of sparrows chirped and bathed in the fountain, while a pair of mockingbirds in a nearby tree took to song. Pristine joined Erica, telepathically, for a quick walk down Memory Lane, remembering events of childhood play in the garden now long past. "I remember GranMarguerite teaching Erica and me the ornithological names of all the birds in the garden," Pristine smiled, "now I'm lucky if I can remember or-ni-tho-lo-gi-cal, or half their names."

"That is a ten sovereign word."

"Nanny, you hear the mockingbirds?"

Nanny raised her head, and looked about. "Flocking birds?"

"Mock-ing birds."

Nanny shook her head. "Too high a pitch for me."

"You don't hear the mockingbirds?"

"Nope."

Pristine took in the sun through her parasol. "I'm trying to figure out which bird they're imitating."

"No idea."

Pristine studied Nanny's face. Her hearing is at its best when you don't want her to hear you. When you do want her to hear you, she's deaf as a doorknob.

The birds flew away, taking with them their song. A family of finches landed on the gravel path, and started pecking at the seeds. Pristine relaxed, and listened to the raging *Torrent Falls* in the distance, dropping thousands of tons of water per second into the arroyo below. "I remember Kensington telling me how many tons of water spew into the Torrent every second, I couldn't even conceptualize the number." Pristine stopped twirling her parasol. "Nanny—are you awake?"

Nanny sat, head slouched forward, mouth half open, snoring. Pristine looked into her face—"Nanny, are you okay? Nanny, wake up. It's time to go in." She shook Nanny's arm, "wake up."

Nanny snored.

Pristine nudged Nanny on the leg. "Nanny—wake up!"

Nanny opened her eyes, and pulled herself up. In the process, she knocked her stick off the bench. "W-where am I?"

Pristine picked up Nanny's stick, and set it on the bench. "You're in the jacaranda garden. You were snoring."

"I was not. I was merely resting my eyes."

"I was afraid you had left me."

Nanny struggled to compose herself. "I'm not going anywhere, Pristine. There is too much keeping me here. You are going to need a

173

nanny, once your heirs arrive. It may as well be me—as long as you allow me to hire my choice of assistant."

"There you go again. While you were snoozing, I reflected on my life."

"I was not snoozing. I was resting my eyes."

"While you were resting your eyes, I had a chance to reflect, and I realized, you have slept through half my life, but you have always been there for me at the most important events. I cannot think of one milestone you missed. You sent Erica and me off to kindergarden. You bandaged us the first time we scraped our knees."

"Both of you, together, the same day."

"You were there when Aunt Flo came to visit—the first time."

"You and Erica both—the same day—twelve minutes apart. You were first."

"That was embarassing. You were there the day Count Russell bestowed the title *Princess of Perfection* upon me."

"I was always there," Nanny nodded, "for both of you. You are my world."

"You stayed awake through the entire presentation."

"I did." Nanny chuckled, "and it was boring."

"It was." Pristine smiled, "you were there when we laid Grandpa Poldi to rest."

"I was, God rest His Majesty's soul. I wouldn't have missed it for the world."

"You were there to see me coroneted."

"I was. In the front row, seated to the left of your grandmother."

"Tomorrow you will attend my wedding."

"And this time next year, I will attend to your heirs."

"You mean so much to me, Nanny."

"You are my world, Pristine—you, and Erica. It has been my honor to mean something to you both. As long as there are Goldspinner babies to look after, I have reason to get out of bed. I expect you will waste no time." Nanny took a swig from her flask, slipped it inside her cloak, and planted her stick. "Are you ready to go in? I need a nap. I am counting on Count Russell tomorrow to make sure I hear you say I do." She lifted herself off the bench, "Now, which is the shortest route to the terrace?"

"Let's go by way of the herb garden, Nanny."

"The herb garden it is. What were we talking about before I was resting my eyes?"

"Prince Godwyn."

"Yes, Prince God—*hic*—Godwyn. Excuse me."

"You need to cut down on the Brandy."

"I told you, Pristine, it's bourbon."

"You need to cut down on the bourbon."

"I will, one day."

"About Godwyn—when we visited Aunt Envie, years ago, she lives on Lake Remembrance and has a teakwood deck that extends out, over the water. Anyway, the last night we were there, under the dancing Northern Lights—it was so romantic, Godwyn floated me around the lake in his arms. It was so romantic. I felt like I had been hypnotized."

"Never forget, Pristine, he may be a prince…"

"But he is a man—and I should not trust him."

"No, I mean yes. Trust God. But that is not what I wanted to say. I was going to say," Nanny stopped walking, "what was I going to say? Give me a moment. What was it? Oh yes, I remember—you must stay on top at all times."

"Stay on top?"

"You must see to it you stay on top." They continued the promendade. "*You* must remain in control, not Godwyn, not the Court, nor the Parliamentarians, Mrs. Thornecroft—or even me. Never allow need to get in the way of exercising your common sense. You are a Goldspinner. Produce a healthy heir, and a spare, and the void you feel will vanish."

"I hope so. It's getting warm. We sat at the fountain quite a while."

As they approached the gravel path, Nanny grabbed Pristine's arm, and clamped on. "The tables and chairs are all set up," she noted.

"It looks like the workers have gone home. It must be after noon. Here are the steps."

"Hold on a second," Nanny stopped. "I need to catch my breath."

"Take your time."

"Pristine, don't worry about Erica. She poses no threat. You are going to be a beautiful bride. I am ready to take the stairs." Nanny stroked Pristine's bosom, "give me your hand."

"Not so tight, Nanny. You bruised me earlier. I didn't say anything because my gown will cover it."

"Easy, Pristine. We are in no hurry."

"Take your time, Nanny."

By the time they approached the landing, Nanny was out of breath again. "I need another break."

"Two more steps, and you can rest on the bench. Come on."

"It looks like two workers out there are still at it." Nanny positioned herself on the bench, and rested her cane on her lap.

"Scooch, Nanny, I'm going to sit down with you." Pristine squeezed in, visualized taking vows the next day before Godwyn, and the world, and smiled. "I know expressing an emotion is a luxury a Queen cannot afford, Nanny, but I have been taught there is one emotion a Queen *can* express, and that is the emotion of well-beingness, contentment, so I want to speak the truth."

"And that truth is?"

"I love you, Carabella Needlepinch." Pristine kissed Nanny on the cheek. "There, I said it. Now get up. We're going to finish these steps, walk across that terrace, and get you to your quarters, so you can take your nap."

Nanny planted her stick, and lifted herself off the bench. "I love you and Erica as if you were my own."

"I know that."

"One last bit of advice, as your wedding night approaches."

"More advice? You're not going to be there."

"I know. Give me your arm. A word for the wise: on your honeymoon night, lay back, and think of Abundance."

"Think of Abundance?"

"At some point, Godwyn is going to want to lock loins."

"Lock loins?"

"The horizontal dance, my dear, the hookie-pookie, the hootschie-kootschie. Never forget, the future of Entitlement lies in your fertile womb, and remember to stay on top."

"And not to trust him."

"Good girl. Trust no one but God." Nanny smiled, "you learn fast."

"Think of Abundance."

CHAPTER XXIII
Royal Wedding

Prince Godwyn Bonheur, the groom in this case, arranged for Nanny Nellie Bickerstaff, and butler Orderic Tibbons, to escort his daughters Possessa and Gezealous to the wedding. As Godwyn left the house, he kissed each on the forehead. "Nanny Bickerstaff tells me you girls behaved beautifully yesterday while I was gone."

"We did," in unison, the sisters nodded.

Godwyn stood at the open door of Villa Leniency, the family home of half a century. "That makes me happy."

"Papa, where are you going?"

"I have an appointment with the taylor for my final fitting, Gezealous."

"When will you be back?"

"Before dinner, and I want to hear a good report from Nanny."

Possessa nodded. "I promise to be good."

Gezealous smiled. "I promise not to fight."

"Good. I am glad to hear it. Have fun with Denise. I will see you at dinner."

The Defender's wedding announcement brought Nellie Bickerstaff's seven year engagement with the Bonheur family to an end. There was afterall, no need for two nannys at the palace. With no better offer on the horizon, she accepted a position in Fou, raising Reverend *McMultiply & Mother McMultiply*'s seven daughters—and now Mother McMultiply is expecting again. "This time, the couple is hoping for a boy," said Nanny.

"At very least, Fou will be a change of wallpaper," said Godwyn.

The opportunity of being in the presence of Queen Pristine again, was one Nellie Bickerstaff was not going to miss. She had Sunday, the twentieth of June marked on her calendar, months in advance.

Music poured out of the Saint Agarapina Cathedral, and echoed across the valley. Amid a thousand other pedestrians, Orderic Tibbons climbed the cathedral steps, and entered the vestibule, followed by Possessa, Gezealous, and Nanny Bickerstaff. They sprinkled themselves (and in the case of the sisters, each other) at the basin of Holy Water, crossed themselves, and proceeded into the sanctuary.

Princess Erica, and husband Sir Buzz, arrived early. Buzz parked the Locomobile at the curb, turned off the ignition, and the V-12 sputtered into silence. Erica leaned forward, and smiled. "You see Buzz, we saved time by *not* taking the short cut."

"My dear, you are right again." Buzz gave her a kiss, through the open separation window, "are you ready to step into the lions' den?"

"Ready as I will ever be."

"Then let us proceed." Buzz stepped onto the cobblestones, opened the rear compartment door, and out stepped a confident princess, dressed in a splashed paisley suit with matching brim hat, dark glasses, and red open toe heels. Around her neck she wore her mother's pearls, and each earlobe donned a single pearl.

Buzz took Erica by the hand, and walked her past the shouting fans, held back by roped barrier posts, and security guards. The couple passed by photographers, and the Press, begging for a comment. Ignoring their pleas, Buzz led the princess up the steps.

"I cannot forget, this is where the Terrorists attacked me, Buzz."

Buzz drew the princess in. "That will never happen again, I promise you. Not as long as I am by your side."

"As much as I trust you, Buzz, I'm not so sure. The lies coming out of Fear has the public disturbed, and the Terrorists remain determined to defend their right to spread violence."

Count Russell and Bishop Martens stood at the top of the cathedral steps, greeting guests. Count Russell wore his usual camelhair flair ensemble, while Bishop Martens chose a white gown with red velvet shoes, and a golden mitre on his head. From the moment Count Russell heard the Locomobile rumble in, he had his eyes on the Runner couple. "Your Royal Highness," he bowed, as they ascended the steps, "Sir Buzz, good to see you."

Erica smiled. "Thank you, Count Russell. Good to see you again."

Buzz nodded, "good morning, Count."

Bishop Martens stepped forward. "Your Royal Highness, welcome home, Ma'am. You look stunning. Sir Buzz, delighted you could attend."

"It's the perfect day for a wedding."

"My thoughts exactly." Count Russell bowed to a group of passing nuns.

Lady Woolsey checked her lipstick in her compact mirror, when she heard princess Erica's gravely voice. She snapped her compact shut, slipped it into her purse, and approached. "Erica—Your Royal Highness," she curtseyed, "my dear, how good to see you."

Erica jumped back, "Auntie Avorah, you startled me. How do you do?"

"I'm sorry. I didn't mean to frighten you."

"But you did."

"Hello, Buzz."

Buzz nodded. "Hello, Lady Avorah."

"I love your feathers, Auntie. What are they?"

"Coque." Lady Avorah checked. "Yes, they're gray bleach cocque."

"They're lovely."

"What a handsome couple you make."

"Thank you, Auntie. Where's Uncle George?"

"He went on a tobacco run. You look radiant, my dear."

"I keep telling her that." Buzz took Erica's hand. "Sweetheart, we should go find our seats."

Erica smiled. "Good to see you, Auntie. Say hi to Uncle George for me."

"I will do that." Lady Woolsey nodded.

"Enjoy the ceremony, Lady Woolsey." Buzz bowed from the neck, placed his hand on Erica's back, and led her to the sanctuary.

"We got through that. Can you believe she's wearing rooster feathers on her head?"

Buzz let out a chuckle. "Gray bleach coque. Could any fashion accessory be more dreary?"

"Thanks for pulling me away. She can talk forever."

"I am always at your side, Erica."

Erica took Buzz's arm. "We should find our seats."

"After we sprinkle ourselves with Holy Water."

"You lead the way, my handsome husband."

Guards held the public at bay behind roped separation poles, as the couple proceeded to the basin of Holy Water. Erica giggled, and held her arms out, "sprinkle me, Buzz."

Buzz flicked his wife with Holy Water, walked her to the double doors, and led her into the cathedral sanctuary. "Look how packed it is."

"It's a royal wedding, Buzz. What did you expect?"

As they entered, they were greeted by head of Security, *Guillermo Garcilaso*. "Your Royal Highness," he bowed, "I want to assure you, the only person you will see here today in white will be the bride."

"Thank you, Garcilaso," the princess smiled. "I appreciate knowing that."

"We appreciate your concern," Buzz nodded.

"Might I usher you to your seats, Your Royal Highness?"

"We appear to be lost. That would be gracious of you."

"This way, please."

The couple followed the security guard up the aisle. Buzz whispered into Erica's ear, "you are finally being treated with the respect you deserve."

Erica squeezed Buzz's hand. "This is exciting. My sister is getting married today."

"That's why we're here."

"Tomorrow we will both be married women."

At the top of the steps, outside the cathedral, the count approached the bishop. "Princess Erica seems to have gotten over her penchant for wearing over-powering perfume," he said. "This princess Erica is easier on the olfactory glands."

"I should say so. She seems more relaxed, more confident."

"It seems the Fifth Tradition, the ride around Market Square did something to restore her faith." The count nodded to a group of passing priests." We are blessed to have not one royal family member, but *three* with us here today."

"Indeed."

Chang and *Chong*, two skew-eyed footmen from Indifference, lugged Entitlement's oldest honorary centenarian, one hundred and seventeen year-old *Old Man Brooger*, up the steps, supporting him with their hands under his armpits. Count Russell shook the super-centenarian's hand, ever so gently, so as not to break a bone, and enunciated clearly: "Mis-ter Bro-oger, how-lovely-to-see-you."

"Oh, eh yesh," the old man nodded, displaying a near toothless smile, "he-he-he, good to be sheen."

"How-are-you-hol-ding-up?"

The old man winced. His teeth clacked as he spoke. "Oh, eh, I might make it through one more winter, provided we don't get another blizzard."

"We-are-hap-py-to-have-you-here."

"Eh? Oh, uh, yesh, happy to be had."

Garcilaso stood in the aisle before the second row of pews, and pointed to two seats. "Your Royal Highness, here is your preferred seating."

"Preferred?" Erica turned up her nose, "I *prefer* front row seats, Mr. Garcilaso."

"I am sorry, Ma'am. That is above my pay scale." He bowed, and walked away.

Queen Mother heard her granddaughter's raspy voice, turned, and reached for her hand. "My dear, and Buzz, how handsome he always looks."

"Hello, GranMarguerite."

Erica kissed her grandmother's cheek. "How are you, GranMarguerite?"

"I am alive. I am holding up."

"Good, good. Stay steady."

"It is always a pleasure to see you, my dear," she smiled. "You look so sophisticated. Both of you."

Buzz took Queen Mother's hand, and kissed it. "You seem spry as ever, Ma'am. We should sit down." Buzz moved forward. "We're blocking the aisle."

"I should have seen that." Erica sat down, and set her purse on the floor.

Buzz removed his cap, and settled into a seat behind an enormous hat. "Could it get any bigger?" he whispered.

Erica laid her gloves on her purse, and set the purse at her feet. "At least you have leg room, Buzz. That's *Lady Celestina*—Lord Cnute's wife."

Lady Cnute heard the princess, turned, and smiled. "Your Royal Highness—you've gained weight."

Erica was not pleased with Lady Cnute's lack of discretion. She smiled, anyway. "Thank you for noticing, Lady Cnute."

Buzz nodded. "Hello, Lady Cnute."

"Sir Buzz, hello." Your Royal Highness, keeping the weight off, that's the hard part. Isn't it?"

"Yes," Erica smiled.

"I know where of I speak. I have lost and gained the same ten pounds several times. Enjoy the ceremony." She turned, and struck up a conversation with Lady *Dragglesdorp.*

"I'm glad we're not in the front row." Erica grabbed Buzz's hand. "The air up there is sour."

George Woolsey entered the vestibule late, and approached his wife. "I had to go all the way to the Tinder Box," he grabbed her hand, "come on. Let's go."

181

"The Runners are here, George. You have to say hello."

"Erica and Buzz don't care if I say hello."

"You're wrong. Just say hello, and we'll take our seats."

"You make me do some of the stupidest things, Avorah."

"There they are, behind Lady Cnute, go say hello."

"Which hat is Lady Cnute?"

"The biggest," Lady Woolsey pointed, "the bird's nest."

Woolsey approached the princess, and nodded. "Your Royal Highness," he kissed her hand, "Erica, delighted to see you."

"Uncle George—how are you?"

Buzz rose from the pew. "Lord Woolsey, hello."

"Good to see you, lad," Woolsey took Buzz's hand.

Lady Cnute heard the ruckus, and turned. "Lady Avorah, how good of you to join us."

"Why would I not join you? I am Her Majesty's godmother."

"But of course…"

"Come George, we should find our seats." Lady Woolsey smiled, and walked away on her husband's arm.

Two fledglings flew out of Lady Cnute's hat, and fluttered about, creating a stir among the congregation. "Buzz," Erica pointed, "look at that."

"Look at what?"

"Didn't you see the birds."

"What birds?"

"Never mind. You can be slow. Sometimes I wonder how you got your chauffeur's license."

"What is it I'm supposed to look at?"

"They're gone. Two calliopes just flew out of Lady Cnute's hat."

"The musical instrument?"

"No, Buzz, calliopes are birds, a genus of hummingbird."

"I thought a calliope was a musical instrument."

"There they go. You see them?"

"Yes, now that I know what I'm looking for. How do you know they're calliopes?"

"When Erica and I were young, GranMarguerite taught us the names of every bird on the palace grounds. Their brightly colored tail feathers tell me they are male, and they're ready to mate."

"With each other?"

"No, Buzz, not with each other. They're looking for females."

"They're not going to find them in here."

"Most unlikely." Erica reached for her purse, and saw on the floor what looked like a pearl, triggering memories of the coronation. She checked her lobes to make sure her pearl earrings were in place.

"Is everything all right, Erica?"

"Everything is fine, Buzz." Erica took his hand, "I never expected to be here in this sanctuary again, so soon after the coronation."

Buzz kissed her hand. "We've come a long way, baby—you and me."

Outside the cathedral, a black carriage, drawn by four white horses, pulled up under the east portico, mirrored under the west portico by a white carriage, drawn by four *black* horses, pulling to a stop. The bride and groom stepped out, entered the cathedral through separate wings, and waited in the wings for their moment in the spotlight.

Lady Woolsey nudged her husband. "Don't forget, George, you are giving the bride away."

"I haven't forgotten, Avorah."

"Uncross your legs, George. You'll get cramps again." Lady Woolsey checked her watch. "Shouldn't you be heading out?"

"I guess so," Woolsey kissed his wife, and walked away.

Count Russell sat down in his seat, next to Queen Mother, as the organist started playing *The Wedding March.* All eyes turned to the bride, draped in white from head to toe, covered in thousands of beads, bobs, and bows, walking to the altar, on the arm of her godfather, Lord George Woosley.

Nanny Bickerstaff led Possessa and Gezealous to their seats in the side chapel, and settled in, late. Nanny Needlepinch, seated to Queen Mother's right, made sure she had nine hours of sleep the previous night, to assure she would stay awake. She smiled, as Pristine walked past. "My Queen, Pristine," she nudged Queen Mother, "she's the perfect bride."

"Yes, she is." Queen Mother smiled.

Lady Woolsey could not contain her pride. "Seeing George in his ceremonial dress reminds me how handsome he was when we first met," she told the woman seated to her right—"so handsome."

Erica tugged on Buzz's arm. "Look at her gown."

"It's lovely."

"It's a Mío original."

Lady Cnute turned. "I read in *Ladies' Monthly,* it's laced with ten thousand beads."

"That is a lot of beads. Thank you, Lady Cnute."

"It took sixteen seamstress four months to sew."

"Thank you."

"You are welcome. Lady Cnute turned around.

"I'd better be careful what I say," Erica whispered into Buzz's ear, "apparently, she has the hearing of an owl. Look at that train—six train carriers. I didn't even have a gown."

"We had a beautiful wedding, Erica."

"Our wedding was nothing like this. It was simple."

"Simple, intimate, and much nicer than this."

"When Pristine and I were little, we dreamed of a big wedding. I guess some dreams don't come true."

"You're the one who insisted we elope. You wouldn't wait for your grandfather to change his mind, or die."

"Grandpa Poldi was stuck on tradition. He would never have blessed our union."

Buzz took her hand. "We could have waited. The best part of our wedding was that I got to keep you."

"Buzz, you are so romantic. I love you."

"Me too. Let's watch the ceremony."

While crossing her ankles, Erica bumped the chair in front of her by accident. Anxiety-ridden over the pomp and circumstance, she pulled a sprig of Baby's breath out of her hair, and shredded it, tossing it bit by bit to the floor. "Erica," Buzz took her hand, "stay calm."

Sixteen maids of honor followed the bride up the aisle, and positioned themselves in a semi-circle before the altar, where the groom waited, in full Tolerance regalia. Count Russell jumped out of his seat. "Oh no, I forgot, I'm the ring bearer." He hastened to the altar, and stepped on his mark the precise moment the groom arrived.

The orchestra conductor brought the wedding march to a close, and Bishop Martens began the officiacion: "Dearly beloved, we are gathered here today to join together these two souls in holy matrimony."

Buzz leaned in to his wife. Pieces of minced Baby's breath lay at her feet. "Remember, Erica, emotion is a luxury a princess cannot afford."

"I am the spare, Buzz," she tossed a stem on the floor, "never before have I been more aware of that. All this attention lavished on Pristine—I didn't even have a bridesmaid."

"You had two bridesmaids."

"We paid them, off the street."

"It worked out well in the end, didn't it?"

"We paid a stranger to be our witness. We picked him up at the hotel bar."

"We're happily married, aren't we?"

"Are we?" Erica reached into her purse, and pulled out a small vial.

"You don't need pills now."

"Just a couple." Erica opened the vial, and shook several tablets into her hand.

Buzz grabbed her wrist, ever so gently. "No more than two, Erica."

"Three."

"Two. Three will make you dizzy."

Erica trembled, as she tried to pick up three tablets. "I forgot to mention it…"

"Mention what?"

"Pomp is one of my triggers."

"Now you tell me." Buzz handed her two tablets, dropped the rest into the vial, replaced the lid, and handed it to her. "Two is all you need."

"I hate you, Buzz."

"I love you, Erica."

"Even Dr. Pastilla let me take four."

"I'm not Dr. Pastilla." Buzz dropped the vial into her purse. "Let's watch the ceremony."

"I hate you, Buzz Runner." Erica popped the pills, and gave him the same forced smile she held in reserve for the Press.

"Relax, sweetheart."

"I hate you."

Bishop Martens stood in front of the stain glass window, lifted his arms, and his sleeves expanded like the wings of an eagle. "If there be anyone here who has reason to believe these two souls should not be joined together in holy matrimony," he scanned the sanctuary, with backup help from the youthful choirboys' eyesight, "let him speak now, or forever hold his peace."

Erica was itching to raise her hand. The thought of losing her sister to a man had bewildered her. Buzz held her in her seat, with gentle force. "Sweethart," he whispered, "bite your tongue."

"I don't like the taste of blood, Buzz."

"Bite gently. The bishop said may *he* speak, not she."

"He also said, speak now, or forever hold your peace."

"May *he* speak, or forever hold *his* peace, is what he said—not *your* peace."

"I am tired of holding my peace, Buzz."

"Bite your tongue." He kissed her cheek, "your pills will kick in soon."

"I hate you right now."

"I still love you."

"I hate you."

"I love you more."

"I hate you more."

"I love you more."

"I still hate you, Buzz."

"I still hate you more, Erica."

"I love you"—Erica sneered—"you tricked me."

"So I did," Buzz kissed her hand. "Watch the ceremony."

Lady Cnute turned, and raised a finger to her lips—"Your Royal Highness—shush!"

"Did Lady Cnute just shush me?"

"I believe she did. We needed to be shushed, Erica. Watch the ceremony."

Bishop Martens spread his arms. "Who giveth this woman?"

Lord Woolsey sucked in his stomach, and held his breath. "I do."

Nanny Needlepinch perked up when she heard the words I do. "Oh no," she cried, "I missed it."

Queen Mother lowered her lorgnette. "You didn't miss it, Needlepinch. That was Lord Woolsey."

"Nudge me if I doze off again, Ma'am."

"Perk your ears, Needlepinch. Don't depend on me."

Nanny drifted off again, but the words 'I do' remained on her radar.

Bishop Martens continued. "Your Majesty, Queen Pristine Marguerite Regina Agarapina Henriette Goldspinner, do you take Prince *Godwyn Gottlieb Friedman Bonheur of Grace*, Defender of the Faith, to be your consort king, your lawfully wedded husband, for richer or poorer, in sickness and in health, forsaking all others until the end of your days?"

Pristine looked into Godwyn's eyes, and saw her reflection. Assured he would never go bald, get fat, or lose his teeth, she smiled. "I do."

"I caught one," Nanny lit up, anxious to catch the next.

"Defender of the Faith, Prince Godwyn Gottlieb Friedman Bonheur of Grace, do you take Her Majesty, Queen Pristine Marguerite Regina Agarapina Henriette Goldspinner of Entitlement, to be your lawfully wedded wife, your sovereign, your Queen, in sickness and in health, for richer and for poorer, forsaking all others until the end of your days?"

Queen Mother nudged Nanny. "It's I do time, Needlepinch."

Godwyn gazed into Pristine's eyes, and smiled. "I do."

"I caught both I do's." Nanny caught a tear with her hankie, blew her nose, and slipped the hankie into her pocket.

"May I have the rings, please?" Bishop Martens held out his hand.

Count Russell stepped forward with a pillow, upon which rested two bands of gold. Bishop Martens blessed the rings, and slipped them onto the bride's and the groom's fingers. He lifted his arms, and nodded. "Defender, you may kiss the bride."

To the accompaniment of *Love, Love You Do,* Godwyn lifted the bride's veil, and kissed her on the mouth, causing the congregation to whistle, and applaud, as the newlyweds walked down the aisle. The commotion joggled Nanny Needlepinch back to life, so she stayed alert to wink at Pristine, as he passed, on the arm of her prince. The bride and groom exited the cathedral through the vestibule, and stepped onto the portico, where the Queen's secretary waited.

"Ma'am, it is time to toss your bouquet." Mrs. Thornecroft pulled the bride off the groom's arm, and escorted her to a platform, where Abel Handsforth stood, before a crowd of uncontrollable females. He took the bride's hand, and helped her onto the platform.

Meanwhile, back in the sanctuary, Buzz took Erica's hand. "You've calmed down," he said.

"Three would've kicked in quicker."

"It was a lovely ceremony. Wasn't it, Erica?"

"It was."

Buzz lifted the princess out of her seat, ducked her, and kissed her on the lips, right there in the pews. Startled, she fell into his arms, to grand applause.

"I've got you, Erica," Buzz fanned her with his programme.

"Buzz," Erica looked up, "why are you fanning me?"

"I thought you had swooned."

"No—I wasn't expecting a kiss."

"I'm fanning you because I love you."

"Oh, Buzz, I love you too."

Buzz walked Erica out the sanctuary, behind Lord and Lady Cnute. Erica whispered, "why would anyone wear a bird's nest on their head?"

Buzz shrugged his shoulders. "I guess it takes all kinds."

Hand in hand, the couple stepped onto the colonnade to shouts, and whistles, and smiled for the photographers. "Long live the princess," the crowd shouted—"can we have a word with you?"

Mrs. Thornecroft stood on the pen-ultimate cathedral step, and still, she was taller than her employer, the Queen, standing on the platform. "Ladies," she shouted, "time for the bouquet toss. Here we go."

Pristine turned her back to the crowd, tossed the bouquet, and hit Mina in the head.

"I caught it," Mina shouted, "I caught the bouquet."

Pristine giggled, and covered her mouth. "I never did learn how to throw."

"I'm next to the altar," Mina waved the bouquet over her head like a teenage cheerleader with a pom-pom, "I'm next!"

"Mina?—next at the altar?" Uppsola laughed, "miracles do occur."

Pristine winked, "wedded bliss is never too late."

After the newlyweds stepped into the nuptial carriage, Erica and Buzz found themselves *The* Number Two attraction. Guards held fans, photographers, and reporters at bay, as the couple stepped onto the colonade. Eight guards escorted them down the steps to the Locomobile, idling at the carriage stop. Buzz thanked guards for cranking her up, and helped Erica into the passenger compartment. "Get in, my love, and let's go."

Erica settled in on the bench, Buzz closed the door, hopped into the driver's seat, and locked the doors. "Safe at last," he assured the princess, "on our way home."

"Good escape, huh, Buzz?"

"It sure was." Buzz shifted into first, stepped on the gas, and off they went. Buzz looked at Erica in the rear view mirror. "Are we going to attend the reception?"

Erica frowned. "I have no interest in those people."

"You are first in line to the throne. You should make an appearance."

"I have no interest in consorting with people, and I *don't* shake hands."

"How about we show up, and stay ten minutes?"

"All right. Ten minutes—no more."

"You are my queen. We shall do as you deem."

"I am not a queen, Buzz. I'm a princess."

"You're *my* princess. You are also my Queen," Buzz shifted gears, and drove off. "That was funny," he chuckled, "over the noise, I couldn't quite make out what those ladies said to you."

"The tall one asked me why I wasn't with my bridesmaids, and the fat one wanted to know why I wasn't wearing my bridal gown."

"What did you say?"

"I told her my bridesmaids were with my sister, and I detest white."

"That's funny."

"It's absolutely true. I prefer color."

The bells of the old cathedral tower rang out across the valley, as guests made their way to the reception, in the palace grand hall. Outside on the terrace, to the east, a bar had been set up. To the west stood a pedestal, showcasing a spectacular six-tier cake. The bar, and the cake pedestal, were positioned at opposite ends of the terrace, each in front of a fountain, into which carved granite lions spued champagne.

Guests mingled, and practices their networking skills. The newlyweds were surprised to run into the princess among the guests, and Sir Buzz, and later Francis, wearing a white suit, white shoes, and a white Bolero hat. After cutting the cake, opening gifts, and mingling with guests, the bride and groom disappeared—with icing on their faces.

Half an hour later, guests gathered into the grand hall to see the newlyweds appear at the top of the staircase, dressed in everyday sportswear. They descended the steps to Mr. Kensington, standing at the base, hand on the Newell post. Pristine took the butler's arm, Godwyn secured a link with the other, and the trio walked out, onto the terrace. Outside, Mr. Kensington released the couple, nearly falling, if not for Fetchett's quick reactions. Guests tossed rice, as the newlyweds walked to the carriage house. To the sound of echoing bells, the coachman whisked the newlyweds away to Play, where Pristine would remember Nanny Needlepinch's advice, lay back, and think of Abundance.

CHAPTER XXIV

Goodbye to Leniency

Orderic Tibbons accepted Queen Pristine's offer to serve as palace butler, and immediately got to work orchestrating the Bonheur family's move to Entitlement. Meanwhile, the Defender of the Faith, Prince Godwyn of Grace, honeymooned at the You-Bet King's Inn in Play, with his bride, Her Majesty, the Queen.

Back in Leniency, Nanny Nellie Bickerstaff was packed, and ready to catch her train to Fou. She approached the butler in the foyer, and set her suitcase on the floor. "Mr. Tibbons, it has been a pleasure working with you these last seven years."

"The pleasure is all mine, Miss Bickerstaff." Mr. Tibbons shook her hand. "You will write, let us know how you are making out?"

"I will send a postcard, as soon as I settle in. Mother McMultiply's baby is due next month, so I might be very busy. I pray I have not taken on more than I can handle—seven girls. This time, they're hoping for a boy."

"Give it time, and remember to breathe."

The sound of horses' hooves crunching the gravel came up the drive. Nanny looked out the door, flung her carry-on bag over her shoulder, and let out an oof—"my carriage is here."

"Let me carry your suitcase," Mr. Tibbons followed her out, and delivered the suitcase to the coachman. "Miss Bickerstaff," he turned to her, "Possessa and Gezealous won't admit it, but they are going to miss you."

"Thank you for saying so, Mr. Tibbons. That warms my heart. May I give you a hug?"

"Of course you may." He embraced her. "We have worked so well together these past seven years, I'm sad to see you go."

"Saying goodbye is always sad, Mr. Tibbons," she squeezed him tighter, "I shall miss you terribly."

"May the wind be always at your back, Nellie Bickerstaff," he pried himself loose. "May God look over you always."

"Thank you. And may Entitlement be everything you ever hoped it would be—and more. God bless you, Mr. Tibbons."

The coachman helped Nanny into the carriage. She waved goodbye, and was driven to Leniency Station, where she boarded her train to Fou. Now the responsibility of keeping Possessa and Gezealous in line rested upon the shoulders of Mr. Tibbons. Possessa tried to bribe him to purchase cigarettes, something the savy butler refused to do. Gezealous tried continually to convince him to take sides—namely hers, something else he refused to do.

Moving day—the action began early. As early as seven o'clock, Mr. Tibbons had the sisters bathed and dressed, ready to be driven to their friends to bid them adieu.

Possessa saw to it she always spoke first. "Mr. Tibbons, if we're moving today, how come you want us to spend the day with our friends?"

"I said the morning, Possessa, not the day. I don't want anything to get in the way of the movers. Today is lockup day, as well."

"What's lockup?"

"Lockup is the day I hand the keys over to the estate agent. You have all morning to be with your friends. *Benjamin* is going to drive you to Melissa's first. From there, he'll take you to see Denise, and whomever else you wish to say goodbye to, but I want you back by noon."

"Noon?"

"Yes, noon, Gezealous. Do you understand?"

"Yes, Sir."

"Possessa?"

"I understand."

"Good." He ushered them out the door, "now into the limo with you."

As Benjamin drove the sisters out, the moving van entered the gates. The driver stopped at the front porch. Two men jumped to the ground, and rolled up the van's back door. Two more grabbed stacks of pre-cut boxes, walked them into the house, and announced their arrival.

All morning, the movers carried laden boxes to the van. Mr. Tibbons, twice the age of any of the moving men, proved himself just as agile. He guided the movers around chandeliers, down stairs, around corners, and out the doors. As the town clock struck twelve, the van drove out the gates, filled with the Bonheur family's possessions, hopes, and dreams.

Benjamin and the sisters returned to Villa Leniency late, and avoided detection by slipping in through the service entrance. On tiptoes, the sisters walked through the empty hall, up the stairs, to their bedroom. As fate would have it, Mr. Tibbons had been detained in his office, on the phone, and was none the wiser when he emerged at ten past twelve to find them in their rooms. Mr. Tibbons bid Mr. Benjamin adieu, and let him know how sorry he was, the Queen of Entitlement requires but one chauffeur.

Minutes later, a carriage pulled up to the veranda. A well-dressed gentleman stepped to the ground, stepped onto the porch, and poked his head in the door. "Hello? Estate agent—anybody home?"

Mr. Tibbons approached the banister, and looked down into the foyer. "Good afternoon," he descended the stairs, "you must be Mr. Cuddlemey."

"I am, estate agent *Wolfgang Cuddlemey* at your service." He held out his card. "You must be Mr. Tibbons."

Mr. Tibbons stepped onto the parquet, hand extended. "I am," he took the card, "Mr. Cuddlemey, how do you do?"

"Very well, thank you."

"Come in, please."

"Your villa has a handsome approach. How many acres is the estate?"

"Sixteen. Not much hospitality I can offer you;. The movers just left."

"Are you ready for me to take you to the station?"

"Let me see if the girls are ready. Excuse me." Mr. Tibbons walked to the staircase.

"Lovely floorplan, high ceilings, beautiful woodwork. Is it early Grace?"

"Yes."

"Mind if I take a look?"

"Be my guest." Mr. Tibbons stood at the Newell post, and looked up the stairs. "Possessa, Gezealous, our carriage is here."

'SLAM.' The sound reverberated through the empty villa.

Gezealous darted down the corridor, dragging a doll, followed by her sister. "Possessa, you miserable witch"—Gezealous clomped down the stairs: 'clomp, clomp, clomp, clomp, clomp, clomp, clomp, clomp, clomp, clomp, clomp, clomp.' She spun at the Newell post, followed by her sister, and raced toward Mr. Tibbons, with the doll held out in front of her. "Look what Possessa did to my doll."

Without touching it, Mr. Tibbons examined the doll. "What did she do?"

"She dyed her hair black, and she got it all over her neck and her blouse. You ruined my favorite doll."

"You brat," Possessa made an ugly face, "she was ruined already."

"You made her ugly. You ruined her."

"She was always ugly—just like you."

Mr. Tibbons took a closer look. "Her hair is tangled."

"Tell her she has to buy me a new doll, Mr. Tibbons."

"Girls, we have company." Mr. Tibbons brought his finger to his lips.

The estate agent looked into the room from behind an arch, and smiled, "good afternoon, ladies."

"Possessa, Gezealous, I want you to meet Mr. Cuddelmey."

"How do you do?" The sisters turned into angels, and curtseyed.

"Th young lady in the red dress is Miss Possessa, Mr. Cuddlemey, and the one with the doll is Miss Gezealous. Mr. Cuddlemey will be driving us to the station, girls. Now take your doll upstairs with you, Gezealous, and bring down your suitcase—both of you."

"Why do we have to bring down our suitcases?"

"Because the footmen have been released."

"You're the butler. That's *your* job."

"You may find relief once we get to Entitlement, Possessa, but for now, I want you to bring your suitcase down, and deliver it to the coachman."

Possessa clomped back up the stairs. "They have a dozen footmen at the palace."

"And they're cute."

"Stop dreaming, Gezealous. Bring your suitcase downstairs.

"Why should we?"

"Because I said so. "NOW GO!"

Gezealous jumped. She hastened up the stairs, behind her sister. He's never shouted at us like that before, she thought, he must be really mad.

Agent Cuddlemey stepped back into the foyer. "This is a fine villa indeed, Mr. Tibbons; gracious living at its best."

"I am afraid you are not seeing much grace here at the moment, Mr. Cuddlemey."

"What can one expect of youth? They are in pain until the limbs stop growing. Are you ready to lock up?"

"As soon as the girls bring down their suitcases."

"I will lock up the service entrance, if you will hand me the keys."

"It's locked. I locked every window and door, except the front. Ninety-eight windows, and seven doors, Mr. Cuddlemey. Excuse me."

A bolt of lightning split the sky, followed by the loud crackle of thunder. Cuddlemey looked out the open door. "It looks like that 50% chance of rain the weatherman predicted just turned into 100%, Mr. Tibbons. It's pouring rain."

"Clouds are rolling in from the east." Mr. Tibbons returned to the foyer. "It's a good thing the movers finished before it started.

Sovereign sized raindrops splattered the windowpanes, like a beating drum.

"Confucius says, 'best thing to do when it rains, let it rain'."

"Leave it to a Confused to come up with that one, Mr. Cuddlemey. Excuse me, while see what's keeping the girls." Mr. Tibbons walked to the stairs, and hollered, "girls, time to go. We have a train to catch."

'SLAM.' The sound reverberated down the corridor.

"We're coming." Possessa dragged her suitcase down the stairs, 'plop, plop, plop, plop, plop, plop, plop, plop, plop, plop, plop, plop,' followed a minute later by Gezealous, 'plop, plop, plop, plop, plop, plop, plop, plop, plop, plop, plop, plop." They stopped at the base of the stairs, and looked out the door, at the pouring rain. Possessa placed her hands on her hips. "I'm not going to deliver my suitcase in the rain." She shook her head, "no way."

"If Possessa isn't going out, then neither am I." Gezealous sat down on her suitcase, and watched the coachman coax the horses to the portico.

"Slip these on, and hop into the carriage," Mr. Tibbons handed the girls their impermeables. The sisters put them on, and watched, as the coachman secured their luggage. "Take your umbrellas, here. Now get into the carriage." He ushered the sisters out the door.

Mr. Tibbons started to hand the ring of keys to the estate agent, but then something in him tweaked. "Might I lock up, Mr. Cuddlemey—just this once."

"Certainly, Mr. Tibbons, if that is your wish."

Locking the front door of the villa he had run for half a century became something of a spiritual event for Mr. Tibbons. It was a moment to be remembered. Whilst one life was closing, another, just across the Gracine Strait, was opening. "You know, I have been the butler in this villa for fifty years, Mr. Cuddlemey, and never once have I found it necessary to lock the front door. Today was a first." He handed the keys to the agent.

"I've heard that before with these grand houses. The gates are secure, the walls are impenetrable, and there is always someone home guarding the fort."

"I am a lucky man, Mr. Cuddlemey." He turned to Gezealous, "I told you to get into the carriage. What are you doing?"

"Nothing. I'm going."

"Never point an umbrella, Gezealous. You could poke someone's eye out."

"I told her that, too, Mr. Tibbons, but she doesn't listen."

"I said I won't do it again."

The coachman helped the sisters into the carriage. Mr. Tibbons looked back, and took a nostalgic trip down Memory Lane. "I am going to miss the old place," he said, "it's been a part of my life for over fifty years."

"I will see to it it goes into good hands, Mr. Tibbons. Let's go. We have a train to catch." Mr. Cuddlemey followed the butler into the carriage, and they were driven out the gates of Leniency for the last time.

CHAPTER XXV
Train of Thought to a New Life

The rain continued, as the coachman pulled up to the portico over Leniency Station. He unfurled a step, and helped Possessa and Gezealous onto the pavement, followed by Mr. Tibbons, and Mr. Cuddlemey, all happy to be dry. The coachman unbelted the suitcases, and a porter rolled in a cart. "Destination, Sir?"

"Abundance, please—Entitlement Station."

"Entitlement it is, Sir." The porter affixed tags to the suitcases, and tossed them onto a rolling band.

"Don't forget your brolly, Miss," the coachman handed Gezealous her umbrella.

"Thank you, Sir." Gezealous struggled to keep her rucksack over her shoulder. She tucked the umbrella under her arm, and followed the entourage into the train terminal.

"Your tickets are inside this envelope." Mr. Cuddlemey handed the envelope to Mr. Tibbons, and checked the clock over the forty foot tall archway. "Your train departs from track 2, at twelve-fifty-six—that's twenty-three minutes from now."

"Thank you, Mr. Cuddlemey." Mr. Tibbons slipped the envelope inside his jacket.

"Let's get you to track 2, Mr. Tibbons." Cuddlemey checked the departure board, and took a look around. "This is it—right here—track 2."

"Ladies first," Possessa ran to the train, followed by her sister.

"Cabin 6," shouted Cuddlemey. "Good luck, ladies."

Mr. Tibbons shook the agent's hand. "Thank you for the lift to the station, and for setting up the travel arrangements, Mr. Cuddlemey. I feel much obliged."

"It was my pleasure, Mr. Tibbons. I see it as my way of serving the

Crown. I wish you good luck in your new home. I hear Entitlement is enchanting."

From the back of the train, standing by the caboose, the station master bellowed: "A-a-all a-bo-o-oard."

"That's my call, Mr. Tibbons."

"Mr. Cuddlemey, it is my wish Villa Leniency falls into good hands."

"It already has, Mr. Tibbons. I have assigned the account to my star saleswoman, Miss *Donna Sloan.* She serves only the finest clientele: dukes, barons, viscounts, and Lords. Miss Sloan was instrumental in helping Princess Erica locate her castle in Gruntle."

"That is good to know."

"With the providence it has, Villa Leniency will certainly land in the best of hands. You had better board," he extended a hand, "Mr. Tibbons, may your new home be all you hope it will be."

"Thank you. And may Grace always be with you, Your Grace."

"A-a-all a-b-o-oard," the station master bellowed his last call.

"Goodbye, Mr. Tibbons, and God bless."

Travelers hugged and kissed loved ones goodbye, and hopped on the train, followed by Mr. Tibbons, proceeding to cabin six, on his way to adventure.

"La-a-ast ca-a-all." The station master blew his whistle. He waved his semaphore, made a telepathic connection with the conductor, and the colossal iron wheels started to churn, sending out tufts of steam. Mr. Tibbons slid the door to cabin six open, and found Possessa and Gezealous, seated in the window seats, arguing over who gets to sit facing which direction.

The door slid shut. "I want you two to stop arguing. We are in public here," Mr. Tibbons reprimanded the sisters.

"But the door's closed."

"All the more reason, Possessa."

"She started it."

"I did not."

"You did so, Possessa."

Mr. Tibbons placed his his attaché, and his hat, in the overhead hammock. "Stop arguing," he said, "it's unladylike." He set his coat on the seat, and approached Possessa, boarding pass in hand. "Excuse me, Miss, it appears you are sitting in a seat reserved in my name." He held up the ticket. "Yes, it says right here: Tibbons, Orderic, 6-A window."

"But I want to see where we're going, Mr. Tibbons."

"You can look out the window from any seat, Possessa."

"Not from over there I can't."

"We seem to have a dilemma. Three passengers want to sit by the window, yet there are only two window seats."

"Me and Possessa should sit by the window 'cause we're young, and we're learning."

"That's *Possessa and I*, Gezealous. What would you say if I were to tell you I should sit by the window, 'cause I am older, and I need to be in the sun to keep my blood flowing?"

Possessa got up, and sat down in a middle seat. Gezealous jumped to fill the vacancy, facing forward. Mr. Tibbons set his gloves on the pull-out tray table, and sat down, facing Gezealous. "The solution is obvious," he said, "Gezealous, you sit facing forward for the first half of the journey, and Possessa, you sit facing forward the second half."

"How come Possessa always gets to be first?"

"Because I'm older. Mr. Tibbons, don't you want to look out?"

"Thank you, Possessa. I appreciate your consideration."

"I was only asking."

"I have traveled this route before." Mr. Tibbons got up, and sat down next to the door. "You take the window seats. Besides, I imagine you'll both be exploring, so what difference does it make?"

"You're swell, Mr. Tibbons. Thank you," Possessa got up, went to sit in the windowseat.

"I have waited a lifetime to hear that. Thank you, Possessa."

The train pulled out of the station, and the sisters watched the world go by. Mr. Tibbons closed his eyes, took a deep breath, and went within. "This is a good time for prayer," he said. "I invite you to join me."

"Do we have to?"

"I cannot make you, Gezealous, but you might patronize me."

"All right." The sisters closed their eyes, and folded their hands.

"As this train pulls out of Leniency, it carries with it all our hopes and dreams. Our lives in Tolerance are now a thing of the past. Everything we have learned over the years, we take with us, as we begin new lives, in hope it will serve us well. Let us be vessels of love, open to change, understanding, and forgiveness, that we may take in the blessings that await us, and bring about peace wherever we go. In the name of the Father, I know it is already done. And so it is. Amen."

Possessa opened her eyes first. "Amen."

Gezealous followed—"wow! We're already out of the train yard."

Mr. Tibbons smiled. "We are off on our new adventure. Now that you girls are maturing, it won't be long before you no longer need a nanny."

"We don't need one now."

"I beg to differ."

"I'm glad Nanny Bickerstaff isn't coming with us. She was mean."

Gezealous sat back. "She was always telling us what to do. And she wouldn't let us go out alone."

"Apparently you both still need somebody to tell you what to do.

"Na-unh," Possessa shook her head. "We don't need a nanny."

"Nanny Bickerstaff was more than fair with you."

Gezealous frowned. "She was not. She was mean to us."

"Your succession of governesses seems to have led you to believe they were *all* mean."

"They *were* all mean," Possessa nodded.

"We only had two."

"I remember three, Gezealous. Nanny Crabtree—you sent her running."

"That was a long time ago."

"Yeah. We were just kids."

"Don't think you can take advantage of me, now that Nanny Bickerstaff is gone."

"We don't think it. We know it."

"I am not joking, Possessa. Things are going to be different once we settle into our new home. Nanny Needlepinch is going to be in charge of you."

"Nanny Needlepinch?—she's like a hundred years old."

"She is not so old she cannot spank you."

"Spank us?"

"Do we *have to* have a nanny?"

"Yes. Someone has to keep you out of trouble."

"We don't wanna stay out of trouble. Staying out of trouble is boring."

Gezealous rose from her seat. "Uncle Orderic, I'm hungry. Will you give me a sovereign so I can get something to eat?"

"What did you do with your pocket money?"

"She spent it."

"And I am not your uncle. You are to call adults by their title, and surname, Gezealous."

"We need to eat, Mr. Tibbons. It's past noon."

"Ple-ease," Gezealous held out her hand, "give me a sovereign, and I promise I'll go away."

"You don't have to beg, Gezealous. He's not gonna let us starve."

Mr. Tibbons pulled a crown out of his pocket. "Go," he handed it to Possessa, "go with my blessing."

"How come you're giving the money to Possessa? I'm the one who asked for it."

"Possessa is more responsible. She will share it with you. I want both of you back here in half an hour—with change."

"Change?"

"Yes, change. And while you are in the dining car, bring me a bag of salted pretzels, a ginger ale, and a Cash-chew-bar."

"There won't be any money left for us."

"There had better be. What do you say?"

"A bag of pretzels, a Cash-chew-bar, and a ginger ale."

"Thank you, is what you say. And I said salted pretzels.'"

"Thank you," Possessa curtseyed.

"Salted, Possessa."

"Yes, Sir," Possessa slid the door open, and her sister followed her out.

"Half an hour," he hollered, as the door shut, "never mind." He got up, and went to sit in the window seat. "How long has it been since I've traveled on a train?" He took in a deep breath. "I can't even remember."

Forty-eight minutes later, the cabin door slid open, and Possessa and Gezealous entered, carrying hotdogs, pretzels, Chio-chips, Cash-chew-bars, and sodas. Mr. Tibbons released the window tray, got up, returned to the middle seat, and looked at his watch. "You are twelve minutes late. Can you explain that?"

"I told Possessa we better get back, but she wouldn't listen."

"Did you bring me what I asked for?"

Possessa nodded. "Chio-chips, a Cash-chew-bar, and a *Loca-Cola.*"

"I asked you to bring me pretzels, and a ginger ale."

"They were out of pretzels, and all they had to drink was sarsparilla and *Loca-Cola.*"

"Where's my change?"

Gezealous set the goods on the tray, pulled the wrapper off a candybar, sat down, and took a bite of sweet before moving on to her hotdog.

"My change, Possessa?"

"Oh, I forgot." Possessa reached into her pocket, and handed Mr. Tibbons three sovereigns, six coppers, and a farthing.

"That's it?—that's all the change I get?"

"That's what the lady gave me."

"From a crown I get three sovereigns, six coppers, and a farthing?"

"That's all the woman gave her, Mr. Tibbons."

"Life en route is expensive." He slipped the coins into his pocket.

Possessa finished her chips, and hotdog, washed them down with sarsparilla, and bit into a Choc-o-la-teer bar.

Mr. Tibbons watched. "That is a lot of food, Possessa, but not very nutritious."

Gezealous wiped ketchup off her chin. "We're still growing, Mr. Tibbons."

"Did you see the daffodil fields?"

"Nope," Possessa kept chewing.

Gezealous dropped a chip, picked it up, and ate it. "I didn't see any."

"We were looking at people."

"Will we be traveling through Grace?"

"Only through border towns, Gezealous."

"Mr. Tibbons, I'm bored. Isn't there anything else to do on a train besides eat?"

"They should have a bowling alley. It'd be the perfect place."

"Read your book, Possessa."

"I don't feel like reading. It'll make me train sick."

"Then I invite you to be quiet, and count cows."

CHAPTER XXVI

A Timely Arrival

Four hours later, after two more visits to the dining car, the train pulled into Entitlement Station. Gezealous jumped out of her seat, and proceeded to gather her things. "We're here," she hollered, "let's go."

"Sit down, Gezealous, until the train comes to a full stop. You too, Possessa."

The massive iron wheels ground to a halt, sending out tufts of cumulous steam. Mr. Tibbons closed his attaché, got up, and put his hat on his head. "Now you may get up."

"All we need do now is find Mr. Crankshaft."

"Who's Mr. Crankshaft?" Possessa swung her carry-on over her shoulder.

"The <u>Q</u>ueen's chauffeur, Dumbo."

"I'm *so so-rry*—I forgot."

"Gezealous, I would prefer you not address your sister in that manner."

"I'm sorry, Mr. Tibbons. It slipped out."

"Don't tell *me* you're sorry, tell your sister. And pick up that wrapper."

Gezealous quavered. "I'm *so so-rry.* I forgot."

"Pick up your trash, and let's go."

"Mr. Crankshaft should be easy to spot, Mr. Tibbons. He's got blue eyes, and he's like seven feet tall."

"His eyes are green, Possessa."

"No they're not. They're blue."

"How would you know? You didn't even remember him."

"I just hadn't thought of him, that's all. He's fat."

"He's not fat. He's big."

"All right you two—stop it. Possessa, you go first." Mr. Tibbons ushered the sisters out the door, down the aisle. "Move along, Gezealous, you're holding up traffic."

Possessa was first to hop off the train. She pointed. "That's him. In the gray suit."

"Please refrain from pointing."

"I'm sorry."

A tall, distinguished man dressed in chauffeur's livery, nodded, and tipped his cap. "You must be the new butler." He extended a hand.

"I am. Mr. Tibbons," he shook the chauffeur's hand.

"Welcome to Entitlement, Mr. Tibbons."

"Thank you. You will remember the Bonheur sisters, Possessa and Gezealous."

"Yes, of course I remember them. Hello, girls."

The sisters curtseyed. "Good afternoon, Crank."

"I am Her Majesty's chauffeur, Ernest Crankshaft. Please call me Crank. Most do."

"I am pleased to meet you, Mr. Crank.

"No mister. Just Crank. The porter has already transferred your luggage to the Isotta, so we can get you straight home. May I take your carry-on?"

"Sure." Possessa handed him her bag first.

"We're finding relief, Mr. Tibbons," Gezealous followed.

"I understand you will be staying this time."

"I guess we'll be calling this home." They followed the chauffeur through the terminal, to the Isotta Fraschini limousine, parked at the curb.

"Mr. Tibbons, if there is anything I can do for you, please call on me. I can drive you anywhere, show you anything."

"Thank you, Mr. Crank. I may take you up on that."

"Just Crank, Mr. Tibbons—no mister."

Possessa nudged her sister's leg. "Did you hear that, Gezealous? He can drive us anywhere." Possessa noticed the rear fender appliqués, the flags of Abundance, and Consciousness, and the license plate, 1-ABC. "We'd better be nice to him," she whispered.

"Here we are." The chauffeur set the carry-on bags in the boot, opened the rear passenger compartment door, and held it open, while the three stepped inside. Crankshaft closed the door, and stepped into the driver's seat. Mr. Tibbons pushed a button, and the separation window descended. "It has been raining in Leniency again. Has it been wet here, too, Crank?"

"We've had more rain than usual this year, but it seems to have cleared." He looked in the rear view mirror. "How was your train ride?"

Silence ensued. "Girls, Mr. Crank asked how your journey was."

"No mister. Just Crank."

"It was okay." Possessa yawned, and covered her mouth. "Excuse me, I'm tired. It's been a long day."

"The train had a dining car, at least."

"We counted cows."

"It sounds like you had an enjoyable journey."

"It was a nice train. The windows were clean."

After a leisurely drive passing fields, and meadows, Crank turned onto Contentment Lane, pulled up to the guardhouse, nodded, and the gates fanned open before them. Crank drove to the portico, stopped the limousine, and pulled the hand brake.

A footman descended the steps, opened the limousine door, and bowed. "Welcome back, ladies."

"I remember you," Gezealous exclaimed, "you're Abel Handsforth."

"I am, and coming down the steps are Randall Quigley, and Gowen Fetchett. We are happy to welcome you. If you will follow us, we will take you to the wardrobe."

"All right."

Handsforth led them up the steps, inside, to respective wardrobes, where a fourth, and fifth footman took their hats, impermeables, and umbrellas. Fetchett rolled in a cart. Quigley transferred the suitcases from the boot to the cart, and together they pushed the cart to the elevator.

The palace housekeeper, a middle-aged woman dressed in a maroon frock, stood before the servants' hall mirror, checking her reflection. She brushed a lock into place, put a smile on her face, ascended the stairs to the foyer, and approached the new butler, hand extended. "Mr. Tibbons, welcome to Entitlement. I am the palace housekeeper, *Feodora Bissiby.*"

Mr. Tibbons bowed from the neck. "It is a pleasure, Miss Bissiby."

"It's missus. Married or not, here in Abundance, housekeepers are always addressed as missus. I don't know why."

"I imagine people believe more is expected of a married woman, in terms of knowledge of products, services, and such."

"I guess so. You may call me *Mrs. B.* Most people do."

Possessa and Gezealous entered the foyer, and curtseyed. "Hello, Mrs. B."

"Welcome back, girls. I should say welcome home."

"How do you do?"

"Things could not be better, now that the rain has stopped, and you have arrived. Might I give you a quick run down on palace life?"

"Please do," Mr. Tibbons nodded. "You girls may want to listen to this."

"Breakfast is served from six a.m. until ten. Come late, you will not eat until lunch, served at one. Tea and biscuits are served from four to four-thirty. At six o'clock the dressing gong is rung. Dinner is served at six-thirty. Come late, you will not eat until breakfast. May I show you to your chambers?"

"Thank you."

"I imagine you will want to freshen up."

"The girls certainly would like to."

"Handsforth, show Mr. Tibbons to his quarters."

"Yes, Ma'am. This way, Mr. Tibbons."

"Fetchett, show Miss Possessa, and Miss Gezealous, to their rooms."

"Yes, Ma'am," the footman stepped forward. "If you will follow me."

Handsforth escorted Mr. Tibbons to the elevator, while Fetchett guided the sisters up the grand staircase. Handsforth and Tibbons exited the elevator, and the butler followed the footman down a long corridor. Anxious to find out which exposure their rooms would have, Possessa and Gezealous skipped ahead, but Fetchett kept them under control.

Within minutes, each traveler was sent a footman to help unpack. Two hours after crumpets with tea, the dinner gong rang, and Possessa and Gezealous slipped into dinner attire. As their first palace dining experience, they savored a delicious dinner of onion soup, chesse souflée, cocque au Resolutión, sautéed patates with caraway seeds, creamed baby corn, and garden vegetables—followed by raspberry pudding, with vanilla sauce.

After dinner, the sisters were excused from the table. With their lives packed, they bored quickly of their books, and Gezealous's washed-up doll.

Possessa sat in the chair, yawning. "We haven't been here a day, and already, I'm bored."

"So am I." Gezealous fanned her legs on the bed. "They're not gonna unpack our stuff until tomorrow."

"I wish I'd packed our backgammon board."

"What's there to do around here? I know," Gezealous leaped off the bed. "This is a palace, isn't it?"

"Yeah." Possessa sat up. "It's a big palace."

"Let's explore. There have to be secret doors, passageways, revolving bookcases, things like that—right? We could play tricks on people."

"We might find a secret room where the Queen hides all her secrets."

"That would give us power over her."

Possessa leaped to her feet. "Why not explore? Papa and stepmother won't be back till Wednesday."

"What are we waiting for? Let's go."

The sisters looked in every room that wasn't locked. Exhausted in their search for that which was not to be found—other than two old pair of roller skates in the attic—they were asleep in their beds by ten o'clock.

Below stairs, Mrs. Bissiby was peeling onions on the butcher-block, when Mr. Tibbons walked in. "Mr. Tibbons," she smiled, "good evening."

"Good evening, Mrs. B."

"What can I do for you?"

"Some time ago, I ran across a copy of the palace blueprints in the shire's office in Leniency. I studied them carefully, but with drapes, vases, furnishings and flowers, the halls and corridors look quite different."

"They do. It took me six months just to memorize the alcoves."

"I would appreciate if, at your convenience, you might give me a tour."

"A tour would take days, Mr. Tibbons."

"Just a brief tour, below stairs for now. Whenever you have time."

"Well, I have time now." She set her knife down. "*Pinguine* can chop these onions tomorrow. Let me put them in the larder. I will be right with you." She grabbed the box, carried it to the kitchen, and her voice faded. "Shall we start with the butler's pantry?"

"That sounds like a good place to start."

She returned to the hall, walked him down a long corridor, and stopped before a door. "Mr. Kensington was not planning to retire, you know, but his stroke seems to have come at an opportune time."

"He had a stroke?"

"Oh yes, while the girls were here. It incapacitated his good arm."

"I understand he celebrated one hundred years of service last year."

"He started as a page, at eleven."

"That's an early age to give up childhood."

"The man was born to serve. The Abundite Centenarian Committee presented him with their ABC award—the Abundite Beloved Centenarian. He came home with a gold watch, and an engraved silver tray."

"Where is he now?"

"He went to go live with his folks, up north."

"His folks?"

"Oh yes, Bereaveés live long lives. I myself have been thinking of moving in with my folks in *Dead Valley*, but why would I chose to live in darkness half the year?" She fumbled with keys, and inserted several into the lock, until the door squeaked open.

"Sounds like those hinges could use some oil."

"Kensington let a few things go after his stroke. He had to."

"If you tell me where I can find an oilcan, I'll take care of that."

"I will set an oilcan on your desk before morning."

"Thank you. I appreciate that."

"Now if I could find the switch," she groped in the dark, "we might see something."

She flicked a switch, and the room lit up. "There we go. This is the butler's pantry."

"It's big," Tibbons's face lit up. "I love it."

"I will never leave Entitlement. As it is, I seldom get out the gates. I'm turning seventy next year. I'm set in my ways."

Mr. Tibbons refrained from making a comment. He noticed the candlestick telephone instead. "I assume there is a master's extension?"

"This is your private line, Mr. Tibbons. There is an extension in the king's bedchamber, the king's library, and Her Majesty's study."

Mr. Tibbons felt himself drawn to the lines of books on the shelves. "Are these record books?"

"They are. They date back to 1832."

"Mind if I take a look?"

"They're yours now. I believe Kensington made the last entry in January of '13. I have never known a more accurate record keeper. He kept a record of every dinner, party, fundraiser, every event for ninety years, including every State Fair. The archives in the storage locker go back even further, hundreds of years, should you ever get bored."

"A wall of history. This will keep me entertained for life."

"I may as well fill you in, Mr. Tibbons."

"Fill me in?"

Mrs. B. stood on the steps. "Ever since King Poldemire passed away, a peculiar vibration has hung over the palace. I am not one to voice an opinion, but the Goldspinner line holds an over-abundance of female genes, and not enough male energy. This is the age-old dilemma that haunts the family. Until recently, it had been kept a secret."

Mr. Tibbons focused on the bookspines. "Too much female blood, you say?"

"For three centuries, the royal family, and the kingdom, were run by queens—until Poldemire's coronation in 1832. If the family is to survive, Mr. Tibbons, your presence, and the presence of your prince, Defender Godwyn Bonheur of Grace, is obligatory."

Tibbons looked up. "I am happy to do what I can, Mrs. B."

She grabbed a ring of keys off a hook. "It is imperative this marriage produce at least one male heir."

"I understand. I shall do whatever is in my power to see to it that happens."

"Good. Now, would you like to see the wine cellar?"

"That would make my evening. What's in the basement?"

"The souterrain?"

"The souterrain; that is what I meant to say."

"You will find the state department there, the dignitary accommodations, Communications Office, post office, beauty parlor, barber shop, and more." She lit a kerosene lamp, and led him down an old stone staircase. "Watch your step," she warned, "the steps are unevenly worn."

"Down the center, I see."

"The palace was built upon these very steps. We have an impressive collection, but there is no electric light in the cellar. You need to bring a lamp."

"I imagine it's not worth the investment for the little time spent there."

"Our cooks, Maurice Le Souffle, and Fradenzo Kookje are delighted to have you join us. They feel they have a family to cook for again. Two families, counting below stairs." She led him to an old oak door. "Now, if I can get the key in the lock, I can turn it...and violá"—the door creaked open.

"Sounds like this door could use some oil, too."

"This door is three hundred years old—more."

"The temperature feels right."

"We keep it at fifty-five degrees." She handed him the lamp. "Take this, so you can see where you're going."

"Thank you." Tibbons took the lamp off her hands, and read the rows of wine and champagne labels. "I have *never seen* such a cellar," his eyes lit up, "this is impressive."

"This *is* Abundance, Mr. Tibbons. We stock only the best."

Tibbons read labels, while the housekeeper read him. "In spite of hearing prince Godwyn's marriage to our Queen is bringing two more females to the table, Mr. Tibbons, staff is delighted to know you will be heading our household."

"Why thank you."

She leaned against the wall, arms crossed. "If it takes three females to draw in one consort and a butler, all is well."

"I am delighted to be here."

"We hope you will be with us for a very long time, Mr. Tibbons."

"As do I. Shall I hand the lamp back to you?"

"Are you done looking?"

"I am for today. It's late." He handed her the lamp. "I have yet to unpack the consort's belongings."

"I understand." With one hand, she locked the door, led the butler back to the servants' hall, and handed him the keys. "If you would like, Mr. Tibbons, I can give you a tour of the main floor tomorrow—or whenever you are ready."

"That would be lovely. Thank you, Mrs. B. Now if you will excuse me, I need to prepare for the consort's arrival."

"Of course. You may want to keep those keys under lock and key, Mr. Tibbons. It wouldn't be the first time a bottle went missing."

"Thank you." He held the ring up. "I will keep that in mind."

The housekeeper extinguished the lamp, and set it on the table. "The bills are likely to be in arrears," she said. "You will find them stacked under the lighthouse on your desk. The kitchen appliances are eighteenth century, and should be replaced. At times the oven goes out, and we have to bake bread in the brick oven in the carriage house."

"I'll tend to the bills tomorrow—along with those squeaky doors."

"I get the feeling you will have things in order in no time."

"That might be a bit optimistic."

"I have faith in you, Mr. Tibbons." She stepped in close. "I took a rhubarb pie out of the oven before you came down. Would you care for a slice?"

"I should be on my way."

"I'll wrap it up, and you can take it with you. I'll give you a fork. Wait here. I'll be right back." She returned, a minute later, and handed him a plate covered in foil. "The rhubard is fresh from the garden. It was picked this morning."

"Thank you."

"Welcome to our family."

"Thank you, Mrs. B.," he nodded, "good night."

"Good night, Mr. Tibbons."

The one hundred and ninety-two palace clocks struck twelve times, in unison, for a total of two thousand three hundred and four strikes—then all was quiet. Upstairs, in the west wing attic, Uppsola Pumba set pips on the board for another midnight game of checkers. Queen Mother draped a cardigan over her shoulders, sat down at the game table, and lost herself in the moon's reflection on Crystal lake. "This is the peace I waited a lifetime for, Uppsola." She cleared her throat. "I thought I'd be spending it with Poldemire, but here I am with you."

Uppsola sat down, set her pouch on the table, and lit her pipe. "How fortunate *you* didn't have to die to find it—eh, Y.M.?"

"Why do insist on contracting me to initials, Uppsola? Time and again, I have asked you to call me GranMarguerite, or Ma'am."

"Y.M. is more efficient."

"I can't teach an old dog new tricks."

"Not this dog," Uppsola toked on her pipe—"light, or dark?"

"Dark," Queen Mother sipped on her lemonade. "Earlier, I was looking down from the balustrade, and saw the new girls skate down the corridor."

Uppsola straightened the pips. "They must have found Pristine and Erica's old skates in the toss-off room."

"What are their names?"

"Possessa and Gezealous, I believe."

"What strange names," Queen Mother chuckled. "Before dinner, I looked out the window, and saw them arguing in the hedgemaze over which was the way out. Mr. Snibbles finally heard them, and rescued them."

"They seem to argue quite a bit. Somebody needs to have a talk with them."

"They are young, Uppsola. It has been so long since young blood has run through the halls, with the exception of Pristine, and that's been decades, it warms my heart to hear them, even if they argue. So what, if they make a bit of a ruckus—it reminds us we are alive."

CHAPTER XXVII

The Honeymoon is Over

Queen Pristine, and consort Godwyn returned from Play better acquainted with each other's freckles, moles, and personalities. The morning of the first day of their return from Play, they met at the grand staircase in the hall after breakfast, so Pristine could give Godwyn a tour of the palace. "Godwyn, I will show you the main floor first," the Queen ascended the staircase three steps ahead of her consort, "I don't know about you, but after last night's good sleep in my favorite bed, I am eager to return to my duties."

"I feel the same. Nothing like you own bed. How delightful," Godwyn smiled, "a tour of my new home, given by my charming bride guide."

"You flirt," Pristine spoke over her shoulder, as she ascended the stairs.

"Where is the souterrain entrance?"

"Why your sudden interest in the souterrain?"

"I want to know where I can get a haircut, post a letter, send you flowers."

"The main entrance is on the north lawn. You can also get there by elevator. You'll find a barber shop, a florist, and a post office. It's located at the end of the hall, inside the Communications Office."

"I would like to see the ballroom."

"It's down there, too—across the hall from the throne room, and the debriefing room. Here we are," she stepped onto the floor, and led him to a large open space—"this is the central gallery."

Godwyn looked out the window, and saw the snowcapped peak of Mount Majesty in the distance. Then he turned his focus to the large open space between wings. "I think this arrangement will serve is well."

"Opposing wings cut down on noise. They also provide privacy."

213

"Mr. Tibbons tells me Possessa and Gezealous behaved well during our absence."

"It seems we are off to a good start."

"I was concerned with us gone they might take advantage of him. Apparently, they didn't."

'SLAM.'

An echo traveled down the corridor. Gezealous darted out of the room, dragging a sweater, with her sister on her tail. "Papa," she hollered, "look what Possessa did to my sweater."

"What did Possessa do to your sweater?"

"She wore it." Gezealous held the sweater out. "Now it has big dirty boobie marks on it."

"You only *wish* you had boobies." Possessa snarled.

"Ugh—she ruined it. Look at it, Papa."

"Settle down, Gezealous." Pristine intervened, "it's only a sweater. Godwyn, are we going to have to put up with this behavior all the time?"

"I certainly hope not. I find this as disturbing as you, Pristine."

Pristine examined the sweater, without touching it. "Tell one of the maids to wash it in hot water, Gezealous, it will regain its shape."

"No it won't, *Mother Majesty*—it's angora."

"It's not even your sweater, Gezealous—"it's mine."

"It is not." Gezealous shouted, "I paid for it."

"You did not."

"I did so."

"You did not. I loaned you the money, and you never paid me back."

"I paid you back, but you spent it so fast you forgot."

"Girls," Godwyn stepped in, "stop arguing."

"I have heard enough." Pristine held her hand out. "Give me the sweater, Gezealous."

"What are you gonna do with it?"

"Hand the sweater to your mother, Gezealous."

"She's not my mother."

Godwyn's voice turned firm. "Hand the sweater to your stepmother."

Gezealous handed over the sweater. "What are you gonna do with it? You said it was ruined."

"It *is*. She ruined it." Pristine snagged the sweater with her ring, and unraveled it. Gezealous gasped, "Mother Majesty—what are you doing?"

Pristine pulled the sweater apart. "There, now we have two halves." She handed half to each, "you are both shareholders with equal equity."

"No, Mother Majesty," Gezealous wheezed—you ruined my sweater."

"But it was already ruined."

"Shareholders with equal equity," Godwyn held back a chortle—"just like your clef."

"You tore it in half!"

"That's what fighting will bring you, Gezealous, division and separation."

"Now what do I do with it?"

"Create a new fashion statement. I am embarrassed to call you girls my daughters. You are grounded for a week."

"But Papa"—

"I said go."

Gezealous clomped up the stairs after her sister, and swatted her with her half of the sweater. "You stay out of my room," she shouted, "I'm not sharing any of my clothes with you anymore."

"And I'm not sharing mine with you, either. Besides, we share the same room, stupid."

"Then stay out of my half."

'SLAM.' The echo traveled down the corridor, and silence reigned.

Pristine waited at the balustrade for Godwyn to catch up. "They seemed less tense when they visited," she said, as they started walking.

"They were trying to make a good impression."

"Are they always this excitable?"

"I've never seen them like this. I don't know what has gotten into them."

"I must say, I was surprised when they started fighting over the clef. I wonder if they played their instruments while we were gone."

"Mr. Tibbons says they did. Every day—as promised."

"Good. At least they put their instruments to use. Turn left here. This is the guest bedroom wing—each with private bath. What a dusty job the installation was. That was completed right before Grandpa Poldi died."

Godwyn studied the portraits on the walls. "Are all of these people your ancestors?"

Pristine stopped. "Most of them are. This is my great-great-great-grandfather, King Aloneous. Sometimes, when I want a little guidance, I come and listen to him."

"What does he tell you?"

"Nothing. He listens."

"Now you have *me* to listen to."

"Will *you* listen to me, and obey?"

215

"You are my Queen. I will always listen to you, and obey."

"Turn right at this next corner. This is the west wing."

"I feel rather ashamed for Possessa and Gezealous."

"Teens tend to be obsessed with themselves, Godwyn. They have nothing better to think about."

"They were never this difficult."

"I imagine the change of environment has something to do with it. Perhaps you should have kept Nanny Bickerstaff on."

Godwyn shook his head. "It's not a nanny they need. They need to get back in school. Their minds have been stagnant these past several weeks. First school was cancelled because of the flood, then the wedding, our absence, and the move."

"Interesting you should bring up school. Before we left for Play, I asked Mr. Snibbles if he would clean out the schoolhouse."

"Who's Mr. Snibbles?"

"Villyum Snibbles—the groundskeeper. He's been here since before Mother was born. Anyway, Mrs. Bissiby says not only did the Gardener brothers step in to help, under Mr. Snibble's supervision, they not only cleaned the schoolhouse, they cleaned the teachers' cottage, and gave both a fresh coat of paint."

"Wonderful. Now all we need is teachers."

"Before we left, Godwyn, I took the liberty of rehiring my former schoolmistress, *Entra Sitwell.*"

"Thank you for letting me know."

"Don't be angry."

"I'm not angry. I'm disappointed."

"Why?"

"They are *my* daughters, Pristine, and you didn't consult me."

"Forgive me. I thought they were *our* daughters."

"They are our daughters. I'm sorry. Forgive me."

"Mistress Sitwell taught Erica, and me. She taught our parents, for God's sake. After Erica and I graduated, she accepted a position in Understanding. The position was not as understanding as she had expected, so I convinced her to come home. She's arriving on Saturday, and will begin lessons on Monday."

"I imagine her standards are high."

"I wouldn't have hired her if they weren't. Trust me, Godwyn, Entra Sitwell will not let them get away with an-y-thing—turn here at the corner. I want to show you the King's library."

The door opened before them, as they approached, and before them stood Quigley. "Your Majesty, Sir," the footman bowed from the neck, and stepped aside.

"Hello, Quigley." Godwyn nodded, as he passed, "thank you."

Pristine turned. "This is the King's library." Godwyn followed her into an eighty foot long room, lined with floor to ceiling oak glass cabinets filled with books. "This is beautiful."

"Perhaps now we should refer to it as the *prince consort's library.*"

Godwyn lulled past the bookshelves, reading spines. "With Possessa and Gezealous back in school," he said, "we should have more time to ourselves."

"Should their daytime lessons not provide us enough free time, we can always enroll them in night school, but for now, Godwyn, let us forget the girls. I need to put you through a security debriefing—in my chambers."

"You said the debriefing room is in the souterrain."

"Who said anything about a room?"

"You did."

"I did not. I said I need to debrief you, in my chambers."

"Pristine, stop. This is the perfect moment." Godwyn took hold of her arm.

"Perfect moment for what?"

"Perfect moment—and the perfect place. Sit down, Pristine, please," Godwyn eased her onto the divan, and got down on one knee.

"What is this?—another proposal?"

"I have something for you." He held up a poem on a sheet of paper. "I call it my marriage determination. This is my personal dedication of love to you, Pristine—my sovereign, my Queen, my wife." He pointed to the sheet. "You see this little man, standing in the sun?"

Pristine nodded. "I do."

"That little man is me." He started reading.

Alan John Mayer

MY MARRIAGE DETERMINATION

I will seek and find a noble aim
    in all you say and do,
See love in all your words and acts
    no motive misconstrue.
Your wishes I will anticipate
    as far as in me lies.
I'll leave you free to be yourself
    no force I'll exercise
I'll take up all your cares and woes,
    and bear them all with cheer,
When minor viewpoints disagree,
    I'll yield without a tear.
And when essential clashes loom
    I'll keep an open mind
And calmly wait till you agree,
    or till I'm wrong, I find.
If harsh remarks (forgive the thought)
    from you should ever slip
I'll answer with a mild reply,
    or button up my lip.
In thought and word and every act
    faithful to you I'll be
My confidence, full and complete,
    you will always get from me.
I'll be, so far as in me lies
    the charming Prince you crave
And on the peak you'd have me reach -- Your flag I'll proudly wave.

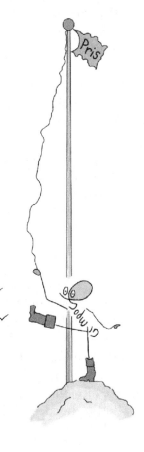

218

CHAPTER XXVIII

The Queen's Debriefing

This determination is exactly what a Queen needs, Godwyn—my Defender." Pristine rose from the divan, sheet in hand. "I shall have Mrs. Thornecroft send it out for framing, and I will hang it over my secretary, where I can read it every day. Now you come with me." She rose from the divan. "*I* want to show *you* what *I* have for *you.*"

Following an exhausting debriefing, Godwyn lay on the bed, smoking a cigarette, while Pristine sat at her vanity table, before the mirror. "Pristine, listen," Godwyn cocked his head, "I hear music."

"Of course you hear music. Your mind has been freed."

"Can you hear it?" He took a drag, and handed the cigarette to Pristine. "It sounds like it's coming from the west wing."

"Now I hear it." Pristine took a puff, and handed the cigarette back to Godwyn, "they're playing."

"Let's pay them a visit." Godwyn took one more drag, and extinguished the cigarette in the ashtray.

"Let me slip into something less comfortable." Pristine rose from her hassock, and walked out, "I'll be right back." Minutes later, she returned wearing a chiffon lounging gown. "Are you ready? Let's go."

Godwyn straightened his tie, put on his shoes, and followed Pristine to the music room, where footman Gowen Fetchett stood at the door. He nodded, knocked, opened the door, and stood back. There in the jamb stood Pristine. She knocked twice, and walked into the room. "Good evening, girls."

"Mother Majesty," Gezealous set her violin on the chair, and bowed. "Papa, hello."

Possessa rested her cello on the stand, and rose from her chair. "Mother Majesty, Papa, you've come to visit us."

Pristine stepped into the room. "Your father and I heard you playing."

"We thought we would pay you a visit, see how you are."

Pristine walked to the window, and looked through the sheers. "Don't stop playing on our account. This is the room Erica and I learned to play in. Well, she learned. I was never any good. This is one of my favorite rooms in the palace. It's got a southern exposure, and the windows let in so much light. Just smell those jacarandas."

"I was going to say that." Godwyn nodded—"oh, to be a bird."

"Next thing I know you'll be reading my mind, Godwyn—like Count Russell."

"One never knows what mysteries lay ahead."

"I like this room a lot," Gezealous stepped in, "it's got a warm feel to it."

"A lot is a collection of jewelry, Gezealous."

Godwyn noticed the ceiling. "The cornice is magnificent. Is it rococo?"

"Late Baroque. This is where Erica and I took harpsichord lessons."

"Isn't the ceiling neat, Papa?"

"Who are all those people up there?"

"There appear to be all sorts of spirits up there, Gezealous."

"I believe the craftsman wanted to create the illusion of heaven."

"I would say he succeeded."

"Erica and I put a name to every face up there. Let me see if I can remember them. That's Tiberius," she pointed, "and that one is Laviticus. There's Propecia, and Clitorious, Huomo-masculinicus, and the voluptuous one in the middle we christened Volumnia."

"What's a harpsichord?"

"It's a string instrument, much like a piano. The one Erica and I played on is in the museum. I have a tin ear, which is why it pleases me so much to hear you play."

"Shall I keep playing?"

"Please."

"The new instruments make a difference."

"I noticed. You play beautifully."

Possessa stopped playing—"not that beautifully."

Godwyn smiled. "You can admit you are good, Possessa. Just don't let it get to your head."

"Your father told me you play the piano. Mrs. Bissiby had it tuned."

"What do you say, girls?"

"Thank you." Gezealous lowered her head. "I'm not very good on the piano. I'm much better on the violin. I can only play two songs: *The Merry Farmer*, and *Silent Night*."

"I can play ten songs."

"But not without a few flat notes, Possessa."

"We'll leave you girls to work it out on your own. Give the piano a try. It's there for the playing."

"Keep playing, girls. Remember, the music doesn't stop playing until you stop playing the music."

"Good night, Mother Majesty." The sisters curtseyed.

"Good night, you two."

Godwyn kissed both on the forehead. "Don't stay up too late."

"We won't." Gezealous positioned her violin on her neck, and raised her bow. "Come on, Possessa, from the top."

The door opened, as Pristine reached for the handle, and she and Godwyn stepped into the corridor. "Being grounded seems to work for them," she whispered.

"It seems to be working for us, too. By the way, I've noticed these doors virtually open and close by themselves. What's the secret behind this technology?"

"You haven't noticed the footmen?"

"Even where there is no footmen, the doors seem to open automatically, as if by magic."

"My great-great-great grandfather, King Aloneous, the efficiency expert…"

"The portrait you pointed out to me in the gallery?"

"That's him. Back in the late eighteenth century, he conducted a study to calculate how many man hours are needed to perform certain duties, among them opening and closing doors. He calculated he could save man hours if he were to replace the footmen. He experimented with various substances, but it was seaweed pods that brought him success."

"Seaweed? Those long things we played with on the beach in Grace?"

"Yes, those slimy things. He crushed the pods into a pulp, then filtered them through carbon fibers, he developed a lubricant that makes hinges swing freely. That is why slamming a door here has such a powerful impact."

"Your great-great-great-grandfather created this lubricant on his own?"

"Well, I don't know if he created it on his own. I imagine he employed a staff, but he was an eccentric, so maybe he did come up with it on his own. It

221

was a hit, particulary with the carriage trade. King Aloneous is credited with a few other inventions too, among them, the Aloneous box."

"What's an Aloneous box?"

"It's a device that clears dust particles out of the air. It was developed to catch the dust in the air in the gold mines. Anyway, after making the invention, he was able to cut down from twenty footmen to twelve. Turn here. I want to show you the library—third door on the right."

"You already showed me the library." Godwyn stopped, and looked at his surroundings, "but this isn't the same corridor."

"What I showed you was the King's library, Godwyn, what we will now refer to as the prince consort's library. Now I am going to show you the petite bibliotheque—petite, like me. It's filled with female autors, women's studies, poetry, medicine, science, and the like."

They approached, and the door swung open. Godwyn followed Pristine in, and looked around. "This is cozy."

"It's smaller than the other, but more inviting. This library contains only eight thousand books, whereas the King's—*the prince consort's* library contains thirty thousand books, and hundreds more manuscripts."

A thump overhead derailed Godwyn's train of thought. He looked up. "What was that?"

"GranMarguerite is always dropping things," Pristine chuckled, "I've gotten used to it. It reminds me she's still alive."

"How do Queen Mother and Miss Uppsola get along up there?"

"Like two bugs in a rug. GranMarguerite says she's finally getting the peace she longed for, but she had to lose Poldemire to find it. Imagine, serving in the public eye for seventy-nine years, then suddenly finding yourself retired to an attic."

"Well, she had a good run of it, and it's not any old attic."

"I hope my run doesn't last that long."

"That would take you well into centenarianship."

"It would make me one hundred-and-nine. Tibbons would have to roll me into Court in a wheelchair."

"If he could." Godwyn calculated. "That would make him one hundred and—fifty."

"Gramma-Pristine," she giggled. "I'll be old and wrinkled."

"Gramm-Pris," Godwyn kissed her neck, "and I will still love you."

"That tickles, Godwyn. Come here. I want to show you something."

"You show me, Ma'am," Godwyn chased her past the bookshelves, and took a swing at her derriere.

Pristine scurried past, but Godwyn caught up—to three paces. He grabbed her from behind, and cradled her in his arms, "Earlier you said you want to discuss the war," he blew into her ear, "would this be a good time?"

Pristine escaped his embrace, threw herself into a chair, and crossed her legs. "No time is ever a good time to talk war, Godwyn."

"But we need to talk about it. What are your feelings?"

"I will tell you." Pristine sighed, "I am Queen of Entitlement, sovereign of Abundance, and I am afraid to face Fear. Terror scares me stiff, and yet something in me is determined to open communication between the two. Does that make any sense? Am I crazy to want to get involved with Fear and Terror?"

Godwyn sat down next to her. "Of course it makes sense, and you are not crazy. I would prefer you *not* get involved with Fear or Terror, but you will do what is right. You are a courageous woman, Pristine—a leader by birth. Like all leaders, you have fears, but only the courageous such as you are determined to overcome them."

"Deep down, I am a coward. Am I crazy, like Erica, I just don't know it?"

"No, no, no, no, no," Godwyn shook his head, "listen to me, Pristine. You are not crazy. If you believe you possess what it takes to face the *Tzarina of Terror,* and you believe you can negotiate with *Minister Ill Literati*—that self-serving tyrant of Fear, and I believe you do and can, then make it your cause. I will stand by you. I just don't want to see you insulted, the way he insulted Queen Mother years ago, at the summit in Timorous, when he brushed her aside and walked ahead."

"She was embarrassed," Pristine shook her head, "embarrassed for *him.*"

"The man is a criminal. He has no respect for anyone, least of all himself. He never learned to love anything but money. Power is love to him. He professes he donates his salary to the needy, but what he steals from the state coffers, his fraudulent charities, and the poor, is a thousand times his salary. The man is without a shred of dignity. He belongs behind bars."

"You are right. He's an imposter, whom only an ignorant Terrorist or a lost Fearling would follow. He's a cultmaster, but I have to deal with him."

"Whatever you choose to do, Pristine, I stand at your side—three paces behind."

"It's tradition, Godwyn. I cannot change that."

"I stand by you, and on that peak you would have me reach, your flag I will proudly wave."

"No one prepared me for what it is to be Queen."

"You've heard of the Peter Principle."

"No. What is the Peter Principle?"

"The Peter Principle is the notion which observes people in positions of heirarchy are promoted to their next highest level of incompetence—as skills from one position do not necessarily transfer to another. It's the reason our world is run so inefficiently, the reason there are so many incompetent fools in charge."

"Are you saying I'm a fool?"

"Of course not, and if you were, you would be my fool. God has placed you in this position so you can develop compassion for *all* of humanity, including Fearlings and Terrorists. God has chosen you, Pristine Goldspinner, to be His mediator here on earth, and he has chosen me to stand behind you."

"Her mediator."

"Her mediator, very well." Godwyn smiled.

"I need you every day to defend my faith, Godwyn."

"Pristine, I shall defend your faith every moment of every day. What more can I offer you than my marriage determination? I stand with you in everything you think, say, and do. You are my Queen, my sovereign, my wife, the love of my life."

"As I always envisioned a husband to be—standing at my side."

"Three paces behind, and I accept that."

Pristine walked over to the globe, and gave it a spin. "Let's go on a trip."

"Where to?"

Pristine dragged her finger across the globe, until it stopped spinning.

"This is where we are going." She opened her eyes, and noted the placement of her finger—"the Isle of Bile."

"The Isle of Bile?" Godwyn checked her finger. "What on earth are we going to do in Bile? I hate cold weather. I don't hunt. I don't shoot. I don't gamble."

"I hear the beaches in Bile are white sand, and they have tons of entertainment on the boardwalk—and you like to fish."

"I hate fishing. I only did it to please my father. Bile? We'd better go during their summer. I hear it's the first week of June."

"You exaggerate. They have lovely white sandy beaches."

"They're all nude beaches, Pristine. Bile is known for its nude beaches."

"Really? Maybe I had better spin again."

"I think so. See if you can place your finger somewhat closer to the equator." Godwyn leaned back in Poldemire's old leather chair, and admired the shelves of books. "I can't wait for a rainy day. It's going to take me a lifetime to check out all these books."

"That's just this library, Godwyn."

"Two lifetimes. The crates from Leniency won't made a dent."

"Not to change the subject, Godwyn, but I would like to talk to you about Possessa and Gezealous."

"What have they done now?"

"Nothing. Mistress Sitwell is ready to begin lessons."

"Finally some time to ourselves."

"Mistress Sitwell will discipline them."

"I hope so. Nanny Bickerstaff wasn't much of a disciplinarian. Neither were Crabtree, or McMeane. Rather than to go through the process of re-hiring and re-training, I turned a blind eye."

"I have good news, Godwyn. I convinced Nanny Needlepinch to come back."

"Was she ever gone?"

"She was with a family in *Clemency*. The family wasn't to her liking, so I convinced her to come back. Carabella Needlepinch is my salvation, Godwyn. You need to know that."

"I'm glad she was there for you during the difficult times, but do we need her now? The girls are old enough to look after themselves."

"She has offered to keep an eye on them after school and on weekends. You were right when you told me I couldn't fill in as a mother. I now realize I cannot tread where others have failed."

"Now you are making sense, Pristine." Godwyn pulled her close. "I told you it's best you not get involved. As a parent, I myself feel inadequate, ever since their mother died. It's been nine years. Here I am, Defender of the Faith, yet there are times when I can't even hold my own. I feel like a hypocrite, defending the faith for others, while questioning my own."

"You're not a hypocrite, Godwyn. You are the prince consort of Entitlement, reigning at my side over Abundance."

"Three steps behind—I'm kidding."

"No, you are not."

"Okay, so what. I feel like I have let both my daughters down."

"Try not to be so hard on yourself. You're a good parent."

"I wish they would stop quarreling."

"Mistress Sitwell will put an end to that."

225

Alan John Mayer

"I would be happy if I could just get them to stop slamming doors. My brothers and I never quarreled. Sure, we played rough—all but Francis. We wrestled, and tumbled, but we seldom argued, and we never slammed doors—except for Francis. He always was temperamental. Why can't girls behave more like boys?"

"They're teenage girls, Godwyn. They are pre-programmed to fight."

"I tired so hard to re-establish a family after Prudence died. I thought Nanny McMeane could step in, and act as a mother. I don't know how I could have been so naiive."

"We're a family now, Godwyn—you and I, Nanny, Possessa, Gezealous. We'll make it work." Pristine rose from the chair. "This library is too cerebral for me right now. Come to my bedchamber. We'll have a pick-me-up."

Godwyn rose to his feet, "I could use a pick-me-up right about now."

"Meet me in my bedchamber, in ten minutes."

Godwyn followed Pristine to the door, and it opened before them. "Mr. Tibbons," Pristine was startled to see the new butler standing before her, in the corridor. "Mr. Tibbons—is everything all right?"

"Yes, Ma'am."

"What can I do for you?"

"I wonder, Ma'am, if you and I could go over the finances together some time this week. I want to be sure I am following protocol."

"How about Monday after breakfast? Nine o'clock?"

"That will do fine. Thank you, Ma'am. If you will excuse me."

Pristine whispered into Godwyn's ear, as she walked him down the corridor, "I ordered a set of silk sheets before we went on honeymoon," she winked, "I thought you might give me your opinion on the thread count."

CHAPTER XXIX
The Payoff

Queen Pristine sat in her consultation chair in the green parlor, across from Count Russell. "Tell me, Count, how is it you can read my mind?"

"I listen, Your Majesty, I let myself be free."

"But we all listen, Count Russell."

"Not all of us; I listen with my heart. Communication occurs not so much through words, but more so in the silent part."

"You mean without words—telepathically."

"Without words, Ma'am," the count nodded, "that's it, being present in the moment, relying upon wit."

"Along with *The 48 Laws of Power*, that gives me something to think about. What a book."

"It's a masterpiece. M'am, might I recommend another book? If I offer a suggestion, will you take a look?"

"Which title might that be?"

"*Speaking Without Words*, Ma'am, by Dr. Friederick van Quirds."

"I'll check it out. Maybe Dr. Quirds will offer some answers to my questions."

Palace gynecologist, portly Dr. *Meddle Fingerling*, was at the height of his career when fertility became a palace issue. The good doctor had brought seven royal family members into the world, including princesses Henriette, Envie, Kimono, Erica, and Pristine. Announcing the birth of an heir was a duty he felt comfortable doing, but delivering the news of Her Majesty's two miscarriages was a different matter—not to mention the stillborn prince, a year later. Dr. Fingerling tried, unsuccessfully, to console the grieving Queen, resigned to her bed in a state of severe depression. With consort Godwyn looking on, the doctor packed his black bag.

"Doctor," Godwyn approached, "it has been months now. How long will it take for Pristine to get over this depression?"

"Do not fret, Sir. At times things go wrong. I prescribed a sedative, nitrazepan, to help Her Majesty through the depression. The Queen is in good health, but she needs rest. These tablets will help her sleep."

"She never wanted children, Doctor. Do you think that could have something to do with her miscarriages?"

"It is possible the psyche could have taken over the soma. Her Majesty needs to rest, avoid stress, and before you know it, she will gain weight, and conceive again. You will know when the timing is right."

"It takes all I have to hold the faith."

"That *is* good news." Dr. Fingerling nodded. "Whatever it takes, keep up the faith, for yourself, Her Majesty, *and* the kingdom. See to it she rests, and she will get better."

"Thank you, Doctor." Godwyn returned to Pristine's bedside, and took her hand. "Did you hear what Dr. Fingerling said, Pristine? He says you should eat well, get plenty of rest, and we will conceive again."

"I guess so." The Queen responded with melancholic cheerlessness. "Two miscarriages, and a stillborn prince. Why Godwyn?"

"You just rest, Pristine." Godwyn ran his fingers through her hair. "I am going to uphold the faith. I will be right here when you wake up."

"I don't think I can sleep."

"Dr. Fingerling prescribed you a sedative. Shall I give you one?"

"I don't want to sleep." She turned. "I don't want to be awake, either."

"Consort Godwyn," Dr. Fingerling nodded for him to come.

"I will be right back, Pristine. Wait right here." Godwyn stepped out. "What is it, Doctor?"

"You might take Her Majesty out for a walk. Some fresh air should lift her spirit."

"I shall see to it she gets out." Godwyn returned to the bed. "Would you like to go for a walk in the garden with me, Pristine?"

"No." The Queen didn't even bother to shake her head.

"The fresh air might do you some good."

"I don't want to leave my bed." She scrunched her pillow. "You run the kingdom for me, Godwyn, as my proxy."

"You want *me* to run the kingdom? I have no right to rule."

"You have the faith."

"You are going to be fine. Get some sleep. When you wake up, I will take you on a leisurely promenade through the garden."

"I can't sleep."

Pristine would not listen to anyone. She stayed in bed, and ordered Mina to lock her doors. Not even Handsforth's meals-on-wheels could lift her spirit. Orderic Tibbons had been privy to more than half a century of Bonheur family laundry. Godwyn knew he could rely upon him for confidentiality. Later that day, he shared his feelings with the butler, while the butler was brushing the consort's suit. "Here I am, Defender of the Faith, Tibbons, a title imposed upon me at birth, and I am powerless to squelch the pain that clouds Pristine's happiness. What can I do? She's down to ninety-seven pounds."

"I will give it some thought, Sir."

"I've not seen her all week. She won't open the door for even Handsforth."

"The good news, Sir, with Miss Possessa and Miss Gezealous in school, you have time to focus on Her Majesty's health."

"I might be able to if she would unlock her doors."

Mr. Tibbons set the clothes brush aside, and hung the consort's pants on a hanger. "Might I offer a bit of advice, Sir?"

"Anything, Tibbons. What is it?"

"What the Queen needs is rest from the pressures of running a kingdom. You need to take her on a vacation."

"We were in Play not so long ago."

"With due respect Sir, that was over two years ago."

"Has it been that long? Pristine did say she wanted to visit the Isle of Bile, but I have no desire to go to Bile. I don't like cold weather. I don't fish. I don't hunt or gamble. Besides, there is so much here to keep us busy."

"Perhaps some entertainment." The butler held up the consort's jacket. "Lift your arms, please."

"Her spark is gone." Godwyn slipped into the jacket. "We must get her to eat."

"Give her time." Tibbons buttoned the jacket." There you are, Sir, ready for the day."

"Have you no immediate suggestions, Tibbons?"

"Not for female trouble, Sir. That is Dr. Fingerling's department."

"This is a kingdom. We need an heir."

"Fate will bring us an heir, Sir. Love is the solution. I will keep a close eye on the Queen, see if Mina will let me into her chambers."

"I appreciate any help you can give me."

"What is it you always say, Sir?—this too shall pass?"

231

Left to their own devices, Possessa and Gezealous took advantage of their stepmother's reproductive misfortune, and rejected all adult intervention. With Godwyn's mind on Pristine, he neglected his daughters. The sisters were irritated with Nanny Needlepinch for sticking her nose into their quarters. Possessa had taken up smoking, and drinking, and Gezealous was following in her sister's tracks.

Mr. Tibbons did his best to uphold standards. "I try not to intervene," he told the consort, "I stay out of the west wing, unless of course, they ring for me."

"What has gotten into Possessa, Tibbons? Her loose language has me concerned."

"Youth, Sir, the times are changing."

"Have another talk with them. They respect you."

"With you paying so much attention to the Queen, Sir, your daughters have gotten the idea their stepmother has run off with their father's affection."

"They cannot believe that."

"I believe they do, Sir. They resent the attention you lavish on Her Majesty."

"Talk with them, please."

"First thing in the morning, Sir."

"By the way, Tibbons, I found an empty bottle of champagne in the west wing hall the other day. Do you know anything about this?"

"No Sir. The cellar is locked, and I haven't noticed any bottles missing."

"About Possessa's smoking, and drinking…"

"I am aware of the smoking and drinking, Sir."

"I hope Gezealous isn't going to follow in her sister's shoes."

"Several times Miss Possessa has asked me to buy cigarettes for her. I refuse, of course, but she seems to have talked one of the footmen into buying them for her. I have yet to find out which. When I do, I will see to it he is placed on probation. In case you haven't noticed it, Sir, the girls are turning into young ladies before our very eyes."

"Unfortunately, they are not not turning into the kind of young ladies their mother would be proud of. They need to be set straight."

"I will do what I can. In the meantime, while I talk with the girls, you might want to have a talk with Mistress Sitwell. It couldn't hurt to have her on our team."

"Excellent idea. I have wanted to hold an audience with her since she arrived. I've been preoccupied."

CHAPTER XXX
The Remedy

All winter, the royal astrologer worked on the Queen's astrological chart, pinpointing fruitful days, identifying fertile windows, down to the minute. In Leniency, Mr. Tibbons had been in charge of planning the family's meals. Now, with Her Majesty in a precarious position, he was putting his dietary training to use to manage her diet. That very afternoon, he went below stairs to speak with Mrs. Bissiby, and found her as he entered the servants' hall, straightening her tie before the mirror. He greeted her, "good morning, Mrs. B."

"Good morning, Mr. Tibbons. Lovely day, isn't it? What can I do for you?"

"I have here an astrological chart pinpointing Her Majesty's fertile days and hours, Mrs. B., along with her minimum daily vitamin and mineral requirements. Familiarize yourself with this chart, please, and see to it Le Souffle and Kookje meet these requirements."

Mrs. Bissiby studied the chart. "Who prescribes this?"

"Dr. Fingerling—Her Majesty's gynecologist."

"I know who Dr. Fingerling is, Mr. Tibbons."

"It is of utmost importance we adhere to this chart, Mrs. B. The kingdom is counting on you to do your part to help us produce a healthy heir."

"My part?"

"Your part—here at the palace."

"I shall see to it Her Majesty gets her daily vitamin and mineral requirements, Mr. Tibbons." She grabbed a pin off the bulletin board, and tacked the sheet to it. "I will see to it staff sticks to this chart as if it were the Ten Commandments."

"Thank you, Mrs. B., what you do is of great importance. Ask them to see me if they have any questions."

The housekeeper's efforts found their way into Le Souffle's exotic culinary delights, Kookje's scrumptious pastries, and Handsforth's congenial meals-on-wheels deliveries. Pristine took to the kitchen's new output like a monkey to bananas. Soon she had gained ten pounds. Her strength returned. The sparkle returned to her eyes. Princess Erica even congratulated her sister on her recovery by venue of a singing telegram—a Jack-in-the Box.

One evening, Pristine decided she was ready to rejoin the family for dinner. The gong rang, and Mina dressed her, but this time, the Queen refrained from wearing a belt. She took the elevator down, and on the arm of Gowen Fetchett, she walked into the dining chamber. As she entered, Godwyn, Possessa, and Gezealous rose to their feet—everyone except Nanny Needlepinch, who lifted a shoulder, and raised a hip.

Godwyn smiled, as the footmen rolled in the dessert trolly. "I have a surprise for you, Pristine."

"A surprise? What sort of surprise, Godwyn?"

"I have engaged some after-dinner entertainment for our amusement."

"Oh, boy," Gezealous's eyes lit up, "finally some distraction from all the boredom."

For once, Possessa spoke last. "It's about time something fun happened around here."

Nanny was just happy to see Pristine at the table. First to enter the dining chamber was the Court jester, dressed in a purple and chartreuse checkered jumpsuit. He flung somersaults around the dining table, while humming the Abundance state anthem. Next came the dancing girls. They swung from ropes and poles, followed by the fire-eating dragon man, and the shirtless sword swallower. While the footmen removed the soiled dessert plates, the skinny lady was rolled in for the grand finale, singing *God Save the Queen*, in a high falsetto. Pristine could barely contain herself. She let all thoughts of holding in emotions go, and laughed so hard, she grabbed her midriff in pain—hoping not to induce another miscarriage. "I've not laughed this hard in years," she cried, "my stomach aches. Stop singing—I can't stand it."

"Stop singing!" Godwyn jumped out of his chair, and ran to her. "We don't want to take any chances. Stop laughing, Pristine, please." The footmen dismissed the performers, waiting on the sideline, and tried to roll the skinny lady out, but she refused to leave until she had finished all three refrains, what she was paid for. Finally, after everyone had been excused from the table, Godwyn and Pristine found time to laugh alone, together.

That winter, following the Queen's monthly checkup, Dr. Fingerling shared good news, as he packed his bag. "Your Majesty, you can expect a healthy little visitor come November."

Pristine sat up. "Doctor Fingerling, third time is a charm, right?"

"Third time is a charm, Your Majesty. You and consort Godwyn are pee-chee again."

Godwyn was elated. "Pristine, isn't that wonderful? We're pee-chee again."

"Finally, I can rest."

"Not only can you rest, Your Majesty, you must eat well."

"I will eat all spring, and all summer, Doctor; I promise. I will eat like a horse."

"That's my girl." Godwyn smiled. "We are going to laugh, laugh, laugh, then laugh some more."

"I will get big as a balloon, Godwyn. I'll get sick. My legs will swell, and you won't find me attractive anymore."

"I will be right behind you."

"Why must I go through this again?"

"This is our greatest joy yet, Pristine. We are going to be parents."

"*Another* pregnancy, why?"

"The important thing is you are healthy, and comfortable."

"Comfortable?" Pristine laughed—"pregnant in bed?"

"We must celebrate. Let me ring for champagne."

"You know I can't drink when I'm pregnant, Godwyn."

"One drink is not going to hurt anyone."

"One sip—to celebrate."

Late that summer, during Saturday tea, Godwyn poked fun at his rotund little Queen. "You kept your promise, Pristine, you are as big as a house," he smiled, "I still find you attractive."

"I believe the word I used was *balloon.*"

"My error. You are as big as a balloon, and sexier than ever."

"You lie, but I did keep my word."

"We did say we were going to laugh, laugh, and laugh some more, and we have—have we not?"

Pristine nodded. "We have."

"Your laughter is sweet music to my ears, Pristine."

"I was going to say the same about you, Godwyn."

"My pee-chee Queen." He kissed her stomach. "You are so beautiful, and so very big."

By October, the Queen had gained twenty-five pounds, and could not make it out of bed without assistance—not to mention making it to the throne, without an accident. Miss Mina, Miss *Competencia*, and Miss Cocoa took turns sitting at Her Majesty's side while she slept, just in case. From then on, Pristine sat looking pretty. By day, she solved crossword puzzles. By night, she chewed taffy, while waiting for her special day to arrive.

Miss Cocoa fluffed the Queen's pillows. "You Majesty, when you are go-ing to de-lever dis baby?"

"You think I have control over this monster, Cocoa? I lay here, listening to the clock, day after day," she bobbed her head up and down, "tic-toc, tic-toc. I can't even see my feet. They've disappeared. All I do is sit here looking pretty for the consort—from the neck up. Help me out of bed, Cocoa. I have to see a change of wallpaper. Take me to the music room."

"You are sure, You Majesty?"

"I'm sure. I want to pay my stepdaughters a visit."

"You need somebody esteady to helep you. I ring de footman."

By noon, the rain had stopped, and a rainbow spanned the sky. The sun's sweltering heat sucked the moisture out of the puddles, transforming hydrogen into a majestic display of cumulous clouds. Possessa stood before the mirror, adjusting her sun hat. "Come on, Gezealous," she prompted, "put on your coat. The sun's out."

"Where are we going?"

"Out."

"Out where?"

"I'll tell you when we get there. Put on your coat."

Gezealous grabbed an umbrella, just in case, and followed her sister to the door. Possessa opened the door, and found the Queen standing before her, propped up on the one hand by Cocoa Rocco, on the other, Gowen Fetchett. "Mother Majesty," Possessa curtseyed—"what are *you* doing here?"

Gezealous curtseyed. "We were just coming to see you."

Possessa nodded. "That's right. How are you doing."

"Don't lie, Possessa. I can read you like a book—both of you."

"How are you feeling, Mother Majesty?"

"Are you not both grounded?"

Possessa set her purse on the table. "That was two weeks ago."

"I thought your father grounded you again. I smell smoke. Have you been smoking?"

The sisters looked at each other, and shook their heads. "Not I."

"I quit."

"Me too."

"You are lying, both of you. I can smell it on you from here. Take your coats off. You are not going anywhere."

"You're not our mother. You can't tell us what to do."

"I should eslap you on de face, boat of you." Miss Cocoa let it fly. "You speaken to my Queen like dis. You girls need learn some respaict."

"That's okay, Cocoa," Pristine calmed the maid. "I can handle this. In case you need a reminder, Possessa, there is only one Queen here, and I am she. I expect you to heed my commands. There will be no smoking in your quarters, and I had better not catch either of you drinking, or I will commit you to the orphanage."

"The orphanage?" Possessa laughed, "you wouldn't dare."

Gezealous giggled. "We're too old for the orphanage."

"They'd laugh at you, Mother Majesty."

"You girls think this is funny?"

"You girls donut know how good you got it. Eshow some respaect."

"I can handle this, Cocoa."

"No, You Majesty, dese girls need learn respaect."

"I am sorry, Mother Majesty," Possessa curtseyed, "I apologize."

"Me too."

"Are you not going to invite us in?"

Gezealous stepped back. "It's your palace, come in."

Possessa positioned herself before her cello. "You're going to come in anyway."

On the arms of the maid and the footman, Pristine floated into the room like a balloon ready to take flight. "I know what it is like to grow up without a mother," she walked to the wall, "I grew up without a mother or a father."

"What happened to them?"

"That's not a polite question, Gezealous."

"It's okay, Possessa, it's been a while. My parents died in an earthquake, while princess Erica watched. It drove her to Insanity."

"Papa told us about Princess Erica. I'm sorry she's crazy."

"Crazy is perhaps not the right word, Gezealous. She suffers from P.T.S.O."

"What's P.T.S.O.?"

"Post Traumatic Stress Occurrence. Her circuits are overloaded."

"I like what she wore to your wedding. She had on really cool cherry shoes."

Pristine pushed herself off the wall. "Help me, Cocoa. The only cure seems to be shock treatment, and medication."

"Love is a cure."

"You are right, Gezealous. Love is a cure. Which is exactly how I am trying to handle the two of you."

"You love us?"

"I do. I would like to love you unconditionally, as you are, without you smoking and drinking behind our backs."

"I told you, Mother Majesty, we quit."

Gezealous piped in, "that sounds conditional."

"Perhaps, but it is what it is."

"Will princess Erica ever recover?"

"In time, perhaps. I hope so." Pristine leaned against the window frame, and scratched her back. "Why don't you play us a tune?"

"You want us to play *now?*"

"There is no time like the present, Possessa. Fetchett, help me to the divan."

Fetchett took the Queen by the arm, and walked her across the room.

"You no want to sit down, Ma'am?"

"I'm fine, Cocoa. If I sit down, I'll never get back up."

"Mother Majesty?"

"Yes, Gezealous."

"I feel like a first grader calling you Mother Majesty. Can we call you something else?"

Pristine chuckled. "What do you think, Cocoa?"

"I donut know. Mother Majesty sound good to me."

"Mr. Fetchett, have you an idea?"

"I couldn't say, Ma'am. Mother Majesty sounds about right."

Possessa frowned. "But it doesn't sound right to me."

"You could call me Mama Majesty."

"*Mama Majesty?*" Gezealous snickered—"that's worse than calling you *Mother* Majesty."

Possessa smiled. "It sounds okay to me."

"It makes us sound like kindergarteners, Possessa." Gezealous shook her head, "na-unh. I am *not* gonna call you Mama. I'll stick with Mother."

"As you wish."

"Do you still want us to play?"

"I would like that."

"Possessa," Gezealous whispered, — "we were going out."

238

"But now now you are not. You are going to play. Help me back to my room, Fetchett. We can hear you from across the hall. I need to talk to Mrs. Thornecroft about birth announcements."

"You Majesty, you can no go downstairs."

"I'm okay, Cocoa." Pristine turned. "You girls behave yourselves. No smoking, and no drinking."

Possessa curtseyed. "Yes, Mama Majesty."

Gezealous positioned her violin under her chin. "Yes Mother Majesty."

Pristine stepped into the corridor, on the arms of her footman and maid, and proceeded to the west wing when they saw Mrs. Thornecroft coming up the stairs.

"Your Majesty, Mr. Fetchett, Miss Cocoa," the secretary nodded, "what are you doing out of bed?"

"I couldn't stand looking at the ceiling any longer. I had to get out. Fetchett and Miss Cocoa have been kind enough to take me on a walk."

"I bring good news, Ma'am."

Pristine leaned against the balustrade. "Well, let's hear it."

Mrs. Thornecroft held out a chart. "Latest statistics show, since the coronation, communication between young and old has improved by six percent."

"That *is* good news."

"As of last month, 82% of the subjects love their Queen."

"Could be better, but that's not bad."

"Tithing has risen to 11.2% per capita."

"Abundites always have tithed more than subjects of any other state. That is why we live in Abundance." Pristine rubbed her stomach.

"Sharing is up seven percent, crime is down eleven percent."

"That's good to hear. Where needs are met, there is little want. Where there is little want, there is little crime. More good news, Mrs. Thornecroft?"

"News, Ma'am, but not so good. Fear and Terror are fighting again."

"The world would be a better place if they would just kill each other off, but that will be the day pigs fly. Thank you, Mrs. Thornecroft. Come with me to my chambers, please. We can discuss the birth announcements there. Fetchett," she reached out, "steady me please—to my bedchamber."

"Me, too, Ma'am." Cocoa latched the Queen's arm over her shoulder, and they walked her across the hall.

"Your Majesty, you are huge," Mrs. Thornecroft looked at the Queen's stomach, "how pregnant are you?"

"Eight months, three weeks, and six days."

"When are you going to deliver this baby?"

"Any day now, Mrs. Thornecroft. I am as anxious as anyone else."

That evening, supported on one arm by Miss Cocoa, and Miss Mina on the other, Pristine stepped into the dining chamber for a final meal with her family, while still waiting for her special day to arrive. Twickenham pulled her chair out. Godwyn rose from the table. "Pristine, I am so glad you are joining us. We have missed you."

"Pristine," Nanny lifted a hip, and nodded. "How are you feeling?"

"Like a cow." Pristine plopped into her chair, and Munchipoo shoved her in. "I barely fit at the table."

Godwyn spread her napkin out on her lap. "I'm sorry you are uncomfortable."

"Uncomfortable?—to say the least."

Godwyn returned to his seat.

Nanny leaned in. "Pristine, when are you going to have this baby?"

"Any day now, Nanny. Godwyn, where are the girls?"

"I sent them to their room."

"Why?"

"They lied about smoking."

"I spoke with them about that the other day. I thought I made it clear there is to be no smoking, no drinking."

"They evidently didn't hear you, Pris."

"Of all the nasty habits, why would anyone take up smoking?"

"Beats me."

"Ow-ow-ow," Pristine flinched—"ow-ow. Another kick."

Godwyn leaped out of his chair." Are you okay?"

"That one hurt. Ow—he kicked me again. He's going to be a soccer player. When will I be relieved of this monster inside me?"

"Probably when he becomes an adult, and moves out."

"Oh Nanny, don't joke like that."

"How are you feeling, Pris?"

"I told you Godwyn—like a cow."

"I mean right now."

Upstairs in their quarters, Possessa backgammoned Gezealous two out of three games, closed the board, and set it aside. "I am so tired of waiting for this brat to be born, Gezealous; let's play something loud."

"What shall we play?"

"Something that will annoy them. Go grab the sheet music to *Raukus*. It's in the bench. We're gonna make them even madder than they make us."

"Here's a copy," Gezealous set the sheet on the music stand, and picked up her violin.

"This should do it." Possessa positioned her cello. "Open the door. We want them to hear this."

Gezealous opened the door, and positioned herself on the chair. "Are you ready?"

"One second. From the beginning. One, two, three—play."

The melancholic timbre of Possessa's cello reverberated down the hall, accompanied by Gezealous's twinged violin playing. The notes came off grief-striken, yet the sisters took delight in playing an annoyance. They smiled. The louder they played, the harder they laughed.

Godwyn rested his head in his hands, elbows on the table. "I know it's not proper to rest my elbows on the dinner table, Pristine, but what have I done to deserve this?"

"Our only hope is to marry them off."

"If we can find men willing to take them."

"Godwyn, how many times have I heard you say 'this too shall pass'?"

"And it will, but when will *this baby* pass? You're a week overdue."

"Nine days, actually. What do you suggest I do? Squeeze my stomach?"

"I'm sorry. I didn't mean it like that. We need to start looking for prospective husbands."

"They have two more years of schooling to go."

"Two more years?"

"Mrs. Sitwell enrolled them in her thirteenth grade program. That should keep them busy. Before you know it, they'll be out."

"Can't Mistress Sitwell put them on the fast track?"

"That is the fast track. Be reasonable, Godwyn. Two years go by fast."

Godwyn leaned back in his chair. "Twickenham…"

The footman stepped forward. "Sir?"

"Bring me a Bromaseltzer."

"Yes, Sir."

CHAPTER XXXI

Redskins & Black Cat

Pristine sat around looking pretty for yet another week, waiting for her special day. She had long passed the balloon stage, and admitted she now felt less like a cow, and more like a whale. She now spent her days squirming in bed, trying to get comfortable. "Godwyn," she tossed another pillow aside, "this is exhausting, not knowing when the stork is going to drop in."

"How are you feeling?"

"Pregnant. How are Possessa and Gezealous? I haven't seen them since last week."

"I don't know if you have noticed, but while you have been growing out, Possessa and Gezealous have been growing up."

"I did notice. Cocoa and Fetchett walked me there last week. They've become young ladies."

"You shouldn't be out of bed."

"I couldn't stand it anymore. Nanny tells me, apparently, our daughters think I have hijacked their father's love, and they are determined to do whatever it takes to get it back, hence the raukus music recital the other night."

"At this stage, they are libel to blame anyone for anything."

"They've been smoking again."

"I know. Mr. Tibbons found an empty wine bottle in the music room last week."

"This has to stop. They are so close to getting their diplomas. I do not want them jeopardizing their future like this."

"I'll have another talk with them, Pristine."

"They don't listen to you. Tell Tibbons to talk with them. He is the only one they listen to."

"How about we forget Possessa and Gezealous for a moment, and focus on ou" —

"Ow-ow," Pristine flinched, "ow-ow-ow—he's kicking again."

"And focus on our baby."

"Ow-ow"—Pristine winced, "ow-ow-ow."

Godwyn jumped out of the chair, "are you all right?"

"Ow-ow-ow-ow—oh—that kick really hurt."

Across the hall in their parlor in the west wing, Possessa lay on a chaise, thumbing through a magazine, smoking a cigarette, while Gezealous walked around the room, spraying lilac water. Possessa took one last drag off her cigarette, extinguished the butt in the ashtray, and waved her arms. "It's smokey in here, Gezealous, "open the doors. We don't want the room smelling like smoke, in case Mama Majesty returns."

"Why do you think I'm spraying air freshener, Possessa. You open the doors. And why do you call her Mama Majesty?—you sound like a retard."

"Open the balcony doors, Gezealous."

"You think she's gonna check on us again? No way. You're the one who told her we quit. You open the doors."

"You sure are testy."

"I am. So are you." Gezealous set the sprayer on the mantle. "This waiting is getting on my nerves. This stupid heir is two weeks overdue, not even born yet—and we're still grounded? I'm going out."

"Gezealous, we can't. She'll ground us permanently."

Gezealous drew back the drape, opened the door, and stepped out, onto the balcony. She rested her arms on the balustrade, gazed into the nighttime sky, and listened to a wolf, howling in the distance. "Possessa, it's a full moon. Come take a look."

Possessa turned the page. "I've seen plenty of moons, Gezealous."

"There's only one moon."

"You know what I mean."

"It's huge. Come take a look."

Possessa extinguished her cigarette, set her magazine on the table, and stepped onto the balcony. "Where?"

"Duh—in front of you."

"Wow. That is big."

"It's close to the earth. That's why it looks so big."

"You think we might become stepaunts tonight yet?"

"She's probably holding it in just to get even with us."

"It's only a matter of time before this brat is gonna take over. And only because the minute he pops out, he'll get a title slapped on his butt."

"You know, it could be a she, Possessa."

244

"I doubt it. Dad's got five brothers, and no sisters."

"Yeah, and look—he has us."

"I overheard Papa tell Mr. Tibbons Mama Majesty's been sleeping on her left side. That's to produce a male. Either way, I'm not gonna let anyone, male or female, usurp me."

"Except Mother Majesty. Not that it matters now. Do you really believe your voodoo doll curse caused her miscarriages?"

"I sincerely believe it. I did everything by the book, and it worked."

"What about the stillbirth?"

"I don't know why that didn't turn into a miscarriage. I still wonder."

"Admit it, Mother Majesty's miscarriages were a coincidence."

"I don't think they were. The voodoo curse worked on her miscarriages. I don't know why it didn't work for the stillbirth."

"You've lost your touch."

"I haven't lost it, Gezealous. It's just been misplaced."

"We have to figure out how we're gonna work this heir."

"This could still be a stillbirth. Whatever. As soon as Sitwell hands me my graduation certificate, I'm outta here."

"Where you going?"

"I'm getting married."

"Married?" Gezealous was stunned. "Married to whom?"

"To a rich, handsome man."

"Why haven't you told me about this before?"

"I have yet to meet him. And I'm not gonna waste my life curtseying to Papa's new brat. I'm gonna have my own palace. This baby is going to threaten our inheritance, Gezealous. This is no longer about just jewelry and furs. This is about property, land, and gold."

"I'm getting cold. I'm gonna grab my stole," Gezealous walked inside, tossed her mother's fur over her shoulder, and returned to the balcony. "You know what I just realized, Possessa?"

"What?"

"The nursery is in our wing, next to the music room."

"Oh my God. You're right. I didn't think about that. We are destined to listen to this brat's crying. I'm telling you, Gezealous, the only way to secure our future is to marry rich."

Gezealous cozied up with her fur. "I thought we're getting high school diplomas to secure our future."

Possessa laughed. "Are you kidding? You don't seriously think a high school diploma signed by Mistress Sitwell is going to secure our future, do you?"

"What about our graduate courses? They should be worth something."

"Get real, Gezealous. She's only putting us through her 'graduate courses' so she can save her job. Without us, she's gone. We need husbands—rich husbands."

"Where are we gonna find them?"

"I don't know, but find them we will. I am not gonna work for a living. I'll tell you this. Unless we marry powerful men, we are not gonna inherit one lousy sovereign. Everything from Leniency is now in Mama Majesty's hands, and possession is nine tenths of the law. You watch—as soon as we graduate, she is gonna tell us to get jobs, and if we don't get jobs, she is gonna assign jobs to us, and if we don't take her jobs, she is gonna cut our allowance, and throw us in the street."

"She wouldn't dare."

"You wanna bet? She threatened to commit us to the orphanage. Remember? What makes you think she won't throw us in the street?"

"Papa wouldn't let her."

"Don't count on it, Gezealous. He's whipped."

Gezealous gazed into the stars. "The moon has shifted."

"The moon doesn't shift, Gezealous. The earth shifts. I'm cold. I'm going in."

"Me too," Gezealous slipped in first.

Possessa closed the balcony door, and locked it. "I am not going to spend my life opening and closing my own doors," she pushed a button, and the drapes drew to a close. "That is for the plebians to do."

Gezealous tossed her stole, and sat down on the chaise. "I miss Leniency, and all our friends."

"Me too. I miss Denise, and Donna."

"We spend too much time in that stupid old schoolhouse. Sitwell's a spinster—isn't she?"

"How about that Civics teacher who pops in every Friday? Whats-his-name."

"*McMaster*—he's sooo affected—Master McMaster. That's his name"

"I think he's as queer as a twelve sovereign note." Possessa opened the icebox, pulled out a bottle, and held up two glasses. "Help me polish off last night's wine?"

"May as well." Gezealous got up, and walked to the bar. "Drinking seems to be the only way to alleviate the pain of all this waiting."

"You said it." Possessa emptied the bottle, and tossed it into the bin.

"That's the end of that. I'm out of cigarettes. Gezealous, be a dear, and ring for a footman."

"You smoked the whole pack? Possessa, you've got to cut down."

"We need more wine."

"You smoke too much."

"And how are *you* handling this pregnancy? Ring the footman, Gezealous."

"You know he's going to smell smoke." Gezealous pulled the cord hanging from the ceiling. "Depending upon which one comes, he might tattle."

"Tell him to put another log on the fire. I hope the rusty haired guy with the can opener teeth doesn't show up."

"Quigley." Gezealous chuckled, "the Scare City look."

"That's the one. Where is he?"

"Give him time."

"How long does it take to get here?"

"The elevator's out again."

"Here's your glass." Possessa sat down. "You know, we're gonna have to curtsey to this brat."

"Remember, it could be a she."

"Even worse. I will marry any husband before I curtsey to a princess."

"You have to be choosy, Possessa. You can't just marry any husband. You have to affirm *a handsome* husband, a *rich* husband."

"A rich, handsome, *accident-prone* husband—oops," Possessa bit her lip—"that slipped out."

"Careful, Possessa. What was it Nanny Bickerstaff used to say?—the walls have eyes, and the windows have ears. This place could be bugged."

"It's the other way around. The *windows* have eyes, and the *walls* have ears. What-ever. Let's try not to fight anymore."

"It's you who starts it."

"I start it?"

"You said it."

"That was a question, Gezealous, not a statement. Where is that footman?"

"Give him time. You need to cut down, anyway." Gezealous picked up a magazine, and started thumbing."

"I'll stop smoking after the monster is born."

"Have you seen the latest issue of *Abundant Life?*" Gezealous held up the magazine. "They ran an exposé on the miners of Abundance."

"What about the miners?"

"They're photographed without shirts on." Gezealous tossed the magazine—"page thirty-two."

Possessa set her glass down, and turned to pages. "Oh, he's cute."

"Which?"

"Him."

"I think *this one's* the cutest. Did you know every mine in Abundance is equipped with a machine that sucks gold particles out of the air?"

"Really? I want one."

"Me too. They're called Aloneous boxes, but they're for industrial use only."

Possessa pointed to the photograph. "I'd marry him—if he brought home enough gold." She turned the page, harrumphed, and tossed the magazine on the coffee table. "Where is that stupid footman?"

"Be patient, Possessa."

"I am patient."

Gezealous folded the magazine in half, and held it up. "This is the perfume I'm gonna ask Papa to buy me for my birthday."

"Nice bottle."

"It's from Mío. Three crowns an ounce."

"I'll tell Papa to buy me some, too."

A knock at the door diverted their attention. "Be nice to him, Possessa—especially if it's Quigley."

Possessa rose to her feet. "I'm always nice. Come in."

"No you're not."

The footman stepped into the parlor. "You rang, Miss?"

"Quigley, where have you been?"

"Beg pardon, Miss. One of the kitchen maids has taken ill. Her duties have been divided among us."

"Which maid?"

"Miss Pinguine."

"I don't know her."

"She's the scullery maid, Miss."

"Is she going to recover?"

"I think so. The heat got to her."

"Good. I want you to bring me a pack of cigarettes, and a bottle of wine."

"Beg pardon, Miss Possessa. I have instructions not to take any more orders from you."

"Instructions from whom?"

"From Her Majesty, the Queen."

"She has some nerve. Don't listen to her, Quigley. She's not in her right mind."

Gezealous rose to her feet. "Listen, Quigley, Her Majesty has been pregnant for almost ten months—she's not quite with the plot anymore."

"It has been strenuous for everyone, Miss Gezealous."

"Quigley," Possessa took back the floor, "I want you to bring me a pack of cigarettes, and a bottle of red wine. Make sure it's chilled."

"If Mr. Tibbons finds out I am your purveyor of alcohol and cigarettes, he will put me on probation, and will dock my pay."

"If he does, we'll stand up for you, Quigley. Now do as Miss Possessa says."

"Put it on the tab, Quigley. I'll sign for it."

"I can't do that, Miss Possessa."

"You can say we forced you."

"I would rather not do that, Miss Gezealous."

"What are you, Quigley?—a man or a chicken?"

"I am a man, Miss. Perhaps if you were to pay cash. That way, the transaction can't be traced."

"Gezealous, hand Quigley a sovereign."

"I don't have a sovereign."

"Liar. You got change for a crown yesterday. Go get it."

"Oh, I forgot about that. I'll get it." Gezealous walked out.

"While Miss Gezealous is getting you a sovereign, Quigley, put another log on the fire, please."

"Yes, Miss," the footman walked to the hearth, opened the screen, grabbed the poker, and stoked the fire.

Gezealous stepped back into the parlor. "Here's a sovereign, Quigley."

The footman placed the poker in its holder, and slipped the coin in his pocket. "Same as last time, Miss?—Redskins?"

"Two packs of Redskins, and a bottle of Black Cat. Make sure it's chilled."

"I don't feel comfortable doing this, Miss."

"Aren't you forgetting something, Quigley?"

"A pack of Redskins, and a bottle of chilled Black Cat."

"You were going to put a log on the fire."

"Oh yes, I forgot." He tossed two logs on the fire, and closed the screen.

Gezealous slipped ten farthings into the footman's pocket, "for your trouble, Quigley."

"I shouldn't be doing this." He walked to the door.

"I'm sorry, Quigley—did you say something?"

"No, Miss."

"Good. You are excused."

"Yes, Miss. I shall return with your cigarettes, and wine."

"Thank you, Quigley," Gezealous mumbled, as the footman walked out the door. "You really should be nicer to him, Possessa."

"I *was* nice."

"You gave him attitude. He may not be handsome, like Handsforth or Twickenham, but he brings you whatever you ask him for."

Possessa lit her last cigarette, blew out smoke rings, and handed the cigarette to her sister. "I'll share with you."

Gezealous took a drag off the cigarette, coughed, and handed it back to her sister. I just don't get this smoking thing. Seems to me, if I cough, it's not right."

"To each his own."

"Best you not sign anything, Possessa. The trail would give us away."

"You think I'm stupid? I've been practicing Queen Mother's signature for months now. I think I finally got it down."

"That's forgery, Possessa. That's not right. Mr. Tibbons or Mrs. B. will know."

"You're such a spoil sport." Possessa exhaled rings of smoke. "What is a few farthings to them?"

Tension was high that evening at the dinner table, as Godwyn, Possessa, Gezealous, and Nanny Needlepinch waited for their entrées to be served. Godwyn was displeased to have heard of his daughters' secret activities. "Why can't you girls get it through your heads, you are not to smoke and drink?" He turned to Nanny. "Needlepinch, are you not capable of controlling two teenagers?"

"I do my best, Sir, but Possessa and Gezealous are headstrong young women."

"Headstrong?"

"Quiet, Possessa. No one asked your opinion. Your mother has told you several times, there is to be no smoking, and no drinking."

"She's not our mother."

"She's our stepmother."

"Stop splitting hairs. Needlepinch, what is it you actually do around here to warrant your pay?"

"I do my best, Sir." Nanny turned to the sisters. "Why do you two insist on aggravating your parents?"

"Mama Majesty is not our parent."

"Can you not see how you are upsetting your father?"

"Possessa, my wife is every bit your parent. She is your sovereign, your Queen, *and* your stepmother. This is her palace. You will respect *her* rules, and you owe her an apology—both of you."

"Why? I haven't done anything wrong."

"I think…"

"I don't care what you think, Gezealous."

"What about Princess Erica? She doesn't respect the rules."

"Get out!" Godwyn rose from his chair, and pointed to the door, "get out—both of you!"

"What did *I* do wrong?"

"Leave." Godwyn turned to the footman, "Munchipoo…"

"Yes, Sir?" the footman stepped forward.

"Remove Miss Possessa's, and Miss Gezealous's place settings. They will be dining in their chambers tonight."

"Very well, Sir."

The sisters set their napkins on the table. Two footmen hastened in to pull out their chairs, and the sisters walked to the door. Gezealous stopped at the threshold, and turned. "I just want to say…"

"Out!" Godwyn was fuming, "Before I throw you out!"

"All right. Geez—you don't have to yell at us."

"Youngsters can be frustrating, Sir."

"You be quiet, Needlepinch. You're half my problem, It is your job to keep them in line, and what do you do? Sleep."

'Stomp, stomp, stomp, stomp, stomp, stomp—clomp clomp clomp—stomp, stomp, stomp, stomp, stomp, stomp,' the sisters made their way up the stairs, to their rooms.

Godwyn sat with his head in his hands, shaking his head. "I thought my problems would be over once they grew up. Needlepinch, I need you to step up to the mark, if you are to continue on palace payroll."

"The girls are still adjusting, Sir."

"Adjusting? We have been here five years, and they're still adjusting?"

"I will talk with them."

"They don't listen to you, Needlepinch. You're excused. Go, please."

A footman stepped forward, handed Nanny her stick, and pulled out her chair. "Thank you, Consort. I *am* rather tired."

251

CHAPTER XXXII

The Crown

Whew-whew," the Queen screamed, "Dr. Fingerling, huff-huff—get the devil out of me. These contractions are different, huff-huff, from what I learned in school." Pristine clamped onto Carabella Needlepinch's arm like a vice grip, in an unconscious moment of retaliation. "A-gaaain"—she screamed "Doctor, shoot me!"

"Keep pushing, Ma'am," the royal gynocologist cheered the Queen on, "you are doing fine."

"Doctor—bring this pain to an end!"

Dr. Fingerling handed a vial to Nurse Chien. "Give Her Majesty another 50cc injection," he said, "you will find a syringe in the inside pocket of my bag."

"Right away, Doctor." The nurse walked away.

"Aaaaaah"—the Queen huffed, and puffed. With each contraction, the screams got louder.

"You are doing fine, Pristine." Nanny pulled her arm back. "Your grip is a *lit-tle* tight."

"Huff-huff"—the Queen huffed, and puffed—"phew-phew."

"That's my girl," Nanny brushed back a lock of Pristine's hair, "you are doing fine."

"Nan-ny," Pristine gasped, "never a-ah-aah-again do I want to experience, a-ah-another contraction. Oh no, here it comes—huff-huff."

Dr. Fingerling checked in on his progress. "Everything looks beautiful, Ma'am. We should see a crown soon."

Pristine took a deep breath. "I don't know why it took the garment industry to invent the zipper when it would have made childbirth so much easier. I never want anything to do with con-con-con-tractions again—no contractions, no more babies. Oh no—a-ah-aah-aaah!"

Nurse Chien approached with a needle. "Your shot, Ma'am."

Pristine clamped onto Nanny's arm, and pinched. "Nanny, am I glad you are here. Here and awake. You have, you have never missed, not one important moment in my life, and here you are, like you said you would be."

"I will always be here for you, Pristine." Nanny dabbed the Queen's brow with a handkerchief. "You can depend on me for as long as I breathe."

Five hours into the delivery, an exhausted Dr. Fingerling sat down in the corner, and took a break.

Nurse Chien checked her watch. "Your shot should kick in right about now, Ma'am."

"Oh no—here comes another."

"Smile, my dear." Nanny patted Pristine's hand. "Remember, this too shall pass."

"Where is Godwyn when I need him?"

"Godwyn is outside."

"Send him in, Nanny."

"Men are not to be present at childbirth, Pristine."

"What is Dr. Fingerling doing here?"

"The royal gynecologist is an exception, of course."

"Oh...finally, the pain is subsiding."

"I warned you, Pristine. Never trust a man. They will only cause pain."

In the King consort's library across the hall, an anxious consort sat in Poldemire's brown leather chair, investing his best into defending the faith. "Pristine and an heir will come through in good health," he repeated the prayer like a mantra, "rest assured, a healthy heir will be born before morning. Mother and child will be fine."

Mr. Tibbons knocked, and entered the library. "The temperature is expected to drop severely tonight, Sir. Shall I set another log on the fire?"

"Please, Tibbons. I don't remember it ever being so cold."

"It is expected to drop below zero before midnight." Tibbons stoked the hearth.

"Any news?"

"Not yet."

Godwyn watched the crackling embers shoot fire into the screen. "The subjects will never know what their Queen has gone through for them; two miscarriages, a stillborn prince, the explosion in the mine, the conflict between Fear and Terror. How can such experiences not affect a woman's emotions?"

"It is a miracle no lives were lost in the mine explosion."

"I prayed hard on that one."

There was a knock, the door opened, and Handsforth entered the library. "This just arrived, Sir." He held out a small silver tray upon which rested a telegram—"and Lord Woolsey is here to see you, Sir."

"What does Woolsey want?" Godwyn rose from the chair, and took the telegram. "Thank you, Handsforth. Send him in."

"Yes, Sir." The footman stepped back.

"Godwyn, my man," Lord Woolsey walked in, covered from nose to toes in argyle, "how are you holding up?"

"What are you doing here, George?"

"Avorah is spending the week at her mothers. I thought I'd drop in. Any news?"

"Not yet. I have been expecting news for two weeks now."

Godwyn returned to Poldemire's chair, and sat down. "Have a seat, George."

Woolsey set his pouch on the table, sat down, and packed his pipe. "How is Pristine doing?"

"Doctor says she's self-controlled. I, on the other hand, am anxious."

"Anything I can do to help?"

"Smoke your pipe." Godwyn cracked the seal, and unfolded the telegram.

"Last night, Avorah's laundry froze on the line. That's how cold it is."

"Her maid should have taken the laundry inside."

Woolsey lit his pipe. "It was inside," he puffed, "it was hanging in the laundry room."

"Pour yourself a Brandy, George." Godwyn read the telegram.

"Shall I pour one for you?" Woolsey reached for the carafe.

"No thanks. I've had five."

"Are you going to just stand there reading, or are you going to share the news?"

"The war is over." Godwyn handed the telegram to Woolsey, opened the top drawer of his desk, and pulled out a box of cigars. "The Terrorists ran out of ammunition, and the Fearlings scattered in a panic."

"Now it will be up to Abundance to monitor the peace." Woolsey read the telegram. "That could prove more difficult than ending the war."

"This means a new world order." Godwyn opened the cigar box, and held it out. "Take two, George—take three, or four. Before morning we shall have more reason to celebrate."

"Mmm," Woolsey passed the cigar under his nose, "Don Coronas— only the best. Thank you." Woolsey helped himself to four cigars, and handed the telegram to Godwyn. "What good timing. It seems an omen that peace should break out the same day an heir is born unto the kingdom."

Godwyn set the box on his desk, returned to Poldemire's chair, and sat down. "If I know Pristine, as I believe I do, she has this thought out, and will deliver this baby before midnight."

"She is the Princess of Perfection."

"Don't ever let her hear you say that, Woolsey. She will ban you from the Court."

"You look tired. You need to get some rest."

"I can't sleep." Godwyn gazed into the crackling fire. "I've dozed off here and there, but every time I awaken, I find myself in Poldemire's chair. I haven't slept in two days."

Woolsey reached for the carafe. "I think I will have another."

"Help yourself, Woolsey. You know, this tiny kingdom has stayed clear of war for three hundred years, and yet, we have had to accept war forced upon us these past four years. This is going to bring about huge changes. Millions are dead, millions more are injured. Lives, families across the globe have been destroyed. Entire cities lay in ruins. And for what?"

Woolsey puffed on his pipe. "The right to a few hundred yards of dirt, to be reclaimed when the Allies move in."

Godwyn opened the screen to the hearth, grabbed the poker, and prodded the fire. "We have peace for now."

Woolsey sipped his Brandy. "If history is any indication, it is only a matter of time before Fear and Terror strike again. They cannot be but fear and terror. Our earth, this home of ours, is enveloped by two magnetic fields that operate in constant opposition to one another. These fields are not uniform in their lines of travel. When they interact with metal, or mountains, they bend, forcing negative to fight positive in an endless battle over the earth. I fear as long as we inhabit the planet, we shall live with fear and terror. Even if humanity were to transport itself to another planet. Wherever we go, there we are."

Godwyn returned the poker to its place, and closed the firescreen. "Both states are going to need rebuilding, and Abundance is going to pay the price."

"If the Fearlings had voted for a respectable leader while they were still able to vote," Woolsey puffed on his pipe, "before they lost their democracy, this last war might not have happened. It is their lack of value for education that brings them loss. Their people refute common sense. Their ministers fight against their own people. They gave power to monsters who ignored science that they may line their pockets at the expense of the people, and the earth."

"Some people will go to any extent to protect their right to breathe in fear, Woolsey. Even if it brings loss upon themselves. Now that their armies have been defeated, should Pristine decide to honor her coronation commitment, and go there, we face no threat."

"Those people are filled with resentment."

"What resentment is that?—Woolsey."

"Greed, born of the ego. As a result, the young Fearlings and Terrorists will now grow up in a defeated world, filled with ruins, with no possible escape. I doubt humanity will ever overcome greed. It lives in too close proximity to fear. Greed and stupidity will be the end of the human race."

Godwyn set the telegram on the table. "Things can, and will change when he value the contributions educators make to society, not with words, and billboards, but with a paycheck comparable to other professions. Without teachers, we have no doctors, no firefighters, no musicians, no scribes, no essential workers."

"And no dentists."

Godwyn checked the clock. "Imagine a world without dentists."

"Pristine is working to elevate the profession. She has Mistress Sitwell working with her on that. We must reward our teachers the way we reward chiefs and managers—according to results. Now that Fear and Terror have been squelched, conditions can change, and it will be up to Abundance to install new institutions."

Woolsey poured himself another Brandy. "I could not agree more."

"It's not just about elevating the teaching profession. Fear and terror start with the parents, in the home. Sadly, they are often reinforced in the schools."

"Indeed." Woolsey set his glass on the table, and relit his pipe.

"I can't wait to share the good news with Pristine. If she would just have this baby. I should ring Tibbons, have him go check."

Mr. Tibbons stepped into the library. "I heard a cry, Sir. I shall investigate?"

"Please do, Tibbons, and watch out for Needlepinch. Be firm with her, or she could bite your head off."

"Yes Sir," the butler exited.

257

Woolsey puffed on his pipe. "So, Carabella Needlepinch is back. How is the old broad?"

"I don't know. Why don't you ask her—if you can catch her awake."

"Is she still napping on the job?"

Godwyn snickered. "Seems to me she sleeps all day. She does nothing to warrant her pay. She carries out no specific duties. She's never around when you need her. All she does is annoy me. The girls find her invasive, but Pristine insists she is family—so she stays. Sometimes, I feel like I married them both."

"You should know, Godwyn, Carabella Needlepinch has been pinching the Goldspinner family for three generations."

"I had an idea. Yesterday she threw a shoe at me."

"A shoe?"

"It really wasn't her fault. I got in her way."

Woolsey chuckled. "*You* got in the nanny's way? That's a laugh. How are Possessa and Gezealous coming along with their playing? They must be what—nineteen and twenty by now?"

"Eighteen and nineteen—going on thirty-two."

"Any prospects of marriage?"

"We have not yet come to that bridge."

"It is never too soon to marry them off. They need to be on the market the moment they are ready to be picked."

"I don't know which man would have them. Ever since Prudence died, they seem so mean spirited. Possessa knows everything better, loves to argue, and she's rude to the footman. Gezealous is sassy, and constantly at odds with Pristine."

"I know how teenage girls can be, Godwyn. I have spent the second part of my life as godfather to two princesses."

"Why did you and Avorah never have children?"

"It didn't seem we needed any. We met when we were in graduate school. After we married, we became engaged with our careers. Reproduction is not for everyone. The world does not need more people. The planet is struggling to heal as it is."

"I agree. All life is precious, but it seems now there is just *too much* precious life."

"The best way to limit our carbon footprint is to not have kids. Think about it. You and your family members have consumed three times what Avorah and I have consumed in the same amount of time—and you are a small family of four. Think of the tons of outused diapers alone."

"I never thought of it that way."

"It wasn't until the earthquake swallowed up Henriette and Alistair, not until Erica and Pristine were orphaned did Avorah and I take an interest in children."

"Sometimes I wonder why I am a father. I suppose to most of us, the idea of having little carbon copies of ourselves walking around is appealing. When they're not angry, I look into my daughters' smiling faces, and I know why I wanted to be a father." Godwyn reached for the carafe, "I think I will have another Brandy. You?"

"Thanks. How is the communication between you?"

"Lately, they won't have anything to do with us. Most of the time, they refuse to even speak to us, and when they do, it's a one word answer."

"Where are they now?"

"In the music room, I suppose, playing records. That is, if they haven't bribed Crankshaft to drive them someplace. Pristine grounded them for a week again. Let's hope they don't make her mad again." Godwyn took a deep breath. "The war is over, George, and I am about to become a father again. Any minute, Tibbons is going to come through that door, and announce the birth of a healthy heir. This will take time to internalize, peace, and an heir. Now it will be even harder to restrain young people. They'll leave for the city. They'll go work in the factories. Possessa and Gezealous will leave us too, once they find husbands—if we ever do. Their refusal to accept a chaperone on dates makes it difficult to find respectable prospects."

"Woolsey sipped, and relit his pipe. "That is where it begins, disrespecting centuries of tradition by refusing a chaperone. Next thing you know they will be painting their faces."

"They already do that. The latest is this ghastly blood red color, and they paint their lips into the shape of a heart. If you ask me, I think it looks ridiculous. Pristine says it's a fad, but she too likes to paint her lips into a little heart. Last week Possessa and Gezealous went on a double date to the Fair. I insisted Needlepinch tag along. I wanted to get back at them for a rather raucus serenade they gave Pristine and me a few weeks back."

"Nanny with her bell?" Woolsey took a sip, and set his glass on the table.

"They abandoned her in the Spook House. Poor woman nearly had a heart attack. They act as if the world owes them something. This is my fault. I spoiled them after Prudence died. I thought I could make up for losing a mother by giving them everything they asked for."

"It's nine-twenty." Woolsey rose from the chair, and lifted his britches. "I'd better be on my way. Avorah is going to call me at ten."

"Well then, you'd better get home."

"How long has Pristine been in labor?"

Godwyn looked at the clock, "nineteen hours, and counting."

Woolsey tucked his pouch into his pocket. "Next time I see you, Godwyn, you will be the father of a healthy baby prince." He finished his Brandy, set the empty glass on the table, and walked to the door.

"Do me a favor, George."

Woolsey turned. "What favor is that?"

"Call Mrs. Thornecroft in the Communications Office in the morning. Ask her to prepare a statement for the town crier announcing armistice, etcetera etcetera, along with details on our heir; height, weight, coloring, etcetera, that she may prepare a statement announcing our double good fortune."

"I will call her first thing in the morning, and have her send you a copy."

"Thank you. I don't know if I'll even be awake."

"Get some rest, Godwyn. Good night."

"Good night, George." Godwyn closed his eyes, boarded the train of thought leading to the kingdom within, and prayed. "Lord, I ask that you bring comfort in the joy of knowing Pristine is well, and our new heir is a healthy one. Bring relief to the war-torn, in whichever state. Free all God's children trapped in cages of war. Send healing vibrations internationally, that we may move forward as a continent united in Consciousness, in peace for all, ruled under liberty, and justice by, and for all. In heaven's name I thank you. Amen."

Downstairs in the gentlemens' wardrobe, Harrison helped Lord Woolsey with his hat and coat, walked him to the front door, and bid him good night.

Upstairs, in the east wing, Mr. Tibbons stood outside the Queen's bedchamber door, and knocked. The door opened a crack, and Dr. Fingerling stuck his head out. "Mr. Tibbons, what are you doing here?"

"I heard crying. I thought we might have an heir."

"That was Her Majesty's cry."

"No news?"

Fingerling shook his head. "No news."

"This is an exceedingly long delivery, Doctor."

"What would you have me do, Mr. Tibbons? Squeeze the baby out?"

"Of course not. It's just that Consort Godwyn is anxious."

"You tell Consort Godwyn childbirth is not something that can be rushed. When the moment arrives, he will hear the cry of an angel. Now if you will excuse me, I hear Her Majesty calling me." The doctor shut the door in the butler's face.

"No staff member in Leniency would have dared speak to me in such a tone," the butler mumbled, as he walked down the corridor, "just because he brought five royal Goldspinners into the world, he thinks he has license to be arrogant. This is my house. *I* will decide who will be arrogant."

Dr. Fingerling returned to the Queen's bed, and checked in on his work. "We are heading into day two, Your Majesty," he cheered her on, "how about we get this show on the road."

"A-a-a-a-a-a-a-a-a-a-augh—what pain!"

"That's my girl," Nanny patted Pristine's wrist, "one more push should do it."

"We're almost there, Your Majesty. Here comes the crown. I see the crown emer-ging, we have an heir—and it's looks like it's going to be a—oh no…"

"Why it took the garment industry to invent the zipper when it would have made childbirth so much easier I will never know," is a credit of Hollywood team Jane Wagner, and Lily Tomlin. Thank you for oiling the gears of prejudice for over half a century, and beyond, by providing the world a menu of brilliance, with a side of laughter.

ABOUT the AUTHOR

Alan John Mayer was born in Casablanca, Morocco. As a dependent of his U.S. Department of Defense father, and Berliner war refugée mother, change was consistent. By high school, he had attended eleven schools on four continents.

From age eleven to fifteen he held a paper route, and ran his own lawn care service. At fifteen, he found himself thrust into a series of foster homes, the fourth in Europe's smog-ridden industrial Ruhr Valley. Determined to escape the dust, he bought a train ticket, and appeared at a favorite aunt's house in the country. Not knowing what to do with a fifteen year-old boy, on his savings in the States, she arranged for him to visit friends of hers who had emigrated to several European capitals on both sides of the Iron Curtain, after World War II.

In 1978, he began a journal, and life in Southern California. He holds a Bachelor of Arts Degree from the University of California in Theater and Television Production, a K through Adult multi-lingual Teaching Credential from the University of California, a Practitioner's licence from Ernest Holmes College in Los Angles, California, and an M.A. in Childhood Development from the University of Life in Contentment. He is a forty year *Course in Miracles* student, a vegetarian since 1989 (one who occasionally cheats with fish and fowl.) His lifetime goals are to speak for those whose voices have been silenced, to create a rescue home run by animals, and human beings, and to prepare himself for the day the Lord calls him Home.

ABOUT the ILLUSTRATOR

S tephen Lubin has worked in the animation industry for twenty years, fifteen on teams at Walt Disney Feature Animation in Los Angeles, California.

He has worked with Alan on several books, and is currently working on a graphic novel with other former Disney artists.

Stephen lives in Los Angeles, California, with family, and his cat Muzzy. He was an active supporter of the 'Free Tillikum' movement, loves animals, enjoys gardening, film, music, and is a student and teacher of *A Course in Miracles*.

You can see more of Steve's work on TicToc@riggolio, and at http://bit.ly/IMDB/SteveLubin.

Congratulations, you are now an *Obsessed* reader. The birth of an heir to Entitlement and the upcoming tour through Consciousness is only the beginning of the many adventures that lay ahead in *Hoodwinked*, book II of the *A Boy Alone* series. If you enjoyed this story, please take a moment to share with others by writing a review. Few take the time to do so, so important in the process of deciding whether to purchase a book, read it, and pass it along.

Cozy up this winter with the royal Goldspinner family, seated around the twenty-foot tall Blue Spruce Solstice tree in the grand hall. Enjoy a traditional Abundite celebration. Now that Nanny Needlepinch has an heir to look after, her life has purpose again. Join school mistress Entra Sitwell, as she chaperones Possessa and Gezealous on rendez-vous after rendez-vous in search for husbands, leading to *the* social event of the decade—a double ring Valentine's Day wedding ceremony on the north lawn. Can the Bonheur sisters adjust to living in separate states?—with husbands? Who was that the groom was seen kissing?

For short stories check out AmericanValuesRestored.com. Feel free to like, comment, and share. (To be updated before I am called Home.)

For canine and feline comedy on YouTube, feel free to like, comment, and share: Meck&Miao. (Any invitation to edit videos is accepted.)

God bless the animals, whose voices need to be heard, and listened to. May all creation find compassion, shelter, and peace.

Thank you, Donna Sloan, for fun at Toastmasters, and for believing in the *A Boy Alone* series.

Thank you, Dr. Doris Palazzo Lubin, and Steve Lubin, for keeping me sustained and on track, and for helping me to bring this book into print.

Thank you, Jane Wagner, and Lily Tomlin.

Lastly, thank *you*, the reader, for joining us on this journey.

END

to a new

BEGINNING

OBSESSED

HOODWINKED

THE GRAND TOUR

THE LIE

POSSESSED

LOST in CONFUSION

VICTORY OVER SELF

Step into a new State of Consciousness.

Hop on board the train to Abundance.

Made in the USA
Las Vegas, NV
05 March 2021

19061968R00154